AN *Aster Bay* NOVEL

WHISKING
It All

CARA DION

Also by Cara Dion

Love Song Series

Irreplaceable

Indiscreet

Undeniable

Aster Bay

Whisking It All

Just For Show

First Comes Marriage

Visit my website to learn more and download free bonus content:

For Ann

Chapter One

Jameson Chase was in hell.

His risotto was undercooked, the chef at this restaurant had clearly never heard of salt, and his date hadn't put her phone down once since their food had arrived.

Trisha snapped another picture of her untouched plate and tapped away on her phone. "Hashtag date night," she said in a sing-song voice as she typed.

When Jamie had agreed to this blind date, he'd been told Trisha was a food blogger. He suspected "Instagram addict" was closer to the truth. *This is the last time I let Helen White set me up on a blind date*, he thought. *This is what happens when you try to humor an old lady.*

He took another sip of his wine and waited for Trisha to notice that he hadn't spoken for the last five minutes. Finally, she set her phone down on the table and turned a wide smile towards him. "So, what were you saying?"

"I wasn't."

She giggled—*did grown women giggle?*—and poked at her food with her fork. "My grandmother said you were funny, Jimmy."

"It's Jamie."

She broke off a piece of the under-seasoned, chewy short rib that sat on top of the undercooked risotto and popped it into her mouth. Her eyes went cartoonishly wide, and she pressed a finger to her lips in surprise. Maybe she knew something about food after all. With a horrified look on her face, she reached for her napkin, spitting the bit of meat into the white fabric.

"Is that *beef*?" she gasped, pinning the blob in her napkin with a withering glare.

"Yes," he said, "It's a short rib."

"Of beef?!"

"What did you think a short rib was?" *Scratch that. She definitely doesn't know anything about food.*

"I don't know! Other animals have ribs!"

At the bar behind them, a petite, dark-haired woman snorted into her wine. He supposed if he weren't the one stuck on the blind date from hell then he might also find Trisha's reactions funny, but as it was, he was having a hard time thinking much of anything aside from all the better ways he could have spent his night.

Trisha took an overly large sip of her wine, gulping it down. "Hashtag gross!" she said with a grimace.

"Why did you order it if you don't like short ribs?" he asked, trying to remain patient. He may never want to see Trisha again, but her grandmother was unavoidable, and he didn't want her granddaughter complaining that he was a total ass.

"Because *you* ordered it! You're the chef. I assumed you had good taste."

Every muscle in his body tightened as the insult landed. Her opinion shouldn't matter; she didn't know anything about food. He took another sip of his wine, focusing on setting his glass back down without shattering it.

"Look, Jimmy—"

"Jamie."

"—I think we can both agree this dinner is a whole plate of yikes, so why don't we skip it and just get to the good part."

He arched an eyebrow at her, anger still simmering on the edges of his vision. "The good part," he repeated.

She leaned forward, giving him a clear view down the front of her already low-cut dress. She glanced down, as if to be sure her breasts were on display, then flashed a grin back in his direction. "Your place or mine?"

He barked out a laugh. *So much for not being an ass.* "That is not happening."

Her grin disappeared, replaced by a tight purse of her lips that looked way too much like her grandmother. "Fine. We done here, then?"

"Oh, yeah. I'd say we're done here."

She grabbed her absurdly tiny handbag from where it hung off the back of her chair, snatched up her phone, and stormed out of the restaurant, her heels clacking along the tile with each furious step and her eyes locked on her phone screen as she, no doubt, blasted him on social media. He didn't exhale until the door swung shut behind her.

Leaning back in his chair, he scraped a hand over his face. "Jesus Christ," he mumbled. He was way too old for the revolving door of bad blind dates he'd been on over the last few months. For fuck's sake, just that morning he'd spotted a new patch of gray coming in.

The woman at the bar chuckled to herself as she took another sip of her wine.

"Something amusing?" he asked, just loud enough that he was clearly talking to her.

She glanced up at him, giving him his first good look at her face. Goddamn, she was beautiful, especially with that knowing smile and sparkle in her eyes. Even if she was young.

"That has to be the worst date I've ever witnessed," she said.

He exhaled a laugh, shaking his head. "Yeah, tell me about it."

"Blind date?"

He nodded.

"Who'd you make angry enough that they did *that* to you?"

"Her grandmother, apparently."

The woman shook her head as though disappointed in his answer. "You have to come up with some better screening questions. Maybe, 'knows how to order their own food' is a good place to start."

He smiled for the first time since Trisha had walked into the restaurant that night, declaring that he was 'hashtag gorgeous.' "I'll take it under advisement, thanks."

The woman grinned, her eyes lighting up. He'd never seen eyes like hers, a blue so dark it was almost black, like a raven's feather.

"Would you—" He stopped himself, flashing an apologetic smile and turning his attention back to his wine. He was clearly too old for her. *Don't be a creep.*

"Would I what?" she asked, the arch of her eyebrow challenging him to ask the question.

"Would you care to join me?"

She made a face that seemed to say, *sure, why not,* then took her plate and glass of wine and carried them over to the now empty place across from him. She was shorter than he'd expected. Curvier, too—the kind of woman who would make heads turn wherever she went and had the swing in her hips that proved she knew it. Jamie slid

Trisha's uneaten food out of the way. The woman set her plate down and they both laughed to see they'd now added a third plate of inedible short ribs to the table.

"Don't worry," she said in a stage whisper. "I know it's beef."

"Thank God." He extended a hand to her across the table. "I'm Jamie."

"Tessa." Her hand was so small in his, so soft against the roughness of his calloused palms. "You really are a chef," she said as she withdrew her hand. "You have chef's hands."

"And what do you do, Tessa?"

"I'm a pastry chef."

His heart beat faster and he straightened up in his chair. He may be too old for her, but at least they'd have some good conversation, which was more than he could say for the woman who'd previously occupied that seat. "Yeah? Where?"

She hesitated, glancing away and pushing her food around with her fork. "I'm getting ready to open a pop-up actually. Hoping to do some traveling before I look for my next long-term gig." She took a bite of the risotto and immediately made a face, dropping her fork. "God, that really is awful."

He chuckled. "Yeah, it's pretty bad."

"No, it's objectively awful. How are they serving this? Does this chef even have salt in his kitchen?"

His blood buzzed beneath his skin, a floaty electric feeling he hadn't felt in ages. "Doesn't appear that way. And the braising liquid for these ribs is—"

"Watered down tomato paste at best. 'Braising liquid' is too kind." She pushed the plate away and took a sip of her wine, half looking like she intended to gargle with the alcohol to clear the taste from her mouth. "Oh, shit," she said. "You're not friends with the chef, are you?"

He smiled. "No. Contrary to popular belief, we don't *all* know each other. This is my first time here."

"Mine too."

"So is Rhode Island home, or part of your traveling?"

She considered the question. "A little of column A, little of column B. I'm in the area to spend some time with family. The pop-up thing is kind of a family business."

"Ah. And where is your family tonight?"

She grinned. "Not here. I caught an earlier flight, and thought I'd give myself a night in the city to mentally prepare... I'm not expected until the morning." Her eyes dropped to his lips and all the blood in his body rushed to his groin.

Jamie let his eyes roam over her face, the dark almond-shaped eyes, high cheekbones, and a pouty mouth. She was even more beautiful up close where it was clear she wore hardly any makeup, the glow in her cheeks just pure *her*. His gaze snagged on her lips. He took a deep breath and shifted in his seat, trying to subtly adjust himself without giving away that he was already half-hard for a woman he'd only just met.

She wrinkled her nose. "That was too forward, right? I'm sorry, I—"

"Not too forward. Just forward enough." Her smile was like a gift, dazzling white against her olive skin. "How old are you, Tessa?"

"Does it matter?"

"If we're going to be that forward, then yeah, I'd say it does."

"Twenty-five."

He sucked in a breath. *Definitely way too fucking young for me. Jesus, I'm probably as old as her father.*

"You alright there?" she asked with a laugh.

"I'm too old for you," he said, regret lacing every word.

"Says who?" she asked, cocking her head to the side.

His eyes dropped to her lips again, mesmerized by the way they tilted up with repressed laughter. Something reckless sputtered to life in his chest, something that very much did not care that he was sixteen years older than the woman sitting across from him. Something he hadn't felt in a long time.

If she didn't care about the age difference, maybe he shouldn't either.

He wouldn't usually entertain the idea of seeing where the night would take them without knowing there was the possibility of a future, but there was something about Tessa... She was far too young for him and only in town for a short while, but he wasn't ready to walk away from her just yet.

"Should we get another drink?" he asked, tilting his chin towards her nearly empty wine glass.

Her smile widened as she picked up her glass and drained the last of her wine. She set the glass down, her fingers lingering on the stem. "Yes, Chef."

Hot damn, he could get addicted to that word on this woman's lips. He had a feeling he could get addicted to her lips in general. His mind was already compiling a mental list of all the things he wanted to hear her say—things like "yes" and "more" and "harder."

When was the last time he'd felt the thrill of meeting a woman and being so instantly attracted to her? How long had it been since he'd found himself doing this particular dance with someone, feeling out the boundaries, testing the limits, wondering if she would gasp or scream when she came? Only a few minutes after meeting this woman and he was already praying he'd get the chance to find out.

"Not here," she said. For a minute he wondered if he'd somehow said that last part out loud. Her eyes danced, lips turning up at the corners like she knew what he was thinking. "Come on, you must know a better place around here to grab a drink and something that's actually edible."

Was it his imagination or did she skim her eyes over his body on that last word?

"It's not fancy," he warned.

"I like rough around the edges," she said. He chuckled. "Show me."

Chapter Two

Jamie took Tessa to a food truck parked a few blocks from her hotel in a small park, Christmas lights strung between the open window of the truck and the edges of nearby picnic tables. They ate fish tacos made with locally caught fish and drank vinho verde out of red solo cups while sitting on the grass watching headlights fly by on the highway below the embankment. The lights glinted off the silver at his temples, shadows playing in the creases at the edges of his eyes when he laughed.

"Most ridiculous order customization," she said, taking another bite of her taco. A bit of the tangy pink sauce clung to the corner of her mouth. She licked it away, awareness prickling at the back of her neck as his eyes tracked the movement.

"Last summer I had a candied ginger salmon and citrus risotto on the menu. A tourist came in and requested the dish without any ginger. Or citrus."

She laughed, nearly spitting out her mouthful of wine.

"Holy shit, that's a good one," she said.

"Your turn," he said, scooping up pieces of mango that had fallen into his cardboard tray and popping them in his mouth.

She watched the tip of his finger disappear between his lips and imagined all the other things she wanted to watch his lips do.

"We served a summer berry pavlova at my last gig. Every once in a while, someone would place an order with the note that they had an egg allergy."

He threw his head back and laughed, his Adam's apple bobbing as the warm sound washed over her.

They swapped kitchen war stories, tales of executive chefs who ran their kitchens like war zones and prep cooks who didn't know a chiffonade from a julienne. They bonded over their shared opinion that it was time for bacon to go back to the breakfast menu and leave desserts alone, and commiserated over the need to write menus that pleased the general public rather than pushing the boundaries of their creativity. By the time they'd finished eating, there was no denying how much she wanted him.

She took his hand and led him back to her hotel, straight through the lobby without a word. She felt his eyes on her as they waited for the elevator, his hand firm in hers, his thumb sliding up and down along the sensitive skin at the base of her wrist. They rode the elevator in silence, the blood rushing in her ears, every one of her nerve endings prickling with awareness of his every breath.

Tessa had never done anything like this—picked up a random guy and taken him home with her. While she was no stranger to short-term flings, she'd never had a one-night stand. She'd never wanted to. But there was something about Jamie that felt like she'd known him her whole life, like she could trust him to break her, but only in the ways she wanted him to. And she wanted him to. She'd seen that wicked glint in his eyes, the confidence with which he moved. She wanted it all.

He pulled out his wallet, removing his ID and holding it out for her.

"What am I supposed to do with that?" she asked, not even looking at the plastic rectangle in his hand.

"Take a picture and send it to a friend. So they know who you're with." At her blank stare, he continued. "So you know you're safe with me."

She batted away his license and took his empty hand in hers again. "I don't need a picture of your driver's license to feel safe with you." Besides, she had no one to send such a picture to anyway...

He frowned, a tinge of pink appearing on the tops of his ears. "Sorry," he mumbled. "I thought that was what people did when they did this kind of thing."

Her heart squeezed in her chest and she brushed a loose wave of his dark hair away from his eyes. "I wouldn't know. I don't usually do *this kind of thing*," she teased.

"Me either," he said, capturing her hand in his and guiding it to rest against his chest.

The elevator doors opened, and he waited for her to move first, to grip his hand tighter and lead him down the hall to her hotel room. At the door, she dropped his hand to dig through her bag for her key card. He moved behind her, his hands resting on her hips, sliding up and down, the thin fabric of her top catching on his rough palms and moving with him. He pressed his nose into her hair and breathed in long and slow, his breath on her neck sending tingles over her scalp.

"Tessa..." he murmured, leaving the question unspoken, but she could feel it in the tension of his muscles, the way he held himself back.

Please don't ask questions, she thought. *Please just let this be simple.*

Finally, she found the key card, swiping it through the lock. The light flashed red and she tried again, her hands beginning to shake as desire pulsed through her veins. Red again. She grunted in frustration. Jamie slid his hand over hers, guiding the key card into the lock and withdrawing it slowly. The light flashed green and she pushed the handle, turning in his arms and gripping his shirt, pulling him in after her.

Her lips were on his before the door slammed shut behind them. He tasted like Portuguese wine and mango salsa and she pulled him closer. He groaned, digging a hand into her hair and angling her head where he wanted it as he deepened the kiss, licking into her mouth. She opened for him as her fingers found the edge of his shirt and pulled it from his pants, her hands sliding beneath the button down to meet the skin of his lower back. He was hot to the touch, and she scraped her nails lightly along his back. A low, guttural sound rose in his throat as his free hand slid down her hips and grabbed a handful of her ass, fingers kneading her full curves.

"Off," she demanded against his lips, pulling at his shirt.

He moved away from her just enough to reach behind himself and pull the shirt over his head, tossing it aside, his eyes never leaving hers. All the breath left her body as she took him in. Jamie had the kind of defined abs and pecs that came from years of hard work, not hours in a gym, the sculpted contours of his biceps, the line of dark hair running from his belly button into his pants. The sprinkle of silver in his hair was mirrored by the dusting of hair on his chest, and she had the most intense urge to slide her fingers through it. His eyes hooded as he watched her, his tongue slipping out to wet his lips.

"Your turn," he said, his voice rough and ragged.

She pulled off her shirt and tossed it aside, leaving her in leggings and a hot pink, cotton bra. These were her traveling clothes, not what she would have usually worn for a date, though she was grateful she'd shaved her legs that morning at least. He didn't seem to mind her comfortable clothes, though. He closed the distance between them and wrapped his arms around her, pulling her hips flush against his so she could feel the steel bar between his legs already standing at attention.

His stubbled chin and lips dragged over her cheek, down her jaw and along her throat, his tongue darting out to lick at her pulse point. He kissed her like he couldn't get enough, like she was something special, like he might go out of his mind if he didn't have his mouth on her. She knew it was all just part of the fantasy of a one-night stand, that it didn't mean anything, but still… It was nice to feel wanted.

He gripped her ass again while his other hand unhooked her bra. He ripped the fabric away and bent to take one tightly furled nipple between his teeth with a gentle tug, the sharp bite sending sparks along her skin.

"That feels so good," she moaned.

He grinned against her chest as he moved to her other nipple, swirling his tongue over the turgid peak and then blowing on the wet skin, her nipple puckering further with the sudden chill until it was so stiff it stung with need.

"It will feel even better when I get my mouth on your pussy," he said.

She gasped at the dirty words, wetness rushing between her legs at the filthy promise.

"Tell me what you want, Tessa," he said, his kisses trailing down her torso, over the curve of her belly.

She dug her fingers into his wavy hair, his locks just long enough for her to grab a good handful and tug, directing his mouth towards the apex of her thighs. He chuckled, a wicked sound, like he knew exactly how much he was driving her crazy and loved every second of it.

"I want you to lick me," she said.

His eyes grew darker, greener somehow, like the wild overgrowth of a forest, and he hooked his fingers over the waistband of her leggings, yanking them and her panties down in one swift motion. He steadied her with an arm around her hips as he helped her step out of the fabric and then backed her up towards the bed. Her calves hit the edge of the mattress and she fell backwards.

No sooner had she hit the bed than he knelt between her knees on the floor, dragging her closer to the edge of the mattress. He threw her legs over his shoulders and ran his hands up her thighs, the roughness of his skin at odds with the gentleness of his touch. Just before he reached the place where she was wet and aching, he stilled, glancing up at her where she'd propped herself up on her elbows to watch.

"Yes?" he asked.

"God, yes."

He didn't need to be told twice.

He parted her with his thumbs and lowered his lips to her before she'd even finished saying the words. Tessa's mouth fell open on a soundless gasp as she watched him devour her, his eyes locked on hers as he teased and sucked and tasted every part of her. She squirmed under the intensity of his gaze, as though he weren't just fucking her, he was *seeing* her, and she wasn't sure she'd signed up for that. She squirmed beneath his touch and he growled, like an animal who'd had their favorite toy taken away, and gripped her thighs harder, pulling her back against his mouth.

She was powerless to stop the wave of pleasure rising

up within her when he looked at her like that and moved his tongue against her most sensitive places like he knew exactly how to make her come undone, so she gave herself over to the tide of her orgasm, crying out as it roared through her. He continued sucking on her clit, his fingertips digging into her thighs, until her hips stopped bucking against his mouth.

As he pulled away from her, his chin glistening with her pleasure, he smiled. "I knew you'd be a screamer."

She laughed, her limbs loose and heavy in the aftermath of her orgasm. "Why are you still wearing pants?"

He smiled, the kind of smile that lit up his eyes and made her briefly wonder if she could keep him. *Impossible.* She wouldn't be staying in Rhode Island for long. She didn't stay anywhere for long. And Jamie seemed like the kind of guy who had a regular order at the local café, who had routines and people who'd notice if he didn't show up somewhere when he was expected. For all they had in common, they couldn't be more different.

With one hand still gently stroking her thigh, he used his other hand to undo his belt and jeans. Why was it so sexy that he could do that one handed? He pulled out his wallet, retrieving a condom.

"Of course, you have a condom in your wallet," she said, rolling her eyes but unable to hide her smile.

"I like to be prepared," he said.

Then his pants were off, and she watched as he rolled the latex down the length of his cock. She'd never understood why some women would wax poetic about that particular male appendage. She liked a dick as much as the next heterosexual woman, but she'd never felt the need to write an ode to one.

That was before.

Jamie's cock was a thing of beauty. Thick and hard with a smooth, flared tip and a map of veins running down the shaft. Sheathed in latex, it glistened in the dim hotel lighting. He watched her watching him, his forest-dark eyes gleaming with a mix of arrogance and wonder, and gave himself a few firm strokes as he advanced on her.

"Like what you see?" he asked.

"You know I do."

He stood between her spread knees, lifting her legs to plant her feet on the edge of the bed. Then, taking himself in hand, he dragged the head of his cock through her folds, using the ridge of his crown to tease her swollen clit. He watched her, like he was memorizing her reaction to every movement, learning just the right amount of pressure to make her gasp and squirm beneath him. As he teased her, that look shifted, cut through with flashes of something different. Like he wasn't just thinking about making her come, but like he was already mentally ordering them breakfast in bed. Like he wanted to swallow her whole and then draw her a bath, fuck her until she could barely form a complete thought and then take her to pick out a Christmas tree that they'd decorate together while a roast cooked in the oven, and it was too much.

That wasn't the look of a one-night stand.

That was the kind of look that led to promises, commitments, and eventually, disappointment and resentment.

"Come here," she said, wrapping her legs around his thighs and pulling him closer as she slid up the bed, urging him to follow. She was done with loaded looks. She didn't want to think about what was going on behind his eyes when he looked at her like that. She didn't want to think at all.

Jamie climbed up after her, crawling over her and lowering himself between her thighs. He captured her lips in a searing kiss that tasted like her own orgasm, and with a single smooth thrust, he filled her completely. She gasped against his mouth as her body stretched to accommodate him, molding herself to him. He adjusted his angle, gripping her thigh and pulling it up around her waist, so that with each slow slide in and out of her, his pelvis dragged against her clit, pleasure radiating out from the place where they were joined.

"Holy fuck," he groaned, lips against her neck. "You feel so good."

Her hands raked over his back, and he captured one wrist in a firm grip, holding her hand above her head as he continued to work himself in and out, each stroke stealing her breath.

"Like this," he said, nipping at her bottom lip. "I want to watch your tits bounce while I fuck you."

Tessa moved her other hand above her head to join the first, gripping the headboard and inviting him to watch her. This was the look she wanted, the one of unrestrained lust, the one that made her thrill with the heady power of making a man like him lose control. He dipped his head to watch her chest move in time to his thrusts, cursing under his breath as he began moving faster.

"So fucking beautiful," he groaned, one hand reaching up to grip her breast in a rough handful, squeezing and plumping her.

"Jamie?" she breathed, arching her back to press herself into his hand.

"Yeah, baby?"

"Harder."

He cursed under his breath and dropped his hand to

brace himself on the bed beside her head, his hips slamming into her harder and faster with each thrust.

"Like this?"

She nodded, panting too hard to answer properly. He released his hold on her thigh, dragging his hand over her skin until he found her clit again with his thumb, strumming that swollen bud like a guitar string. A sharp spike of pleasure shot through her at the touch, growing stronger with each movement of his thumb.

"I wanna hear you, Tess. Wanna hear you scream my name when you come."

She moaned, her eyes falling closed as her climax gathered at the base of her spine. A few more strokes of his thumb, a few more deep thrusts, and her orgasm ripped free, shooting fire down her legs, the soles of her feet burning with the pleasure. She screamed his name as he continued to fuck her, shouted it over and over in an unintelligible jumble of words as he drove her from one orgasm into another until he finally lengthened and jolted within her, and collapsed forward, his sweaty forehead pressed to her chest as he filled the condom.

When he'd discarded the condom and crawled back into bed beside her, she turned her back to him, letting him gather her into the little spoon position, his half hard cock pressed against her backside. He dropped a kiss on her shoulder and spoke against her skin, "That was... fuck, that was amazing."

"Yeah," she whispered.

And it was. Too amazing.

Stupid. No such thing as too amazing when you're talking about orgasms.

"We're lucky the room next door didn't call the manager," she said, forcing laughter into her tone.

"Were you holding back on me?" he teased sleepily.

"Maybe a little."

Another kiss, this time further up the curve of her neck, his teeth barely grazing her pulse point. "Next time, I'll have to fuck you somewhere you can be as loud as you want, then." Another nip, this time on her ear.

Next time...

Her body was tired and sore in all the best places, but she couldn't make herself relax. Jamie nuzzled his face into her hair, hot puffs of his breath warming her neck as he drifted off to sleep, and her mind reeled from the sudden sensation that the walls were closing in.

Next time.

In the early hours of the morning, before the streetlights had turned off, Tessa soundlessly wheeled her suitcase from the hotel room, closing the door behind her with a soft snick while Jamie slept. *It's better this way,* she told herself as she rode the elevator to the lobby and ordered a car service to drive her to Aster Bay.

Chapter Three

"You outdid yourself this time, my friend," Jamie said, running a hand lovingly over the top of a wooden crate piled high with beets, the deep purple orbs leaving a fine layer of dirt over his palm. He looked up at the grinning farmer who stood beside his pickup truck in the gravel parking lot of Jamie's restaurant, Lemon and Thyme.

The restaurant was constructed on a wharf so that the building appeared to be floating on the water. The raised garden beds on either side of the main entrance were overflowing with herbs, scenting the warm September air thick with dill and thyme. The sight of his restaurant in the early morning usually set Jamie at ease, the reflection of the sun as it gleamed on the water slowing his racing thoughts, but not that morning. That morning he'd woken up in a strange hotel room alone, every trace of Tessa gone as though she'd never even existed. He'd thought they'd had a real connection, that he'd take her to the greasy spoon that made killer eggs benedict and find out how long she was in town, convince her they had the potential for something that went beyond incredible sex, that it was worth seeing each other again. Clearly, he'd misread the situation. It was a frustration and unease that even the water gently lapping at the pilings beneath his restaurant couldn't quell.

Ricky gestured to another crate. "I also got those Brussels sprouts Anabel was asking after, and the leeks. I'm a little short on the arugula, though, and I'll send someone by with the apricots later today. Couldn't fit it all on the truck," he said, gesturing to the overstuffed bed of his run-down pickup.

"I appreciate it." Jamie dug into his back pocket for his wallet, pulling out a wad of crisp bills and holding them out to Ricky. "You've got the best produce for twenty miles."

Ricky accepted the bills and shoved them into his pocket without bothering to count. "I bet you say that to all the farmers."

"You and Cheryl come on by any time you want. Dinner's on me. I owe her with all the work she's going to be doing for the festival anyway."

Ricky's smile faltered as he ran his hand over the back of his head, leaving bits of soil in his crew cut. "I guess you haven't heard yet."

Jamie's brow furrowed. He shifted on his feet, crossing his arms. "Heard what?"

"Cheryl's been put on bed rest," Ricky said. Jamie moved to ask more, but the farmer held up one hand, dirt embedded in the lines of his skin. "She and the baby are alright. It's just a precaution."

"Do you need anything?" Jamie asked.

"Not right now, thanks."

"But you'll let me know?"

"I will," Ricky said with a smile.

"Guess I'll need to find a new pastry chef for the festival," Jamie said.

"'Fraid so. But Ethan said he's got an idea, someone

you haven't considered yet, so maybe he's already got you covered."

"Maybe," Jamie said. Though why his best friend had failed to mention this mysterious new pastry chef—or how he even knew one that Jamie didn't—was beyond him.

If only I had Tessa's number... He shook off the thought. *It's my own damn fault. This is exactly why I don't have casual sex.*

Once all the crates had been moved inside the restaurant and Ricky had gone on his way with a promise to send someone by with the rest of the order that afternoon, Jamie went in search of his chef de cuisine. He found Anabel in the small office at the end of the hall off the dining room, poring over the complicated scheduling sheet. She was a short Portuguese woman, but anyone who underestimated her based on her size was in for a rude awakening. Despite her diminutive stature, she was a force, and not just in the kitchen.

He knocked twice on the door frame and Anabel held up a finger to him as her eyes scanned the sheet and her mouth continued to move wordlessly. After a moment, she leaned back in the chair and looked up at Jamie, a wide smile spreading across her face.

"What's up, Chef?" she asked.

"Produce delivery's here. Ricky's sending someone back later with the apricots."

"Great. How's Cheryl doing? I heard she's on bed rest."

"How does everyone know these things before me?" Jamie asked.

"I heard it from Natalia at yoga this morning, but I'm pretty sure she heard it from Carla over at the diner. Oh! That reminds me." She shuffled through some papers on the desk before locating the one she wanted, holding it out to him. "The university wants to know if we'll take on an apprentice again this semester."

Jamie stepped back, refusing to take the paper. "No. I need to focus on the food and wine festival, which means I need you focused on the restaurant. I'm not going to be able to jump in as much for the next few months, so I can't have you distracted with breaking in a new apprentice right now. Tell the university we'll gladly take someone on in the spring. It's bad enough that Brodie still has the training wheels on," he said.

"He's a good kid. He just…"

"Doesn't like to work?" Jamie finished for her.

Anabel laughed. "Yeah. That about sums it up."

"Come check out the haul," he said, motioning for Anabel to follow him back into the kitchen. "Ricky sent a few crates of Brussels and leeks, but the arugula crop isn't as abundant as I'd like. The beets, however…"

Jamie trailed off as Anabel took in the line of crates filled with the purple root vegetables.

"You aren't kidding." She planted her hands on her hips, her eyes narrowing as she stared at the produce, as though she could intimidate it into being what she had originally wanted. Hell, if anyone could do it, it would be Anabel. "So what are you thinking? Cut the arugula with the—"

"Beet greens, yeah," Jamie said, taking up a position beside her. "And change up the vinaigrette, to something with—"

"A bit more bite. Got it. What are you thinking for the beets themselves?"

"Gnocchi," Jamie said, glancing at his chef de cuisine. She nodded, pressing her lips together as she considered the idea. "With a sage brown butter. Maybe some walnuts."

"We got a nice delivery of scallops that would go great with that," Anabel offered.

"Let's get some of those beets roasting then. We'll need to roast them off and purée them with enough time for it to cool before—"

"I got it," Anabel said, cutting him off. "Now get out of here. You're going to miss your meeting. Say hi to the guys for me!" Anabel called over her shoulder as she disappeared into the walk in.

Alone again, Jamie's thoughts strayed back to Tessa. The idea of never seeing her again was a low simmering irritation, like a too-itchy tag on a sweater. Jamie didn't do one-night stands, and he hated that the first time he strayed outside those bounds was with a woman he was certain he wanted more than one night with.

Jamie shifted a few crates of the beets, but Anabel was right—his friends were waiting. But he also knew he couldn't show up there with a head full of thoughts of the night before. They knew him too well, especially Ethan. Ethan would take one look at Jamie and know immediately that he was thinking about a woman.

If he couldn't make himself stop thinking about Tessa, maybe he could at least shift his thoughts to another, equally unobtainable woman. He picked up two overlarge beets in one hand and snapped a photo of the round vegetables cradled in his palm, firing off a message with the photo attached. It only took a second for his phone to ding in response.

WhiskyBusiness: You know what they say about men with big hands.

Jamie smiled to himself as he typed out his reply, glancing up from his phone every few seconds to make sure he didn't walk into a wall as he made his way out of the restaurant. He didn't know why he hadn't thought of it sooner—if anyone could help him shake the restless anxiety of being ghosted by the best sex of his life, it was Whisky.

DiceDiceBaby: They would be correct.

WhiskyBusiness: Please tell me you're doing something more creative than a beet salad.

DiceDiceBaby: Give me a little credit.

WhiskyBusiness: Then what're you making, hot shot?

DiceDiceBaby: Gnocchi, sage brown butter, walnuts, and scallops.

WhiskyBusiness: I'll allow it.

DiceDiceBaby: What would you make?

He swung into the driver's seat of his car and waited for her reply. He and WhiskyBusiness had met in an online chat forum for their favorite show, *Brilliant British Bakes*, six months ago. What had started as a heated debate about judge Peter London's choice for the season's frontrunner had turned into months of near constant messaging. Eventually the forum's moderator had encouraged them to move their conversation into a private message thread. They'd been messaging each other daily ever since.

He didn't know much about WhiskyBusiness—not her real name or what she looked like, or even where she lived, aside from knowing she was in the United States. She was a chef, like him, though she favored desserts, and he suspected she was younger than him, given her pop culture references.

A few months back when he realized that messaging with her was the highlight of his day, he'd asked her to divulge more details, offered to send her a picture of himself, to fly somewhere to meet her. After all, he was a master of long-distance relationships. Wherever she was, he'd make it work. She'd turned him down, insisting it was better if they kept things online and anonymous. Just friends. He couldn't say he agreed. Then again, Jamie had never been good at keeping things casual.

His date the night before was the latest in a string of bad blind dates he'd gone on over the last few months. Ever since word got out that he was single again, it seemed every elderly woman in Aster Bay was desperate to set him up with their granddaughter or niece or cousin's daughter's friend. For a while, he'd held out hope that Whisky would come around and agree to meet, to bring their online connection into real life, but if she hadn't changed her mind by now, it was time to admit that she wasn't ever going to. Agreeing to the blind dates was meant to be a first step in letting go of the dream of ever taking his connection with Whisky off the internet, but each date had been worse than the last.

Though if he hadn't gone on that awful date, he never would have met Tessa…

He couldn't help the sprout of guilt growing in his gut at texting with Whisky like he hadn't spent the night before in bed with another woman, but Tessa was gone and Whisky had no interest in taking their relationship to the next level, so he had nothing to feel guilty about. Hell, he didn't even know Whisky's *name.*

WhiskyBusiness: Beet cake with a bourbon custard and vanilla bean ice cream.

DiceDiceBaby: Well, shit, where do I get some of that?

WhiskyBusiness: Sending you the recipe now.

A moment later, his phone chimed with a link to one of her recipe cards. Whisky had tons of these digital recipe cards, each one a scan of a handwritten recipe—mostly just a list of ingredients, temperatures, and times with very little of the method. It had taken him a while to figure out her shorthand, but by now he had his own folder of the digital cards, each one another piece of her story that she was willing to share with him. He collected them the way teenagers collected mementos of their high school crushes: a molten lava cake recipe instead of a movie ticket stub, the ratios for her sangria granita instead of a note passed in pre-calculus.

For a moment he wondered what Tessa would make with the beets, what she'd think of Whisky's cake idea…

Another chime.

He closed the recipe and opened the message, barking out a surprised laugh at the image that filled his screen. A feminine hand was wrapped suggestively around a half-shucked corn cob, husk and silk peeled back to reveal the bright yellow and white kernels. It was the first glimpse of her skin he'd gotten, and his eyes fixated on the olive undertones, the tiny white line of a scar at the base of her thumb.

DiceDiceBaby: I see I'm not the only one with impressive produce.

WhiskyBusiness: *wink emoji*

Jamie glanced at the clock. If he didn't get going, he was going to be late and his friends would never let him live it down. They already teased him mercilessly about his friendship with Whisky.

DiceDiceBaby: You around later?

WhiskyBusiness: Sure thing. Rewatch season 2?

DiceDiceBaby: Definitely.

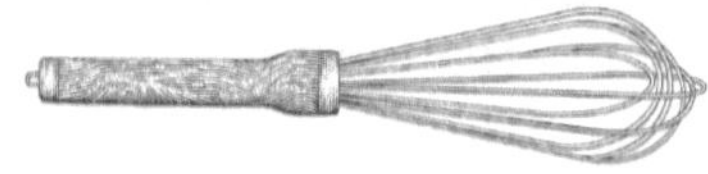

As Jamie had suspected, Gavin and Baz were already there when he arrived at The Barclay. The boutique hotel just outside of the downtown center of Aster Bay had an expansive lawn and connected to a private section of the beach. That past summer, Jamie had spent a week at The Barclay for his brother's wedding festivities, and while he'd always loved the beachfront spot, that week had cemented it as one of his favorite places in Aster Bay. It also had the only ballroom in town large enough to even consider hosting the opening dinner for the food and wine festival.

When Jamie had agreed to chair the town's largest annual festival, he hadn't realized just how much was involved. It had seemed easy enough—plan a menu, pair it with wine from Ethan's vineyard, get Gavin to put together some publicity, sell enough tickets that Baz didn't worry about the finances. But there was so much more to it, venues and vendors and finding enough volunteers and liquor licenses. Thank God his friends were on board to help. He would not be the reason the festival failed, not when the town was counting on the tourism it would bring, and certain members of the merchant's association were already wary of letting someone who wasn't originally from Aster Bay take the lead.

"Sorry I'm late," Jamie said as he climbed out of his car. "Is Ethan here yet?"

"No," Baz said. "He said to go ahead without him. Something came up, but he'll come by Lemon and Thyme tomorrow morning."

Jamie glanced at his phone to confirm what he already knew—he hadn't missed a call or text from his best friend. "Wonder why he didn't tell me," he mumbled.

"Said he has a surprise," Baz said with a shrug.

Jamie tensed. "I hate surprises. Did you guys hear about Cheryl?"

"Yeah. I hope she's alright," Gavin said, brushing his shaggy blonde hair out of his eyes.

"I saw Ricky this morning. He said it's just a precaution," Jamie assured his friend.

"Look at you," Gavin teased, "up on the town gossip like a local."

Jamie ignored the way his friend's comment rankled, like an unexpected brush with a nettle bush. Even after twenty-three years in Aster Bay, he still wasn't considered a local. He knew Gavin hadn't meant anything by it, but he couldn't help but feel that familiar twinge of not belonging, the certainty that he would *never* belong, no matter how many festivals he chaired.

He planted his hands on his hips and surveyed the hotel parking lot, squinting in the late September sun. "Lot's smaller than I remember," he said.

"So's the dining room," Baz replied.

Jamie sighed. "We're going to have to make it work. There isn't anywhere else."

Baz grunted and disappeared inside the hotel, prattling on about deposits and administration fees.

Jamie began to follow, but Gavin caught his arm. "Hey, rumor has it you went on a date with Trisha White last night."

Jamie groaned. "Where did you hear that?"

"Mrs. White and my mom are in the same book club. So?" A knowing grin spread across Gavin's face. *Jerk.* "She's cute."

Jamie scrubbed his hand over his face, his fingertips pressing into his eyes. "She didn't even know that short ribs are beef."

Gavin laughed. "Well, it was a date, not an interview, right?"

"It was a disaster."

Even though it was true that his date with Trisha had been awful, he didn't regret it. He never would have met Tessa if he hadn't been on that date. And Tessa was worth meeting.

"I know that look," Gavin said, pointing at the smile that had slipped across Jamie's face. "Must not have been that big of a disaster."

"Oh, it was every bit that big of a disaster. But after—"

"There's an after?"

"There was this other woman. At the bar. We may have… had a drink."

Gavin snorted. "Is that a euphemism? Good for you, man. How long has it been since you…*had a drink*?"

A long time. Since I started talking to Whisky every day. That couldn't be right, and yet… *Damn.*

"When are you seeing her again?" Gavin asked.

"I'm not. It was just a one night thing." His stomach

twisted, his body rebelling at the idea that he wouldn't ever see Tessa again. But it was out of his hands. She'd disappeared the first chance she got. He pursed his lips against the bitterness rising within him.

Gavin frowned, visibly confused. "Was it bad?"

"What? God, no. It was... No, it was definitely not bad." Jamie lowered his voice, pushing away thoughts of just how *not bad* the night before had been. "You cannot say a word to anyone. Helen White will have me tarred and feathered and run out of town if she knows I left a date with her granddaughter and went back to another woman's hotel room."

"Hotel room?" Gavin's eyes lit up at the new bit of gossip.

"Not a word."

Baz appeared in the hotel doorway, his dark features pulled into his usual scowl. "Are you two coming?"

"Jamie hooked up with someone last night. In a *hotel*," Gavin said, flashing one of those all-American smiles that made his students in the marketing program at the university swoon.

"What happened to not a word?" Jamie asked, shoving his friend, who only laughed in response.

"The guys don't count," Gavin protested.

"Weren't you out with Trisha White last night?" Baz asked.

"I was, but—"

"But that's not who he went back to a *hotel* with," Gavin gleefully offered.

Baz huffed out a laugh. "Don't tell Mrs. White."

Chapter Four

"Planning your escape already?" Ethan asked, leaning in the doorway to his guest room.

Tessa looked over her shoulder at her father, a handful of push pins balanced precariously between her lips. She stood on the bed, her feet sunken into the mattress and her hands pressed to the world map on the wall.

"Jesus, TJ, don't put push pins in your mouth," he said, coming into the room and holding his hand out beneath her chin. She rolled her eyes and spit the pins into his palm. "Not something I expected to have to say to my twenty-five-year-old."

"I was fine. And I go by Tessa now. Remember?" She selected a pin from his outstretched hand and jammed it into the corner of the map.

"Right. Sorry. I keep forgetting."

"It's okay," she said as she pinned down another corner.

She knew he was trying. She wouldn't even be there if he wasn't trying. But she hadn't used the nickname since she started working in professional kitchens a decade ago. *You also haven't seen your father more than a handful of times in the last ten years.*

Guilt coursed through her veins, a familiar sensation ever since she'd admitted to herself that she hadn't done her part to meet him halfway. It was one thing when she was a kid, but she was an adult now. She could have tried harder to rebuild their relationship. Should have.

You're here now, she reminded herself as she jabbed another pin into the wall. *You're trying.*

"What are all the 'x's?" Ethan asked, gesturing to the map. It was covered in tiny red 'x's—Sri Lanka and Portugal, Peru and Denmark, Belgium and Thailand. "Places you've been?"

She huffed out an amused breath. "Places I want to go." She turned to him with her brightest, most charming smile. "Some of which I'll actually get to visit now. Thanks to you."

Ethan scrubbed his hand over the back of his neck, ruffling the short hairs there. "Not me. Your grandparents are the ones who set up that trust for you, Teej—Tessa. I don't know how far twenty grand will get you, though."

Tessa hopped off the bed and surveyed her work. The map was slightly crooked, but it was good enough. "Farther than I've been."

"You know you don't need to do this to get the money," he said, his brow crinkling with concern. "Work here, I mean. The rules of the trust are clear. You turn twenty-five, the money's yours. No strings attached."

"You trying to get rid of me?" she asked. She'd meant it as a joke, but her smile slipped and for a moment, she was flooded with fear that maybe he didn't actually want her there.

"No! Of course not. I'm so glad you're here, T. I'm afraid I'm gonna wake up and realize it's all a dream." Ethan sank down on the edge of her bed and she took a seat next to him, waiting for him to continue. "I just don't want you to think you are under any obligation to do anything you don't want to do."

"I know. But like I told you on the phone, I want to spend some time with you, work together on this pop-up. I'm sorry I haven't come back before now—"

"Hey, hey, no one blames you for that. Least of all me."

She drew in a deep breath through her nose. She blamed herself.

"I want to be here. I want us to get to know each other." His eyes were misty and she absolutely could not handle another second of this heart-to-heart. How had things gotten so heavy so fast? "And in three months' time, I'll be out of your hair."

"You're not in my hair."

"You know what I mean. Besides, I don't like the idea of taking a hand-out. At least if you let me run the pop-up this year, I'll feel like I've earned some of that money. Mom always said not to take anything you didn't earn." She ignored the twinge of grief, still so tangible even after three years, and barreled on. "Besides, you're out a baker for the season and I'm currently unemployed. It just makes sense. I've always thought I might want to open my own place. This is kind of like a test drive to see what it would be like."

"Maybe you'll even open something around here one day. You know, I know folks who have a few open storefronts in town. I could—"

"We've been over this," she said as gently as she could. "I don't see myself staying here long term."

"Right," Ethan said, taking a step back and flashing a strained smile.

Shit. She didn't want to hurt her father's feelings, but did he really not see that being in Aster Bay, even for the few months she had promised him, was going to be hard enough? She'd only been in town for twenty-four hours and already she could feel everyone's eyes on her. And when she closed her eyes to hide from their staring, all she could see was Jamie tangled in her hotel room sheets, his hair falling over his face as he slept. It would have been so easy to climb back in bed, to just…stay.

Staying had never been Tessa's strong suit.

"But I'm here now," she said. "Why don't you take me over to the vineyard and show me around? It's been so long, I'm not sure I'd even recognize the place. And I'm dying to see the kitchen."

"Yeah, alright, kid. Let's go."

Ethan's house sat on a small lot at the edge of the Nuthatch Vineyards property. The vineyard had been in Ethan's family—Tessa's family—for generations, but Ethan was the first to build a proper home on the land. A line of tall pine trees served as a privacy fence of sorts between the house and the rest of the property, so while she wouldn't have a view of the sprawling grounds with row after row of grape vines, she also wouldn't have to contend with curious workers trying to catch a glimpse of Ethan's estranged daughter through the kitchen window.

The farmhouse-style main building of the vineyard that housed the winery and tasting room was on the other end of the property, so they rode over the bumpy dirt roads of the grounds in Ethan's pickup. It also was home to Sugar Grapes. When Tessa was a kid, her grandmother ran Sugar Grapes, a bakery that specialized in dessert and wine pairings and had been famous for its red wine brownies. But when her grandmother had retired, the bakery had closed down. It'd been shuttered ever since, though Cheryl, a local farmer's wife, ran a pop-up shop out of the kitchen every holiday season, providing pies and cakes for the townspeople's Thanksgiving and Christmas dinners. This year, Cheryl was very pregnant and unable to open the shop. When Ethan had called a few days ago to arrange for the transfer of her trust, she'd been unable to give him a permanent mailing address and he'd invited her to come stay with him and open the bakery for the three-month season. She'd accepted on a whim.

Ethan assured her that the kitchen was kept in good repair and well-stocked with equipment since caterers still worked out of the space when people rented the vineyard for weddings and big events. But she would need to create a menu from scratch, make sure the kitchen was fully stocked, and hire staff. It was going to be a lot of work, but she couldn't wait. And it would give her something to focus on while she and Ethan tried to establish a new relationship—other than obsess about Jamie, that is.

She didn't know why she couldn't get the man from the night before out of her head, but she told herself she'd done the right thing. Jamie didn't seem like the kind of guy you could have a fling with and then leave behind in three months. He was the kind of guy you kept. The kind of guy who kept you.

She stepped out of the truck, dropping the last few inches to the dirt when her short legs didn't quite reach. Why couldn't she have inherited her father's height? Staring up at the wood-shingled building with its dark green roof and a faux grain silo on one side of the building that she knew housed a winding staircase up to the second floor tasting room, she was hit with an unexpected feeling of déjà vu.

She knew this place, remembered her grandmother scolding her as she slid down the railing, the metal digging into her hands and leaving awful red marks across her palms. Her father building block towers with her in his office while they waited for her mother to get back from her GED classes. The way her grandfather would bring her bunches of fresh grapes for her school lunches, claiming each one to be the most delicious one yet.

Her breath caught with a sudden wave of longing for those grandparents she'd hardly seen over the last seventeen years, grandparents who had helped raise her, who'd never stopped calling or sending birthday cards, even when she hadn't always returned the favor.

"Are Grama and Gramps here?" she asked, glancing around like her grandmother might appear over the slight rise of the hill that led off to the production facility where the grapes were processed into wine.

Ethan scrunched up his brow. "No, T. Grama and Gramps moved to Florida two years ago."

"Right. I knew that," she said. Had she known that? She wasn't sure. Her mother hadn't been big on sharing news from Aster Bay, and Tessa was still disoriented by the sudden nostalgia for a place she couldn't have described two days ago even under duress. "Sorry." She smiled up at Ethan, squinting in the sun. "It feels weird to be here without them."

"To me, too, kid." He looked away and cleared his throat. "Come on. Let me show you around."

The kitchen was beautiful, all gleaming stainless steel and high-end appliances, well maintained and well equipped. It was also sterile, devoid of any personality. She'd worked for chefs who preferred their workspace that way, a blank canvas so nothing distracted them from their work. But not Tessa. She needed color, vibrance, inspiration bursting from every seam. How could you be creative in a white and steel box?

As she surveyed the kitchen, she could see exactly what she'd change, starting with the shelf of solid white plastic containers, each with a fading label for various cake decorations. It was a travesty to conceal all that joy in opaque containers. As soon as she could find the closest restaurant supply, she'd be replacing those with clear plastic jars filled to the brim with every color of sprinkle she could find.

"What do you think?" Ethan asked.

"Can I hang things on the walls?" she asked.

"Of course. Just run anything more permanent by me first, okay? Don't go knocking down any walls or redoing the tile without me at least signing off on it."

"I can work with that. I'm going to take a peek in the walk-in."

"Have at it. I've got a few calls to make. Come find me in the office when you're ready to go, yeah?"

She watched him leave, making sure she was alone, before she pulled out her phone.

WhiskyBusiness: What's better? Robin's egg blue or fire engine red?"

It only took a moment for the three dots to begin dancing at the bottom of the screen.

DiceDiceBaby: That depends on where you're putting the color?

WhiskyBusiness: Dish towels. Oven mitts.

DiceDiceBaby: Go with the blue. Calming and creative at the same time.

WhiskyBusiness: And if I'd said the color was going

somewhere else?

DiceDiceBaby: Like where?

WhiskyBusiness: I don't know. Fondant?

DiceDiceBaby: Does fondant need a color?

WhiskyBusiness: *eye roll emoji* You're no fun.

DiceDiceBaby: What can I say? I like the look of a white cake.

Tessa snorted and rounded the corner into the walk-in refrigerator. She'd be starting from scratch with stocking the place, but it had plenty of space to store the larger baker's racks that would house cooling cakes and setting custards. She snapped a picture and sent it off to DDB.

DiceDiceBaby: New kitchen?

WhiskyBusiness: New to me.

DiceDiceBaby: Where?

WhiskyBusiness: No identifying details, remember?

DiceDiceBaby: Can't blame a guy for trying.

She liked DDB. Too much. She had enough years of proof to know that liking something that much was a sure sign it would never work out—jobs, homes, families…

She'd been clear with him from the beginning. This was

an internet friendship, even if their messages had grown increasingly flirtatious. Even if she did spend more time messaging the mysterious chef she'd met in the *Brilliant British Bakes* online forum than any of the guys who matched with her on the dating app she'd reluctantly installed last year. Come to think of it, she couldn't remember the last time she'd even logged into the dating app.

Flashes from the night before swirled through her mind—Jamie staring up at her from between her legs, burying his nose in her hair, banding his arm around her chest to hold her tight to his body as he pistoned into her from behind in the middle of the night. Heat rushed through her, and she swallowed down the twinge of regret that she'd never see him again.

It's for the best.

The night before had felt like a dream, somehow out of time and place. It had all felt so unreal and yet somehow more real than she could afford to indulge. None of that mattered now, anyway. Jamie was gone and DDB would stay safely confined to her message inbox where he could never look at her like he was making plans. Tessa didn't make plans, especially not with men.

WhiskyBusiness: One more color question.

DiceDiceBaby: Hit me.

WhiskyBusiness: Panties.

The three dots appeared. Disappeared. Reappeared.

Tessa smirked, biting her lip to keep from outright laughing as she imagined him trying to find the perfect response. She didn't know what he looked like, but she imagined he was tall, with warm eyes and a sexy smile. Big hands, rough from years of working in kitchens. In her mind, he was big all over.

Like Jamie.

No.

DiceDiceBaby: Bikini cut?

She laughed. DDB was nothing if not a stickler for details.

WhiskyBusiness: Thong.

DiceDiceBaby: Go with the red.

Chapter Five

Jamie knew he could be a grumpy asshole—his brother Daemon, the grumpiest of assholes, delighted in telling him so— but he didn't generally consider himself an angry person. That was before he arrived at his restaurant to find the one-night stand who had run out on him before sun-up *in his kitchen.*

A kitchen was a chef's castle, or temple, or whatever the fuck meant it was a sacred goddamn place. His crew knew better than to so much as rearrange the pot rack, which is why he could not figure out how the hell Tessa had come to be there, unaccompanied and without his knowledge, two days after she'd disappeared while he was sleeping.

When he pushed through the doors from the darkened dining room, he found her blasting some God-awful pop music and singing off-key into one of his wooden spoons, her back to him as she danced in front of the gas range. He was momentarily distracted by the way she moved to the music, her full ass almost hypnotic as she shimmied her hips in jeans that looked practically painted on. His cock kicked behind the placket of his pants. She was all curves and softness, and his body remembered how it had felt to lose himself in that softness less than forty-eight hours before.

His eye caught the telltale glint of edible glitter on the workstation and suddenly no amount of perfect ass shaking could distract him from the ways in which she had sullied his kitchen, even if he also wanted to drop to his knees and bury his face between her thighs until she swore not to walk out on him again. Was it possible to want to berate someone and also be overwhelmingly relieved to see them? He wanted to shake her until she understood how fucked up it was to leave without saying a goddamn word and then beg her not to do it again. The emotional whiplash was exhilarating and exhausting.

Still bleating into the wooden spoon and oblivious to his presence, Tessa grabbed a bottle of rum from the workstation—the good stuff that he used for creating rum caramel sauce for bread puddings—and poured a heavy splash into the skillet in front of her. *And now she's wasting my best rum.* She tilted the pan until the alcohol caught on the flames from the burner, a sudden pillar of fire erupting from the pan as she swirled the contents with a practiced motion of her wrist.

Jamie swallowed the rebuke he'd been prepared to bark in her direction, instead silently leaning against the doorway, crossing his arms over his chest as he watched her cook. Her dark hair was piled on top of her head in a messy bun, but she'd clearly taken the time to be sure each strand was tucked away. She'd foregone a chef's coat in favor of her street clothes—tight jeans and a V-neck shirt covered in a cherry print—but the towel over her shoulder had only the barest hint of soiling where she'd wiped her fingers as she worked. A professional knife roll sat on the workstation next to the offending vial of edible glitter.

She belonged in the kitchen.

But why the hell was she in his? And how had she even found him?

She gave the pan another shake, then set it down. She spun around, shimmying and singing the whole time. As her eyes snagged on Jamie, she dropped the spoon, the wood clattering to the floor.

"Holy shit!" she shouted, pressing a hand to her chest. She grabbed the remote for the stereo system from the counter beside her and switched off the music, the silence settling around them. "What are you doing here?"

He arched an eyebrow at her. "This is my restaurant. What are *you* doing here?"

Her face paled and she narrowed her eyes at him like she was trying to make out a fuzzy image in an old photograph. "You're Jameson Chase?"

She used his full name, like they were at the goddamn DMV, like he hadn't been inside her the night before last.

"Most people call me Jamie. Or Chef. Thought you'd remember that. You certainly screamed it loud enough the other night."

She retrieved the spoon from the floor and tossed it into the sink. Her hands rested on her hips, her chin tilting up defiantly and her blue eyes blazing. "Not sure I know what you're talking about."

He pushed off from the doorway, stalking towards her. Yes, he was angry with her, and yes, he wanted to know why she was there, how she had found him, but he wanted to taste her again more. "Maybe I should remind you then."

She took a step away, her eyes going wide, and he froze. *What the fuck is that about?*

"What are you doing here, Tessa?" he ground out, her reaction to him setting his nerves on edge. He wanted her, but he wasn't about to make a move on someone who wasn't into it. *What changed?*

"I would think it's obvious," she said, tilting her head towards the pan on the stove. Her eyes were too wide, darting all over the kitchen, from the door to him, like she'd seen a ghost.

"I've never known someone to break and enter just to fix themselves a snack," he said.

"I have permission to be here."

"Not from me. How'd you find me?" When she continued to stare at him blankly, he tried again. "Why bother tracking me down, after you took off without even saying goodbye?"

She had the good graces to look embarrassed, pink spreading up her neck and into her cheeks. "I didn't track you down."

"No? Looks that way from where I'm standing."

He meandered through the workstations in a wide loop to assess the damage she'd done and give himself time to process the fact that she was in his kitchen, to put some distance between them while she was doing the whole deer-in-the-headlights thing. He trailed his finger along the edge of the counter, affecting a stance that was far more casual than he felt, but he was pleased when his finger came away clean. She worked neatly, edible glitter aside.

He stopped just in front of her, close enough that he could speak softly but not so close that he was tempted to touch her. "The other night didn't have to be a one time thing, you know?"

She recoiled, reaching over to shake the contents of her pan. "Yes, it did. It should never have happened in the first place."

"That's not how you felt then." He peered into the pan on the stove. Bananas foster before noon was a little unconventional, but he supposed there were worse vices.

"Wow." She shook her head, pulled the pan out of his reach, and turned off the flame. "You are even more arrogant than I thought."

"You're going to tell me you didn't have a good time?"

"Whether I had a good time is not the point." Her cheeks were crimson, and she glanced warily at the door again. Why did she keep doing that?

"Then what is the point?"

She leaned against the workstation, crossing her arms in a way that pushed her breasts up, like she was daring him to look, to remember how her nipples had pebbled beneath his tongue. As if he could forget.

"The point is, it can't happen again."

He took a step closer, crowding her against the workstation. She tilted her chin up to meet his gaze, a challenge glinting in her eyes. He loved how she went toe-to-toe with him, holding her ground.

The slight parting of her lips and the way her eyes widened betrayed her, though—if he wasn't mistaken, she was just as turned on as he was. But given how skittish she was acting, she'd have to touch him first if she wanted to do more than verbally spar. He wouldn't touch her until he was absolutely certain that she wanted him to, no matter how badly he was dying to feel her against him.

Jamie reached around her and dragged a tasting spoon through the sauce in her pan. He took his time licking the sticky concoction from the back of the spoon, enjoying the way she watched him. A flush crept up her cheeks as her eyes followed the movement of his tongue. He tossed the spoon into the sink with a satisfied hum. "Cardamom? Interesting choice."

Her eyes dropped to his lips. Just for a second, but long enough for him to notice. "It's delicious and you know it."

He wasn't used to people talking back to him in his kitchen, but he found he liked it more than he would have expected, especially when it was Tessa doing the talking in that almost breathless tone of voice.

Again, she glanced at the door.

"Expecting someone?" he asked.

She swallowed, looking a little sick all of a sudden. "There's something I should tell you."

He gripped the edge of the counter on either side of her hips, digging his fingers into the metal to keep himself from putting his hands on her. "Then tell me."

Her gaze turned wary and she worried her bottom lip between her teeth. He took a half step back, letting his eyes sweep over her, but giving her the space she clearly wanted. He drew a long breath in and out through his nose. Leaning against the counter across the aisle from her, he braced his hands on the countertop behind him.

"I thought I would have recognized you," she mumbled, mostly to herself.

"What does that mean?"

There was that wariness in her eyes again as she scanned his face. "I didn't come here today for you."

What the hell is she talking about?

"Then who did you come to *my* restaurant for?"

"Ethan Hart."

"Ethan?" Jamie glanced over his shoulder at the door to the kitchen. "How do you know Ethan?" She opened her mouth and closed it again without making any sound, her expression turning pained. *Fuck.* "Are you and Ethan—"

"Sorry I'm late!" Ethan's voice echoed through the kitchen as he burst through the doors.

Jamie took another step away from Tessa, knocking over her edible glitter in the process. He cursed under his breath as it exploded in a puff into the air, sending bits of glitter into his hair. He tried to shake it loose as he grabbed a side towel, setting to work cleaning her station of the offending sparkle.

"No worries. Didn't realize you'd invited someone to join us," Jamie said, careful to keep his tone free of the confusion and frustration slowly bubbling up through his blood.

Tessa was somehow involved with his best friend.

No wonder she'd snuck out of the hotel room that morning. Had she used him to cheat on his best friend?

"Sorry about that. I know how strict you are about your kitchen," Ethan said. He wrapped an arm around Tessa's shoulder. She visibly tensed beneath his touch.

Good. I hope she feels guilty as fuck.

Ethan gave Tessa a soft smile before turning back to Jamie. "You remember my daughter."

All the air knocked out of Jamie's lungs and the world tilted on its axis.

He hadn't slept with Ethan's girlfriend—he'd slept with his best friend's *daughter.* How the fuck had that happened? The last time he'd seen TJ, she was a gangly eight-year-old with a permanent scowl on her face, nothing like the woman in front of him.

TJ—also known as Tessa Jayne.

Fuck!

"TJ's setting up the pop-up bakery at Sugar Grapes this year since Cheryl's on bed rest. I figured she could step in as your pastry chef for the festival, too, but I know how picky you are and that you'd want to taste her food yourself before you commit. It made more sense for her to prepare it here than at the bakery. Sugar Grapes isn't stocked yet." Ethan paused in his monologue just long enough to notice the death glare Jamie was shooting at Tessa across the room.

Did she know who I was when we met last night? Did she have any idea that she was taking her father's best friend back to her hotel room? Was this all just another way for her to hurt her father?

Tessa swept away from Ethan towards the walk-in freezer, the movement breaking Jamie from his horrified litany of questions. "Let me just plate this up and I'll come out and join you," she said, her voice brittle and too bright.

Before Jamie could find out what exactly she was plating from his freezer, she was gone around the corner. He glanced up just in time to see the mesmerizing sway of her hips as she disappeared into his kitchen, his gaze snagging on the way her ass moved beneath the tight denim. He immediately looked away, closing his eyes against the onslaught of unwanted lust. It was no wonder he hadn't recognized that surly kid in the confident woman she'd become.

No excuse. His stomach twisted. *No excuse for betraying your best friend.*

And when he'd come into the kitchen that morning, and she'd realized who he was, she still hadn't told him.

Fucking fuck! What kind of game is she playing?

"Jame? You alright?" Ethan asked, assessing Jamie where he'd resumed scrubbing his towel aggressively over the counter that would never again be free of glitter.

"You didn't tell me TJ was in town," Jamie said, moving on to make coffee. He needed a task to focus on so he couldn't think about all the inappropriate things he'd done to his best friend's daughter.

"It all happened kind of fast. I called to set up the transfer of her trust, and we got to talking."

The trust.

Jamie, his back to Ethan as he futzed at the coffee machine, squeezed his eyes shut. This was all about money for her. She didn't care that Ethan would be crushed when she left. And what was worse, Jamie had been a party to hurting his best friend.

Ethan, oblivious to Jamie's mental self-flagellation, continued on. "She mentioned she was between jobs, and with Cheryl not being able to run the pop-up this year... You know how I've been trying to get her to come back to town, especially since her mother died. When I think of all those years I missed out on really getting to know her, all the times Steph lied to me about my own kid... Well, this seemed like a good chance for us to get to know each other. Without her mother's lies getting in the way." When Jamie didn't say anything, Ethan lowered his voice. "You're not mad that I let her into your kitchen, are you?"

"No!" Jamie jammed his finger into the button on the coffee maker, the machine whirring to life. "No. Just surprised, that's all. You know I hate surprises."

"Okay," Ethan said, dragging a hand through his hair.

He turned to face Ethan, guilt clawing at his throat. "You sure it's a good idea to let her in on your business, even for a few months?"

"Why wouldn't it be?"

Damn Ethan and his too-trusting nature.

"Seems awfully convenient. She just happens to be between jobs and willing to come back here, for the first time in years?"

"I told you—Steph lied to us both for years. Told TJ she wasn't welcome and told me she didn't want to be here. Who knows if she would have come back sooner if she'd been given the choice?"

"Exactly. Who knows? Maybe she's angling for more than just the trust."

"Like what? Like a father? A family?"

Jamie cursed under his breath. "See, that's what I mean. You want her to be here so badly, you wouldn't even see it if she was playing you."

"Is it so unbelievable that she actually wants to be here?" Ethan asked, hurt cutting through his voice.

"That's not what I meant."

"Then what did you mean?"

Jamie shook his head, reaching for the coffee mugs. Even if Tessa was taking advantage of him, Ethan would never hear it, and pushing the issue would just drive him away. Jamie's stomach lurched. He would not lose Ethan's friendship over this. If it meant he had to keep an eye on Tessa himself, he would.

"Nothing. I'm sorry. If you're happy, I'm happy."

Ethan exhaled, a wary smile sliding across his face. "I'm hoping you two will get along. From what I understand, she's been working under some impressive chefs on the West Coast but they've kept her name off most things." Jamie nodded. It was typical behavior for a certain type of superstar chef. "She wants to open her own place. I'm hoping I can convince her to do it here."

"You think that's something she'd want to do?" Jamie asked, avoiding Ethan's eyes under the guise of shaking more glitter out of his hair, hoping the movement masked his panic at the idea of Tessa becoming part of Aster Bay on a permanent basis.

"Not today, it's not. She's got a head full of Steph's bitterness. Decades of those old hurts between Steph and her parents. She seems to think everyone in town thinks like them, that she's got a scarlet letter on her chest or something. But if she can work with you on the food and wine festival and make a mark on this town that's all her own, I think she'd see that there are more people who want her here than don't."

Jamie nodded. It was a good plan, and exactly the kind of thing Ethan would come up with—helping his daughter, his best friend, and his town in one clean sweep, with a side of healing family trauma for good measure. Jamie wanted to get on board, he did, but he also wanted to scrub his skin until it was raw and he no longer remembered the way it felt to sleep pressed against Tessa.

Ethan sighed. "This feels like my chance to actually get to know my kid, maybe convince her to come home for real, ya know?"

Jamie's grip on the handle of the coffee mug he was retrieving faltered, the mug slipping through his fingers and clattering on the counter. "How long is she staying?"

"Through the holidays."

"That long?" Jamie winced, knowing as soon as the words had left his mouth that they were the worst words he could have chosen in that moment.

Except maybe, hey, I fucked your daughter last night. Jesus fucking Christ.

"She's my daughter," Ethan bristled. "Her mother's been gone for three years now and who knows where the hell the rest of the Cordeiros are. My family is the only family she has left and I've been waiting for years for a chance to be there for her. She can stay as long as she fucking wants."

Jamie waited, knowing Ethan well enough to know there was something he wasn't saying.

"She's just here until Christmas. She'll make a salary while she works for me, and I'll sign the trust over to her before she leaves. She's always wanted to travel. Now she can do that without taking on any debt. And if the next few months go well, maybe she'll come back when the wanderlust wears off."

"Sounds like she's getting more out of this deal than you are."

"She's my kid—that's the way it's supposed to be. Besides, it's the first time she's wanted to know *me* and not the version of me that Steph filled her head with for all those years. I don't know... I'm not expecting us to become close overnight, but maybe with a few months in the same place..."

"I get it," Jamie said.

He just didn't trust her not to break his best friend's heart. And he wished he hadn't slept with her before he'd found out who she was.

Tessa reappeared carrying a small stainless-steel container, frosty wisps rising into the air above the container. "What are you guys still doing in here?" she asked. "Shoo. I'll be out in a minute."

"You did not just shoo me out of my own kitchen," Jamie said, narrowing his eyes.

She cocked a hip and an eyebrow at him, the corner of her lip quirking up. "No, Chef."

Fuck me.

Chapter Six

Tessa took her time plating. While pristine plating might not be her style, Ethan had been very clear that it was Jamie's and, if she wanted to prove herself, she needed every advantage she could get. Most men weren't inclined to partner with women they'd seen in pigtails, never mind someone who'd ghosted them after earth-shattering sex, but from everything Ethan had told her, working on this festival with Jamie could help her start to make a name for herself, separate from the temperamental chefs she'd worked under for the last few years. Besides, it was important to Ethan that she and Jamie get along, that she work with his friend on this festival. It was too early in their relationship for her to start letting her father down already. She didn't want either of them to hand her this job—she wanted to earn it, and their respect. Both of them.

She only had vague recollections of Jamie from when she was a kid, but she knew he'd been around back then, the guy Ethan called when he and her mom were fighting again. The one who would show up at the house in the middle of the night if Ethan needed to take a walk through the grapes and blow off some steam. She thought she would have had at least a twinge of recognition for the man before she'd pulled him into her bed.

The dining room of Lemon and Thyme was sparsely decorated in creams and sage green, three walls of floor to ceiling windows proudly displaying the view of the ocean. She'd missed that view. When she'd last lived in town, the building had been more of a pub than the upscale restaurant Jamie had turned it into, but it still offered its patrons a stunning view of the bay. It was like you weren't even on land anymore, surrounded by the waves and the bobbing boats on three sides. It was like floating.

Ethan and Jamie sat at a four-top in the corner, three mugs of coffee waiting on the table. She set a shallow bowl in front of each of them before taking a seat next to her father. Each bowl was dressed with a swirl of caramel sauce, half a flambéed banana, a perfect quenelle of white ice cream, and a sprinkle of pecan-studded granola, little flecks of edible glitter dusting the pecans. The presentation was a bit subdued for her taste, but she hoped it was just the right amount of refined to prove to Jamie that she was all grown up. A true professional.

"You had time to make ice cream?" Jamie asked.

Tessa shrugged, pouring sugar into her coffee cup. "I made it last night. I wanted to test the ice cream machine at the bakery."

He shot daggers at her with his eyes as he slid his spoon across the bowl, gathering a bit of everything into the perfect bite, and ate. She held her breath, anticipating the moment the ice cream melted on his tongue.

His eyes flew to hers. "Goat cheese."

She leaned back in her chair with a satisfied smirk. The complexity of flavor, the cool ice cream with the still warm banana, the crunch of the granola and the smooth caramel, the peppery cardamom and the earthiness of the rum—the dish was a masterpiece. She knew it and now he did too.

"Teej, this is fantastic," Ethan said, digging into another bite.

"Thanks, Ethan." She saw the hurt flicker across her father's face at her use of his first name, there and gone before anyone else would notice. But what was she supposed to call the man she only saw twice a year for the last decade and a half—*dad?* Then, as if she couldn't help rubbing salt in the wound, she added, "I go by Tessa now."

"Right. Sorry. Old habits," her father said with an apologetic smile.

"It's good, but it won't work for the festival. You can't flambé bananas to order," Jamie said.

"I'm aware," she replied. "It wasn't meant as a possible menu item."

"Then what was it meant as?"

Ethan's head snapped back and forth between his daughter and his best friend as they lobbed barbs at each other across the table. He took the final bite from his bowl and pushed it aside. "Jame, this dish might not be appropriate for the festival, but I think you should bring Tessa in on the menu planning, just like you were going to do with Cheryl. She's got some really interesting ideas—"

"Do they involve edible glitter?" Jamie asked, gesturing to the granola with the tip of his spoon.

"What's wrong with edible glitter?" Tessa asked, crossing her arms over her chest.

Jamie scoffed. "It's edible glitter. If you need pyrotechnics to make your dish memorable, then it's not a very good dish."

"Hey, now," Ethan said.

"That dish went viral when one of my customers posted it on Instagram last month."

"The people on Instagram only have to look at the food. Not taste it."

Tessa's blood thundered in her ears at the challenge. "I guess you don't want any more of it then," she said, reaching across the table and pulling his bowl away from him.

A low growl formed at the base of his throat as he gripped the bowl and pulled it back towards himself. "I didn't say that."

"I wouldn't want to diminish the pretentiousness of your restaurant with something as low-brow as edible glitter," Tessa fired back, pulling the bowl back towards her.

Jamie tugged it again, dragging the bowl across the table and Tessa with it. She lurched forward to keep her grip on the rim of the bowl, the movement bending her over the table. Jamie's eyes dipped to the flash of her cleavage, her electric blue lace bra now very visible down her shirt. He only looked for a second, but it was long enough to send a shiver of awareness down her spine.

He still wanted her. He might not like that he did, but she knew that look in his eyes—she'd seen it the other night right before he'd put his mouth between her legs.

"Was there something you wanted?" she asked, staring daggers at him, and arching her back just to watch him squirm.

Jamie released the bowl like it had burned him, sending Tessa reeling backward until she landed, with a humph, in her seat. Jamie held her gaze as he licked the last of the caramel off his spoon. For all his griping, the man certainly enjoyed her food. And she enjoyed watching him eat it, maybe a little too much.

Her father's eyes darted between Tessa and his best friend. "Are you done?" He shot a pointed look at Jamie. "Tessa's food is very popular—"

"On social media," Jamie said with just enough derision in his voice to make it clear exactly how he felt about her internet fame. "I heard."

"She's *good*, Jamie. That dish was fucking incredible," Ethan said, pointing at his own empty bowl.

A lump formed in her throat and tears sprang to her eyes that she quickly blinked away. It shouldn't matter that her father liked her food, that he was standing up for her, but it did.

"And you need her—"

"I'll be fine on my own," Jamie ground out, avoiding Ethan's eyes.

"Cheryl is unavailable for the foreseeable future and, I love you, man, but your bread pudding is not going to wow the foodie tourists who come to the festival every year," Ethan said.

Tessa snorted. Typical that a chef of Jamie's caliber would rely on bread pudding to fill out his dessert menu. For a moment, she imagined what it would be like to teach him to make real pastries and plated desserts worthy of being on his menu. To watch the triumph on his face the first time he made a perfect macaron, or the muscles bunch in his forearms as he kneaded dough for fresh bread. To lick frosting off his fingertips…

Enough.

Ethan continued. "I don't know what bug crawled up your ass and died today, but I have to get back to the vineyard, and I need to know you can handle working with my kid without behaving like an asshole over garnishes."

"Edible glitter is *not* a garnish," Jamie said, sounding like a sullen teenager.

"Enough about the edible glitter! The last chef I worked for didn't have a problem with it," Tessa said. "Marisa

Sinclair. Maybe you've heard of her?"

She cocked her head with a mock quizzical lock on her face, but the way Jamie's nostrils flared and his jaw clenched told her all she needed to know. He'd heard of her former boss alright, though there weren't many people in the food industry who weren't familiar with the James Beard Award-winning chef. She just hoped he hadn't also heard that Marisa had unceremoniously fired Tessa a few weeks ago for that very same viral Instagram post, complaining that it didn't fit the Marisa Sinclair brand, by which she meant it wasn't about Marisa Sinclair and therefore wasn't allowed.

Ethan turned to Jamie and said, "I know how important this festival is to you, and I wouldn't have invited her to be a part of this if she wasn't the best at what she does. If you don't trust her yet, can you at least trust me?"

Jamie blew out a breath and nodded. Finally, he looked up and met Tessa's eyes. It took a conscious effort not to shrink in the face of the anger simmering in his gaze. He drew a long breath in and out through his nose, schooling his features into something that more approximated indifference. Somehow the indifference stung more than the anger.

"Cheryl is a solid baker, but her recipes are nowhere near as original or exciting as what you just put together," he said, nodding towards his empty bowl.

She glowed under his praise. *As if you've never received a compliment from a hot guy in a chef's coat before—get it together, Tess.*

"But I have one question," he continued.

"Shoot," she said.

"What's in it for you?"

"Jame—" her father started.

"No, I want to know. You're already opening a pop up during the holidays. Taking on the festival, too, is a lot."

"It sounds like Cheryl was going to do both," Tessa replied, bracing for a fight.

Jamie continued on like he hadn't heard her. "It's long hours, thankless work. Ethan and I—and our friends—are doing it because we love this town. This is our home."

"It's her home too," Ethan protested.

Jamie didn't take her eyes off her. "But you're only here for a few months before you cash out, so I want to know why you're interested in the extra work?"

"I'm not afraid of hard work," Tessa said, glancing between her father and Jamie and ignoring the way Jamie's stern voice sent heat curling low in her belly.

"Jamie? Can someone give me a hand?" A woman's voice rang out from the back office.

Jamie started to stand, but Ethan held up a hand, getting to his feet. "I'll go help Anabel. You two get to know each other." Then, to Jamie, in his most no-nonsense dad voice, "And *be nice.*"

Before either of them could protest, Ethan had disappeared down a dark hallway.

As soon as they were alone, Jamie got to his feet, crowding her space and hissing, "Did you know who I was?" She scrambled to her feet so he wasn't towering over her quite so much. "That night—did you know?" he demanded.

"No! No more than you knew who I was."

"This is a fucking disaster," he growled, prowling away from her and tearing at his hair, little specks of glitter falling from the strands. He circled back, coming at her fast until they were toe to toe. "Your dad can never know."

"Jesus, of course not! Do you really think I'm dying to tell my father that we—" She stopped herself mid-sentence, forcing herself to take a deep breath and meet his furious gaze. "No one needs to know."

"I want the truth. Why are you really here?"

"What do you mean?"

"Is it just about the money? Because if you're just here to con some more cash out of dear ol' dad—"

"What the fuck?" She took a step back, her breath coming faster as her own anger built. "First of all, not that it's any of your business, but he was willing to transfer the money without me ever setting foot in this God-awful town. *I'm* the one who insisted on working for it. Why would you even—"

"You haven't come back here in seventeen years, Tessa. Why now?" he asked, crowding her again.

"I needed to sign the paperwork for the trust."

"Ethan would have come to you."

"I—I needed a job."

"Get a different one," he snarled.

"I want to know him, Jamie. He's all I have left. I…I want this time with him."

"And then what?" he asked, his voice low, his face so close to hers she could feel his breath on her cheek. "You disappear for another ten years?"

"Why the hell do you even care?"

"He's my best friend!"

"He's my *father*!"

Jamie stumbled backwards a step, scraping his hand over his face, and watching her like she might suddenly sprout snakes from her head and turn him to stone.

She planted her hands on her hips and stared him down. Getting into a screaming match with her father's best friend wasn't going to help anything. "I don't like this any more than you do, but Ethan wants us to work together on this festival. It's important to him, and I don't intend to let him down."

"Me either," Jamie said, though the furrow of his brow and tight set of his lips made it clear that he thought they'd both already done so.

"I'll help you build a menu, but I expect equal input and full billing as the pastry chef for the festival."

Jamie nodded, and she thought, just for a moment, she saw the disdain in his eyes melt into a grudging respect. "Done," he said, pushing past her and back towards the kitchen.

Tessa called after him, "You won't regret this."

"I already do."

Chapter Seven

DiceDiceBaby: What is this show's fascination with honeycomb?

WhiskyBusiness: Have you tried it?

DiceDiceBaby: No. It's toffee right?

WhiskyBusiness: Pssh. Sending you a recipe now.

Tessa tapped out the few instructions from memory as the nervous contestant on the screen waited for the judges' reaction to her latest confection. Honeycomb was easy enough to make and a trained chef like DiceDiceBaby would be able to follow her shorthand.

DiceDiceBaby: Thanks. Recommendation for how to serve it?

WhiskyBusiness: I like to mix it into ice cream. That's how they serve it in New Zealand, but they call it hokey pokey there.

DiceDiceBaby: When were you in NZ?

WhiskyBusiness: Haven't been yet. But it's on my list.
WhiskyBusiness: Oh! He's gonna do it!

A smile slid across Tessa's face as she watched Peter London extend his hand to the flustered home baker on the screen. Something about this show always soothed her when she was feeling on edge, and after her run in with Jamie that morning, she was seriously fighting the instinct to bolt. The woman on screen made a sound somewhere between a gasp and a strangled laugh as she accepted the coveted handshake.

DiceDiceBaby: Why do women lose their minds over this guy?

WhiskyBusiness: It's the eyes.
WhiskyBusiness: And the confidence.
WhiskyBusiness: Peter London has BDE if I ever saw it.

DiceDiceBaby: BDE?

WhiskyBusiness: Big. Dick. Energy.

She bit her lip, her fingers hovering over the screen of her phone as she considered her next words. She shook her head, going with her first instinct. She and DDB had been messaging—and flirting—for months; there was no point in stopping now.

WhiskyBusiness: Know anything about that?

DiceDiceBaby: I know all about that.

"I'm off," Ethan said, coming into his living room where Tessa sat in the armchair, her leg hooked over the overstuffed arm as she watched *Brilliant British Bakes.* "Are you sure you don't want to come with me?"

"To bar trivia with your friends?" she asked, doing her best to look like someone who hadn't just been on the verge of soliciting a dick pic from a stranger on the internet. "No thanks. I'm good." The last thing she needed to do was spend any extra time around Jamie.

"Well, if you change your mind we'll be at The Rookery. I'm sure the guys would love to see you."

She gave him a skeptical look. "More like the town biddies would love to see me so they can have fresh gossip for church coffee hour."

She was prepared to run into people throughout town who'd known her as a child, people she and her mother had worked hard to forget. They'd ask about her mother, unaware that she'd passed three years ago—somehow that bit of gossip hadn't made its way around town—and throw out the same things she'd heard every day when she'd lived in Aster Bay as a child: "Look how you've grown," or "You are the spitting image of your mother," followed promptly by an assessing look as though she might actually be Stephanie Cordeiro, returned to the town that ran her off.

He chuckled and ran his hand over the back of his neck sheepishly. "That too. But Gav and Baz haven't seen you since you were a kid. I don't think Jamie even recognized you today."

He most certainly did not, she thought, heat rising in her cheeks.

She was prepared for all those awkward encounters

with the people who would never forgive her mother for the sin of being a teenage mother. She hadn't been prepared for her one-night stand to turn out to be her father's best friend, or for the way the hunger in his eyes would turn to disgust when he realized who she was. Yet even his anger sent need pulsing between her thighs. Somehow that fire in his eyes and the way he clearly got off on being called 'Chef' made him even harder to resist.

You cannot fuck your dad's best friend...again.

"You're sure I can't convince you?" Ethan asked. "First round's on me."

He was so damn earnest and she wanted to spend time with him, to get to know the father she'd hardly seen for the last seventeen years. That was the main reason she'd come back to Aster Bay after all these years—that and her determination to earn the money her grandparents had left her. If her mother had taught her anything it was to earn what you took. But she didn't know how to do this, how to be Ethan's daughter or his friend, never mind both.

She'd long ago figured out that her father's absence in her life was more her mom's doing than his, and now that her mother was gone, it felt like time to go back to Aster Bay, even if the town made her itchy. She wouldn't be staying for long. A few months to build a relationship with the man she couldn't bring herself to call 'dad' and give her resume a boost along the way, and then she'd be out of Rhode Island and off on her next adventure, with enough cash to finally travel before she had to find a new place to land.

Her phone chimed again, and she glanced down to see a new message from DDB. "Get out of here," she said to her father with a smile. "You don't want to keep your friends waiting."

"Next time then." Ethan knocked on the door frame once and left the room, the rumble of his truck pulling out of the driveway following a few moments later.

DiceDiceBaby: So is that your type? Snarky British dudes who withhold affection and praise?

Tessa snorted.

WhiskyBusiness: Nah, too proper. I'd freak him out.

DiceDiceBaby: Why do you say that?

She sighed and considered her answer. She hadn't intended to take their conversation from flirting to mining her childhood trauma, but that just seemed to be the way things went with DDB. One minute they were debating whether or not someone could realistically have an orgasm in public without anyone knowing, and the next he was spilling his guts about the death of his parents when he was in college. He understood what it was like to have that empty hole in your heart that could never be filled in, only patched over.

They messaged daily, but they'd never shared real names, photos, or locations. She knew he was the chef-owner of a restaurant, that he favored unique twists on classic dishes. He shared her love of *Brilliant British Bakes* and her disdain for the bastardized American version of the show. He lived somewhere near the beach, had a brother he didn't see often, liked to watch British period dramas, and had an inexplicable dislike for Brozone, the most popular boy band in the world. And he made her laugh. She looked forward to their conversations so much that it was sometimes hard to remember that they didn't *actually* know each other.

He'd asked her to meet in person a few times, but she couldn't bring herself to risk losing the fantasy of him. It was just easier if DDB stayed a fantasy, the mythological perfect guy who she might someday run into in line for a croissant in Paris. If they met, what were the odds that he'd actually live up to the Henry Cavill clone in her head?

WhiskyBusiness: He couldn't handle calling me "good girl" *wink emoji*

Easier to flirt than say anything real. Safer. If she was going to make it through the next few months, she couldn't afford to let her demons out to play. They had a habit of not going back in the box when she needed them to. Better if she never opened the lid in the first place.

DiceDiceBaby: Have you been?
DiceDiceBaby: A good girl?

Definitely not.
Tessa slid down further into the armchair. The conversation was rapidly moving from flirting to full-on sexting. While she was definitely intrigued by the idea, sexting in her own cramped apartment in Vegas was one thing; doing it in her father's living room was another. And for some stupid reason she felt guilty about sending sexy messages to DDB now that she was going to be spending more time with Jamie.

Working with Jamie, she reminded herself. *Just working.*

Not that she owed any kind of fidelity to DDB, or to Jamie for that matter, but her overdeveloped sense of guilt didn't seem to have gotten the memo.

Before she could decide how best to reply—encourage this line of conversation or gently steer them back to debating whether short crust pastry was superior to American pie crust—the doorbell rang.

She opened the storm door to her father's house to find a curvy, petite blonde on the front porch. Her hair was pulled back in a ponytail that highlighted sharp cheekbones in her otherwise round face, and her eyes were rimmed in a dark, smoky liner that made them look too large for her face. She held a basket of assorted scones and muffins and greeted Tessa with a crooked smirk, one edge of her mouth rising higher than the others.

"You must be TJ."

Tessa winced. "It's Tessa. But yes, that's me."

"Oh," her confident grin faltered, clearly embarrassed by the mistake. "I'm Kyla. I help Cheryl bake for the farm stand—well, I *did* until she got put on bed rest. She said you were opening the pop-up at Nuthatch this year. I've worked the holiday pop-ups with Cheryl for the last three years, so if you need help..." She straightened her shoulders, adopting the posture of a confidence she clearly didn't feel. "I'm punctual, always prepared, and a fast learner."

Tessa smiled, hoping to set Kyla at ease. "Come on in, Kyla. It's nice to meet you."

Kyla followed Tessa into the large farmhouse-style kitchen, setting the basket of baked goods down on the poured concrete island in the center of the room.

"What's with the muffins?" Tessa asked, gesturing to the basket.

"Cheryl sends over a basket from the farm stand every week. If she doesn't, Ethan won't take the time to eat breakfast. Since she's on bed rest now, I made most of this one myself." She turned a few of the muffins in the basket, nervously adjusting them as though they were on display in a shop and not in a basket on the kitchen counter.

Tessa's heart clenched at the idea that her father's friends looked out for him that way. If she had lived in town, she'd be the one to fill his kitchen with breakfast pastries, to make sure he took care of himself... "That's really thoughtful. I'm sure he appreciates that."

"It's not a big deal," Kyla continued. "Just some ginger scones and blueberry muffins."

"It's perfect," Tessa assured her. "Thanks for bringing it by."

"I made them myself. If you like them, maybe you'll give me a call if you need help with the bakery? Or if you want me to take over making the weekly delivery. Now that Cheryl's closed the farm stand until after the baby's born, I've got some time on my hands. The ginger scones are my own recipe, and my number's on the card in the basket," Kyla said, pointing out the little square of cardboard sticking out of the side of the basket.

Tessa pulled out a scone and took a bite.

Kyla flushed. "Oh, you don't have to do that now. I mean. You can try it when I'm gone."

"This is good," Tessa said as she went in for another bite. Not the best scone she'd ever had, but it was a solid recipe. "Your ginger could be candied a bit more, but I can teach you that. How about you come by the vineyard on Monday and we'll work out the details?"

"Yeah?" Kyla shook off the moment of excitement that had bled through her nervousness. "I mean, yeah, sure. I could do that."

"Great."

Kyla headed for the front door, but paused and swung

around to face Tessa again, a sheepish look on her face. "I was going to head over to The Rookery to meet my boyfriend for a drink. You could come. If you wanted to. I mean, I know you don't really know anyone in town yet and—"

"Thanks, but I—"

"There's this trivia thing every Monday night and it's usually good for a few laughs. A bunch of the people in town have standing teams."

"Yeah? Who's on your team?"

"Oh, I don't play. I go to watch. It always comes down to the same two teams," she explained, her eyes lighting up as she talked. "One is your dad and his friends, which is reason enough to go."

"Why's that?"

"Have you seen those guys? The eye candy alone—" She stopped, cleared her throat, her cheeks turning pink, and began again as if she hadn't just called Tessa's father 'eye candy.' "The other team is this group of retired elementary school teachers." A wicked gleam flashed in her eye. "They taught all of the guys on the other team—except Jamie, since he didn't grow up here."

"Who usually wins?"

"The old ladies," Kyla said with a grin.

Tessa barked out a laugh. Maybe it wouldn't kill her to go to the bar for one drink. And if she got to see Jamie get his arrogant ass handed to him by a bunch of grandmas, well that was just all the more reason to go.

Chapter Eight

DiceDiceBaby: Have you been?
DiceDiceBaby: A good girl?

Jamie stared at the open message thread and took another sip of his gin and tonic. It had been nearly twenty minutes and WhiskyBusiness hadn't written back. Had he gone too far? Usually, she was the one to send him risqué texts, but after spending the day trying to convince himself that he could not sleep with his best friend's daughter (again), he'd hoped he could blow off a little steam with Whisky, someone infinitely more appropriate, even if equally inaccessible.

"Will you put your damn phone away?" Baz barked as he took his seat at the table with Jamie.

"She still hasn't written back?" Gavin asked, taking the seat opposite him.

Jamie tossed his phone down on the table. "Nope. Forget it."

"Hey, now, is that any way to talk about your internet girlfriend?" Ethan asked through a shit-eating grin.

"She's not my girlfriend," Jamie grumbled. For the millionth time.

Baz arched a sardonic eyebrow. "Right. You just spend half your time texting her."

"Does she know about the woman from the hotel?" Gavin asked.

"What woman from what hotel?" Ethan asked.

Jamie scowled at Gavin, his stomach lurching. "It's nothing."

"Jamie went back to a woman's hotel room the other night. He's being very secretive about it."

"Why does Gavin know about hotel woman and I don't?" Ethan asked.

"I don't want to talk about it. It was just a one night thing," Jamie said, hoping Gavin would let it rest. The last thing he needed was for Ethan to start asking questions about that night.

"Yeah, right," Baz huffed in disbelief. "You don't do one night things."

"One night or not, at least that woman was real." Ethan reached for Jamie's phone, his eyes going wide as he read the latest texts in the thread. "Shit. Are you having cyber-sex with the internet girl?"

Jamie snatched the phone out of his hands. "Give me that."

"Is it still called cyber-sex?" Gavin asked. "Isn't it just called sexting now?"

"What if you get on video though?" Ethan asked. "That's more than sexting."

"They're not getting on video. She won't even send him a picture," Gavin pointed out.

"Are you even sure she's a woman?" Baz asked. "She could be a sixty-year-old man for all you know."

"She's not a sixty-year-old man," Jamie snapped. "She's a—actually, I don't know exactly how old she is. But she is an adult, human woman. Not that it matters because she's *not* my girlfriend. Can we talk about one of *your* love lives for a change?"

"Oh, Jamie, I don't think we're quite done talking about yours." Jamie squeezed his eyes shut as the older woman's hand fell onto his shoulder, her familiar Chanel perfume hovering like a cloud around her. "I hear it didn't go so well with Trisha."

"There's a *third* woman?" Ethan blurted out.

Jamie ignored his best friend. "Trisha was lovely, Helen," he said carefully. "But we didn't have much in common."

The older woman sucked her teeth. "I was afraid that might be the case. Though it sounds like maybe you *did* hit it off with some other young ladies." Helen clicked her tongue and shook her head. "You won't be able to bounce from woman to woman forever," she chided, and Jamie caught the glee in his friends' eyes at Helen implying that Jamie, the serial monogamist of the group, bounced between women. "When are you going to settle down?"

"Not yet, Helen," Jamie said. "You keep turning me down."

Helen laughed and patted him on the shoulder. "You couldn't keep up, young man," she said with a wink.

Bullet dodged. Helen White and her friends were regulars at brunch at Lemon and Thyme, but more than that, they had the ear of everyone who was anyone in Aster Bay. Getting on their bad side was the death knell for any business in town.

"Where's the rest of your team, Mrs. White?" Ethan asked.

"Right over there," she said, gesturing with a perfectly manicured hand to a table near the announcer's stand where Ruth, Dot, and Judy waited for her to join them. "Are you boys ready to lose again?"

"Not this time, Mrs. W," Gavin said. "This is our lucky week. I know it."

Helen laughed. "Alright, boys. If you say so. Next round's on me. Least I can do for embarrassing you like this every Monday."

"Thanks, Mrs. White," Baz, Gavin, and Ethan chorused as she walked away, joining her friends who each raised a hand to wave in their direction.

"We cannot keep losing to our elementary school teachers," Baz grumbled once Helen was out of earshot.

"Yes, that must be really embarrassing for you," Jamie said as he checked his phone again.

Still no reply from Whisky.

"Will you put that thing away?" Ethan said. "Even if she wrote back right now, you don't want it to look like you've been sitting around waiting for her to text."

"That's exactly what he's been doing," Baz said.

"I've got a good feeling about our chances tonight," Gavin said, setting down his beer. "Brodie's been catching me up on all the Marvel movies."

Jamie took another sip of his gin and tonic to keep from saying that Brodie should spend a little more time focused on his work at the restaurant and a little less time watching *Captain America*. Gavin's son had been slacking off lately, too busy flirting with the waitresses to pay attention to the things Anabel was trying to teach him. The kid said he wanted a future in the restaurant business, but from what Jamie could see, all he wanted was to get laid. Not that Jamie could tell Gavin that. Gavin would feel the need to defend his son and it just wasn't worth the conflict with one of his best friends. Anabel would set the kid straight eventually.

"I still can't believe Brodie's old enough to drink," Baz said, his eyes drifting to the crowd at the bar where their friend's son was holding court with a group of local twenty-somethings.

"Me either," Gavin said. "I think that officially makes me old."

"That's what happens when you have kids before you graduate from college," Jamie said.

Ethan shook his head. "Can you believe you were his age when he was born?"

All four friends stared at the twenty-one-year-old at the bar with his cocksure grin and shuddered. No one wanted to picture Brodie being responsible for a baby.

"Can you believe you already had a four-year-old when Brodie was born?" Baz asked.

"Speaking of TJ, is that her?" Gavin asked. "I thought you said she wasn't coming."

Jamie's head whipped around, following Gavin's gaze to where Tessa and Kyla, Cheryl's baking assistant, were standing by the front door. Kyla searched the crowd, clearly looking for someone. Jamie and Tessa locked eyes. A cautious smile tipped up the edge of her lips and his cock stirred at the sight of her sinful curves in those painted-on jeans and a cropped sweater, slivers of her olive skin taunting him as she moved.

"It is, right?" Gavin asked. "I hardly recognized her. Little TJ, all grown up."

"She goes by Tessa now," Jamie said, before he could think better of it.

Thankfully, Ethan didn't seem to notice that his best friend and his daughter were staring at each other across the bar.

"She just got in yesterday," Ethan said. "She's going to open the pop-up bakery this year since Cheryl's on bed rest. And she'll help out with the festival."

"That's great, Ethan," Gavin said, grinning. "Must be nice

to have her home. I don't know how you do it. I'd go nuts if I didn't see Brodie for months at a time. Oh! We should introduce them. They're about the same age." Gavin twisted in his seat, ready to flag down his son.

Jamie's stomach sank. No way was he going to sit by and watch Tessa get cozy with *Brodie.* She deserved so much better than that horndog. She deserved—

What? You?

No, he needed to stay as far away from Tessa as physically possible.

Before he could suggest that they leave well enough alone, Kyla linked her arm through Tessa's, dragging her across the bar and straight into the crowd clamoring for the bartender's attention. Jamie followed them with his eyes over the top of his glass, watching as Kyla walked straight into Brodie's arms, rising up on her tiptoes to plant a kiss on his lips. *That's new.* The blonde pulled Brodie's arms around her waist and made introductions as a wave of relief flooded through Jamie. Tessa wouldn't be getting cozy with Brodie because her friend already was. *Thank God.*

"Ethan Hart!" The scolding tone cut through the noise as Dot made her way to their table, an arthritic finger capped with a hot pink acrylic nail wagging in his direction. "I have half a mind to call your mother."

"What's wrong, Mrs. Blumenthal?" Ethan asked, his brows narrowing as he watched the irate former kindergarten teacher approach.

"You didn't tell us TJ was back in town!" Dot said, finally reaching their table and giving Ethan a tap upside the head.

"He didn't tell us right away either, Mrs. B, if it makes you feel any better," Gavin said.

"Suck up," Baz mumbled into his scotch.

"How old is TJ now? No, wait, don't tell me—you and

Stephanie were sixteen when you had that beautiful baby girl, and that was the year Mikey Greenhall got detention for skipping school to see a midday showing at the movie theater, so she must be…" Dot screwed her face up and waggled her fingers, silently counting. "…Twenty-five! Already!"

"How do you do that?" Gavin marveled.

Dot winked and tapped a finger to her temple. "We haven't seen that girl in *years,* Ethan. You've been keeping her from us."

"I promise you I have not," Ethan said, his voice unnaturally even, but Jamie saw the way his hand flexed and closed around his beer bottle.

"She is the spitting image of Stephanie." Dot turned to Jamie, always eager to fill him in on the things he'd missed by not growing up in Aster Bay with the rest of his friends. He'd been around long enough to have met Stephanie, though, before she and Tessa had moved away, and while there was a certain similarity about their coloring, he didn't think Tessa looked as much like her mother as Dot claimed. Jamie glanced towards the bar, searching for another glimpse of Tessa, but she'd already been swallowed up by the crowd of locals. "That girl was always a looker. Turned heads everywhere she went. But she only had eyes for this one. High school sweethearts. Such a shame about—"

"You'll have plenty of time to catch up with her, Mrs. B. Tessa's staying for a few months. She'll be helping with the festival," Ethan interjected, ending Dot's monologue on the tragedy of high school sweethearts who didn't stay together.

"Oh! That reminds me. I need to call Pastor Davis and start a meal train for Cheryl and Ricky. Judy!" Dot called as she left to rejoin her table. "Judy, did you remember to call Pastor Davis? I need to know how many pans of macaroni to make."

Jamie's phone chimed.

WhiskyBusiness: You don't strike me as the type who wants a good girl. I think you like your women a little bad.

As he tapped out a reply, Baz groaned, "Here we go again. Are we ever going to play some trivia?"

DiceDiceBaby: Why's that?

WhiskyBusiness: You appreciate an all-butter pie crust. That means you like a challenge.

DiceDiceBaby: Maybe I just like butter.

"Not your girlfriend, huh?" Gavin said. "That's a pretty big grin for a text from someone who's not your girlfriend."

At the announcer's stand, Mike Greenhall held up an old school bell, ringing it until the bar quieted down. "Are you ready for this week's game?" he shouted. The crowd clapped and hooted, the four older women at the front the loudest of then all, Helen's whoops cutting through the rest of the noise. "Round one's theme is Hollywood scandals of the past decade."

Baz, Ethan, and Jamie groaned. "Well, there goes that. We might as well just concede now before Mrs. White gets a chance to gloat," Baz said.

"Come on, guys. We can do this," Gavin said, ever the optimist.

"First question!" Mike called. "What former child star turned pop star made headlines for having an on-set relationship with the actor playing her father in a recent

Broadway musical film adaptation?"

Jamie laughed, shaking his head as he reached for the answer sheet in front of Gavin. "Give me that. I actually know this one."

Chapter Nine

Everything in the room was beige. Beige carpet, beige walls. Tessa wasn't sure what she'd expected from the church community hall, but it hadn't been this.

From the outside, the church was lined on three sides by rows of intricately detailed stained-glass windows. At night, when the church was lit up from within, the stone building resembled the gingerbread houses she made at Christmas with crushed candy windowpanes. But this room was in the church basement, and the attention to aesthetics clearly had not made its way underground.

Gavin, Ethan, Tessa, and Baz stood in a line at the back of the room in front of the pathetic coffee and Danish table like the four horsemen of the disappointing pastry apocalypse. Tessa made a mental note to bring something to contribute to the table for the next meeting. Maybe her cinnamon buns or apple spice bread.

When Tessa and Ethan had arrived at St. Anthony's, Gavin had bounded over to greet her with a wide, genuine smile and a warm, if awkward, hug. With his shaggy, sandy blonde hair and his overly friendly demeanor, he was the human equivalent of a golden retriever. He was the only person—aside from her father—who seemed genuinely happy to see her, and not because she was a town curiosity.

Half the people in the room kept craning their necks to catch a glimpse of Stephanie Cordeiro's child, the prodigal daughter all grown up. The child that had disgraced both the Cordeiro and Hart families by her very existence. Ethan swore that wasn't true, that no one in his family—*her* family—felt that way, but that's not what her mother had always said. And Tessa remembered the whispers in the grocery store when she had lived in town as a kid. The way people stared as she and her mother selected apples for the week, the saccharine smiles of the church ladies who sidled up to them at the deli counter in hopes of a bit of salacious gossip about the teenage mother and her bastard child.

Tessa planted her feet firmly, crossing her arms over her chest and focusing her gaze on Jamie and his presentation at the front of the room. She would not let small town narrow-mindedness run her off again.

Kyla appeared at her side. "Hey, did I miss anything important?"

Tessa tried to hide her surprise at seeing her there. "You know you didn't have to come to this, right? Just because you're working at Sugar Grapes doesn't mean you're obligated to work on the festival too."

"I was planning on helping Cheryl anyway," Kyla said with a shrug. "It's not a big deal."

But it was a big deal to Tessa, having someone who had her back, and not out of familial obligation. She nodded, flattening her lips to hide her smile so as not to embarrass Kyla, but she couldn't help the warmth in her chest.

At the front of the room, assembled local business owners sat in rows of beige folding chairs and sipped weak coffee out of beige cardboard cups while Jamie explained his plan for the food and wine festival.

"But how will you get more tourists to come?" a confused-looking woman with short-cropped, brown hair asked.

"Gavin and I have been in touch with several media outlets and we're planning an advertising and press blitz to explain how our festival will be different from the hundreds of other festivals around the country," he answered.

Jamie turned a dimpled smile on the assembled group and Tessa could feel their anxiety calm under his reassuring gaze. Couldn't they tell that was a fake smile, that it didn't reach his eyes? It was nothing like the way he'd grinned at her that night while they'd sat on the grass eating tacos.

"We are confident that our food will be top notch," Jamie continued. "Ethan's daughter Tessa is in town temporarily to reopen Sugar Grapes for the holidays and has agreed to help with the festival's menu. While we will miss Cheryl's red wine brownies, Tessa has an impressive pedigree and some exciting new ideas to contribute. Make no mistake—culinarily, Aster Bay's food and wine festival will be one of the best festivals in the country."

Did he mean it? The words were glowing but the dimple in his cheek had disappeared, his eyes gone steely as he'd spoken about her. Even if he respected her food, he didn't like her.

"That's great for once the tourists are here, but you gotta get them into town first," a large man in a plaid flannel shirt and knit beanie said.

"I hear you, Norm, but Gavin's the best. He's going to get us featured in all kinds of news outlets."

"Which is exactly what we've done every other year," Norm fired back. "This year's gotta be bigger. You said you could make it bigger."

Jamie glanced at Gavin at the back of the room, as if to

confirm, before addressing Norm. "We're going to highlight what makes us different, the things that only Aster Bay can offer."

"Like what? We're not the only beach town hunting for tourists in the winter," Norm said.

"Like our restaurants, our vineyard. Like package deals with tickets to the festival and a stay at The Barclay," Jamie said, glancing again at his friends at the back of the room. Beside her, Tessa could feel the men stand a little taller, as though they could project their support across the room to their friend.

"That's what we've always done. It's not enough!" someone shouted from the crowd.

The concerned murmuring rose to an all-out barrage of unease, accusations of false promises starting to fly as Jamie struggled to regain control of the meeting. But he just kept repeating the same thing about advertising, and the more he doubled down on the talking points he'd clearly rehearsed, the more the crowd grew incensed.

Kyla shook her head. "They've got to target a different demographic," she mumbled.

"What?" Tessa whispered back.

"Every year they advertise to middle aged people and senior citizens. People who have families and too many things to do in the run up to the holidays as it is," Kyle explained. "They have to start going after a younger crowd if they want to bring in more people."

It was brilliant. As Kyla spoke, Tessa could see it, the way they could draw in childless couples and groups of friends looking for a weekend getaway before they had to face all the drama of the holidays, how they could turn this run-of-the-mill festival into a townwide vacation destination.

"You should tell them," Tessa said, nudging Kyla's shoulder.

Kyla's eyes widened. "No way," she hissed, the sound nearly lost in the pandemonium of anxious business owners.

"Kyla, it's a great idea."

"*You* can tell them," she said. "It's not my festival."

Tessa glanced at Jamie, at the tension around his full lips, the blank expression in his eyes as his head whipped around trying to keep up with the crowd. Her father and his friends shifted on their feet, glancing at each other, but made no move to intervene. Someone had to do *something*.

"We can market to twenty-somethings," Tessa shouted from the back of the room, loud enough to cut through the cacophony. The noise died down as the assembled business owners turned to see who had spoken. "We put Jamie's face on the ads and target single women looking for a girls' trip." A few bursts of laughter punctuated the low rumble of the group, bolstering Tessa's confidence. She glanced at Kyla, taking her wide-eyed nod as encouragement, and took a step forward, moving towards the front of the room. "We don't just do tickets to the festival and a stay at the hotel in those packages—we throw in options for a yoga class or a manicure, things to highlight the other businesses that aren't directly tied to the festival or tourism."

"I could offer a lingerie fitting. Women love to do that as part of a bachelorette weekend," a tall woman with a perfect hourglass figure and a single streak of silver in her dark hair said, turning an encouraging smile her way.

Tessa smiled back, taking up position beside Jamie at the front of the room.

Jamie glared at her. "This festival is supposed to be about the food. The best food and wine the region has to offer."

"Who said you can't have some fun while you're doing that? Food doesn't need to be so serious all the time," she said, genuinely confused as to what his objection was. She turned back to the crowd, who suddenly seemed much more welcoming and open to her ideas—to Kyla's ideas—than the man standing beside her. "When I lived in Vegas, I used to run these bake and sip nights. People would come and I'd teach them how to make a dessert while they drank their wine. It was a big hit. We could do something like that here. If you want to be different, you have to be interactive."

"That's a lot of moving pieces to organize," Jamie countered. "We don't—"

"Then I'll organize it."

"You're not in charge," Jamie snapped. "You can't—"

"Maybe she should be," Norm shouted.

Gavin made his way to the front of the room, hands raised to quiet the wave of murmured concern and agreement. He shook his head, good-natured smile firmly in place. "Let's all calm down. I don't think anyone is implying that Jamie doesn't have this under control."

Norm got to his feet. "I am. I'm implying."

"Look, Tessa's got a point," Gavin said, avoiding Jamie's death glare. "Narrowing our target audience and really speaking to what they want to see is a solid marketing strategy. And bringing in the strengths of the rest of the community is a great way to highlight how Aster Bay is different from all the other festivals. But we only have a few months before the festival. We need to be advertising now. We just don't have time to—"

The woman from the lingerie shop got to her feet. "I'll help." She turned to Tessa. "Just tell me what you need."

"Thank you, Natalia," Jamie said, "but I'm not sure—"

"TJ should co-chair!" someone at the back of the crowd shouted. Their suggestion was met with a wave of agreement.

"I don't think that's really necessary," Jamie said,

pinching the bridge of his nose like he was in physical pain at the idea of working more closely with her.

"You said it yourself. It's a lot of things to organize. Let the girl help," Norm said. "Aster Bay is in her blood."

Tessa shot a desperate glance at Jamie. "I'm happy to help, but that doesn't mean I need to be—"

"All those in favor of TJ Cordeiro as co-chair for the food and wine festival?" Norm shouted. A resounding "aye" rose up from the crowd. "There you have it. I have a hotel to run. Meeting adjourned."

"What just happened?" Tessa asked, glancing between a fuming Jamie and a baffled-looking Gavin.

"Congratulations," Gavin said. "You and Jamie are now co-chairs of the food and wine festival."

WhiskyBusiness: I would kill for a Starbucks.

DiceDiceBaby: In need of a caffeine fix?

WhiskyBusiness: I am plenty caffeinated. Starbucks is not about needing caffeine.
WhiskyBusiness: Starbucks is about a moment of the day that's just mine.

DiceDiceBaby: And here I thought it was a coffee shop.

WhiskyBusiness: I've had so much coffee today. Bad diner coffee, bad home coffee maker coffee. But there is not a Starbucks to be found for miles!

DiceDiceBaby: Is this a recent revelation? Did all the

Starbuckses in your area get up and move in the middle of the night?

WhiskyBusiness: Starbuckses? Is that the plural of Starbucks?

DiceDiceBaby: How else would you say it?

WhiskyBusiness: Starbucksi?
WhiskyBusiness: Or is this like a "moose" situation.

DiceDiceBaby: You're going to need to be more specific.

WhiskyBusiness: You know, how the plural of moose is moose.

DiceDiceBaby: Ahh yes. So did all the Starbucks (plural) disappear?

WhiskyBusiness: I'm sure they did not. I'm sure the Starbucks around the corner that I've been going to for the past year is still there, still serving the best damn iced caramel macchiatos with two pumps of mocha. But I am not there to drink said beverage.

DiceDiceBaby: Are you on vacation?

WhiskyBusiness: Sort of.

DiceDiceBaby: What's a sort of vacation?

WhiskyBusiness: Apparently a forced Starbucks detox!

DiceDiceBaby: I see.

WhiskyBusiness: Do you though? I don't feel like you're sufficiently sympathetic to my lack of caffeinated beverage options.

DiceDiceBaby: You caught me. I never really understood the whole Starbucks thing.

WhiskyBusiness: I'm sorry, can we even be friends anymore?

DiceDiceBaby: Give me a good cup of regular coffee, fresh ground beans, some cream. I don't need the half caf double shot swirly drizzle extra whip stuff.

WhiskyBusiness: I don't know what you just described but it sounds delicious.

DiceDiceBaby: I think that's the withdrawal talking.

WhiskyBusiness: Maybe.
WhiskyBusiness: More likely it's the sense that my life is one big joke to the universe. Sugar usually helps with that. I have not had enough sugar to cope with this new thing I just got volun-told to do.

DiceDiceBaby: Uh oh. What did you agree to?

WhiskyBusiness: Just working with a chef who hates me for the next few months.

DiceDiceBaby: I'm sure they don't hate you.

WhiskyBusiness: You didn't see the way he was looking at me.

DiceDiceBaby: How was that?

WhiskyBusiness: Like he hates me.

DiceDiceBaby: Can you say no?

WhiskyBusiness: Not really.
WhiskyBusiness: And I kind of don't want to. I think I could be good at it.
WhiskyBusiness: I like that they're trusting me with this project, ya know? It feels important.

DiceDiceBaby: Important how?

WhiskyBusiness: It's complicated. Like, details-we-don't-share-with-each-other complicated.

DiceDiceBaby: Do you ever wonder if everything would be less complicated if we just went crazy and shared those details with each other?

WhiskyBusiness: All the time.

Chapter Ten

"We'll definitely use the chardonnay," Jamie said, taking the half empty bottle and moving it to the left side of the table where he and Tessa had been placing the wines around which they intended to build their menu.

"And the Vidal Blanc," Tessa added, pointing to that bottle with her wine glass before taking another small sip.

"We don't need the Vidal if we have the chardonnay. They'll both pair with cream sauces and seafood." Jamie took the bottle and placed it on the right side of the table with the rejected wines.

After two hours in the vineyard's tasting room, Jamie was starting to get the distinct impression that they were just playing a game of musical wine bottles as they shuffled them back and forth across the table rather than getting closer to any solid decisions. As much as he resented having Tessa foisted upon him as co-chair, forcing him to spend extra time with the one woman he should not be spending *any* time with, he couldn't deny that there was some relief to having a partner in the planning for the festival, to know it wasn't all on him.

Tessa glared at him and moved the bottle to the left side

of the table with the other keepers. "The Vidal has hints of pineapple and grapefruit, and the chardonnay is more apple and nuts. One is bright citrus and the other is silky butterscotch. They're totally different."

Jamie blinked, his mind struggling to process the revelation that her palette was refined enough to taste those subtleties in the wine. "We don't need both."

He wasn't sure why he was arguing with her. She was right, and now that she'd pointed out the differences, he could picture it—a pumpkin ravioli with lobster tails and a chardonnay browned butter. Pineapple marinated in the Vidal Blanc, bruléed and served with herb crusted fried goat cheese. He scribbled the thoughts down on his notepad before the inspiration left him.

Tessa leaned in close, watching as he wrote. "Fried sage." He glanced at her, waiting for her to complete her thought. "And pine nuts. For the ravioli. Agnolotti would be even better, but I'm not the one making fresh pasta, so that's up to you."

Well, shit. Tessa's suggestions would take the dish to a whole new level. Anabel wasn't as confident in her filled pastas, so he'd have to make the agnolotti himself, but it would be worth it to achieve the more delicate dough to filling ratio.

"You could demonstrate the pasta making technique. I'm sure women would line up to see you kneading pasta dough," Tessa said, her eyes lingering on his forearms before she swallowed another sip of the wine.

A wave of lust spread through him as he stared at her faux-innocent smile. They were in her father's vineyard, for Christ's sake. What the fuck was she trying to do?

Tessa tapped his notebook with a smug smile. "Write it down."

"Do you have any of your own recipes to contribute or are you just going to piggyback on mine?" he grumbled, gesturing to where her own notebook lay closed in front of her.

It was one thing to build on someone else's recipe, and entirely another to conceptualize a dish all on your own. At least, that's what he told himself. His snarky question had nothing at all to do with the frustration that he hadn't thought of adding pine nuts himself—he would have eventually—or that, for a minute, he wanted to bend her over the table and drink the wine straight from her lips.

Was she flirting?

Fuck, he didn't even know anymore.

Who cares if she's flirting? Nothing can happen.

She leaned back in her chair, taking another sip of the Vidal before setting her glass down. "Skip the pineapple. It sounds great, but there are no pineapples growing in Rhode Island and if we want to highlight the area, we should stick with local produce."

"No grapefruits either," Jamie replied.

She smirked, her eyes sparkling, and he found himself holding his breath waiting to hear what she'd say next. Out of purely professional curiosity, of course. Not because the light streaming through the high windows of the tasting room had changed, reflecting and refracting and highlighting every shade of blue in her eyes.

"Cranberries," she said at last. "A take on an Indian pudding with a cranberry sorbetto made with the Vidal. Maybe with whole cranberries candied in a ginger simple syrup as a garnish." She tapped her finger against her mouth, and he forced himself to look away from the soft give of her lip beneath the slight pressure. "That could be something."

He cleared his throat and nodded once. "Good. We'll

keep both the Vidal and the chardonnay. Eighty-six the blend."

"Agreed." She took the bottle of Nuthatch's house white blend and moved it to the reject section of the table. "Doesn't seem like enough."

"It's plenty for the opening dinner. But we'll need a plan for the rest of the festival," Jamie agreed.

"We need something unusual. Something different." Tessa pushed away from the table, getting to her feet, and began walking in wide arcs around the other side of the table. Back and forth like she was on some kind of loop, her gaze locked on the line up of wines. "We need to get out of this room. Get inspired."

"The wine is supposed to be the inspiration."

She spun around in a circle, gesturing to the dark wood and leather décor of the room. "I need light. Sunshine. Maybe some music."

"Or some glitter?" he mumbled.

She shot him a withering look. "Something other than this country-club-meets-secret-society room."

Indignation flared on his best friend's behalf and Jamie began to rise from his seat. "This is the premiere vineyard in the area. Your father—"

She sighed, waving her hand at him. "Down, boy. I know this place is great."

"Did you just talk to me like I was a *dog*?" He clenched his jaw to keep his mouth from kicking up at the corner because there was nothing amusing about her tone of voice. And certainly nothing attractive about the way she cut through all his shit.

"My father doesn't need you to protect him from me," she said, her voice steely in a way that wiped any sense of fun away.

"Right. Sorry," he mumbled. He hadn't meant to offend her.

"It's fine."

She turned her back to him again, staring up at the photograph from her grandparents' wedding that hung on the opposite wall. The huge gilt frame took up half the height of the room.

"Henry and Louise loved this festival," he said, looking up at the photo of the two people who had become like second parents to him after his own parents had died.

"That's what Ethan said."

"How're they doing?"

She glanced at him over her shoulder. "You probably know better than I do. I haven't spoken to them in a while."

"Why not?"

She was quiet for a long time, long enough that it was clear she had no intention of answering his question, though she kept her eyes on the photograph.

"We need to try it from another angle," she said, almost to herself. "The dinner is basically set, but we still need to come up with brunch and the small bites for the tasting. Let's go see what local ingredients spark something and then try to pair those with the wine. Maybe take a walk on the beach? Nature's always good for inspiration."

"That's a wild goose chase."

"But how will we know that we've picked the best options if we don't see what's available to us?" she asked.

"Because I know."

She threw up her hands and turned to face him again. "Fine. Then how will *I* know? We could go to that art gallery downtown and see what calls to us. Peruse the fish market? The worst thing that happens is we waste an afternoon."

Jamie pushed back from the table. He needed distance,

not another day spent watching the light play across her skin. "I don't have another afternoon to waste with you, Tessa."

Her eyes went wide, the way his words had wounded her visible in her gaze for a fraction of a second before she wiped her expression clean. He closed his eyes and forced himself to take three deep breaths before he said anything more. It wasn't her fault that he was on edge every time she was near, like his nerves were misfiring, bees buzzing beneath his skin. She was his best friend's daughter, for Christ's sake, and the more time he spent with her, the more confident he was that she had no ulterior motives for being in town. For Ethan's sake, Jamie should be making her feel welcome. Wanted. *As a part of the town, a colleague, nothing more.*

"I just meant—"

"I know what you meant," she muttered. "Don't worry. I'll go exploring on my own. I won't waste any more of your valuable time. Chef."

Fuck.

She swiped her notebook from the table and stormed towards the spiral staircase that led down to the main floor of the vineyard. Jamie cursed under his breath and strode across the room after her.

"Tessa, wait."

"It's fine," she said without looking at him or slowing her stride. She was halfway down the stairs before he even began descending. "Don't you have to get back to the restaurant anyway?"

"Will you slow down?"

How the hell did she walk so fast?

At the bottom of the stairs, Tessa turned and pushed through the French doors into Sugar Grapes. Jamie followed, just catching the door before it smacked him in the face. The lights were all off, café chairs stacked neatly on top of tables, the display case empty.

He pulled up short, his leather shoes squeaking on the black and white tile floor, as his gaze fell on the wall behind the counter. Giant glass jars lined the back wall, each filled to the brim with a different color of sprinkle, arranged in rainbow order. One jar contained nothing but edible pearls. Another was filled with tiny nonpareils. Above the row of jars, a series of brightly colored paintings hung on the wall, each one a close up of a different fruit or vegetable rendered in messy brushstrokes and paint splatters. A bunch of rainbow carrots, an assortment of berries, a perfectly ripe peach. They were somehow at once childlike and sophisticated, unpretentious subject matter and exuberant art.

"Tessa…"

She turned to look at him, her face falling when she noticed the way his eyes darted around her redecorating.

"Please just…don't." He turned a questioning gaze her way. "I don't want to hear it if you hate it."

"Why would you assume I hate it?"

He followed the counter around the corner to a series of Fiestaware cake stands, each a different height and glossy color, each waiting for a creation as outrageous as the lime green and mauve porcelain. At the end of the counter, next to the station where cakes would be cut and plated, a stainless-steel cylinder held an assortment of spatulas and cake servers, each with a robin's egg blue handle. For a moment he thought of Whisky, stocking her kitchen with oven mitts and dish towels in the same color.

Tessa crossed her arms over her chest and glared at him, though her glare was more sad than angry. He took a step towards her, compelled to touch her, but stopped himself, shoving his hands into his jeans pockets.

He held her gaze and dropped his voice, hoping she could hear the sincerity. "I don't hate it."

"You kinda do, though. A little bit," she said.

"Not even a little bit," he said, taking another step towards her. He tilted his head towards the painting of the peach. "Though that one's borderline obscene."

She barked out a surprised laugh, and he couldn't help but smile at the sound.

"If we're going to do this—be partners for this festival—you need to trust me," he said.

"And you need to respect my process."

"Okay," he said. He held out his hand to her. "Partners?"

She gripped his hand in his and gave it a firm shake. "Partners."

Jamie pulled his hand away, that buzzing feeling overtaking his skin, and shoved it back into his pocket. "If you want to be inspired by the local ingredients, you aren't going to find them in an art gallery or on the beach."

Tessa rolled her eyes. "I thought you were going to respect my process."

"Will you listen for two seconds?"

"Will you talk faster?"

He bit the inside of his cheeks to keep from laughing and met her challenging stare with one of his own. *Mistake.* He had a feeling he could stare into her eyes for hours and still not discover all their secrets, the way the color shifted like water beneath moonlight.

"I have an idea for the brunch menu," he said. "Tomorrow morning. Seven o'clock. I'll pick you up."

"And take me where?"

"Where all the inspiring ingredients are."

WhiskyBusiness: Happy October!

DiceDiceBaby: Happy October. Is that a thing people say to each other?

WhiskyBusiness: *eyeroll emoji* It is if you say it.
WhiskyBusiness: Don't you just love the fall?

DiceDiceBaby: I guess? I'm more of a spring guy myself.

WhiskyBusiness: This weather makes me want to wear cozy sweaters and drink hot chocolate and make pies.

DiceDiceBaby: Don't you make pies year-round?

WhiskyBusiness: Not fall pies. Apple and pumpkin and pecan.
WhiskyBusiness: I just found my grandmother's recipe for sweet potato pie. I'm dying to make it.

DiceDiceBaby: That's one of my favorites. My friend's mom used to make it for me every Thanksgiving. It's a fall classic.

WhiskyBusiness: Then I'll definitely have to make it.
WhiskyBusiness: This is my first real fall in years.

DiceDiceBaby: You didn't have fall where you lived before?

WhiskyBusiness: Not like this. Not like leaves-changing-color, chill-in-the-air, time-to-make-soup fall.

DiceDiceBaby: What kind of soup would you make?

WhiskyBusiness: I'm no good at making soup. I always burn the bottom of the pan.

DiceDiceBaby: Then what kind of soup would you want me to make for you?

WhiskyBusiness: I love a good chouriço and kale soup.

DiceDiceBaby: I would gladly make you chouriço and kale soup.
DiceDiceBaby: If you were here.

WhiskyBusiness: I know you would. And I would make you a pie.

# Chapter Eleven

Ethan wandered into the bakery long after the vineyard had closed for the day to find Tessa sitting on the counter, crumpled pieces of notebook paper scattered around her as she tried to finalize the bakery's opening menu. She'd discovered a box of index cards full of her grandmother's recipes in a drawer beneath the front counter and had been slowly setting aside the ones she wanted to revive (or reimagine)—like the sweet potato pie.

But she didn't want to just resurrect the bakery as it had been. She wanted to make it her own. Being a pop-up shop allowed for room to experiment, try new things to see what worked, and hopefully by the time she left Aster Bay, she'd leave Sugar Grapes with a few new tricks up its sleeve in case her father decided to make the bakery a permanent fixture of the vineyard someday.

Ethan took one look at the exhaustion in her face and insisted on taking her out to dinner. He'd wanted to go to Lemon and Thyme, but Tessa had had enough of Jamie for one day. Every time they were together, she got more confused. They'd bicker and snipe at each other one minute and then suddenly they'd be flirting and he'd look at her with all that banked heat in his eyes until she didn't know which way was up. Tessa was all too familiar with never standing on solid ground, and she was tired of it. Her time in Aster Bay was meant to be simple, but she should have known better. Nothing was ever simple about Aster Bay.

In the end, Ethan agreed to take her to the Dockside Diner, a little hole in the wall on the edge of town. The sparkly red vinyl booths and chrome and faux-marble linoleum tabletops gave the place a vintage vibe, and every surface was pristine. The metal napkin holders on each table gleamed in the fluorescent lights, no drippy ketchup bottles in sight, and a teenager in a spotless white apron was diligently scrubbing the counter when they arrived.

Tessa slid into the booth opposite her father as their server, a woman in her mid-sixties with curly dark hair piled high on her head, approached.

"You folks here for dinner or dessert?" the woman asked as she set coffee cups in front of each of them and filled them to the brim from the pot in her hand, the word "decaf" scrawled across a piece of masking tape affixed to the pot.

"Dinner," Ethan replied. "How're you doing today, Carla?"

The woman smiled. "Any day above ground is a good day. Who've you got with you today?" she asked, tilting her head towards Tessa.

"You remember my daughter—" her father began, but he was promptly cut off by the woman's delighted squeal.

"Is that little TJ all grown up?" She turned her head over her shoulder, hollering towards the kitchen. "Frankie! Steph Cordeiro's baby is here!"

Tessa's stomach dropped and she worked to keep her face neutral, not to betray the way all of her internal organs were recoiling at the unexpected and unwanted attention.

"What?" came the shouted reply from the disembodied

voice that was, Tessa assumed, Frankie.

"Tessa Jayne Cordeiro is here!" Carla repeated, her shouting now drawing amused and interested looks from the other tables.

An older woman across the diner pursed her lips and straightened her spine, pointedly not looking in Tessa's direction as the man across the table from her leaned forward to whisper something, his eyes trained on Tessa.

"What?" This time the shouted reply was even louder.

"Oh, forget it, you old coot." Carla turned back to their table with a wide grin, completely oblivious to the scene she'd just caused and Tessa's overwhelming desire to slide under the table and out of sight. "Look at you, sweetheart! You're all grown up! And the spitting image of your mother," she clucked.

Ethan cleared his throat and shot Tessa an apologetic look. "Tessa's opening up the holiday pop-up bakery at Nuthatch this year," he explained.

"And co-chairing the food and wine festival, I heard," Carla said. "We're all glad to have you on board, darling. Especially since Cheryl won't be able to make her brownies. Oh! Speaking of—I hear Dot Blumenthal is putting together a meal train so Ricky doesn't accidentally poison Cheryl with his cooking."

Ethan shook his head. "Can't poison someone with canned soup and grilled cheese."

"You can if you try hard enough," Tessa replied.

Ethan glanced at her, a hint of a conspiratorial smile tugging at the corner of his mouth. Almost like they were in on the same joke. Like they knew each other well enough to have inside jokes.

"Alright, what'll you have?" Carla asked, retrieving a notepad and pen from her apron pocket. "Frankie's got a burger with caramelized onions and a lemon aioli that is to die for, but we're all out of avocado so don't ask for any guac with your nachos." She looked up at them expectantly.

After they'd ordered, Carla moved on, hollering at Frankie to hurry up already with that order of loaded tater tots for table three.

"She seems nice," Tessa said.

"Sorry about that," Ethan said with a wince. "The whole, 'Steph Cordeiro's baby' thing."

Tessa shrugged, but she didn't meet his eyes. "Not the first time. Won't be the last. I knew what I was signing up for when I agreed to come back here."

"It won't always be like this," Ethan said. "They'll get to know you and you'll stop being anyone other than Tessa who makes the fancy pastries I can't pronounce."

"You don't have to lie to me," Tessa said.

"I'm not—" Ethan began.

"Have you ever been someone other than the guy who knocked up mom when you were a teenager? Has anyone in this town ever let you forget that that's who you are?" She looked up at her father, her own sadness and that lingering shame making her voice tight. If she was going to spend the next several months in Aster Bay, she needed to face the facts, and the fact was that this town would never forget the greatest scandal to rock Aster Bay High.

Ethan's eyes narrowed at her across the table. "Yes, of course. That was a long time ago, T. I volunteer with the Merchants Association. I run the toy drive for the women's shelter every year. And I—"

"Right, you do all of those things, but have you ever, even for a day, not also been the kid who caused a scandal when he was sixteen?"

Tessa watched her father's face. She wanted him to say

no, that no one treated him differently anymore; it was all in the past. Maybe if he said those things, she'd believe him. Maybe it would mean she could have a different life in Aster Bay this time around.

"You'll never not be a teenage father. I'll never not be the baby who brought shame to the Cordeiro and Hart families."

"Teej—"

"There's no point in pretending that's not who we are," she said before taking a sip of her coffee. She hated decaf, but she needed something to do with her hands, something to make her stop talking.

"But that isn't who we are," Ethan insisted. He reached across the table, gripping her wrist and staring into her eyes like he could make her understand. "Most of the people in this town are good, kind-hearted people who don't hold what you did when you were sixteen against you—or your kids. I run the best damn vineyard in the state, so who cares if some of the old ladies at St. Anthony's have nothing better to do than rehash something that happened twenty-five years ago? That's their issue, not ours. Together, we're going to put on the biggest, most profitable food and wine festival this town has ever seen. We are going to put Aster Bay on the goddamn map. The only people's opinions I care about are the family I was born to and the family I've made for myself. So, if a few people want to gossip about the fact that I was a teenager when the best thing to ever happen to me was born—"

The loud mechanical music of Ethan's default ringtone rang out and he mumbled an apology as he dug the phone from his jeans pocket. His brow furrowed as he read the name on the caller ID.

"Hi, mom. Can I call you back?" Tessa watched as her father's face morphed into confusion, his words tumbling over each other and his grip on his phone tightening. "Mom, slow down. I can't understand you. What about dad?" Tessa's stomach dropped. A few more cryptic exchanges, his face growing paler by the second and his eyes darting nervously to Tessa, then he hung up with a promise to "be there as soon as I can."

He'd barely pulled the phone away from his ear when Tessa pounced, unable to hold back the question that had sunk into her gut like a lead weight. "Is Gramps okay?"

He looked at her like he was seeing a ghost. "I…I don't know, kid." He paused, cleared his throat and started again. "Gramps had a heart attack."

Tessa's throat was too tight. When was the last time she'd talked to Gramps? She hadn't seen her grandparents for years. After she and her mom left Aster Bay, they hadn't exactly kept in touch with the family they'd left behind, though she'd been getting better at calling her grandparents on the holidays at least. She'd always told herself that there would be time to get to know them again once she figured out the rest of her life, once she'd become someone they could be proud of. She'd never considered that time might be limited.

You should have known better. After mom died, you should have known how little time we get with people.

"Grama says he's stable, but he needs surgery," Ethan said robotically, still staring at the phone, as though he were repeating back the words he'd been told but hadn't yet processed them.

"Stable is good."

"They're all alone," Ethan whispered. Guilt twisted in her gut. "I think…I have to go to Florida." His voice broke. "If I drive to Boston, I can probably get a flight out tonight or first thing in the morning. You just got here, but I—"

"Go," Tessa said. "I'll be here when you get back."

Ethan stumbled to his feet, pulling Tessa into a hug. She hugged him as tightly as she could, giving herself over to the crush of his worried embrace. He pulled away, shifting into problem-solver mode, his to-do list almost visibly scrolling through his eyes.

"Park your rental car on the left side of the driveway so it doesn't get stuck in the ruts from my truck, and make sure you leave the porch light on if you're going to be out late. The top step can be dangerous in the dark. The landscaper can charge the card on file and the crew at Nuthatch know how to keep everything running. If you need petty cash, Margo knows the combination to the safe."

"How long will you be gone?" Tessa asked.

"I don't know. I don't know if—" He broke off again, shook his head, and picked back up where he'd left off in his list. "I'll call the guys from the road. If you need anything while I'm away, any one of them would help you, but Jamie knows the most about the operations at the vineyard. I'll send you his number."

"I already have it," she said, feeling oddly detached from the whole thing. This was her grandfather who was in the hospital. She should be worried, right? But did she even have a right to be worried when she hadn't called her grandparents in months? She shook off the uncomfortable mix of worry and shame and focused instead on her father. "Go. Give Grama and Gramps a hug from me. I'll be fine."

He dropped his gaze, shaking his head as though he could clear the emotion from his voice. After a long moment, he looked back up at her, and a lump formed in her throat as she took in the ferocity in his eyes.

"Don't give anyone the power to make you feel like you aren't magic, Tessa Jayne. This is your home. You belong here. And if anyone has a problem with that, fuck 'em. Put your head down, work harder, and fuck 'em."

She nodded, "Yeah," she said, her voice hoarse. "Fuck 'em."

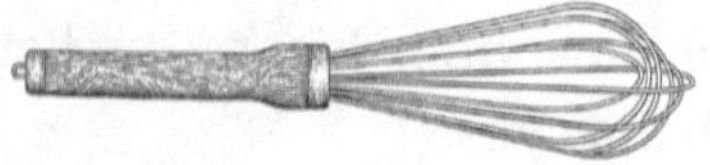

Tessa couldn't sleep. She'd never spent the night alone in her father's house before, and even though he'd called from the airport to say he'd gotten a seat on a flight to Florida that night, the pit in her stomach from earlier hadn't dissipated.

It didn't help that her father's house was too big, too old and creaky, too empty. She knew, logically, that the weird whistling sound was probably something in the pipes, that the door slamming at the end of the hall was because she left the bathroom window cracked open and not because of some malevolent spirit come to haunt her for being a shitty daughter. For wasting the time she could have had with her grandparents. For betraying her mother's memory by being in Aster Bay in the first place.

She knew, but she still jumped every time the house groaned.

The neon red numbers on the alarm clock on the bedside table said it was late. She should try to get some sleep before her alarm went off, but between the many mystery noises, the yawning sense of unease ever since Ethan received that phone call, and the restless tension in her muscles at the thought of seeing Jamie in a few hours, she knew she wasn't getting to sleep any time soon. She shouldn't be so excited to spend the morning with Jamie— he'd been hot and cold with her, a grumpy asshole one minute and then flirtatious and teasing the next.

Unless of course he wasn't actually flirting with her

and she was completely misreading things. After all, why would Jameson Chase, her father's best friend, be flirting with her? Not that she *wanted* him to flirt with her anyway. Not like she'd spent the last few days wondering what it would have been like if they hadn't been connected by her father, if they'd just been two people who had an amazing night together and then kept running into each other.

Shit.

Jamie might not have been flirting with her, but DDB definitely was. Over the last few days, they'd been sending each other increasingly ridiculous photos—his hand wrapped around an eggplant held at crotch level, her holding two pumpkins in front of her chest. Each photo kept any identifying details out of the picture—no faces, no tattoos, nothing to give away a location, though she noted that DDB wore the same kinds of close-fitting Henleys and dark jeans that Jamie favored. Each image sent a thrill down her spine. It was harmless fantasy, pure escapism, because nothing was ever going to happen with DDB.

Just like nothing is ever going to happen with Jamie.

WhiskyBusiness: Are you up?

DiceDiceBaby: I am. What time is it where you are?

WhiskyBusiness: Just after midnight.

DiceDiceBaby: Here too.

Her heart pounded. DDB was in the same time zone. For a fraction of a second, she considered asking him where he lived.

What if he's close?

WhiskyBusiness: What are you wearing?

It was the most forward she'd ever been with DDB. No suggestive vegetables to hide behind. This was just her, crossing this line that she very much hoped he wanted to cross with her.

A moment later, a photo appeared on her screen. The angle was odd, just barely hiding his face from the frame, though the edge of a stubbled jaw was visible in the upper right corner. He wore a heathered blue t-shirt, the fabric pulled tight over his biceps and pecs, and gray sweatpants. He was fully clothed, yet the image was downright indecent, the way his shirt clung to every ridge and contour of his body, the all-too-clear outline of his dick apparent beneath his sweatpants. She sucked in a breath, heat pooling low in her belly.

WhiskyBusiness: Damn. That's a good picture.

DiceDiceBaby: Your turn.

Tessa kicked off the comforter and angled the camera to hide her face, though her dark hair spilled over her shoulder, curling between her breasts. She wore a turquoise V-neck t-shirt, stretched out from years of wear and dipping scandalously low. The fabric, thin from repeated washing, betrayed her lack of bra and the tight furls of her nipples. The top of her pink pajama shorts and a stretch of upper thigh appeared at the edge of the frame.

DiceDiceBaby: It's good to see you, beautiful.

WhiskyBusiness: You too.

WhiskyBusiness: What are you doing up?

DiceDiceBaby: I just got home from the restaurant. You?

WhiskyBusiness: Hiding from the ghost in this house.

DiceDiceBaby: There's a ghost in your house?

WhiskyBusiness: Not my house. I'm staying with family for a bit.

DiceDiceBaby: In a haunted house?

WhiskyBusiness: It might be. I keep hearing all these creeeeeeeak whoooosh eerrrrrrr noises.

DiceDiceBaby: Well, that settles it. It's clearly haunted.

WhiskyBusiness: I'm glad you agree.

DiceDiceBaby: You could burn sage.

WhiskyBusiness: Excuse me. I don't burn my cooking.

DiceDiceBaby: No, like a bundle of sage. You light it on fire and wave it around.

WhiskyBusiness: And that helps my ghost problem how?

DiceDiceBaby: I don't really know. My sister-in-law's friend mentioned something once.

WhiskyBusiness: I'd rather forget about the sage and cuddle up with you instead.

She waited for his reply, knowing maybe this time she'd gone too far. Saying she wanted to cuddle was definitely more serious than suggestive produce and, more than that, it would never happen. But at that moment, she really did mean it. She wanted nothing more than to bury her face in the soft fabric of his t-shirt and wrap herself in his strong arms. Funny how when she closed her eyes and pictured it, DDB smelled like Jamie, like soap and cedar...

DiceDiceBaby: Me too, princess.

Chapter Twelve

Jamie drove up the gravel driveway to Ethan's house at 6:59 a.m. Ethan had called him the night before on his way to the airport, making Jamie promise he'd help Tessa find her footing with the bakery and the festival. "She's feeling like an outsider," Ethan had said. "She doesn't know the area, or which vendors to use. She wants to be taken seriously on her own merits, and you could help her make the right connections to get her started."

Jamie knew no better way to welcome Tessa into the food scene of Aster Bay than a trip to the farmer's market. But as he walked up to Ethan's front door to pick Tessa up for their hunt for "inspiration," Jamie suddenly had second thoughts. He was not the right person for this job, for teaching someone how to assimilate into Aster Bay. After twenty years, he still didn't feel like the town had fully embraced him, aside from the guys who had become more family than friends.

Tessa threw open the front door, turning and walking back down the hallway before he even had a minute to say anything. "I just need to brush my teeth!" she called over her shoulder before disappearing into the bathroom.

When she re-emerged, Jamie was still standing in the foyer and she skidded to a stop, her eyes raking over him. He cleared his throat, arching an eyebrow at her and trying not to enjoy the fact that she was checking him out. He was supposed to be helping her build a name for herself as a chef, like her father would have if he were in town, not like a man who couldn't stop thinking about her raven-wing eyes, or the sounds she made when she came.

He held out a cardboard coffee cup to her.

"Oh, thank God." She reached for the cup, speaking directly to it. "Hello, lover." As she took a sip, she caught his amused smirk. "I...really like coffee."

"So I gathered. Nice shirt."

She glanced down as though she were seeing the hot pink t-shirt with a picture of a giant frosted donut over each breast for the first time. "Thanks," she mumbled, adding something about laundry day before taking another sip of her coffee and releasing a happy sigh. The sound warmed him more than coffee ever could. He thought it best he not examine why.

He cleared his throat. "Did I get it right?" At her questioning look, he gestured to the coffee cup. "How you take it?"

"Oh! Yes! I mean it's no Starbucks, but still. How did you know?"

"It's how you prepared it at the restaurant the other day."

She let out a surprised laugh. "And you remembered?"

He shrugged, like it was no big deal. Like he didn't remember every second he'd spent in her presence over the last two weeks. Every snarky remark, every flutter of her eyelashes, every sigh... *Stop.*

"Any word on your grandfather?"

"Ethan called about a half hour ago. Gramps is scheduled

for surgery on Wednesday, but he's stable for now. He got mad at the nurse for not letting him have bacon with his breakfast this morning."

Jamie smiled. "That sounds like Henry. I'm glad your dad is there. I'm sure your grandmother appreciates it." He gestured to the front door. "Shall we?"

The roads of Aster Bay were mostly deserted this early in the morning, making the small town with its perfect rows of trees along each sidewalk appear more like a movie set than an actual town. He loved fall in Aster Bay, the baskets of flowers hanging from each lamppost color coordinated for the season—orange, yellow, and deep burgundy mums declaring that fall had arrived, even if the trees hadn't started changing colors yet—and the air just beginning to take on the crisp smell of autumn.

Whisky was right. It made him want pie and soup. Maybe he'd make chouriço and kale soup later, even if Whisky couldn't taste it.

He pulled the car into a parking spot in the small lot next to the town common, an entire block in the center of town devoted entirely to a playground, gazebo, and green space. That morning, the green space was covered with row after row of white pop-up tents, each one occupied by a local vendor. A few customers were already milling about, but this early in the morning, it was mostly just the vendors.

"Ready to be inspired?" Jamie asked.

"Always," she said, withdrawing her small, leather-bound notebook from her back pocket.

The first tent boasted an assortment of baked goods and a giant coffee urn. Jamie nodded to the woman as they walked past, then leaned down so only Tessa could hear him. "Don't eat Linda's muffins if you value your digestive health."

She laughed mid-sip of her coffee. "Thanks for the warning."

They walked past the next few tents, Jamie greeting each person by name, tossing out well wishes for their spouses and asking after their children. He'd worked hard to learn every name, to remember little details about each person so they would know he cared about them. So they'd forget he hadn't always been one of them.

He paused in front of a tent filled with crates of vegetables in every color of the rainbow—beets and cabbages, multicolored beans and what must be the last of the eggplant crop. The back of an old pickup truck was pulled up behind the tent, the bed piled high with ears of corn. Tessa ran her hand lovingly over the vegetables before she began scribbling in her notebook. What he wouldn't give to see what she was writing in there.

"Don't tell me you're out of beets already," Ricky said as he pulled a crate of peppers from the cab of the truck.

Jamie smiled. "Not even close. I wanted to introduce you to Tessa." He dropped his hand to the small of her back, his palm barely making contact with her and yet the touch still made his mouth go dry. As his hand met the curve of her spine, she looked up from her notebook as though emerging from a trance. "Tessa, this is Ricky DaSilva. He owns DaSilva's Farm on the edge of town and has the best produce in the county."

"Are you Ethan's daughter?" Ricky asked, setting down the peppers and taking a step forward. He extended his hand to her.

"I am," she said.

The farmer broke into a wide grin. "So you're the one taking over the pop-up. Oh! *And* the festival."

"This is Cheryl's husband," Jamie explained.

Ricky's grin somehow grew wider. "That I am. She'll be glad to know I've met you, though Kyla's already been by to tell us how much she likes you. My wife would want me to thank you for hiring Kyla on."

"No thanks needed. She earned that spot on my staff," Tessa said. Her cheeks darkened under Ricky's continued thanks, and Jamie forced his thoughts away from the last time he'd seen her skin turn that particular shade of pink.

"You see anything you want for Sugar Grapes, you just let me know and I'll have it delivered," Ricky offered.

"Thank you," she said, wandering to the end of the table to examine the raspberries. She moved beyond Jamie's reach and his hand fell away from her back. He shook it at his side, as though he could shake off the memory of her skin.

Keep your distance.

Jamie and Ricky chatted while Tessa browsed, occasionally jotting something down in her notebook. Ricky thanked Jamie for the chicken dinner he'd delivered a few nights prior, and Jamie recounted the story of Brodie's alarmed discovery that beets could change the color of your urine. Eventually, Tessa placed an order for corn, raspberries, and blueberries, and they said their goodbyes to Ricky, moving back out of his tent.

"Inspired?" Jamie asked, gesturing to her notebook.

She smiled, taunting him with the closed book. "Starting to be."

At the tent displaying jars of colorful jams and preserves, Tessa bought a variety of unusual flavors, adding a jar of caramelized onion and fig chutney to her selection at Jamie's urging. "It's the best chutney on this side of the bay," he'd said. When they arrived at the tent for the goat farm, Jamie introduced her to Michelle, a woman who made all kinds of goat cheese on her goat farm, commenting that Tessa might enjoy trying some of the lesser-known varieties in her next batch of ice cream.

"You really love it here, don't you?" Tessa asked when they'd said goodbye to Michelle, Tessa promising to stop by the farm soon to bring her a sample of the ice cream she made with it.

"I do," Jamie confirmed.

"But you're not from here?"

He focused on making sure the heavy bag of preserves didn't swing against the bag of produce hard enough to bruise anything. Maybe then she wouldn't notice the tension creeping into his shoulders. "No. I'm from Massachusetts, but I moved here for college and never left. Now Aster Bay is home."

Tessa was quiet for a moment, and he was aware of her eyes on him as he waved in greeting to a passing couple who frequented Lemon and Thyme. The woman always ordered the seafood special, regardless of what it was, and he made a mental note to get their names the next time they came in.

"I don't think I've ever felt that way about a place before," she said softly.

He stopped walking and turned to look at her, waiting until she raised her downcast eyes. "It's not about the place. It's about the people. If these people didn't live here, Aster Bay wouldn't be the same. Gavin and Baz and your dad—they're my family."

"What about your real family?"

"My brother and sister-in-law are theater actors in New York. We don't get to see each other much. And my parents died shortly after I moved here. Car accident."

Her eyes creased in empathy. "I'm sorry. I didn't know."

He nodded in acknowledgment but kept talking so the

ball of tension behind his sternum couldn't take root. "Your dad and I had a few classes together in college and… I don't know. I don't know why he took me in, but once Ethan Hart decides you're a part of his family, you can't shake him."

He began walking away, needing to move so he didn't do something foolish like think about how it would feel for Tessa to be part of his family. Across the common, a cluster of women who had gone to school with Ethan and his friends eyed Tessa warily, one even going so far as to point at her while she said something that made the rest of her friends laugh. Jamie positioned himself between Tessa and the women, steering her towards the other side of the farmer's market and hoped she hadn't noticed.

"Your dad introduced me to Gavin and Baz and his parents," he continued, forcing himself to focus on answering her question so he wouldn't have time to think about the choice words he wanted to say to those women. Who the fuck *pointed* at people in public?

"Ethan said, 'we're your family now.' And he meant it." He glanced at her, hoping she understood. Needing her to understand. "Family isn't necessarily about blood, Tessa. It's about the people you let in, the people you would do anything for, who would do anything for you."

She looked away from him. "I don't have people. Not like that."

"Maybe you'll find them in Aster Bay."

"Maybe." She smiled a sad sort of smile, like she didn't really believe him, her eyes darting to the group of women who were still laughing. He swallowed down the impulse to say that he could be one of her people, if she wanted him to be.

They made their way through tents selling farm fresh eggs and rounds of crusty artisan breads, an entire tent just for various kinds of mushrooms, and a stall selling freshly made dog biscuits that looked more like giant peanut butter cookies than something you'd give your pet. With each stall they visited, each bag of new things added to her stash, Tessa seemed more at ease, the tension of their conversation slowly leaving her stance. She even stopped looking abashed when someone would give a startled laugh after noticing her shirt, instead leaning into the joke.

She selected a final jar of giardiniera and paid for her bounty, and Jamie took up the bag before she could, as he'd done with every other bag before.

"I can carry my own bags, you know," she said.

"I know," he said, though he made no move to let her do so.

They'd fallen into a comfortable rhythm, like she'd been a part of the town all along, like she belonged there. *Because she does,* Jamie thought. *This is her hometown. Not yours.*

At the end of the row of tents, they came to a food truck. Lindsay, a petite woman with long wavy brown hair, was setting out an A-frame sign with a chalkboard menu as they approached. For a moment he thought of the taco truck they'd visited that first night, of the taste of mango and lime on her lips...

"Jamie! To what do I owe the pleasure?" Lindsay asked, clapping chalk dust off her hands.

"'Morning, Linds. Have you met Tessa?" Jamie asked, his hand once again landing on the small of Tessa's back, like some magnetic pull kept bringing them back together.

Lindsay squinted as she stared at Tessa, like she was trying to place her and couldn't quite do it. Suddenly her eyes flew wide and her gaze darted between Jamie and Tessa. "TJ?" Jamie gave a slight nod and Lindsay squealed, stepping forward and taking Tessa's face in her hands. "TJ

Cordeiro! Will you *look* at you!"

With a delighted squeak, Lindsay pulled Tessa into a hug. Tessa shot a confused look at Jamie, who shrugged and bit back a laugh.

Lindsay continued speaking into Tessa's hair, rocking her back and forth as she did. "I haven't seen you since you were just a little girl. And now you're all grown up!" She pulled back, keeping her hands on Tessa's shoulders. "Let me get a look at you."

"I'm sorry," Tessa said, shooting another questioning look Jamie's way. "Who are you?"

"No need to be sorry, sweetheart. We haven't seen each other in years. I just can't get over how *grown* you are!"

"This is Lindsay Bradford. She owns this food truck," Jamie offered.

"Your mother was my best friend from kindergarten all the way until—well, until you were a very little girl," Lindsay said with a sad smile.

Shit. I didn't know that, Jamie thought, wondering if he'd made a mistake in bringing Tessa there.

"How is Steph? Is she here?" Lindsay asked, glancing behind Tessa like her mother might materialize.

Jamie saw the question hit Tessa, saw the way her eyes shuttered and her stance stiffened. Before he could interject, she answered. "No. She passed away a few years ago."

Such a simple statement of fact, but Jamie recognized the lingering grief that fluttered around the edges. Maybe only someone who'd also lost a parent could see it.

"Oh, sweetheart, I'm so sorry. I didn't know," Lindsay said.

"It's fine," Tessa replied tightly.

If Lindsay noticed the way Tessa's jaw tensed, she didn't show it. But Jamie noticed, his hand curling at his side as he fought the urge to touch her again. To rub soothing circles on her back and knead the knots from her shoulders until that grief had receded again, like a wave receding from the shore. It would be back—it would always come back—but if he could help her find a reprieve... He lifted his hand to touch her, but something in the sharpness of her gaze held him back.

"Did your mother ever tell you about the time she and I went sledding on that hill behind St. Anthony's and she was too scared to even try the inner tubes? Swore they went too fast." Lindsay smiled, lost in her own memories. "So where have you been all these years? Rumor has it you've come from Vegas?"

Tessa swallowed and recited her history like it was a list of facts in a textbook and not her own story. "We were in Phoenix for a while with my mom's first husband, and when he didn't work out, we spent some time in South Carolina. Mom met Lou, her second husband, and we moved with him to Vegas. And when Lou left, mom met Richard. They moved to Colorado and I stayed behind." She smiled, but Jamie could see the way her own lips fought the unnatural movement.

"My, you have been busy," Lindsay said, her own fake smile plastered on her face. "I guess when Steph said she wanted to be anywhere but here, she really meant anywhere."

Tessa tensed, the lines of her face becoming sharp as Lindsay's comment sent Tessa's hackles up. Jamie's hand settled on Tessa's back again, unable to resist the pull to touch her, to soothe her. She leaned into the gentle pressure and he stroked his thumb over the thin fabric of her t-shirt.

"Tessa and I are co-chairing the food and wine festival," Jamie said, steering the conversation away from the ghosts of Tessa's past.

"So I heard! Any way I can help, anything you need, you just holler," Lindsay said, resuming her pre-opening routine.

"I'm glad to hear you say that, Linds. This morning we're in the market for some inspiration," Jamie said.

"Inspiration?" Lindsay shot him an amused look. "That's a tall order for a Saturday morning."

"We're hoping to nail down the brunch menu. And if anyone knows what to serve with mimosas, it's you," Jamie said. He turned to Tessa, dropping his voice to a faux-whisper. "Lindsay is a genius with a quiche."

"Genius? Ha!" Lindsay cackled and cast a fond smile in his direction. "You always were a flatterer." She turned to Tessa. "You got a special someone in your life, Tessa Jayne?"

Tessa glanced at Jamie warily, taking a step away from him so his hand fell away. "No. No one special."

He wanted to eliminate the distance between them, to keep his hands on her, to show her that he could be someone special... none of which was okay. Because he couldn't be someone special to Ethan's daughter, and when she walked out of that hotel room two weeks ago without so much as a goodbye note on the pillow, she'd made it perfectly clear that she didn't want him to be anyway. He needed to remember that no matter how much she haunted his thoughts, she would always be someone who had decided she didn't want him around for more than one night.

More than that, she would always be his best friend's daughter.

So maybe she was right. Maybe where Tessa was concerned, he really was no one special.

Chapter Thirteen

"Coming!" Tessa hollered at the incessant knocking on the front door. *What is it with small towns and people just dropping by unannounced?*

She pulled open the door to find a quartet of white-haired women on her front steps, each grinning wider than the last.

"Can I help you?" she asked.

The woman closest to the front clicked her tongue. "TJ! Look at you!"

Tessa grimaced as the woman prattled on about some silly thing Tessa had done as a six-year-old. She was really getting tired of the non-stop walks down memory lane from every person she met, each one seemingly remembering everything about her even though she had no memories of them. Granted, she'd worked pretty hard over the years to block out thoughts of Aster Bay and her mother had hated discussing her hometown, but still...

"So that's why we're here!" the woman concluded with a satisfied smile.

Shit. What did she say?

"I'm sorry. I think I missed something..."

"We're taking you to dinner," the woman on the end said. She pointed to each of them in turn, starting with herself, "Dot, Ruth, Helen, Judy. Don't worry. We won't hold it against you if you don't remember right away."

"Speak for yourself," Ruth said.

"So? Ready to go?" Judy asked.

"Go where?" Tessa said, struggling to keep up.

"To dinner," Helen repeated. "We heard you were here in this big house all by yourself and we thought, that's no place for a young woman on a Saturday night. So here we are. We're taking you to dinner. Our treat."

"Oh, I couldn't—"

"It wasn't a request, dear," said Dot.

That is how Tessa Cordeiro found herself at dinner at Lemon and Thyme on Saturday night with four elderly women, all of whom had apparently taught both her mother and father in elementary school.

"Then there was the time your father caught a frog at recess and chased your poor mother all around the schoolyard trying to get her to kiss it," Judy laughed between sips of her pinot grigio.

"And did she?" Tessa asked.

"Heavens no!" Judy laughed. "When he caught up to her, she turned and planted one right on Ethan's lips. Surprised the hell out of him."

Tessa smiled. She'd never heard these stories of her parents' youth together. Her mother hadn't liked to talk about Aster Bay—other than to tell her how judgmental everyone was—and her father... well, she'd never asked him.

"They were always circling each other. For years," Helen said with a chuckle as she dipped her bread into the plate of seasoned olive oil in the center of the table. "We all knew they'd end up together. Even when she dated Mikey Greenhall."

"That was only for a few weeks," Dot said, as though it was hardly worth mentioning.

"You certainly know a lot about the love lives of two teenagers," Tessa chuckled.

"Oh, sweetheart, we know everything that goes on in this town," Helen said. It felt like a warning.

"If you ever want to know what *really* happened, you come talk to me," Dot said with a smile and a wink.

"Excuse me? Are we not just as capable of telling Tessa Jayne about her parents' courtship?" Ruth asked, and Tessa wasn't sure if she was actually offended or just teasing her friend.

"Dottie's memory does keep the most faithful record of events," Judy said.

"How would you know? You'd forget your own hat if it wasn't on your head," Ruth said.

"It's true!" Judy laughed. "But you go see Ruth if you want to hear how things *should* have been. Talk to Helen if you want to know what everyone said about it after the fact. But if you want to know what they actually *did,* that's when you talk to Dottie."

"So I suppose talking to all of you is the only way to get the full story," Tessa said, grinning despite herself.

"Precisely," Helen said.

"Evening, ladies," Jamie said as he appeared beside their table.

His dark hair was mussed in that sexy just-rolled-out-of-bed way. He wore dark fitted jeans and a long sleeve t-shirt with Lemon and Thyme's logo screen printed over his left pec, sleeves rolled up to reveal his sculpted forearms, the front in a French tuck that drew attention to the shiny silver of his belt buckle.

Jesus Christ, Tessa, don't look at his belt buckle.

He turned his dimpled smile on each of the older women in turn, the curve of his lips only faltering slightly when his gaze landed on Tessa.

It was her own fault. They'd had a perfectly good time at the farmer's market until they'd run into Lindsay. After that, Tessa just hadn't been able to shake the urge to run, to put Aster Bay and these people who wanted to dredge up memories of her mother she didn't share and the man who wouldn't stop circling her thoughts—who kept touching her like she somehow belonged to him—far behind her. Once Lindsay and Jamie had gotten to chatting about the ideal mimosa pairings, Tessa had excused herself, waiting in the car until Jamie had finally returned and driven her home in tense silence. None of it had felt right for the man who ate fish tacos with her on a grassy hill overlooking the highway and then growled his way through the hottest sex of her life.

Jamie thanked them for coming, assuring Dot that he had in fact sent the chicken dinner over to Cheryl and Ricky as promised, and then, guaranteeing that their food would be out shortly, he disappeared. He hadn't looked at Tessa once after that initial glance and something twisted in her stomach as she watched him walk away, the tense muscles of his back shifting beneath his shirt.

Halfway through their entrées, as Judy and Helen debated whether her mother had been the one to throw the dodgeball that gave her father a bloody nose in the second grade, Tessa caught sight of Jamie slipping from the kitchen and down a dark hallway at the back of the restaurant. She excused herself from the table—not that the women really noticed, they were so deep in their argument—and followed. It would have been easier to text him, a simple sentence or two to apologize for being grumbly and aloof when he had been doing a nice thing by showing her around, but that didn't feel right. Not when the last time she'd hurt him she had left without saying goodbye. He deserved a face to face conversation.

There were two doors off the hallway, one that led to an empty office, neat stacks of folders on the edge of the perfectly clear desktop, and another that led to a set of stairs. At the top of the stairwell, the door opened out onto a rooftop terrace. She gasped as she took in the stunning view of the harbor, lights shining on the opposite shore in the darkening sky and the black shadows of boats bobbing in the water.

"What are you doing up here?"

Tessa turned to meet Jamie's cold stare. He sat on the floor of the rooftop terrace, facing out over the water, his elbows resting on his bent knees, a beer bottle dangling from his fingers.

"I wanted to apologize. For this morning," she said, taking a tentative step onto the roof and letting the door slam shut behind her.

"Don't worry about it," he said, taking a sip of his beer. Her gaze snagged on the bottle. It was the same brand that DDB drank.

"You were so nice, and I ruined it," she said, coming to stand beside him. He grunted in agreement and took another sip. "It just messes with my head when you're like that."

"Like what?"

"Nice to me."

"I shouldn't be nice to you?"

"You should hate me."

"Why would I hate you?"

"Because of who I am."

"Don't see a reason to hate you for that."

"Because of the other night. Because I left."

He nodded, focusing his attention on his beer. "Well, joke's on you. We're stuck with each other now."

"Right." She swallowed down the lump in her throat, determined not to let the jaded edge in his voice hurt her. "Anyway, I'm sorry."

"Apology accepted."

She stood there in silence, watching the wind ruffle his hair, the stiffness in his shoulders, all coiled tension that he steadfastly focused anywhere but on her. She should have left—that's what she was good at, and she'd said what she came to say. But she wasn't ready to go. He'd opened up to her at the farmer's market, and then she'd gone and shut down on him, and she knew he said he accepted her apology, but she didn't want just that. She wanted him to understand.

"This is hard for me. Being here."

"No one asked you to come to my restaurant, Tess." He sounded tired, like just talking to her was exhausting.

"I meant in Aster Bay," she said. *Does he really not want me in his restaurant?* "You're the only one here who seems to want to know me as Tessa, as the person I am now. Even my dad can't stop calling me TJ, like he still sees me as the kid I used to be. All these people think they know me—"

"Maybe they just want the chance to get to you know," he snapped.

"But I don't know them. All these people who knew my mother... I was eight years old when we left. Why don't I remember them?" She bit her lip to stop from talking. She hadn't meant to say so much.

Jamie stared at her, his brow furrowed like he was trying

to peel away her layers. She wrapped her arms around herself as though that would help. "Your mom kept you on a pretty short leash," he said at last. "Maybe you didn't know we were all around."

She sat next to him on the ground, careful to leave a few inches of space between them. "Do you remember me? From back then?"

He nodded and took another sip of his beer, keeping his gaze out over the open water. "A bit. Your mom didn't like you being around Ethan's friends much."

"Why?"

"I don't know." He glanced at her, his gaze softening. "Your mom had a rough time of it. I don't think she knew who she could trust. And she always made it clear that she had no intention of staying in town. Maybe she didn't want you to get attached."

Tessa nodded and looked back over the water. "Mom used to say it was us against the world. But I think maybe that wasn't true."

"She felt like it was."

"Yeah." She ran her eyes over him again, ending back on his face, the stubbled line of his jaw. "She wouldn't like me being here now."

"At my restaurant, or in Aster Bay?"

"Both."

He stared at her, his eyes darting between her own. What was he thinking? About her mother keeping a young child away from her father and his friends? Or about what she would say if she knew what had happened between Tessa and Jamie in that hotel room?

She reached for his beer. "May I?"

He handed it to her, and she took a long pull of the hoppy liquid before passing the bottle back. Her lips tingled when he took his own sip as though he were pressing his mouth to hers and not just to the same curved piece of glass where her mouth had just been.

"Be honest with me, Tessa. That night... Did you remember me?"

"No." She turned to face him, her knee pressing against his thigh. "I swear to God, Jamie, I didn't know who you were."

"I believe you."

Relief washed over her as his words settled between them. She hadn't realized how badly she wanted him to trust her.

"What are you doing here, Tess?" His voice was low, almost hoarse.

She blinked, thrown off-kilter by the question. "I told you. I needed a job and I—"

"Not in Aster Bay. Here. On my roof." He met her eyes, the moonlight glinting off his irises like the eyes of a predator in the dark.

She swallowed, her mouth suddenly dry. "I wanted to apologize."

"Yeah. You said that."

"I meant it."

He grunted, his eyes dropping to her mouth and then back to meet her gaze.

"I thought," she said, her voice soft, barely audible above the breeze coming off the water, and she scooted closer to him, "we could be friends."

"Friends," he repeated, shaking his head, though there was no joy in his chuckle. "I don't want to be friends with you, Tessa."

Her heart sank. "Oh."

"I don't feel very *friendly* when I look at you," he continued, his voice rough in ways that did delicious things

136

to her insides.

She reached for his beer bottle again, the rough pads of his fingers brushing against hers as the glass slid into her grasp. She took another long pull, nearly draining the bottle. He tracked each movement, his eyes darting over her face, her throat.

He took the bottle back from her, and downed the last sip, setting the bottle aside. When he turned back to her, the lust in his eyes was deep enough to drown in. She reached up with one hand and brushed a lock of hair from his eyes. He caught her wrist, his eyes growing darker as his hand curled around her wrist, fingertips digging into her skin. But he didn't push her away. He just held her there, as though he could freeze time.

She leaned closer and tentatively brushed her lips against his. He sucked in a breath and there was a fraction of a moment where he was frozen against her, but then he released her wrist and slid his hands into her hair as he kissed her back, deepening the kiss. She gripped his forearm, holding his hand in her hair with one hand, and slid her other around his waist, using the leverage to pull herself closer to him. He tasted like beer and orange and smelled of cedar and soap. She moaned against his kiss as he licked into her mouth, tangling his tongue with hers.

Jamie wrapped an arm around her back and pulled her into his lap, her legs closing around his waist as he continued to kiss her, the hand buried in her hair tightening just enough to send gentle sparks across her scalp. For the first time since she'd set foot in Aster Bay, she felt like someone really wanted her, not the memory of the child she'd been, but *her*, the woman she'd become. She rocked against the hard length of him and dug her nails into his back. He pulled away, wild eyes searching hers, before he leaned his forehead against her.

"You're my best friend's daughter," he said, the words harsh, like they'd been ripped from his body. And yet he still rocked against her, torturing them both with the friction.

Her breathing was labored, their chests pressed together as each breath moved them closer. She wasn't ready for the moment to be over.

"We could pretend I'm not," she said.

He brushed his lips against hers, softly. "I can't pretend. And I can't be your friend. Not if I'm still going to be his after you leave."

"Then what are we?"

He brushed her hair behind her ear and let his hand fall away, meeting her gaze with pained eyes. "Just two people who happen to be working together." She raked her fingers through his hair, brushing the longer strands that had been caught by the wind out of his face, and he closed his eyes like he was savoring her touch. His voice shook when he said, "You should go."

"Jamie—"

"I'm hanging on by a thread here, Tessa. Please go."

His voice was so raw, so broken, and she knew she'd done that to him. Shame flooded her veins.

She got to her feet on shaky legs and left him on the roof, staring out at the water, the same way she'd found him. When she returned to the table, she told the ladies she wasn't feeling well and excused herself, insisting they stay and enjoy the rest of their dinner, but allowing them to call a car to take her home.

She lay in bed in her father's guest room and touched her fingertips to her lips, as though she could preserve the feeling of Jamie's kiss. As though the one person in Aster Bay who really saw her for who she was hadn't just sent her away.

For the first time in months, she didn't want to message DDB. She didn't want to watch *Brilliant British Bakes* or daydream about the bakery she'd open one day. Instead, she rolled over, curling up into a ball, and closed her eyes, pretending she was back in that hotel room with Jamie's arms around her and his lips on her neck.

Chapter Fourteen

Jamie placed the last tray of stuffed shells in the chest freezer in Cheryl and Ricky's basement and made his way back up to the living room where Cheryl sat, enthroned in a pile of pillows with a plate of waffle fries balanced on her very pregnant belly.

"Shells are in the freezer and there's a turkey dinner with all the fixings in the fridge," Jamie said.

"Honey, do you think you could maybe get the baby to stay in a little while longer?" Ricky asked with a goofy grin. "We've never eaten so well."

Cheryl placed her hands on either side of her pregnant belly, cooing to her unborn child. "Don't you listen to your daddy. You come on out of there. Any time now would be fine." She bit into another waffle fry and a practically indecent groan fell from her lips. "Jamie, you are a godsend. How did you know I was craving waffle fries?"

Jamie shot Ricky a grin and a wink, before rummaging in the bottom of the cooler bag he'd brought with him. He retrieved a small plastic container and held it up for Cheryl. "And nacho cheese."

She groaned again, reaching out for the container. "I

swear to God, if I wasn't already married—"

"But you are," Ricky said, dropping a kiss on her forehead and swiping the container before heading for the kitchen. "I'll just heat this up."

Cheryl ripped off another piece of waffle fry. "So, tell me everything. How's the festival planning coming?"

Jamie took a seat in the armchair across from the couch, leaning his elbows on his knees. "Good, good."

"You are such a bad liar. Even worse than Ricky."

He sighed. "It's fine, it's just not what I expected. There are so many moving parts, and we still need to figure out how to incorporate Tessa and Kyla's ideas about marketing to twenty-year-olds—"

Cheryl laughed through a mouthful of waffle fry. "Yeah, I heard about that. Please tell me they're filming you walking in slow motion on the beach."

"Don't give Gavin any ideas. But really, it's fine. If it brings in more tourists, then it's worth it."

"And how are things with Tessa working out?"

"What do you mean?" He glanced away, hoping he didn't look as flustered as he felt. At some point that had to go away, right? The immediate flash of memory of her naked and stretched out beneath him every time someone said her name.

"Are you guys working together alright? I know how much of a dictator you are in the kitchen."

"I am not," he protested.

She laughed again, reaching out to accept the nacho cheese from Ricky before he'd even fully re-entered the room. "You most certainly are. I was nervous about working on the festival with you and we've known each other for years."

"You were? Cheryl, if I ever made you feel—"

She waved him off with half a fry. "You didn't. But you're this big professional chef and I'm just a farmer's wife who sells brownies at a farm stand."

"And you run the most successful holiday bakery in town."

She laughed. "It's the only bakery in town. The only reason the pop-up does well every year is that nobody in this state likes to cross bridges, least of all to get a pie."

"That's not the point. You're a fantastic baker. I'm hardly in the kitchen anymore. Ever since I bought Lemon and Thyme, Anabel does most of the cooking." It was the thing they didn't tell you about becoming a restauranteur—there wasn't a whole lot of chef-ing for the chef-owner.

"But Tessa's more on your level. Mrs. Kemp and Mrs. White were telling me she worked for some fancy, award-winning chef in Vegas."

He nodded. "Yeah, she did."

"I can't wait until she opens Sugar Grapes. I already told Ricky—'Ricky,' I said, 'when Tessa Jayne opens Sugar Grapes, you are going to buy me one of everything.' Ethan's mom used to make the best banana bread. I hope Tessa has that recipe."

"You make pretty good banana bread yourself."

"Not like this. It had some spice in it. Oh, what's that spice called? Ricky, what's that spice called?"

"What spice?" he asked.

"The one in Mrs. Hart's banana bread."

"Something with a 'c'," Ricky said.

She dipped a fry in the bright yellow cheese. "Cardamom." She groaned, as though she were eating it then. Jamie didn't blame her. If Louise's cardamom banana bread was anything like Tessa's cardamom bananas foster, it was certainly groan-worthy.

Jamie's phone vibrated. He pulled it free from his pocket

and immediately got to his feet. "It's Ethan. I have to take this," he said to Cheryl with an apologetic smile.

"Say hi to him for us and send our best to Mr. Hart. And thank you for all the food, Jamie. Really." Cheryl squeezed his arm and shooed him off.

Jamie answered his phone as he stepped out onto Cheryl's front porch, pulling the door closed behind him. "Hey. How's your dad?" he asked.

Ethan chuckled, a tired, happy sound, on the other end of the phone. "He's just as opinionated as ever, and really not happy that mom's siding with the doctors about changing his diet."

Jamie laughed as he climbed into his car. "He'll come around. How's your mom holding up?"

Ethan filled him in on the thousand ways his mother had found to fuss over him in the last few days, insisting he add a salad to his lunch tray in the hospital cafeteria, grilling him on when he was going to find a 'nice girl' and settle down.

"She's just happy you're there," Jamie said, ignoring the tightness in his chest that his own mother would never do those things again. It was an old hurt, but one that ripped itself open at the most unexpected times. For a moment he thought of Tessa, having to recount her mother's death at the farmer's market the day before, and he cringed. No wonder she'd shut down.

"It looks like she's going to have a while longer to force me to eat my vegetables," Ethan said, his voice sobering. "It'll be six to eight weeks before dad's back on his feet after this surgery. He can't even drive for at least a month." Jamie cursed under his breath. "Yeah, my feelings exactly. I can't just leave—"

"No, of course not. What can I do?"

"You're already doing it, man. I just need you to be there for Tessa, make sure she has what she needs. I hate that I'm not there. She finally comes to town and the first thing I do is leave."

"I'm sure she understands," Jamie said, guilt twisting in his gut.

"I just spoke to her before I called you. She's not as tough as she wants people to think, you know?" Again, Jamie thought of the hurt in her eyes when he'd turned her away. He leaned his head back against his headrest, closing his eyes as he listened to his friend talk. "She's trying to get people to take her seriously as a chef and she doesn't have any friends in town—"

"She and Kyla Mitchell seem to have hit it off."

"—and now I'm not even there."

Jamie smiled, despite himself. "Worrying like that, you sound like your mother."

Ethan huffed a laugh. "I guess you never stop being a parent, no matter how old they get. I know she's not a kid anymore. Just...do what you can to help her see that she could have a life here, okay?"

"Yeah," Jamie said, squeezing his eyes shut against the irrational desire that he be a part of that life. "Okay."

Jamie stood on the roof of his restaurant as the wind whipped around him watching the boats bob in the harbor. He pulled his jacket around himself with one hand, his other loosely holding a mostly-full beer bottle at his side. From his position on the roof, he could see the entire harbor and the large, stately homes on the opposite side lining the waterfront of the peninsula at the end of Aster

Bay. He loved this spot, despite the fact that the rooftop terrace remained unfinished even three years after he'd taken ownership of the restaurant.

When he'd bought the place, he'd had big dreams of putting outdoor dining up there during the warmer months. He'd yet to find another place in town that had the same uninterrupted view, the waves gently lapping at the sides of the boats almost hypnotizing. On the roof, he felt like he was at the center of the town—not just *in* it, but a part of it, connected to it, integral to it. It was what had attracted him to the location in the first place. Well, that and the incredible kitchen.

As the sun set over the harbor, painting the water in streaks of pink and orange, and the sounds of clattering silverware and muted conversation floated up to him from the restaurant below, he fought for that sense of peace. But it eluded him. Instead, the roof practically vibrated with the reminder of the night before, when he'd pulled his best friend's daughter into his lap and kissed her like she was his to kiss. When he'd sent her away so he wouldn't do more than kiss her. The hurt in her eyes as she'd walked away from him was seared into his memory, added to the list of moments he'd stolen with her that flashed through his mind like an old, flickering movie projector. No matter how hard he tried, he couldn't stop picturing the fan of her eyelashes across her cheeks when she closed her eyes, the hypnotic ripple of her abdominal muscles contracting when she orgasmed, the high gasp when he tugged her nipple between his teeth, the scrape of her fingernails down his back, the salt of her skin—

Enough.

It was the worst kind of betrayal of Ethan's trust, thinking of his daughter that way. Maybe that's why Jamie had gone up to the roof that night, to torture himself with the memories he couldn't escape, and the knowledge that each one could cost him the family he'd built for himself in Aster Bay. That they could cost Tessa a chance at building the life in Aster Bay she deserved, one free from whispered scandals.

He took a sip of his beer and dug into his pocket for his phone. Still no message from Whisky. She'd been quiet all day, only sending a few hurried replies here and there. His last message to her stared back at him.

DiceDiceBaby: How's your ghost?

He had just stuck his phone back in his pocket when it dinged. He pulled it out so fast he almost dropped his beer. Pausing, he forced himself to take a breath and set the bottle down on the ground, sitting beside it on the cold ground, his elbows resting on his bent knees in front of him.

WhiskyBusiness: He's just fine. His name is Bob and I've decided we're going to be friends.

Yes, this was what he needed, to spend a night being DiceDiceBaby, the kind of guy who could laugh and flirt and not end up infatuated with his best friend's daughter. The kind of guy Whisky thought he was.

DiceDiceBaby: You named your ghost?

WhiskyBusiness: I read online that if you give a ghost a name, it feels acknowledged and is less likely to bother you.

DiceDiceBaby: But Bob? Really?

WhiskyBusiness: It was the least threatening name I could think of.
WhiskyBusiness: And I've been cooking with a lot of sage.

DiceDiceBaby: You're supposed to burn it. Not cook with it.

WhiskyBusiness: That seems like a waste of perfectly good sage.

Jamie took a sip of his beer and looked out over the water. This was nice. Conversation with a woman about nothing at all. Conversation that had no chance of going anywhere or hurting anyone or meaning anything.

For a moment, he wondered what Whisky would say if he told her about Tessa. They'd never made promises to each other, there was no expectation that they weren't dating other people, especially since they weren't dating each other—but sometimes it felt like they were. Sometimes all their nothings felt like…something.

Which made what he'd done with Tessa, what he still wanted to do with Tessa despite all the reasons he shouldn't, all the more complicated.

DiceDiceBaby: You ever wonder what things would be like if we'd met in person instead of on the internet?

WhiskyBusiness: I don't like to think about 'what if's. If I started, I'd never stop.
WhiskyBusiness: What if I hadn't moved around so much growing up? What if I took this job instead of that one? What if I popped my popcorn tonight in avocado

oil instead of coconut oil?

WhiskyBusiness: You see how quickly that can get out of hand.

DiceDiceBaby: Point taken. Though I think the avocado vs. coconut oil thing might be overstating your point.

WhiskyBusiness: I like to think that no matter how we met, we would have ended up here.

DiceDiceBaby: Sending anonymous messages on a TV show fan forum?

WhiskyBusiness: Friends.

The memory of Tessa sitting beside him in that very spot the night before flooded his senses.
I don't want to be friends with you, Tessa.
I don't feel very friendly when I look at you.
He dug the heels of his hands into his eyes and raked his hands through his hair. What was he doing? Sitting there moping over two different women, neither of whom he could have, like some kind of sullen teenager.

WhiskyBusiness: Do you ever wonder 'what if'?

DiceDiceBaby: No. I think I know exactly what would have happened if we'd met some other way.

WhiskyBusiness: Oh yeah? Tell me, oh wise one, what this alternate timeline looks like.

DiceDiceBaby: I would have asked for your number.

And I would have called you right away.

WhiskyBusiness: Calling? How very 1998 of you.

DiceDiceBaby: I would have wanted you to hear my voice, so you would know I meant it when I said I wanted to take you to coffee.

WhiskyBusiness: Even if I ordered a double mocha half caf extra whip monstrosity?

DiceDiceBaby: Even then.
DiceDiceBaby: And I wouldn't have stopped calling you to ask you to go for coffee, or drinks, or dinner and a movie.

WhiskyBusiness: Or a rewatch of *Brilliant British Bakes*?

DiceDiceBaby: With plenty of coconut oil-popped popcorn for your snacking pleasure.

WhiskyBusiness: Don't forget the parmesan cheese, lemon zest, and black pepper on top. That's the most important part.

DiceDiceBaby: I would never forget the toppings.
DiceDiceBaby: And then one day I wouldn't need to call because we'd already be together. And the only thing I'd have to call you for is to ask what you wanted me to pick up for take out on the way home.

WhiskyBusiness: You wouldn't need to call for that. You'd already know.

DiceDiceBaby: Shrimp pad thai, extra lime, hold the peanuts.

WhiskyBusiness: Who even likes peanuts in savory food?

DiceDiceBaby: Not you.

WhiskyBusiness: It's a lovely dream.

Chapter Fifteen

Jamie stood in the doorway to his kitchen, watching as his sauce pots were displaced in favor of a giant spotlight. As if the kitchen weren't bright enough as it was. Kyla hoisted herself up on top of the steel workstation and he winced at the idea of the marks her sneakers would leave behind.

"How badly do you want to tell her to get down?" Gavin asked at his side.

He shot his friends a pained look. "Tell me again why this is necessary."

"Fuck if I know," Baz said. "Kyla and Tessa are the geniuses behind this one."

"Then what are you doing here?"

"Did you seriously think I would miss this?" Baz asked with a smile. "Hell, Ethan made me promise to send him behind the scenes photos."

"Don't do that."

"A promise is a promise, man," Gavin said as Jamie shot daggers at him. They had no effect. Gavin was unflappable.

"Have you heard from him today?" Jamie asked.

Gavin shook his head. "He said he'll call after the surgery."

The surgery was supposed to start hours ago... Jamie

sent up a silent prayer to whoever was listening that everything was going okay in that operating room.

Across the kitchen, Kyla instructed Brodie in the exact placement of yet another reflector, ignoring her boyfriend's complaints as she adjusted the angle of the light she'd set up on his counter. "Jamie," she called, waving him over, "Could you stand right over there so we can test the light?"

"Your adoring public awaits," Baz snickered.

"Fuck you," Jamie said with a laugh as he walked away, taking his place at the staged workstation as Kyla had instructed.

"I didn't know you were a photographer," Jamie said, holding up his hand to block out a particularly bright light aimed directly at his face.

Kyla made a few more adjustments to the reflectors. "It's not a big deal."

"It looks like a big deal," Jamie said, gesturing to all the equipment.

"Kyla got her degree in photography. Graduated early. Last May," Gavin said, smiling softly at his son's girlfriend with pride. Kyla blushed, but kept fiddling with the lights without responding.

"I had no idea. I know you worked with Cheryl, and that Tessa was glad to have you sign on, but I didn't know you did all this, too," Jamie said.

"I am a woman of many talents," Kyla deadpanned before hopping off the counter, pausing to wipe off the dirt left behind by her shoes. "Now we just need Tessa," she said.

"I'm here!" Tessa burst through the kitchen doors, Natalia trailing behind her with a wardrobe bag. "Sorry. It took longer than I thought to get camera-ready."

Kyla and Natalia chatted with Tessa as she dropped a to-go cup of coffee and her phone on the counter and made her way through the maze of wires and lights occupying his kitchen, but Jamie hardly heard any of it. He felt like he was in a wind tunnel, the blood whooshing past his ears and his vision hazy, except for the woman walking towards him. Her hair had been styled in loose waves around her shoulders, her eyes were done up with the kind of makeup that he'd only seen on movie stars, and her lips were painted a deep crimson.

"Doesn't she look great, Jamie?" Gavin prompted.

"What? Oh, yeah," he said, meeting her eyes. She smirked at him, a knowing gleam making her eyes sparkle. "You look amazing."

"Damn," Brodie said, appearing at Kyla's side. He slung an arm over her shoulder. "Why don't you dress up like that, babe?"

"Because I'm not the one being photographed," Kyla said, slipping out from under his arm.

"Your turn, Jamie," Natalia said, gesturing him over to where she'd hung the wardrobe bag from a pot rack. As Aster Bay's most fashionable resident—and one of the only people who'd volunteered to help with this marketing experiment—Natalia had been appointed the photoshoot's impromptu stylist and she was taking the role very seriously.

Jamie let Natalia fuss over the precise rolling of the sleeves of his chef's jacket, muttering something about forearms as she did, but he didn't take his eyes off Tessa. Instead of a chef's coat, she wore a navy-blue sweater, the weave shot through with sparkling silver threads that caught the light, and a deep V-neck revealing the high, firm swell of her breasts. Dark jeans hugged her hips and ass and disappeared into calf-high, camel-colored boots, the heels clacking against the tile floor of the kitchen with every step she took. Tessa was always gorgeous, but standing there in front of the lights, laughing with Kyla as she affected exaggerated poses for the lighting tests, she looked like an honest-to-God model. He wanted to peel the expensive clothing from her piece by piece until he found the girl he knew underneath, the one who hardly wore makeup and preferred novelty tees to the kind of overtly sexy clothing Natalia had put her in.

"She's pretty, right?" Natalia said with a too-knowing smirk as she adjusted the lapels of his coat.

"She didn't need the makeup or the clothes for that," he said.

"No, she didn't."

"She looks great," he said. "She just doesn't look like her."

Natalia hummed, as though he'd said much more than he'd meant to. Before he could ask what that sound meant, though, Gavin was calling him over to review the plan with Tessa and Kyla.

"We're just going to have fun with it," Kyla said, fidgeting with the camera in her hands. "The more it looks like you don't know you're being photographed, the better. We want it to look authentic."

"Like I always happen to wear heels and a push-up-bra in the kitchen?" Tessa asked.

Kyla laughed. "Exactly. Brodie, can you kill the overheads?" she called.

Brodie flipped a switch, turning off the overhead lights and leaving them under the bright beams of the spotlights Kyla had placed throughout the kitchen. Suddenly his kitchen looked more like a movie set than the heart of his restaurant.

"When you told me you took photos, I had no idea you meant like this," Tessa marveled, gesturing to the extensive set-up. "It's so professional."

"My girl takes all kinds of photos," Brodie said with a chortle. Kyla's face turned bright red.

"Brodie," Gavin barked, scowling.

Jamie pinned the kid with a withering glare. "Where's that *mise*?"

"On it," Brodie grumbled as he disappeared into the walk-in for the prepared cutting board of diced and julienned ingredients for Jamie and Tessa to pose with.

"It's not a big deal," Kyla said, not meeting their eyes. "It's just a hobby."

"She's being modest," Gavin said gently, but he let it drop. "We really appreciate you doing this, Kyla. Really."

Kyla blushed. "Let's start with the wine," she said, taking her camera and boosting herself up to sit on the edge of the workstation opposite them.

As Gavin and Natalia looked on, Jamie fumbled with the wine opener, finally succeeding in opening the bottle of Nuthatch's cabernet sauvignon and pouring he and Tessa each a glass. He tried to ignore the clicking of the camera as they each raised their glass and took a sip.

"Scoot closer," Kyla directed. They each took half a step towards each other. "Look at each other," she called. They locked eyes over the top of their wine glasses and took another sip, their eyes unnaturally focused on each other.

The clicking stopped and Kyla lowered the camera while Brodie set the cutting board down on the edge of the workstation nearest Jamie and Tessa. Kyla glanced around the room, chewing her lip.

"What is it?" Tessa asked her.

Kyla thought for a minute, then shook her head. "Nothing. Let's try again. Pretend we're not here."

Three more times they tried to take her direction and three more times they succeeded only in looking like some kind of deranged automatons.

"Jesus. Wouldn't think it'd be so hard to take a good picture," Brodie grumbled.

"Okay, this isn't working," Kyla said. She set her camera down and slid off the workstation. "Everyone out." Jamie took a step towards the door and Kyla spun on him. "Not you two. Everyone *else* out." Kyla ushered their protesting friends out of the kitchen and into the dining room. She turned back to them with a determined set to her jaw. "New plan."

Thirty minutes and a glass and a half of wine later, Jamie and Tessa were much more relaxed. Tessa and Kyla had set up the Bluetooth speakers in his kitchen to blare that awful pop music Tessa liked, and Tessa was delighting in tormenting Jamie with each new song.

"You can't rhyme 'love' with 'love!'" Jamie said. "That's just lazy songwriting."

"What else should they have rhymed it with?" Tessa asked, refilling their glasses.

"I don't know. Dove? Glove?"

Tessa laughed, her hair swaying around her shoulders as she did. A strand of hair caught on her lipstick. Before he'd even processed the impulse to move, Jamie reached out and swept it away, brushing it behind her ear. *Click.* He looked up as Kyla snapped a photo, a wide grin spreading across her face.

"Don't mind me," she said. "Pretend I'm not even here."

Tessa took another sip of her wine, arching an eyebrow at him over the top of the glass. *Click.*

"I think we've had enough wine for now," Jamie said, taking her glass in his hand. *Click.* He set their glasses down and retrieved the cutting board, doing his best not to notice how rosy Tessa's cheeks had gotten over the last half hour.

"What are we cooking?" Tessa asked as she scanned the ingredients arranged before them.

"It's mostly cooked already. We're just assembling," he said, moving glass dishes of diced, roasted butternut squash and a fine chiffonade of parsley off the board and onto the workstation. Tessa reached over him and swiped a cherry tomato, popping it into her mouth. *Click.*

They worked together to assemble crostini from the various ingredients, Tessa pausing occasionally to sneak another sip of her wine, accompanied by the soundtrack of Brozone's greatest hits and the clicking of Kyla's camera.

"You can't put the apple on that one," Jamie said as Tessa moved to sprinkle tiny cubes of apple over the crostini he'd assembled with scallops and herb oil.

"I can't?" she asked.

"The apple is for the squash and ricotta one."

"Why can't it be for both?" She stared him down as she dropped the bits of apple over the scallop crostini.

"There's not enough for both."

"Then we'll put the walnuts with the squash and ricotta," she said, reaching for that bowl.

He stayed her hand. *Click.* "The walnuts are for the red pepper."

"Come on, take a risk." She met his eyes, a challenge gleaming in those raven-dark depths. "Chef." The word was soft but it reverberated through his body like a siren's song, vibrating in his bones.

He released her hand, triumph flaring in her gaze as she dug her fingers into the walnuts, sprinkling them over the crostini.

Tessa reached for the squeeze bottle of balsamic glaze, leaning over the workstation so that her chest brushed against Jamie's forearm, the contact like a burn radiating across his skin. "Sorry," she said with a smile.

"No, you're not," he rumbled, recognizing the edge creeping into his voice. It was a tone not meant for his kitchen, under bright lights. It was a tone best suited for darkness.

She threw her head back and laughed, his eyes drawn to the movement of her throat. "You're right. I'm not." *Click.*

He wasn't sure if he was drunk on the wine or the proximity to Tessa or both—he suspected it was both—but inebriation was his only explanation for what he did next. He stepped behind her, bracing his hands on the workstation on either side of her hips, caging her in with his body. He swept the hair from one of her shoulders, exposing the long line of her neck to him. A shiver moved through her at the brush of his fingertips and he was instantly hard, barely able to keep himself from pressing his lips to the place where her pulse pounded beneath her skin.

"You're chaos," he murmured.

"You like my chaos."

He hummed in agreement, watching as she lifted her latest crostini creation and held it up to him. He had been the one to top the crisp slice of bread with perfectly roasted asparagus and shaved Parmesan, but she had drizzled it with the balsamic glaze. His eyes were drawn to a tiny, white scar on her hand, exactly like the one Whisky had. Scars were common enough in a kitchen, but something about seeing that particular mark made him want to press his lips to that small imperfection on her skin. Instead, he took a bite of the crostini, the bright vinegar coating his tongue, and a low thrum of approval sounded in his throat.

"I do," he said.

She turned partially towards him, still in the cage of his arms, and popped the other half of the crostini in her mouth. Something deep and primal flared in his chest as he watched pleasure bloom on her face when she ate the food they had prepared together. Her tongue appeared at the corner of her mouth, skating over that red lip as she sought out every drop of the dark, sticky glaze. For half a moment he pictured those lips wrapped around his cock, the streaks of lipstick they'd leave behind.

"I think we've got it!" Kyla said, her voice breaking through the little bubble he and Tessa had created.

Jamie cleared his throat and took a step back, turning to hide the erection pressing against the placket of his pants from Kyla's view.

"Great," he grunted. "We done here?"

"Yeah," Kyla said. "I'll have these pictures over to Gavin by the end of the week."

"Thanks," Tessa said.

He caught Tessa's gaze, the heat of the last few minutes melting away into something closer to confusion, but he had no answers for her. For a few moments, he'd not only forgotten about the camera—he'd forgotten all the reasons that he needed to keep his distance from her. Distance that was getting harder to maintain with each passing day.

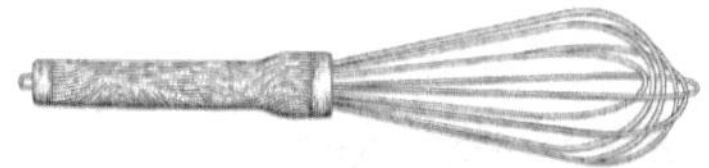

Ethan: The surgery's over. The doctor said it went well. He's in recovery now.

Jamie: That's great news.

Gavin: You must be so relieved.

Ethan: Now the hard part begins. I have no idea how I'm

going to get my dad to do all his PT. The man is stubborn as a mule.

Baz: Now there's the pot calling the kettle black.

Ethan: Tell me something about what's going on at home. I don't want to think about hospitals for a little while.

Gavin: We did the photoshoot today for the ad campaign.

Ethan: I saw those shots Baz sent over.

Gavin: And?

Ethan: It was a nice set up.

Jamie: ?

Baz: That means he doesn't know how to comment on his daughter being all glammed up and getting cozy with Jamie.

Jamie: We were not getting cozy.

Ethan: It did look pretty cozy.

Gavin: I mean I wouldn't say it *wasn't* cozy.

Jamie: Can we stop using the word cozy?

Ethan: I'm sure they'll be nice shots. Even if I am regretting asking you to send me a sneak peak.

Baz: Be careful what you wish for.

Ethan: But T's doing alright? Settling in?

Gavin: Seems to be.

Ethan: Jamie?

Jamie: Yeah. I haven't talked to her much, but I think she's doing alright.

Ethan: You think? What a robust report from the guy who's supposed to be mentoring for my kid.

Jamie: She's fine. You don't have anything to worry about.

Chapter Sixteen

"What does 'stir until it looks right' mean?" Kyla called from the kitchen.

"Kind of like ribbon stage," Tessa called back.

She placed the last nesting doll in its place on the high shelf and leaned back to examine her work, careful not to lose her balance on the countertop. She'd found the dolls in a box in a local thrift shop the day before and had been unable to resist the brightly painted designs adorning the fragile wooden shapes. Retail therapy had never failed Tessa before, the perfect burst of serotonin to replace any uncomfortable feelings: a voicemail she had no intention of returning from the family she'd left behind, a snide remark from an older member of the Vegas kitchen staff with a chip on his shoulder about his expensive culinary degree, an unexpected wave of grief when she was caught off guard by a memory of her mother—they could all be softened by the joy of discovering a long-forgotten treasure in the corner of a thrift shop.

But apparently the one thing thrifting couldn't soften was the growing ache in her chest every time she thought about Jamie, and the needy pulse between her legs that hadn't yet gotten the memo that he was off limits. If anything, after the photoshoot the day before, that pulse had become more insistent.

"The *what* stage?" Kyla shouted, a thin thread of panic edging her tone.

"Hold on, I'll be right there!"

Tessa hopped off the counter and headed back into the kitchen. Kyla stood over one of the giant stand mixers, flour dusting her apron and streaked across her face as she peered into the stainless-steel bowl.

"Show me what you've got," Tessa said. Kyla tilted the head of the mixer up, lifting the whisk from the bowl. "Ahh, you're not quite there yet. The batter should fall off the whisk in thick lines, like ribbons that kind of pool on the top of the bowl when they fall." Tessa dropped the whisk back into the bowl and turned the mixer back on. "You'll know you're almost there when the batter looks kind of foamy and pale."

"Foamy and pale. Got it," Kyla repeated, staring at the mixture intensely.

Tessa's phone chimed and she pulled it from her jeans back pocket, smiling at the name on the screen. "Why don't you take a break and go grab us some sandwiches from the diner," she said. "Take the credit card from the register." Kyla nodded and left Tessa alone.

DiceDiceBaby: I give up. I'm officially out of ideas for what to do with beets.

DiceDiceBaby: And my produce guy just showed up with six more crates of them!

WhiskyBusiness: Don't give up yet. Did you try the beet dip recipe I sent you?

DiceDiceBaby: I did. It was a big hit—thanks for that. The hazelnuts were unexpected but the perfect addition to that recipe.

WhiskyBusiness: What else have you tried?

DiceDiceBaby: We had beet quiche at brunch, beet flatbreads as an appetizer. I even put it in the veggie burgers. Pretty soon people are going to think the only thing I serve is beets.
DiceDiceBaby: What are you cooking today?

WhiskyBusiness: Working my way through some old family recipes. Apparently my grandmother had a thing for Swiss rolls. There must be thirty different kinds of Swiss rolls in her recipe box.

DiceDiceBaby: I wonder if it's a generational thing. My friend's mother always made Swiss rolls. She had one that was all the flavors of a Bakewell tart.

WhiskyBusiness: So does my grandmother! It's on my list to make this week.

Tessa leaned against the workstation, and wondered what the odds were that they both had a recipe for a Bakewell tart-flavored Swiss roll. She'd have to do an internet search later. Maybe DDB was right and it was a generational thing.

DiceDiceBaby: Is your grandmother the one who taught you how to cook?

She blew out a breath and sank to the floor, leaning against the cold metal leg of the workstation counter. She could claim it was a personal detail and shut down the conversation, but more and more lately, she didn't want to shy away from the personal details with DDB. And with the confusing jumble of lust and frustration still simmering in her veins after the photoshoot, she was craving connection in a way she hadn't let herself admit in a long time.

Maybe it wouldn't be the worst thing to let a few personal details slip.

WhiskyBusiness: No. I didn't see her much growing up.
WhiskyBusiness: We moved around a lot.

DiceDiceBaby: That must have been hard.

WhiskyBusiness: It's not hard when it's all you know.
WhiskyBusiness: My mom was always working, sometimes two or three jobs, so I watched a lot of TV. Specifically, the Culinary Channel. After a while, I started trying out the things I'd seen on TV. The rest is history.

DiceDiceBaby: You taught yourself. That's incredible.

WhiskyBusiness: I had some amazing mentors.
WhiskyBusiness: As soon as I was old enough, I got a job in a kitchen and I just never stopped. Worked my way up.

DiceDiceBaby: And now you have your own kitchen.

She glanced around the kitchen. *Not quite.*
In just two days, Sugar Grapes would re-open. Ethan

had insisted that she not delay the opening until his return, but she couldn't help the odd sense of disappointment that he wouldn't be there on opening day. Stupid, that. It's not like he'd been there for most of the important moments in her life—why should the opening of her first bakery be any different? Besides, it was just a pop-up, and she knew he'd have been there if he could be.

Still, it would have been nice to feel like someone who cared about her was cheering her on.

WhiskyBusiness: I wish you could see it.

DiceDiceBaby: Send me a picture.

Tessa smiled to herself. Kyla would be gone for at least a half hour...

She pulled off her shirt and took a high angle photo of herself, just the edge of her jaw visible at the top of the photo. The rest of the image was dominated by the curve of her neck and breasts, thinly covered with electric blue lace, the dusky points of her nipples straining against the fabric. Before she could think better of it, she sent the photo and waited anxiously as the three dots appeared and disappeared at the bottom of the message thread.

DiceDiceBaby: Holy shit, princess. Warn a guy before you send a picture like that.
DiceDiceBaby: You've got me in the office with a hard on when I'm supposed to be doing payroll.

WhiskyBusiness: Prove it.

A moment later, an image appeared on her screen of a

man sitting in a chair, his face cut off, chef coat unbuttoned and undershirt pulled up to reveal the firm, tan skin of his stomach and a dark line of hair below his bellybutton. At the bottom of the shot, his forearm, thickly corded with muscle, lay across his thigh and his large hand gripped the outline of his impressive erection through his jeans.

Holy shit.

She sucked in a breath and pressed her thighs together, a tingling sensation growing at her core.

WhiskyBusiness: Damn. All for me?

DiceDiceBaby: All for you.
DiceDiceBaby: I wish you were here.

WhiskyBusiness: Yeah? What would you do if I were?

DiceDiceBaby: Get you out of that bra to start.
DiceDiceBaby: I'd want to taste those pretty tits.

As she typed, her hand drifted over her chest. She dragged her nails over her nipple, circling as the flesh puckered beneath her touch.

WhiskyBusiness: I bet your mouth would feel amazing.

DiceDiceBaby: Where else do you want my mouth?

She hesitated for a fraction of a second. *Fuck it.*

WhiskyBusiness: On my pussy.

DiceDiceBaby: Touch yourself, princess. Use your fingers and pretend it's my tongue.

She switched to voice-to-text so she could use her right hand to follow his instructions. Flicking open the button of her jeans, she slid her hand inside, skating her fingers through the damp curls, not at all surprised to find her clit already stiff beneath her touch.

DiceDiceBaby: Are you doing it?

WhiskyBusiness: Yes.

DiceDiceBaby: Good girl.
DiceDiceBaby: How does it feel?

WhiskyBusiness: So good. Wet.

Fumbling with her left hand, she took a few seconds of video of her hand disappearing inside her jeans, the movement beneath the fabric making it clear exactly what she was doing. She ended the recording just as she let out a low moan and hit send.

DiceDiceBaby: Fuck. I want to be inside you.

WhiskyBusiness: You are.
WhiskyBusiness: Are you jerking off?

A short video clip appeared on her phone. She drove two fingers inside herself, bucking against the friction as she continued to work her clit with her thumb, and hit play. His jeans were undone, his hand beneath the fabric of black jersey boxer briefs moving quickly, the unmistakable sound of skin against skin as he stroked himself. Her pussy clenched around her fingers and she imagined it was him inside her. She played the clip again, wondering if he was circumcised, if the veins along his length were pronounced, if she'd be able to feel them on her tongue when he pushed between her lips.

WhiskyBusiness: I want to ride you. I want you to fuck me until I don't remember my name.

DiceDiceBaby: The only name you'll remember is mine.

WhiskyBusiness: We shouldn't do this here. In my kitchen. We could be caught.

DiceDiceBaby: But you can't wait for my cock long enough to go somewhere else.

WhiskyBusiness: You're right. I need you now.

DiceDiceBaby: Are you close?

WhiskyBusiness: So close.

DiceDiceBaby: Fucking get there, princess.

She fucked herself harder, imagining it was him. His fingers on her clit, his cock driving her towards orgasm. And as she imagined him, his hands became Jamie's hands, the sting of his stubble became Jamie's stubble. She fell over the edge with the image of Jamie above her, the memory of his hips holding her open beneath him as he fucked her.

WhiskyBusiness: I'm coming.

DiceDiceBaby: Me too

Jamie's breath on her neck. Jamie's hand on her breast. Jamie's cock buried so deep within her she'd still felt him the next morning.

Jamie, Jamie, Jamie.

As her climax receded, panic replaced lust. *Shit.* She'd just masturbated with DDB. While thinking about Jamie.

Shame soured in her stomach—for letting their flirtation get that far, for touching herself in her *kitchen* for God's sake, thinking of someone else when she was supposed to be thinking about DDB, for fantasizing about her father's best friend. She scrambled to her feet, buttoning up her jeans and rushing to the sink to wash her hands, as though she could wash away the last few minutes.

DiceDiceBaby: You okay? You've been quiet for a few minutes.

Fuck. He'd texted her several times while she'd been too busy freaking out to notice.

WhiskyBusiness: Yeah, I'm fine. Why wouldn't I be?
WhiskyBusiness: Thanks.
WhiskyBusiness: You know, for the orgasm.
WhiskyBusiness: *laughing emoji*

She winced.

WhiskyBusiness: I gotta go.

Jamie stared at her last message as he tucked himself back into his pants, the wad of tissues in his wastebasket like an accusation. Just a few minutes ago, he'd been barreling towards bliss, jerking off at his desk, his phone propped up against the edge of his computer monitor and playing the video clip she'd sent over and over again, just a fraction of a second of her moan at the end teasing him towards an explosive climax. He pulled his undershirt, now stained with his own cum, over his head and tossed it in the wastebasket as well, slipping his chef's coat back on and buttoning it to hide the fact that he no longer wore a shirt.

It had been so fucking hot, thinking of her touching herself in her kitchen while she talked to him. Imagining laying her out on a workstation in his own kitchen and sucking on her clit until she screamed.

Somewhere along the way, he'd stopped thinking about Whisky, though, and started thinking about Tessa, the taste of her coming back to him as he fucked his fist. Suddenly he heard Tessa's moan in Whisky's, felt the tight squeeze of Tessa's climax around his cock moments before he came all over himself like a fucking teenager.

And then Whisky had shut down on him. Shut down and shut him out.

He could hardly blame her. If she had even the slightest inkling that he'd been thinking about another woman—about his best friend's daughter, no less—while they'd just done...that... Fuck, he'd shut himself out, too.

His office door flew open, Baz standing in the opening.

"Fuck, don't you knock?" Jamie barked. Two minutes earlier and he would have walked in on—

"Here?" Baz snorted like it was an absurd question. And Jamie supposed it was. He'd never asked his friends to knock before.

You've also never jerked off in your office before.

"What do you need?" Jamie asked.

"I ran the numbers on The Barclay. It'll work for the opening dinner if we host cocktail hour out on the patio, but that's not in the budget," Baz said.

"It'll be pretty cold outside in December," Jamie said.

"You got a better idea?"

Jamie blew out a breath and shook his head. "Let me talk to Norm and see if he'll donate the use of the patio and the heaters."

"You should have Tessa talk to him."

"Why?" Jamie asked, his skin prickling with an irrational possessiveness and a sudden spike of fear that Baz somehow knew what he'd been up to in his office just minutes before.

"He likes her," Baz shrugged. "He likes her ideas. You heard him at the Merchants' Association meeting."

Aster Bay is in her blood. Yeah, he'd heard Norm alright. He also heard what Baz wasn't saying. Norm liked Tessa more than he liked Jamie, he liked her ideas more than he liked Jamie's.

"Fine. We're meeting Gavin over there the day after tomorrow anyway. I'll see about having her talk to Norm."

"Good." Baz turned to leave, but stuck his head back in the door at the last minute, wrinkling his nose in disgust. "You should get a cleaning company to come through here. Smells funky. But if you do, remember, it's not—"

"—in the budget. I know."

Chapter Seventeen

Jamie was already standing in the parking lot when Tessa arrived at The Barclay. How did he manage to look so good just *standing* there? He was even more handsome than he was in her imagination, and despite her best (okay, moderate at best) efforts, she'd imagined him a lot over the last week while managing to avoid him.

Every time she closed her eyes, she pictured Jamie, the filthy things she'd imagined him doing while she'd messaged with DDB, the even filthier things he'd actually done to her a few weeks ago in that hotel room in Providence, all the things she'd wanted him to do to her in his kitchen during the photoshoot.

An irrational fear that somehow he would know that she'd sexted with someone else while thinking about him settled in the pit of her stomach, mingling with her growing guilt. Bad enough to fantasize about her father's best friend, but even worse to do so while talking to someone else. Even if she couldn't be with Jamie, she needed to change directions with DDB, put up some boundaries and remind them both that they were only supposed to be friends. They'd hardly spoken over the last few days, but eventually the awkwardness would dissipate and it wasn't fair to him for her to flirt with him the way she had, to send him pictures and videos, while she was wishing she was with someone else.

She threw her rental car into park and jumped out, nearly spilling her coffee in the process. She had worked too damn hard to get that coffee to spill it now. That was her emotional support coffee, and she definitely needed it if she was going to get through this meeting with Jamie. At least she'd have Gavin as a buffer.

"Sorry, sorry!" she said as she made her way across the parking lot to Jamie, coffee cups in hand. "Traffic was a nightmare."

"From the other side of town?" he asked.

"No. I had to go two towns over to find a Starbucks and apparently you can't turn left out of their parking lot so I had to turn right but I didn't want to turn right, so then I had to figure out how to turn around so I was going the right direction and I picked *the worst* side street to turn down because I got stuck behind this school bus that stopped at every other house. But I got my Starbucks," she said with a grin, taking a sip of the caramel mocha goodness so she'd stop anxiety-babbling at him.

"You needed two?" he asked.

"What? Oh!" She shook her head with a little laugh and handed him the other cup. "No, this one's for you." *To make up for thinking about you when I definitely should* not *have been thinking about you.* "Cream, no sugar. Right?"

"Right. Thanks," he said, taking the cup and eyeing her like the coffee might suddenly jump up and bite him. He blinked, his eyes clearing, and gestured towards the hotel. "After you."

She followed him through the hotel lobby into a large

restaurant dining room. A bar with a mirrored backsplash was situated on one side of the room, and a baby grand piano sat at the front of the room, precisely angled spotlights shining on the gleaming wood. On the opposite side of the room, a wall of windows overlooked the expansive lawn, which gave way to the most breathtaking view of the ocean. The space was beautiful, if a bit small, but she could already picture it: a Christmas tree on either side of the piano, someone in black tie performing as servers brought course after course out from the kitchen. She walked to the wall of windows, pressing a hand to the cool glass.

"If it's not too cold out, we should hold cocktail hour on the patio," she said.

"That's what Baz said too," Jamie said, coming to stand beside her. "It will cost more to use both spaces but—"

"It'll be worth it," she said. "We just have to make sure we pack the house."

She turned a smile his way and was momentarily struck by how handsome he was with the golden light coming in through the windows and gilding the contours of his face. She turned back to the windows, focusing on taking another sip of her coffee.

She had resolved not to think about how handsome he was, or how he made her skin feel all tingly, or the fact she'd been sexting with DDB while thinking about Jamie. Those were not professional thoughts, and she was determined to be a professional. *Since he's made it clear he has no interest in being anything else.*

Swallowing down the disappointing thought, she forced a lightness into her tone that she didn't feel. "Where's Gavin? I thought he was meeting us here."

"He was." Jamie frowned, glancing over his shoulder like perhaps his friend had materialized without him noticing.

"It's not like him to be late."

"I'm sure he'll be here any minute."

"Yeah, I'm sure you're right. Anyway, Baz was hoping you'd be willing to talk to Norm about donating the use of the patio."

"Sure. But wouldn't it be better coming from you? He knows you better," she said.

He gave a tight smile. "Baz thinks you'll have more luck with Norm than I will. You're a local."

She huffed out a laugh. "Hardly."

"More than I am. At least as far as Norm's concerned." They stared at each other, their frozen smiles becoming increasingly awkward, until Jamie finally cleared his throat and looked away.

"Do you want to see the patio?" he asked at the same time she said, "Should we head outside?"

They both laughed, a grating, uncomfortable sound, and shuffled through the double doors out onto the back patio. The leaves on the trees that lined the edge of the lawn, obscuring the view of the parking lot and the road beyond, had just begun to change, but the day was still warm as the October sun beat down. The grounds were gorgeous, an endless stretch of perfectly manicured grass, breaking off into a rocky pass before a sandy beach disappeared into the ocean.

Silently they wandered towards the edge of the lawn, their shoulders brushing against each other every few steps. At one point she could have sworn his pinky brushed against her hand, but the touch was fleeting and over before she could react.

"I forgot how beautiful it is here," she said, her voice carried away on the breeze off the water.

"People don't think about going to the beach in the

winter. We've got to show them that it's just as magical all year round," Jamie said.

She glanced at him, taking in the way he watched the waves crash on the beach below with such pride it was as though he had personally sculpted the shoreline. For the first time in a long time, she wished she felt that way about Aster Bay, like it was hers to be proud of, hers to celebrate.

Maybe it could be.

"What if we do a bonfire on the beach?" she asked.

"No one does bonfires on the beach in December."

"That's the point."

"It'll be too cold."

"So we make that part of the fun."

"Cold is fun?" He cast a doubtful look in her direction.

"Picture it," she said, setting her nearly empty coffee cup down and holding her hands out as if they were the lens of a camera. "Bonfires all up and down the beach, lots of cozy flannel blankets to snuggle up in, everyone wearing knit hats and mittens and puffy coats. I have a killer red wine hot chocolate recipe. Oh! We get an artist to sculpt a giant gingerbread house out of sand and everyone can help decorate it with seashells and beach glass." She dropped her hands and turned to him, practically dancing with the excitement of it.

"That sounds...amazing." He furrowed his brow, confusion marring his finely shaped features. "How did you come up with that?"

She shrugged, suppressing a smile at the unexpected praise. "Don't ask me to explain my genius. I couldn't even if I tried."

He barked out a laugh, the first unselfconscious sound he'd given her all day. She wanted more.

She grasped his hand and tugged. "Come on. Let's go check it out."

He fell into step beside her, but he didn't release her hand, though their grip on each other was so loose that, had he been anyone else, she wouldn't have even noticed the warmth of his skin against hers. It was at least ten degrees cooler at the water's edge, but between the man beside her and the sun on her back, she didn't care.

At the bottom of the stone steps, she plopped down in the sand, pulling off her sneakers and socks.

"What are you doing?" he asked.

"What does it look like?"

"It's too cold to—"

"Are you always so worried about the cold? I haven't been on a real beach in years. You better believe I'm digging my toes into the sand."

She set her shoes aside, socks tucked neatly inside, and burrowed her feet beneath the sand. Jamie was right— it was too cold. But she didn't care. It felt like drippy ice cream cones and the stiffness of salt water drying on skin, the smell of sunscreen and hot dogs on a charcoal grill. Like playing cards with Gramps and helping Grama make cookies. It felt like home.

The thought planted itself deep in her gut, roots wrapping around her vital organs. *Home.* How had she forgotten that this was how home felt?

"Hey." Jamie's voice, soft and concerned broke through her thoughts as he knelt down beside her. "Hey, what's wrong?"

"Nothing," she said, looking up at him with a watery smile. When had she started crying?

"Then why are you crying?"

"I don't know," she laughed. She drew in a deep breath

of salty ocean air as her hair whipped around her face, sticking to the wet places on her cheeks.

A moment later, Jamie's large shoes landed with a thunk next to hers and she looked over to see him rolling up the legs of his jeans and digging his toes into the sand beside her.

"I thought you said it was too cold," she teased.

He shot her a glare, but she caught the twitch of his lip, the way he clenched his jaw to keep from smiling. She laughed, knocking his shoulder with hers.

"What's that?" he asked, pointing to the small tattoo on the outside of her ankle.

"It's a whisk," she said, moving her foot closer to him so he could see the delicate lines of grey-green ink.

"Why a whisk?" he asked, his voice strangely stiff.

"Why not?" At his exasperated glance she took pity on the man and continued. "I like what it represents."

"Baking?"

"No. I mean, yes, obviously baking, but it's more about what a whisk does. How it's used."

"It breaks things down," he said slowly. "Pulls them apart."

She shook her head. "No, you're thinking about it all wrong. It doesn't pull them apart; it winds them together. It incorporates ingredients until they can never be separated again."

He ran his thumb over the small tattoo, his finger wiping the last grains of sand away and making her shiver. When he spoke, the words were nearly lost to the crash of the waves. "I don't know how I didn't notice it before."

"Before," she repeated. He glanced up at her, the low simmering heat there making it clear exactly what *before* he was thinking of. "You weren't exactly focused on my ankles *before*."

He chuckled, dragging his thumb over her ankle one

more time before he dropped his hand away and broke the spell. "Let's walk a bit. I want to scope out the best spots for the bonfires." He got to his feet and held out his hand to her, helping to pull her to standing. "We'll still need to get approval, probably call the fire marshal—"

"Okay, Mr. Negativity. Can we just dream for a minute, please?"

He rolled his eyes in mock annoyance, not even trying to hide the way his lips curled up at the edge this time. "Just for a minute."

Jamie needed to keep moving. His head was spinning as pieces of conversations with Tessa and Whisky blurred together in his mind.

It probably wasn't that uncommon of a tattoo for a baker, just like so many chefs had knives tattooed on their arms and hands. He didn't even know if Whisky had any tattoos. But the discovery of the quarter-sized whisk permanently inked into Tessa's skin had him reeling. So many small moments colliding in his mind, the similarities between the two women feeling like much more than coincidence.

It's just because of the sexting, he told himself. *Whisky and Tessa are all mixed up in your mind now.*

That had to be it. Because the alternative… He shot a look at Tessa at his side, blissfully dragging her toes through the sand to leave patterns in her wake, stopping every few feet to examine a shell or rock half buried on the beach.

It's just that you want it to be her.

A splash of freezing water crashed across his calves, momentarily stealing all thoughts from his brain. He swore and turned to find Tessa doubled over with her hands in the waves just before a second splash broke over his feet. He cursed louder this time and she roared with laughter.

"That's freezing!" he complained.

She glanced down to where her own feet were submerged in the water up to her ankles. "It's refreshing."

"If by refreshing you mean masochistic."

She wound up and whipped a large splash his way, this one crashing over his chest. He gasped as the water broke over him, plastering his shirt to his skin.

"Oh, you're gonna pay for that," he promised as he advanced on her.

She squealed and took off running down the beach, her feet sinking into the wet sand at the water's edge. It only took a moment for him to catch up to her. He sent a giant splash her way, the water breaking against her torso, soaking her shirt.

"Jamie!" she shrieked, twisting to splash him back.

That's how Gavin found them a few minutes later, soaked through and splashing each other like children, breathless from laughter and the icy shock of the water.

"What's going on, guys?" Gavin asked, grinning as he approached, though he kept a careful distance out of the splash zone.

"You made it," Jamie said, trying to catch his breath. "We were just talking about a beach bonfire. For the festival."

He shot a warning glance at Tessa when she sent a final burst of water in his direction. She bobbed her eyebrows playfully and he barely managed to hold on to his serious expression.

"I don't think you can build a bonfire *in* the water," Gavin laughed.

"Why don't you tell him your idea, Tess, and I'll run up to the hotel and see if they can loan us some towels." Jamie took off back towards the stone stairs.

"See if they have any hot chocolate!" Tessa called after him.

Jamie turned to face her, continuing to walk backwards away from her. "Let's dry off and I'll make you some *good* hot chocolate back at the restaurant."

"Deal!" She smiled, the expression lighting up her entire face.

Even soaked to the bone, sand in her hair, she was stunning. His eyes dropped to her chest, to the pale fabric plastered against her body. It had gone see-through with the water, revealing a bright purple bra. When he met her gaze again, the smile was gone, replaced by a fire in her eyes.

"Hurry up, Jamie. I think Tessa's getting cold," Gavin called as both men watched a shiver move through her. A shiver Jamie was quite sure had little to do with the temperature.

Still, he turned and jogged down the beach. He didn't want anyone else seeing Tessa like that, so exposed, so goddamn pretty it hurt to look at her. Not even Gavin.

By the time he returned to the beach, towels in hand, Gavin and Tessa had walked most of the way back to where they'd left their shoes. She gratefully accepted the towels, wrapping one around her chest and using the other to dry her hair.

"I think you guys are onto something," Gavin said. "I can't think of anything like what Tessa described ever happening in Aster Bay."

"But there is precedent," Tessa chimed in. She recited the facts as though it were a school book report. "There's a little town near Brighton in England whose beach is a popular tourist destination. People specifically visit in the winter to see the clear views of the bay. They even do yoga on the beach year-round."

"And you've been there?" Jamie asked.

"No, I've only read about it," she said, looking longingly out over the ocean. "Someday I'll see those white cliffs for myself." She turned to Jamie, the brilliance of her smile catching him off guard with its warmth. "For now, I'll settle for a gingerbread sandcastle in Aster Bay."

"I might be able to get some kids from the art department at the university to take care of that part."

"That would be great," Tessa said, beaming.

"I'll get Baz working on the logistics with Norm and the fire marshal and make sure we're a go," Jamie said.

"Perfect. I was just telling Tessa that I was late because I was meeting with Natalia. She's rallied half the businesses in town to come up with ideas for add-on programs and packages we can offer, all targeted to people in their twenties and thirties, both singles and couples. I think this just might work."

"Of course, it will work," Tessa said, handing one of the towels back to Jamie. She shot a conspiratorial glance at Gavin. "Tell him the best part."

"What's she talking about?" Jamie asked.

"Those photos of you two that Kyla took last week are getting a lot of attention on social media. They're even getting some local media attention from some of the outlets that we hadn't been able to connect with yet," Gavin said.

"Okay. Why do I feel like you're about to say something I'm not going to like?" Jamie asked, a weight sinking into his gut when Gavin had the good graces to look abashed.

Tessa laughed, drawing her bottom lip between her teeth. "I hope you're not camera shy."

"What is she talking about?" he demanded.

"*Sunrise in the City* wants to do a feature spot. They're the biggest morning news show in New England and they're offering us a prime spot the week before the festival."

Understanding dawned. "No. Absolutely not. It's bad enough you're going to put my face on billboards."

"Not just you," Gavin clarified. "You and Tessa both."

"Why don't you do it? You're the marketing genius," Jamie said.

"They don't want me, Jamie. They want—"

"Chef Broody McHottie," Tessa said, practically bursting with barely contained laughter.

"Chef *who*?" he asked, turning again to Gavin.

"That's what they're calling you online," Tessa said.

Gavin cut in, attempting to soothe Jamie. "Authenticity sells. You can't get more authentic than the two of you. That's the deal with the network—you and Tessa on *Sunrise in the City*. We couldn't ask for better PR."

Jamie glanced between Gavin and Tessa. "I'm not getting out of this, am I?"

"Nope," she said, popping the 'p,' and he was momentarily distracted by her lips.

"I'll take care of all the details," Gavin promised. "I'll prep the talking points, help you pick out your outfit, book the hotel rooms—"

"The *what*?"

"We have to be on set by five a.m. Gavin said it would be easier if we stayed overnight in the city the night before," Tessa said.

He met her eyes, memories of the last time they'd been in a hotel together racing through his mind. Her eyes dipped to his chest, to where the water had molded his shirt to the contours of his pecs and abs. She swallowed hard and met his eyes again, a question there that he didn't want to answer.

She cleared her throat and looked away, her cheeks blazing. "You know what? Silly me. I forgot that I'm meeting the rest of my new staff at the bakery to go through the opening day recipes."

"What about the hot chocolate?" Jamie asked, suddenly very much not wanting her to walk away.

"Rain check. If the bakery's going to be ready to open this weekend, I've got to whip my staff into shape," she said, mimicking a whisking motion and practically falling over herself to gather her shoes. She handed Jamie her towel, once again revealing the shadow of her bra through the wet fabric of her shirt, and ran up the steps that led back to The Barclay.

"Tessa!" he called after her.

"Talk to you later!" she shouted over her shoulder.

And then she was gone.

"What was that?" Gavin asked when they were alone.

Jamie sat on a nearby rock and began wiping sand off his feet and putting his socks and shoes back on. His socks stuck to the damp skin and chafed against hidden grains of sand he couldn't see. "Who knows?" he grumbled.

"I think you know."

Jamie glanced at his friend, his heart pounding in his chest. Did Gavin know about him and Tessa? *Impossible.*

Gavin gestured behind them to the area of the beach where he'd first found Jamie and Tessa. "You two were… having a good time," he said carefully.

"She started it." Jamie collected the used towels just to have somewhere to look that wasn't Gavin's face.

"Sure. She's a kid."

"She's not—" He stopped at the sound of the growl in his voice, gathering himself before he continued. "She's not a kid. She's twenty-five."

"She's Ethan's kid," Gavin said, his voice suddenly harsher than Jamie had ever heard it.

"I know."

"Didn't look like you know."

"I *know*." Jamie scrubbed his hand over his face. "Jesus, *fuck*, I know."

Gavin looked at him with such empathy that Jamie had to look away. After what felt like an eternity, Gavin cleared his throat. "We should go. It's supposed to rain soon."

Jamie nodded, keeping his eyes focused on the wad of towels in his hands.

"Jamie." He glanced up at Gavin, the compassion in his friend's face making him feel even lower than he already did. "You can't."

Jamie nodded, sure that if he said anything, he'd say too much.

"If you ever want to...talk...or something...I'm here to listen. About anything. Stays between us."

Jamie met Gavin's concerned gaze and nodded again, swallowing around the tightness in his throat. He didn't deserve his friend's understanding, not for this. And yet somehow, he still had it.

Why did that make him feel even worse?

Chapter Eighteen

Jamie stared at the box on his desk as though it contained a dangerous animal, a tarantula or a snake or something, and not a bundle of yellowed note cards, their edges soft from years of handling and the ink gone blurry in places. He glanced at the clock. Sugar Grapes had been open for nearly three hours, and he hadn't moved, his computer screen long since gone to sleep as he lost a staring contest with a fucking box.

Outside his office, the clank of silverware and muted din of conversation spoke to another busy brunch rush. Soon the crowd would shift towards lunch and the smell of frying bacon that suffused the air would give way to grilled fish and the house red sauce, a rich ragu simmered for hours with a full bottle of Nuthatch's best red wine in each batch. He checked his phone again, but Whisky hasn't written back.

That's not who I want to talk to anyway.

Fuck.

At some point, he was going to have to go over to the bakery. He'd promised Ethan that he would stop by on opening day and report back with all the details so

Ethan could pretend he hadn't missed yet another major moment in his daughter's life. Just ten more minutes, and then he'd go.

He'd been promising himself 'just ten more minutes' for hours.

His office door opened, a cloud of Chanel rushing through the small crack before Helen shouted triumphantly, "Found him!" She threw the door open and Ruth, Judy, and Dot appeared at her side, disapproval on all of their faces.

He forced his most charming smile on his face, though he felt anything but charming, and affected the posture of someone who had been casually working rather than hiding out. "Good morning, ladies. To what do I owe the pleasure?"

"We have a bone to pick with you," Ruth said, her tone thick with disappointment, the kind he suspected she'd used to great effect when scolding second graders.

"Was there something wrong with your meal?" he asked. It was unlikely with Anabel at the helm, but anything was possible.

"The food was wonderful. As always," Dot said with a smile. She suddenly seemed to remember that they were supposed to be angry about something, and her smile quickly morphed into furrowed brows and pursed lips.

"What are you doing here?" Ruth asked.

Jamie glanced around. "In my restaurant?"

"He's hiding, that's what he's doing," Judy said.

"Hiding?" Jamie asked, his eyes darting between the women as he tried to keep up with their rapid-fire accusations.

"Yes, hiding," Judy repeated.

"You weren't at Sugar Grapes this morning," Ruth said.

"For the grand opening," Judy added.

"The *grand opening*, Jamie," Dot repeated, each word dripping with the kind of guilt trip that only a grandmother could bestow.

"I haven't gotten there yet, but I was just getting ready to head over," he said. It was sort of true.

"You should have been there when Tessa Jayne unlocked the doors," Ruth chastised.

"Gavin and Baz were there when she unlocked the doors," Dot added.

"I know."

The guys had texted him and invited him to go over with them, but he'd said he was too busy helping Anabel prep for brunch. And he had been, though he could have let Brodie take over the prep work—it was Brodie's job, after all. There was a part of him that was afraid that if he walked into Sugar Grapes with his friends, Baz would see what Gavin had seen on the beach, and the last thing he needed was anyone else knowing how goddamn much of his brain space was occupied by Tessa Cordeiro.

"How was it?" he asked.

"You should go and see for yourself," Judy said.

"I'm sure Ethan and Tessa would both appreciate it," Dot offered with an encouraging smile.

He got to his feet to emphasize the point. "I'm on my way, ladies. Thank you for stopping in."

Dot, Ruth, and Judy turned and disappeared down the hallway, Judy's voice trailing behind. "Oh! We have to stop back at the table. I forgot my leftovers. I hope they haven't thrown them away yet."

Jamie chuckled to himself. Judy always forgot her leftovers. His staff knew to mark the container and stick it in the fridge for when she inevitably circled back later that day to retrieve them. The fact that she'd remembered before she left the premises was an improvement.

He glanced up to see Helen still standing in his doorway, watching him, her lips screwed up to the side and emphasizing the deep lines around her mouth where her pink lipstick had smudged.

"Was there something else, Helen?" he asked.

She took another step into his office and leveled him with the kind of look that he knew had gotten children to confess to misdeeds for generations. His heart pounded, as though she could somehow read every inappropriate thought he'd ever had about Tessa all over his face, but he kept his expression blank. She gestured to the box on his desk with a bob of her perfectly penciled eyebrows. "You need a ribbon," she said.

Of all the things he thought Helen White might say, he hadn't anticipated a criticism of his gift-wrapping skills.

"Then I'll find some ribbon," he said.

She sucked her teeth. "See that you do."

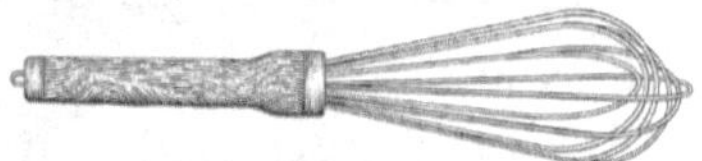

Tessa placed the last apple cupcake in the case, careful not to touch the swirl of cream cheese frosting on top, and took stock of the nearly empty display. Her next batch of donut dough had just finished rising, so at two minutes per side for frying, plus a few minutes to cool, then decorating— she ran through the calculations in her head. It would be fifteen minutes at least before they had more donuts for the case, and that was if she went easy on the decoration and didn't stop to breathe.

"When did we run out of pear tarts?" she asked Kyla, who was working as fast as she could to grab items for the never-ending line of customers.

Tessa had diverted all of her staff—all four of them, that is—to the front of house to help run the register and serve customers when the line was still out the door by their second hour of operation, leaving her alone in the kitchen. But the volume would die down any minute now—it *had* to. They'd been open for four hours and she couldn't restock the cases fast enough.

"What was that?" Kyla asked, before handing a box of cheesecake bars to the man at the register with a frazzled "thank you!"

"The pear tarts. How long have they been sold out?" Tessa repeated.

"Only a few minutes. Pastor Davis' wife bought the last half dozen for a dinner party they're throwing tonight." Kyla boxed up two of the apple cupcakes Tessa had just brought out and slid them across the counter. "Thanks so much for coming!"

"Shit," Tessa mumbled under her breath.

She glanced around the crowded space, every table occupied by happily chattering customers, a line so long it wound around the room, and Kyla and the rest of the team moving so quickly they were red-faced and sweating. Half the eyes in that line had turned to watch her when she'd emerged from the kitchen, her hair a frizzy mess of a knot at the back of her head. Not exactly the picture of calm professionalism she had planned to present on her first outing.

She felt those eyes boring into her, each one judging her. 'She couldn't even bake enough cupcakes on her first day,' they'd say, and, 'Are you really surprised? After all, she is Steph Cordeiro's kid and that girl didn't even graduate from high school,' and, 'This Swiss roll is nothing like her grandmother's.'

"Are there any more sangria cupcakes?" Kyla asked.

"They're still in the oven," Tessa replied, her eyes darting around the near-empty displays and cake stands as panic began to simmer in her stomach.

We're going to run out of product. Why didn't I make more ahead of time? Why didn't I hire more help?

Why the fuck is half of Aster Bay starving for baked goods all of a sudden? Are they really that eager to point and laugh at my failure?

Oh, God, this is just like Vegas all over again.

That stupid picture had gone viral and suddenly Marisa Sinclair's bakery had been overrun, the crowd clamoring for her bananas foster quickly turning into strings of nasty comments on the bakery's social media, the phone ringing off the hook with people who wanted to be sure her boss knew that they didn't think there was anything special about her goat cheese ice cream and granola crumble. All while Marisa Sinclair watched her thriving bakery gain a reputation as "that banana place." Tessa hadn't needed to be told it was time to leave—she'd seen it in her boss' face.

"Tessa! ETA?" Kyla asked, clearly for the second or third time.

"Thirty minutes," she said, shaking off the memories.

"And the donuts?" Kyla asked.

"Fifteen minutes!" Tessa said, turning to head back into the kitchen, hugging the now-empty sheet pan to her chest.

She pushed through the doors to the kitchen and dropped the pan onto the metal workstation, the clatter echoing like laughter. She squeezed her eyes shut and ran her hands over her face, releasing a strangled scream behind her closed lips.

No time for the pity party. Get to work.

First things first. She grabbed one of the myriad colors

of dry erase marker in the cup affixed to the wall and began scribbling a new prep list: fry the donuts; while they're draining, get the cupcakes out and cooling in the pan; poach more pears for the tart (the chocolate cream is already setting in the shells); cupcakes into the freezer; glaze and fill the donuts; make more of the vanilla mascarpone whipped cream for the tarts; frost the cupcakes; assemble the tarts—shit, she'd also need to cut up more fruit to decorate the cupcakes, and run the finished product back out to the display cases. She started adding in more items, arrows pointing to their proper place in the order. There wasn't a minute to waste, not when her entire staff were out front manning the counter and she'd hardly had time to train Kyla on the intricate assembly of the desserts anyway.

Why had she insisted on such a large menu for opening day? Hadn't Marisa taught her to always start small and grow?

This is what happens when you try to show off.

She dropped the marker back in its holder and spun around just as the kitchen door swung open and Jamie stepped inside. "Hey, it's a madhouse out there," he said.

She was so damn relieved to see him until she remembered that relief wasn't an appropriate emotion. What was the appropriate emotion to have when she saw Jamie? She didn't know and she sure as hell didn't have time to figure it out just then.

She pulled the donuts out of the proofing box and unwrapped the first tray. "Kinda busy here, Jamie. Whatever it is you wanted to talk about, can we do it later?"

When she glanced up, he'd wandered over to her scribbled prep list, a deep furrow forming between his brows as she scanned the list. With a grunt, he set the small box in his hands down on the empty workstation by the door and rolled up the sleeves of his shirt. It was a testament to how frazzled she was that she only paused for a fraction of a second to appreciate the view of his muscled forearms.

"What do you need?" he asked as he made his way over to the sink and began washing his hands.

"What are you doing?" she asked over her shoulder as she took her unwrapped tray of donuts over to the fry station.

"Put me to work."

She shook her head. "I've got it."

He sighed and grabbed a side towel to dry his hands. "Your entire staff is needed in front of house, and you have a prep list longer than you can possibly handle on your own. Put me to work."

"You don't know the recipes," she protested as she checked the temperature on the fryer.

The oil had cooled—that was going to set her back. She glanced at her list and tried to mentally reorganize. She couldn't take the cupcakes out for another five minutes, but she could start poaching the pears.

"Then tell me what to do," he said. "I'll be your sous."

"My what?" she asked, not sure she'd heard him correctly. She grabbed a stock pot and set it on the stove, dumping in a bottle of port wine.

"Your line cook. Your prep. Whatever you want to call it. Tessa," he barked her name, causing her to stop throwing vanilla bean pods and cinnamon sticks into the wine and look at him. "Let me help."

Something unexpected twisted behind her ribcage, a flutter that threatened to turn her vision misty. Instead, she tilted her head towards the basket of pears on the counter. "Can you peel the pears?"

He nodded once and strode across the kitchen, retrieving a paring knife from the knife bar. "Yes, Chef."

She moved back to the fryer, dropping in the balls of dough while Jamie made quick work of the pears. By the time the poaching liquid was ready, he dropped the fruit in without needing to be asked, crossing them off the list on the board and moving on to the mascarpone whipped cream while she filled and glazed the donuts.

They worked in silence, aside from the occasional call of "behind" or "corner," and before she knew it, he was arranging the last strawberry (cut in a perfect rose as she'd requested) and placing the last few pieces of brunoise-cut mango on the sangria cupcakes. By the time she returned from refilling the case in the front of the shop and pushed back through the doors into the kitchen, he had taken to scrubbing down the counters.

Tessa stood for a moment and watched him work, the hypnotic bunching of his arm muscles as he cleaned the counters with precise, circular movements. Completely in control. He was always completely in control. And he'd wandered into her kitchen and somehow, without ever once taking over, still kept everything under control. He was sixteen years her senior with a culinary degree from one of the best schools in the country, an accomplished executive chef, and yet he'd whipped cream and dusted pastries with powdered sugar with no ego. Even more than the way the muscles of his back shifted beneath his shirt as he bent over at the workstation, the way he had made order from her chaos without pulling rank made her heart flutter. He glanced up at her, catching her watching him, and a smile tilted up the corner of his lips.

"What?" he asked, laughter in his voice.

"Nothing. You don't have to do that," she said, gesturing

lamely to where he continued to wash the counters as her cheeks heated.

"I know."

It was too much. She'd barely survived him spending the last who-knows-how-long chiffonading mint and chopping fruit and responding to her every request with a quiet "yes, Chef," but having him clean her countertops was more than she could take.

She reached for the towel. "No, really."

He pulled the towel away from her, challenge flashing in his eyes as he held it just out of her reach. "Really. I don't mind." His eyes flickered to her lips, just for a moment. "Chef."

She was on fire. This man was standing in her own kitchen and burning her alive. Who the hell had given him permission to *smolder* at her?

"Thank you," she said, her voice shaky. "Chef."

Again, his eyes traced her mouth, and for a moment she thought he might kiss her. But that would be a terrible idea, the worst idea, because the last time she'd kissed him, she'd left humiliated and feeling so goddamn alone that it almost wasn't worth kissing him in the first place. Almost.

He grunted and pushed past her, moving to clean off another counter on the opposite side of the workstation, placing a giant metal table between them. If that wasn't an indication that she was reading far too much into his eye movements, then she didn't know what was. She pulled her hair out of its tangled bun and began finger-combing out the knots just to have something to do with her hands that wasn't embarrassing herself by throwing herself at a man who had just bailed her out and was definitely *not* flirting with her.

Jesus Christ, stop thinking with your pussy.

"Successful opening," he said, glancing up from the

already-clean spot he was wiping.

"Yeah." She glanced over her shoulder at the doors to the bakery, where the crowd had finally started to die down, six hours after opening. "Apparently everyone in Aster Bay had a burning need for baked goods this morning."

He laughed a sort of snort laugh that shouldn't have been noteworthy but was somehow adorable. Where did he get off being *adorable*?

"What?"

"They didn't come for your baked goods."

"Excuse me?" she asked, crossing her arms over her chest, a thin layer of armor.

He paused in his pointless cleaning, pressing his hands to the edge of the counter and leaning towards her, though they were still separated by the expanse of the metal workstation. "I'm sure the pastries were delicious, but they didn't come because they had a desperate desire for donuts." He shook his head like she was out of her mind and started wiping down the counter again. "Though I suspect they'll be back now that they've gotten a taste for those raspberry rosé jelly ones."

"Then why did they come?" She braced herself for him to confirm her worst suspicion.

They didn't come for your food—they came to gawk and see for themselves if you're really as much of an embarrassment as they always thought.

He dropped the side towel into the laundry bag at the end of the counter. He leaned his hip against the workstation, crossing his own arms over his chest, and met her eyes. "To support you."

"To support Ethan," she corrected him.

"That too. But also *you*, Tessa. All those people are so glad you're here."

"Glad for new gossip, maybe." She moved to the sink, ready to start in on the pots and pans that had piled up during their sprint to restock. This reprieve wouldn't last, and she needed to come up with a new game plan for getting through the day that didn't involve relying on Jamie coming to her rescue.

"I had four elderly women track me down in my office to scold me for not being here when you unlocked the doors. That's not about gossip," he continued.

She closed her eyes. Of course, he had come out of some misguided sense of obligation, some guilt trip that had compelled him to leave his own kitchen and come work in hers. She began aggressively scrubbing the nearest stock pot as embarrassment flooded her system. Why had she ever thought that he was there because he might actually care about her? He had told her in no uncertain terms that he could not—would not—be her friend, never mind anything more than that. Just because they'd splashed around on the beach and had a couple laughs didn't mean he'd changed his mind.

"The people of this town love you," he continued.

"They love *you*," she shot back, her tone sharper than he deserved. "They're just curious about me."

"You're wrong."

"The only reason anyone missed my mom and me at all was because they didn't have new dirt on us so they couldn't talk about us behind our backs anymore," she continued, slamming the pot in the drainer tray and moving on the large stainless-steel bowl. "I should have known nothing would be different. She's dead," she said, her voice catching on the word, "and they're still lined up around the block to watch me fail."

"Tessa—"

"Even my own grandparents wanted us to leave!"

She blinked back the stinging in her nose, determined not to cry about this in front of Jamie. She knew she'd always be a curiosity to the people of Aster Bay, living proof of the cautionary tale they told their children. She'd known that when she agreed to come back and open the bakery in the first place.

She supposed she should be grateful for the reminder that this was exactly why she couldn't stay in Aster Bay, not long term anyway, no matter how many mixed signals Jamie sent her or how many festivals the townspeople roped her into co-chairing. She didn't belong there, and everyone knew it.

She startled when his hands landed on her biceps, the heat of him warming her back. "Tessa, stop," he said softly, sliding one hand down her arm to still her hand in its hostile scrubbing.

She set the pan down and he shut off the water before pushing gently on her arms until she turned around to face him. He was so close she had to look up to meet his eyes.

"Your grandparents were devastated when you two left town." She looked away, shaking her head, and he caught her chin between his thumb and forefinger, forcing her eyes back to his. "I was there, Tess. Everyone was devastated."

"I wish I could believe that," she said.

He dropped his hands and took a step back, his lips pressed together. She missed his touch immediately.

"Maybe this will help," he said, reaching for the long-forgotten box that he'd brought with him when he arrived.

He held it out to her, and she smoothed her finger over the gold satin ribbon. "What's this?"

"Open it," he said, urging her on with a tilt of his chin.

She carefully undid the ribbon and removed the lid of

the box to reveal a stack of yellowed, weathered notecards. She recognized the handwriting as her grandmother's—she had a similar stack of notecards with her recipes from the bakery. But these were different: shepherd's pie and Salisbury steak, chicken cacciatore and tamale casserole. She flipped through them, noting the staining on the chicken pot pie card and the slight tear in the card for Sunday ragu.

"Those were your grandmother's, all her favorite recipes for Sunday family dinners." Tessa continued flipping as Jamie spoke—pot roast and sausage with peppers, lasagna and meatballs. "You might not remember, but your grandparents used to host dinner every Sunday for the whole family. Including your mom and you. And me."

"I remember," she murmured, running her finger over the ingredients list for her grandmother's dinner rolls.

She remembered her mother arguing with her own parents about going to those dinners instead of Mass, the way her mother's parents would rage about Steph's need to repent, their demands that she 'stop playing house' and 'marry the boy already' so Tessa would no longer be a bastard. She remembered asking her mother what 'bastard' meant as they drove to the Hart family home for dinner, her mother's mascara smudged around her eyes where she'd been rubbing at them. She remembered the way those arguments flavored every meal her father's parents had served—chicken pot pie with a side of guilt, Sunday ragu seasoned with a dash of casual condemnation.

Jamie kept on talking, oblivious to Tessa's bitter walk down memory lane. "When I opened the restaurant, Louise gave them to me. 'Passing the baton,' she said. I hosted family dinner at the restaurant every Sunday using these recipes—with some modifications of my own—until they moved to Florida. Turn the cards over."

She glanced at him in question, but did as he asked. She read the words scribbled on the back of the card over and over, gasping when she realized what they meant. One by one, she flipped over the cards, each one covered in the same neat handwriting.

"Louise liked to note when she'd made a meal for a special occasion, to help her remember," Jamie explained.

Tessa read the lists of dates, each one accompanied by a note: TJ's fifth birthday dinner; celebrating Steph getting her GED; Ethan's first day on the job at Nuthatch; TJ's first day of kindergarten; TJ's first loose tooth; TJ's most expressive stick figure drawing; TJ's first time swimming in the ocean, TJ, TJ, TJ... On and on, the everyday moments of her first eight years documented in her grandmother's handwriting alongside the food they'd eaten that day.

"I think she'd want you to have them," Jamie said.

"Thank you," she said, the words thick. A tear slipped down her cheek and she dashed it away, hoping he hadn't seen.

But then he was there, setting the box down and wrapping her in his arms, his chin resting on the top of her head. She pressed her face into his shirt and breathed in the cedar and soap scent of him.

"Why would she do that?" she whispered into his chest.

His arms tightened, hands pressing into her back. "She loves you."

"She wanted us to leave," she repeated the only truth she'd known her whole life.

No one had wanted Tessa and her mother to stay in Aster Bay except Ethan; everyone had wanted them to go. That's what her mother had always said. But what if she'd had it wrong? Was it possible that the guilt and condemnation hadn't actually been passed around the dinner table in her father's family home alongside the rolls and salt shaker? Was it possible she and her mother had brought that baggage in with them, forgetting to leave it behind when they'd hung up their jackets and scarves on the coat rack in the front hall?

"She didn't," he said, softly.

The deep timbre of his voice reverberated through her where their bodies were pressed together. His thumb stroked across her lower back in barely-there movements, each arc sending fizzy tangles of comfort and longing through her blood. When he swallowed, she felt the working of his throat against her forehead.

"And everyone is glad you're here now."

She tilted her head up to meet his gaze, still clutching his shirt, still tracking the maddening strokes of his thumb. "Everyone?"

He held her gaze and swallowed again. For a moment she considered pressing her lips to his Adam's apple.

"Everyone," he repeated, his voice low and rough.

His eyes heated, the green gone liquid and lush. She tightened her grip on his shirt as his hands flexed on her lower back, like he was straining to keep from digging his fingers into her. The tip of his nose skated against hers, and she let her eyes drop closed, anticipating the heat of his lips on hers.

A plate shattered in the other room and they sprang apart, as though the sharp pieces of ceramic dishware had fallen at their feet and not on the other side of the double doors. Tessa backed up until she hit the edge of the counter, bracing her hands behind herself on the lip of the sink. He stared at her with wild eyes, breathing heavily through his nose.

He's your father's best friend, she reminded herself. *He's not yours to have.*

After what felt like an eternity, she broke their eye contact, gesturing to the still-full sink behind her. "I should clean this up."

"Right." He blinked as though coming out of a dream and took another step back. "Right. I should get back to the restaurant."

"Thank you. For today. For all of it."

He met her eyes again with such intensity it felt like the wind moving over her. "You're welcome." He turned to leave, but after only a few steps, he turned back to her, his hands dug deep in the pockets of his jeans. "This was an incredible opening, Tessa. You should celebrate."

She gave a self-deprecating chuckle. "I've got a bowl of popcorn and an episode of *Brilliant British Bakes* with my name on it tonight."

His eyes narrowed, like she'd said something that required contemplation rather than revealing how lame her idea of a celebration was. After a second, he shook his head, clearing the thought. "Right. Well, enjoy."

She watched the door swing shut behind him and tried very hard not to think about how sad she was to see him go.

Chapter Nineteen

WhiskyBusiness: Hey. Sorry for the radio silence. It's been a hectic day.

DiceDiceBaby: No apology necessary. Good hectic?

WhiskyBusiness: Great hectic.

Jamie had been sitting in the parking lot of The Rookery staring at his phone for the last ten minutes, and he still was no surer about what to say to Whisky.

Actually, that wasn't true. He knew exactly what he needed to say. Spending the day in the kitchen with Tessa had only made it clearer. That clarity didn't make him feel like any less of a dick, though.

His phone dinged again.

WhiskyBusiness: I think we need to talk about it.
WhiskyBusiness: The other night, I mean.
WhiskyBusiness: Last week.
WhiskyBusiness: Fuck, this is awkward.

DiceDiceBaby: I know what you meant, and I agree.

WhiskyBusiness: I shouldn't have sent you that picture.
WhiskyBusiness: And then asked for one back.
WhiskyBusiness: And then sent that video.

DiceDiceBaby: I did all those things, too. And I shouldn't have.
DiceDiceBaby: I really like you, but I know you don't want more than my friendship. And I respect that. It was a mistake to cross that line.

WhiskyBusiness: If things were different, if you were some guy I met at a Starbucks, then maybe we would have stood a chance.
WhiskyBusiness: But you're too important to me now.
WhiskyBusiness: You're too perfect.

DiceDiceBaby: I assure you, I am far from perfect.

WhiskyBusiness: In my head, I mean. No man could ever live up to the you in my head.

DiceDiceBaby: And no woman could hold a candle to you, princess.

WhiskyBusiness: The truth is, I did meet someone.
WhiskyBusiness: And I can't be with him, but I also can't stop thinking about him.
WhiskyBusiness: It wasn't fair for me to do those things with you when I'm hung up on him.
WhiskyBusiness: So I'm sorry.

He stared at the texts as they appeared rapid-fire on his screen and waited for the jealousy to curl in his stomach. But it didn't. Instead, relief washed over him like a wave.

DiceDiceBaby: I'm sorry, too. You aren't the only one hung up on someone else.

WhiskyBusiness: Really? You're not just saying that to make me feel better.

DiceDiceBaby: Really.

WhiskyBusiness: Who is she?

DiceDiceBaby: Someone impossible. Someone brilliant.
DiceDiceBaby: She's not for me. But I wish she was.

WhiskyBusiness: Well, aren't we a pair?

DiceDiceBaby: Can we go back to how we were before?

WhiskyBusiness: I would really like that.
WhiskyBusiness: I've missed my friend these last few days.

DiceDiceBaby: Me too.

WhiskyBusiness: And I promise that any pictures I send you from now on will be G-rated.

DiceDiceBaby: It's a deal.

WhiskyBusiness: Thank God, because I really need to

talk to someone about Bob and you're the only one who doesn't think I'm insane.

DiceDiceBaby: Bob, the guy you're hung up on?

WhiskyBusiness: No! Bob, my ghost!

Jamie laughed, tapping out a reply before heading into The Rookery. Gavin and Baz were already at their usual table, Baz scowling at the trivia registration card in his hands while Gavin chatted with Helen.

"There he is! I told you he wouldn't miss our weekly showdown," Helen clucked, patting Gavin on the shoulder as Jamie approached.

"And let you claim victory so easily? Not a chance," Jamie laughed.

"Your team is still down a man," Helen teased. "Not that you had much better luck when Ethan was here."

Jamie's phone dinged and he glanced at the flurry of messages from Whisky, each detailing another encounter with her ghost, though he was pretty confident that it was nothing a can of WD-40 and some weather-stripping couldn't solve.

"At least Ethan didn't spend half the night texting some girl from the internet," Baz grumbled.

"Mrs. White is right. We are down a person," Gavin said, glancing towards the back of the bar where Brodie, Kyla, and Tessa were having a drink, though Tessa seemed to be more focused on her phone than the company she was keeping. "Maybe we should ask Brodie to—"

"No," Jamie and Baz said at the same time.

Gavin's eyes widened.

"Sorry," Jamie said with a grimace.

Gavin shook his head. "It's fine. I know he can be a bit... much."

"If you ask me, the person you should be inviting to join your team is TJ," Helen said.

"Tessa," Jamie corrected automatically.

Helen's eyes gleamed dangerously. "As you say."

"It's not a bad idea," Gavin said. "One of this week's categories is 'viral videos.' We could use someone who actually enjoys watching those."

"Excellent!" Helen said, before turning to the back of the bar and waving a hand over her head like she was waving the flag at the end of a race. "Tessa Jayne!" she hollered. "Come join us, sweetheart."

Tessa wove through the crowd, making her way towards their table with an amused look on her face. "How are you, Mrs. White?" she asked.

"Just perfect now you're here. Sit," she said, gesturing to the empty seat beside Jamie.

Tessa arched an eyebrow in question but took the seat. "What's going on?"

"Congratulations. You are taking your father's place with his trivia team. Now these boys won't be able to complain that the numbers aren't fair when the girls and I win— again," Helen said with a smile. As she turned to go, she winked at Jamie before sing-songing, "Good luck."

"You don't have to do this if you don't want to," Jamie said.

"But maybe you could stick around long enough for the 'viral videos' category?" Gavin asked.

Tessa laughed. "You buy me another drink and I'd be happy to."

"Done!" Gavin said with a smile.

"I'll get it," Jamie said, getting to his feet.

All the relief from his conversation with Whisky was

rapidly dissipating the longer he sat next to Tessa, his calm replaced by a restlessness that demanded he do something with his hands. Getting her a drink seemed like a better option than hauling her outside and kissing the hell out of her like he'd wanted to do since he'd left her in her kitchen two days ago. Truth be told, he'd thought of nothing else since. Pressing her up against the wall and tasting her lips, wrapping her legs around his waist and carrying her to his bed, settling between her thighs...

"What're you drinking?" he asked, forcing his mind away from the thoughts that threatened to give him a hard-on right there in the middle of his favorite bar.

"French 75. Thanks." Her smile turned shy as Jamie nodded and headed towards the bar.

While he waited for the bartender to get her drink, he glanced at Whisky's latest messages.

WhiskyBusiness: I can't just buy a bottle of WD-40. What if Bob feels unwelcome?

WhiskyBusiness: I know I was trying to get rid of him before, but now it's kind of comforting to have him around.

WhiskyBusiness: He's my emotional support ghost.

WhiskyBusiness: Sometimes when I need to clear my head, I blast some music and talk to Bob while I bake. By the time the oven timer goes off, I usually feel better. Even if Bob never talks back.

DiceDiceBaby: Do you want him to talk back?

WhiskyBusiness: God, no! Can you imagine?

DiceDiceBaby: Maybe if you talked to someone who

wasn't incorporeal you could clear your head and let poor Bob be at rest at the same time.

WhiskyBusiness: I'm talking to you right now, aren't I?
WhiskyBusiness: Unless you're a ghost, too, and just haven't told me.

DiceDiceBaby: I think you've been watching too many Halloween movies.
DiceDiceBaby: Maybe you should talk to your guy. The one you're hung up on.

WhiskyBusiness: He doesn't want to be my guy.

DiceDiceBaby: I find that hard to believe.

WhiskyBusiness: And your brilliant, impossible woman? Are you talking to her?

DiceDiceBaby: Trying pretty hard to avoid it actually.

WhiskyBusiness: You should talk to her. Tell her how you feel.

DiceDiceBaby: Yeah? You taking your own advice on that one?

WhiskyBusiness: Maybe I will.

Jamie accepted the frothy drink from the bartender and made his way back to the table, where Tessa was blushing furiously and shoving her phone in her back pocket.

"Tessa's almost as bad as you are about being on her

phone," Gavin teased.

"Isn't that exactly why we wanted her on our team?" Jamie asked as he held out the drink to Tessa and slid into his seat next to her.

"Difference is, I'm pretty sure she's talking to real people," Baz said before taking a sip of his Scotch.

"What's he talking about?" Tessa asked with an amused grin.

"Nothing," Jamie grumbled.

"Jamie has a fake internet girlfriend," Baz replied.

"She's not fake. And she's not my girlfriend." He met Tessa's gaze, curiosity and something that bordered on wariness mixing there. "She's just a woman I met online. A friend."

"Don't complain about the internet girlfriend, Baz," Gavin chided. "Without her, Jamie never would have made that killer beet deep."

"Oh, yeah. I liked that one. With the hazelnuts," Baz confirmed.

Tessa spluttered as she choked on her drink.

"You alright?" Jamie asked.

"Fine," she said, coughing a bit, her eyes scanning over him as though she were seeing him for the first time.

The clang of Mike Greenhall's old school bell announced the start of the trivia match.

"Round One," Mike said into the microphone, "is all about that most popular of cooking competition shows, *Brilliant British Bakes*!"

"The trivia gods are smiling on us tonight!" Gavin said, sliding their answer sheet over to Jamie.

"I wouldn't have taken you for a Peter London fan," Tessa said, watching him carefully. "Do you watch the show?"

"I never miss it," he replied. His mouth went dry, as

though by admitting to watching a wildly popular reality cooking competition he had actually admitted to much more. He just couldn't pinpoint what exactly.

"Guys! Do you know the answer or not?" Baz asked.

"What was the question?" Jamie asked.

"Which contestant accidentally used another contestant's rough puff for their cream horns in season five?" Gavin recited.

"David," Jamie and Tessa said simultaneously.

Something twisted behind Jamie's sternum, a dull scraping away of his certainty. It was an ache so familiar the edges had been softened with repeated wear, a heaviness that had settled in his body for the last six weeks and showed no signs of dissipating.

"This is our week. I can feel it," Gavin said, grinning.

"If these two can pay attention to the questions," Baz grumbled.

Jamie glanced at Tessa, his brow furrowing as he took in the pink rising in her cheeks. *It's just a coincidence*, he told himself. Imagining that the similarities between Whisky and Tessa were anything more than that would be dangerous.

Chapter Twenty

"I'll just be a minute," Jamie said over his shoulder as he moved through the dark, deserted dining room of Lemon and Thyme, Tessa on his heels. The door closed behind her with a quiet snick. "I promised Ethan I'd send him my clam chowder recipe so he can make it for your grandparents tomorrow."

"And he needs the exact measurements," Tessa said, her mind only half on the conversation. "My grandmother gave me a ten minute monologue on my father's lack of improvisational skill in the kitchen this morning when I called to check in."

"You'd think he'd be able to wing it at least a little bit by now. The man's in his forties," Jamie said as they made their way through the dark to his office.

"Ethan is useless when it comes to cooking. Did you know Kyla and Cheryl used to drop off weekly deliveries of muffins so he would eat breakfast?"

Jamie laughed. "No, but it doesn't surprise me. Every Thanksgiving your grandmother used to bake all these pies and Ethan always tried to help. But I'm sure you can imagine how 'helpful' he was. I'll never forget the year he insisted on making the sweet potato pie by himself." He shook his head. "He couldn't have offered to make the apple. He had to pick my favorite to mess with."

"Sweet potato pie is your favorite?" she asked, that fizzy feeling that had been bubbling up inside her chest intensifying.

"Your grandmother's sweet potato pie. No one makes it like her." He opened the door to his office, flipping on the lamp on his desk and sinking into his desk chair. "This will only take a minute."

"Take your time."

Tessa leaned against the doorframe, watching the concentration settle on his face as he clicked through his laptop in search of the recipe her father had requested. A deep furrow formed between his eyes and she had the strongest urge to drag her thumb over the spot, to smooth the creases from his skin.

"Thanks for giving me a ride home," she said. "Brodie was driving home with Kyla and I didn't really feel like being the third wheel to that." *And I think we need to talk.*

"It's no trouble," he said as he continued clicking through folders on his computer.

Just the idea of testing her new theory had her skin tingling in anticipation. Until that night, she'd chalked it up to wishful thinking, but sitting across from him at trivia—where they'd swept the *Brilliant British Bakes* category, thank you very much—she'd begun to wonder. What if it wasn't wishful thinking? What if it wasn't just a coincidence? The fact that Brodie and Kyla had been on the verge of a massive fight was the perfect excuse to ask Jamie for a ride and get some time alone with him. By the end of the night, she'd know for sure—was Jamie DDB?

Tessa looked away, gesturing over her shoulder. "Do you

mind if I go up to the roof?"

"Sure. Go ahead. I'll let you know as soon as I send this recipe off to your dad and then we can be on our way."

Tessa turned and made her way up the stairs and out onto the rooftop terrace. The bay shimmered in the moonlight, the October breeze off the water fanning her hair out around her shoulders. Across the water, porch lights winked in the dark.

With shaking hands, she raised her phone and snapped a selfie, the view of the harbor behind a clear image of her face. If she was right, this picture would change everything. And if she was wrong...

She knew she wasn't wrong.

Before she could talk herself out of it, she sent it to DDB. She watched as the message status changed to 'read,' then blew out a breath and tucked her phone in her back pocket while she waited for his reply.

She didn't have to wait long.

The door to the roof slammed open. Jamie stood in the doorway, his phone clutched in his hand with the photo she'd sent still illuminated on the screen. His chest heaved as though he'd taken the stairs two at a time. Her heart pounded in her chest, and she thought she might cry from the relief.

It was him. All this time.

How many times had she pictured Jamie's face while messaging DDB, or recognized something of DDB in Jamie's words? How many times had she wished they were the same person?

He stalked across the roof towards her, his path lit only by the stars and the moon's reflection off the water. He didn't stop coming for her until they were so close she had to tilt her chin up to look him in the eye. His gaze darted around her face, the corners of his eyes crinkling as his gaze softened.

"It's really you," she whispered.

He ate the words from her lips, crushing her against him with a hand around her waist, his other buried in her hair and tilting her head so he could deepen the kiss. She clung to him, grasping handfuls of his hair, his shirt, pulled onto her tiptoes by the force of his hold on her. He dragged his lips over her jaw to the sensitive hollow beneath her ear.

"I wanted it to be you," he said against her skin, his voice rough and jagged.

She caught his face in her hands and kissed him again, deeper, tasting the words on his lips, reveling in the way those words set fireworks off within her chest. When he licked across her bottom lip, she opened to him, lost to the way his tongue stroked hers, the lush heat of his kiss.

"I wanted it to be you, too," she said.

He lifted her into his arms, her legs wrapping around his waist, as he walked her back against the wall behind her, pinning her with the press of his hips. She dropped back against the wall, her feet falling to the ground so his hands were free to roam her body again as his mouth explored the length of her throat.

"Impossible woman," he grumbled, dragging his teeth along her collarbone.

"Don't forget brilliant," she chuckled, her laugh breaking off on a moan as he pressed a powerful thigh between her legs.

"I haven't forgotten anything," he said, encouraging her to grind against his thigh with a firm hand on her hips. He buried his face in the crook of her neck, nipping at her skin in between hot, sucking kisses. "Not the way you feel, or the way you taste. Not a goddamn thing."

She pulled his head back with a fist in his hair so he had to stop kissing her. She stared into his eyes, panting as they caught their breath. "Take me home," she said, her voice shaky.

He dropped his hands and stepped away, out of her reach, as though her words had been a lash to his skin. Frustration and hurt warred in his face. He looked away from her and swallowed hard. "If that's what you want."

"Jamie," she said, stepping towards him and letting her hands float down his chest until she hooked a belt loop with her finger and tugged him towards her. "Take me home *with you*," she clarified, softer. Then, to make sure he understood her this time, she rose on her tiptoes and sucked his earlobe into her mouth, dragging the sensitive skin between her teeth until he released a shuddering breath. "Please."

He growled, planting a searing kiss on her lips, before he took her hand in his and practically dragged her down the stairs, through the restaurant, and out to his car.

The streets of Aster Bay were mostly deserted that late at night, only the occasional car passing them on the main road through town. As Jamie drove, he kept one hand intertwined with Tessa's and resting on her thigh. They didn't speak, the weight of the decision they were making hanging heavily between them as they drew nearer to Jamie's house on the edge of town. Tessa held Jamie's hand tighter. She'd made her choice.

She followed him up the steps to his small cottage, his porch concealed from the street by a line of pine trees. She wrapped her arms around his waist and pressed her forehead to his back as he fumbled with the lock in the dark. After the second failed attempt to open the door, she planted a kiss between his shoulder blades, remembering the last time they'd fumbled with a lock. She'd hardly known him then.

"Take a breath," she whispered. He drew a deep breath into his lungs, the movement pushing against her arms around his rib cage before he succeeded in opening the door.

No sooner had the door closed behind them than his mouth was on hers again in an urgent, desperate kiss. Tessa broke away, panting, and dropped to her knees in front of him, right there in his front entryway. As she worked his belt, he leaned his head back against the door and cursed. She slid the button of his jeans through its hole and lowered his zipper. She was still holding the zipper pull when Jamie's hand closed over hers.

"You don't have to do that," he said.

She arched an eyebrow at him. "Do you not want me to?"

"I don't want you to do anything you don't want to do."

"What makes you think I do *anything* I don't want to do?" She huffed a disbelieving laugh through her nose and looked up at him through her eyelashes. "I didn't get to taste you last time."

He swallowed, his Adam's apple bobbing in his throat, and sank a hand into her hair, cupping her head gently. Reverently. She'd never felt more wanted than she did kneeling at his feet.

"You don't know how many times I've thought about this," she said, sliding a hand into the open placket of his pants and wrapping her fist around the hard length of him.

He jolted against her touch, thickening with each slow slide of her palm along the hot flesh. He held her gaze, his own eyes growing darker, that deep, wild green color she loved so much barely visible around the pools of black.

"You've thought about sucking my cock, princess?"

"Yes, Chef."

The hand in her hair tightened, gentle pressure guiding her closer to him. "Then be a good girl and put me in your mouth."

She smiled, heat pooling low in her belly as she finally pulled his cock free from his boxer briefs. His erection jutted hard and rude from the open placket of his pants, framed by the dark fabric of his clothing. She gave him a slow pump with her hand, before guiding the tip of him to her lips. With slow, teasing licks, she bathed the head of his cock with her tongue. Her fingers played with the heavy weight of his balls as she memorized the taste of his skin.

"Tessa," he groaned.

She answered his unspoken plea by sliding him between her lips, flattening her tongue along the underside of his erection. He released a string of curses, his hips rocking gently towards her, as though he couldn't control it. She didn't want him to control himself. He'd done nothing but control himself since the second she'd arrived in Aster Bay. She wanted him unrestrained, undone. For her.

"Tessa, baby, if you don't stop, I'm going to come," he said, pulling her off of him. His cock bobbed between them, glistening with her saliva, and she eyed it hungrily. She was just getting started. He chuckled and pulled her to her feet with his grip on her hair. "Another time. You're not the only one who's been thinking about this."

She kissed him and a deep, primal sound rumbled in his chest.

"Fuck, I love tasting myself on your lips."

"Mmm, I love that too," she said, chasing his kiss.

"Take your pants off, princess. I need to know if your pussy tastes as good as I remember."

He didn't need to tell her twice. Together, they removed her jeans and panties, Jamie tossing them aside as he fell to his knees before her. He lifted one of her legs and rested it on his shoulder as he dragged his stubbled cheek in a slow trail up her thigh. He drove his tongue into her, steadying her with a firm hold on her ass, and she gasped at the heat of his mouth against her cunt. Soft groans and grunts fell from his lips as he devoured her with his tongue and teeth.

"As good as you remember?" she panted.

"Better," he rumbled.

He sucked on her clit while teasing at her entrance with a single finger. But every time she felt her climax begin to rise within her, he gentled his touch. She whimpered as he teased her, denying her an orgasm yet again, her legs trembling with need. He lapped at her clit, each stroke of his tongue sending a jolt of desperation through her, a tight, buzzy feeling shooting down her legs, the soles of her feet burning in anticipation of the oncoming pleasure.

She gasped his name, grinding her pussy against his face, desperate for release. At last, he plunged two fingers into her as he took her clit between his teeth, scraping the sensitive bud in an unexpected rush of pleasure pain that tipped her over the edge. She doubled over, folding herself over him as her thighs shook around his head and he held her up with a firm hand on her ass and curling, probing fingers within her.

As soon as her climax subsided, she pulled him to his feet and kissed him hard, sucking the taste of herself from his lips.

"Bedroom. Now," he demanded between kisses.

"Yes, Chef."

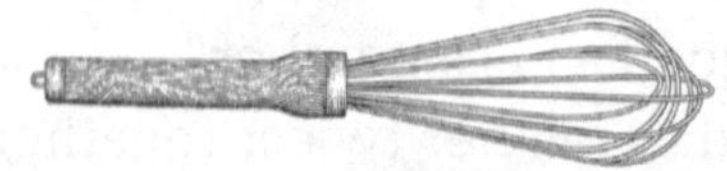

Jamie followed her down the hall to his bedroom, watching as Tessa shed her shirt and bra along the way, dropping them in his hall. He liked the way her clothing looked scattered about his home, like it belonged there, like *she* belonged there. Her perfect ass jiggled as she walked and it took everything he had not to drop to his knees in the hall and eat her again, this time from behind. Instead, he pulled his own shirt over his head, tossing it to the floor along with her clothing, leaving a trail of their impatience behind them.

He kicked the bedroom door closed behind them, unable to take his eyes off her as she crawled onto his bed. She settled amongst his pillows and looked up at him with that sparkle in her raven wing eyes that never ceased to captivate him. With a mischievous grin, she let her knees fall to the side, revealing the place where she was pink and wet and waiting for him, her skin abraded from his facial hair, and her curls damp from his tongue. He couldn't help but pump his hand over his cock as he approached her, his eyes glued to the most beautiful pussy he'd ever seen. He wanted to lick it and fuck it and *own* it, to bury himself inside her in every way possible, to drown in her scent and her taste and never come up for air.

At the back of his mind, his conscience prickled with a warning. *Last chance to stop this*. But that wasn't true. He'd never stood a chance of stopping it. She was Whisky, Tessa, the woman he'd been fantasizing about for months. The woman he woke up hard as stone dreaming about, aching with the need for her. They were always going to end up here.

He climbed onto the bed and ran his hands over her legs, tracing from the tattoo on her ankle to her knees to her thighs. He pressed on her thighs, opening her up even more to him. He wanted to memorize this moment, where she was glistening with her desire for him. As he watched, she circled her own nipples with her fingers, teasing them into tightly furled peaks and roughly plucking at them, her hips rocking against the phantom of his touch.

He fell on her, kissing her, and placing one hand over hers where it teased her nipple, plumping and squeezing her breast with their joined hands. How had he gone so long without touching her? Without tasting her?

With her free hand, she reached between them and took hold of his cock, drawing the tight circle of her fist up and down his length.

"Need you," he grunted.

"I need you too."

He leaned away from her to pull open the bedside table drawer and retrieve a condom. With shaking hands, he ripped open the little foil package and rolled the latex over his erection. Lining himself up at her entrance, he pressed her knees apart as he slid the head of his cock inside her. He froze, swearing as pleasure tore through him at the hot clutch of her pussy around just those first few inches.

She whined, swiveling her hips. "More."

He pressed in a bit further, his eyes glued to the way she stretched around him. It was crude and invasive and the hottest fucking thing he'd ever seen, her soft, pink flesh parting for him, molding to him. With another push he was seated fully, the entire length of him sunk into her wet warmth.

"Fuck, princess." Her eyes sparkled and he couldn't help but kiss her. "You like when I call you princess?"

"I've always liked it," she confessed, rocking her hips up to meet his slow thrusts. She cradled his face in her hand, and he turned to plant a kiss on her palm.

"I like *you*," he said.

She laughed. "I couldn't tell."

He chuckled, fucking her harder until her laughter dissolved into soft gasps with each thrust.

"I like you too," she said.

He smiled, that simple admission making his heart swell in his chest in a way that would have terrified him if he wasn't so focused on making her come again. He pressed two fingers into her mouth, cursing as she sucked on them in long pulls, before winding those fingers between their bodies to stroke her clit as he continued to fuck her.

"Need you to come at least once more," he directed, his fingers moving faster as she began to writhe beneath him.

"Only once?" she joked.

He pinched her clit, hard enough to make her gasp and her back to arch off the bed. "I'll make you come as many times as you'll let me, princess. As many times as you can handle. Until you're so sore you can't imagine ever coming again."

"Yes, please," she whimpered, her hips driving up off the bed, impaling herself further.

"Yes, what?" he asked, tightening his grip on her clit.

"Yes, Chef," she cried.

He released his hold on that sensitive bud and began stroking it again, hard and fast, as he drove into her again and again. Her gasps grew louder, higher, until she reached up and gripped his forearm, digging her nails into his skin.

"Such a good fucking girl," he growled as she convulsed beneath him, her inner walls clamping down on his cock in a maddening grip that made his vision go blurry. He ground his teeth together, determined not to come yet. Not to let it be over yet.

Her gasps turned to heavy panting, her grip on his arm

relaxing, and he fucked her harder as he chased his own orgasm. The rough slap of flesh on flesh resounded in the room and she dug her hands into her hair, her head turning back and forth on the pillow as she chanted his name. Fire licked down his spine, electricity shooting through his pelvis. An image of fucking her bare, of watching his cum drip out of her, of licking her clean, flashed through his mind and he pumped the condom full of his release.

Jamie collapsed on top of her with a groan, gathering her against his chest and kissing her until they could both hardly breathe. He rid himself of the condom, tying it off and tossing it in the wastebasket beside his bed. With her head resting on his chest, Tessa dragged a finger over his cock, the light touch almost unbearable on his oversensitive flesh. Lifting her finger between them, she showed off the cum she'd gathered with an unmistakable gleam of pride in her eyes. Holding his gaze, she slid the finger between her lips, sucking it clean.

"Fuck, Tessa," he cursed as his cock kicked hungrily at the sight. "Give a guy a minute to collect himself."

She eyed his rapidly hardening length and pressed a kiss to his chest. "Doesn't look like you need a minute." He pulled her against his chest, kissing her deeply. When they broke apart, she grinned so hard it made him forget how to breathe. "Aren't old guys supposed to need a longer rebound time?" she teased.

"Old?" he asked, incredulous, as she loosed a laugh that settled in his bones, becoming a vital part of him.

He flipped her over on her back, pinning her hands on either side of her head and kissed her again, rocking his hips against her so she could feel just how little rebound time he needed.

With her. Only with her.

The thought threw him off balance, like standing in a wind tunnel, but instead of hiding from the storm, he turned his face up and reveled in it. Gave himself over to it. He wanted to get lost in her tempest. As he sank into her for a second time that night, he had the sneaking suspicion that he just might find himself there, too.

Chapter Twenty-one

Jamie woke to the lazy glide of fingertips over his cock, already hard and ready to fuck. Again. As if he and Tessa hadn't fucked so many times throughout the night that he'd lost count.

"What time is it?" he asked, his voice rough with sleep, as he gripped a handful of her delicious ass.

"Early. We have time," she said. She wrapped her fingers around his erection and began stroking him in earnest, teasing him until he was throbbing against her palm, leaking with every pass of her fingers.

He reached for the bedside table, retrieving the last of his condoms. She took the packet from him, ripping it open and sliding the condom over his length mere seconds before she threw her leg over his hips and sank down onto him. She sighed as he filled her, the kind of sigh usually reserved for sinking into a hot bath, or freshly washed sheets. The kind of sigh that he could see himself getting used to.

She rode him in slow undulations, lifting her hands over her head and gripping her elbows so her breasts swung freely with each movement of her hips, inviting him to look his fill. And, Christ, he could watch her all day, the way her nipples puckered and her chest flushed as she used him to chase her pleasure. He reached up and bracketed her tits with his hands, lifting them so they bounced against his palms.

"You feel so good," she groaned as she adjusted her angle and continued bouncing on him.

"Let me cook dinner for you tonight. A real date," he said, lifting his hips to meet her.

"Is that what we're doing? Dating?" she asked with a grin, her breathing becoming more labored with each thrust.

He dropped one hand from her chest to draw light circles over her stiff clit. Not enough to make her come, just enough to let her find the edges of her orgasm, to feel it just out of reach.

"What would you call it?" he asked.

She dropped her hands back on his shins. At that angle, even more of her was on display, each bounce and ripple of her flesh, each slick glide of her over his cock. He watched, mesmerized by the sight of her impaling herself on his erection, the way he disappeared inside her and reappeared coated in her pleasure.

"You can't expect me to have this conversation right now. I can't think clearly when you're inside me."

"Good. I don't want you to think clearly," he said, driving into her harder. "I want you to say what you really mean. What you really want."

"I want to come," she said on a frustrated breath.

"I'm not done watching you, princess." He stroked her clit faster, loving the way she squirmed as she tried to get closer to his touch. "I'd watch this forever, if I could," he said to himself.

She lifted her head, eyes sparkling dangerously. "Do it."

"What?"

"Record it." She leaned to the side, retrieving his phone from the bedside table and opening up the camera app. "No faces," she said, handing it to him.

"Fuck." His cock jolted inside her, growing impossibly harder. "You're sure?"

"We can watch it later. On our *date*," she said, resuming her previous position and bouncing with renewed vigor.

He cursed again, aiming the phone's camera at the place where they were joined, the video capturing every obscene slide of his cock, every bit of her stretched and swollen pussy, every stroke of his finger over her stiff clit.

"Fuck, princess," he growled. "Look at you, taking my cock like such a good girl." Her pussy fluttered around him and he grinned. "You like being my good girl, Tess? You like when I tell you how pretty you look with my cock stretching you open?"

"You know I do." Another flutter. "Make me come," she demanded, bouncing faster.

He worked her clit harder, faster, in a dizzying rhythm, mesmerized by the image on the screen of his phone. When she fell over into her orgasm, the camera caught each contraction of her pussy, the clenching of her ass, every quiver and shudder. It captured the throbbing of his cock as he came, the rush of her wetness when he slid from inside her.

Ending the recording, he tossed the camera to the side and sat up, capturing her chin between his thumb and forefinger and bringing her in for a bruising kiss. "That was the hottest fucking thing I've ever done," he said.

"You better send it to me." She nipped at his bottom lip. "I may want to watch it later. In preparation for our *date*," she teased.

"Here." He sent the video to her and then deleted it from

his own phone.

"Why'd you do that?"

"So you don't have to worry about it going anywhere. You have the only copy."

She narrowed her eyes at him. "I trust you, Jamie. I know you wouldn't show it to anyone. Besides, who would you show it to? It's not like you can tell your friends—"

They both froze. His scalp prickled and something in his throat constricted, pressure pounding on the inside of his rib cage.

"Sorry," she whispered. "I didn't—"

"It's fine," he replied, his voice too sharp, too terse. "You're right."

He lifted her off of himself and stood, moving to the closet and pulling on a clean pair of sweatpants.

"Not that I would ever show my friends something like that," he said as he pulled a long sleeve t-shirt over his head. His voice sounded harsh even to his own ears, but he couldn't stop himself. "But you're right. No one can know anything about this."

"Jamie, come on."

"We should get going. I want to get you home before there are too many people around."

"I didn't mean—"

"I said it's fine." He flashed a strained smile he didn't feel, his chest too tight, his lungs refusing to take in enough air. "I'll get your clothes," he said, opening his bedroom door and moving out into the front entryway to gather the clothing they'd discarded the night before.

He picked up her shirt and bra, holding them loosely in one hand as he slumped against the hallway wall. Closing his eyes, he fought to control the pounding of his heart and the panic bubbling beneath his skin.

What was he doing? He'd just spent the last twelve hours in bed with his best friend's daughter. If Ethan ever found out—hell, if Gavin or Baz ever found out—he'd lose them all. All the friends who had become his family after his parents' deaths, who'd stood by him and been the brothers he needed when his own brother was off touring the world and becoming a minor celebrity. He'd have to move. He wouldn't be able to stay there with his friends despising him the way they would. Which meant he'd lose the restaurant, his customers, his co-workers, the tiny piece of home he'd carved out for himself over the last twenty years.

He'd lose everything that mattered to him.

Except her.

Maybe he could keep her?

He scraped his hands over his eyes. No, he'd lose her, too. Tessa was only in town through the holidays. And he knew her well enough from his conversations with Whisky to know she had no intention of staying in one place for long. But Jamie didn't want a nomadic existence. He wanted roots, a family, and a place to call home. He wanted Aster Bay, so he could never be more than a layover for her, a diversion before she was off on the next adventure.

"Jamie." Her voice was soft, unsure.

He turned to find her wrapped in a sheet and standing in his doorway, her movements hesitant, like she was afraid he'd startle.

He held a hand out to her and she went to him, curling against him and tucking her head under his chin. He wrapped his arms around her and breathed in the scent of her, filling his lungs with it.

"I'm sorry," he said, pressing his lips to her tousled hair. "I've never kept a secret this big from them before."

"From my father, you mean," she said.

"Yes."

"He wouldn't like this."

"No, he wouldn't."

"Jamie…I'm only here for two more months and we both need to have a relationship with Ethan for much longer than that." She looked up at him, her head still resting on his chest. "I'm not the kind of girl who stays in one place for long, and definitely not in a place that barely wants me here."

He dug a hand into her hair and tugged just hard enough for her to tilt her head back. "Haven't you figured out yet that we all want you here?"

"I mean, I guess I'm starting to understand that maybe *you* like having me around," she teased.

"Not just me," he said.

What would it take to convince her that she belonged in Aster Bay? That she'd always belonged?

He kissed her until the worry melted from her eyes, as though a kiss could rewrite a lifetime of belief.

"Can't we just enjoy the time we have together without making this more complicated that it already is?" she asked.

"And how much time is that, princess?" he asked, knowing that no matter what she said, he was going to hate her answer.

"I leave the day after Christmas."

It wasn't enough time. It would never be enough time.

"Maybe we could just…do this?" she said, looking up at him with those big raven-dark eyes.

"This?" he asked, needing her to clarify.

"Enjoy each other," she said, her hands wandering over his back. "Enjoy this time together. Without needing it to mean anything. Without anyone else having to know about it."

He knew he should say no. He should end it now. She already meant too much to him for that.

Instead, he smoothed her hair and plastered on a smile even as every bone and muscle and tendon in his body fought to reject the idea that Tessa could never really be his.

"Yes, of course. You're right. No one needs to know."

Chapter Twenty-two

Baz threw the tennis ball against the wall of Jamie's office with a maddening *ka-clunk*, over and over and over again, as though Jamie's head weren't pounding from lack of sleep and too much caffeine. Not that he was complaining. He'd gladly take a headache in exchange for the last few nights of having Tessa in his bed.

"Norm wants a cut of the bonfire ticket sales," Baz said. "He'll give us a break on the patio rental fee and the heaters, but he intends to make it up on the back end."

"Which means?" Jamie asked.

"Which means we need the bonfire to be a sell out to make it worth it. Otherwise, we still end up spending money that isn't in the budget," Baz explained.

Ka-clunk.

"How many tickets are a sell out?" Gavin asked.

"Two hundred. That's the most the fire marshal would approve," Jamie said. "Tessa tried to get him to go to two-fifty, but you know Marty. He wouldn't budge."

"Tessa talked to Marty?" Ethan asked, his face slightly out of focus on Jamie's computer screen.

"And Norm," Gavin said.

"Geez, guys, send her into the deep end, why don't you?" Ethan said.

"She held her own just fine," Baz said. "We all knew Norm wasn't going to just give us the patio for free. He cares too much about his bottom line for that."

Ka-clunk. Ka-clunk.

"It's your call, Gav. Do you think we can sell two hundred tickets?" Jamie asked.

Gavin caught the tennis ball on its next pass across the office, sending Jamie a smug smirk behind Baz's back as he set the ball down on Jamie's desk, out of Baz's reach. "Early sales are going well, especially now that the social media ads are going with the photos Kyla took."

The photos in question were much more suggestive than the first batch Gavin had used on billboards and print ads. The ones Gavin and Kyla had selected for the social media campaigns were borderline indecent, the sexual tension between Tessa and Jamie practically crackling off the screen. He and Tessa had looked through them together that morning right before she rode his face while swallowing his cock.

Jamie adjusted himself subtly under the table and forced the vivid memories from his mind. He could not think about those things while talking to her father.

"I saw those photos," Ethan said with a grimace. "You guys conveniently left them out of the last batch you sent me."

"I thought you looked very nice in the photos, Jamie," Ethan's mother called to the camera as she passed by behind Ethan, a basket of laundry balanced on her hip.

"Mom, I'll take care of that after my meeting," Ethan said. Louise waved him off and continued on her way. He turned back to the camera. "Mom printed out some of those shots from Facebook and has them on the fridge. Every damn day I have to look at your face when I go for the OJ."

Every inch of Jamie's skin was on fire, shame eating him alive as he thought about the photoshoot, about the way he'd practically come out of his skin with wanting every time Tessa smiled at him, how badly he'd wanted to smear her lipstick. Those heated thoughts were practically burned into his gaze in the images, the flirtatious curve of her smile like a dare. To think those photos were on her grandmother's fridge was unbearable.

"You were saying something about the sales picking up?" Jamie asked Gavin, once again trying to steer the conversation away from him and Tessa.

"They won't really pick up until next week," Gavin continued. "Locals will wait until the last minute to buy their tickets."

"The packages Natalia put together are selling fast. There are only three or four spots left in the girls' getaway package," Baz said, reaching for his tablet to pull up the numbers.

"Is that the one with the manicures and massages?" Ethan asked.

"And the lingerie fittings and boudoir photo shoot," Baz confirmed. "Even the guys' weekend packages are more than half sold at this point. Paintball and axe throwing are a big hit."

"What about day passes? Seats to the opening dinner?" Jamie asked.

"Both are doing well, but not as well as the packages."

Just as Tessa had said would happen. Her strategy was working, better than any of them had expected it to. Jamie couldn't help the flare of pride in his chest.

"We'll see an uptick in those sales after Jamie and Tessa go on *Sunrise in the City*," Gavin chimed in.

"*Sunrise in the City*?" Ethan asked, his eyes wide. "You guys have been busy."

"Well, we can't all fuck off to Florida for two months," Baz joked.

"Sebastian Graham, I heard that!" Ethan's mother said, appearing at the edge of Jamie's screen, just behind her son. Baz's face went red, and Gavin barely hid his laughter. "You watch your language, young man, or I won't send Ethan home with any cookies for you."

"Sorry, Mrs. Hart," Baz grumbled.

Louise winked at Jamie and then disappeared from the screen again.

"Don't worry, Baz. Mrs. Hart would never actually withhold cookies," Gavin said.

"And, with any luck, I'll be delivering them before the festival," Ethan said.

"You'll be home that soon?" Gavin asked, sitting on the edge of Jamie's desk so he could better see the screen.

"Dad's doing really well. It looks like he'll be back to his old self with just a couple more weeks of therapy. Well, minus the bacon and Big Macs. He's really pissed off about that last part," Ethan chuckled. No one loved a Big Mac like Henry Hart.

The throbbing in Jamie's head moved behind his eyes and an uncomfortable weight settled on his chest. As much as he missed his best friend, Ethan's return to Aster Bay would make whatever was going on with him and Tessa significantly more complicated. Would they have to end things before she left town? No, that would be unbearable. They'd just have to figure out how to keep their secret once Ethan was home.

"That's great news. Tessa must be thrilled," Gavin said, beaming.

"She's so busy with Sugar Grapes and the festival she's hardly had time to miss me," Ethan said, a hint of sadness coloring his smile. "You three are doing such a great job of making her feel welcome. She can't say enough good things about you all. Especially you, Jamie. The way you jumped in and helped in the kitchen on opening day—" Ethan broke off, shaking his head. "It means a lot to us both. Thank you, man."

Jamie's stomach twisted. "Yeah, of course," he said, looking away. If he looked in Ethan's eyes, even through a computer screen, he might vomit. That or tell him everything. Neither was an acceptable option.

"You didn't tell me you did that," Ethan said. "It's exactly what I would have done."

"Only a lot more helpful," Baz said, "since you can't cook for shit."

Ethan chuckled. "That's true. But seriously, I had no idea. You never mentioned it. I didn't realize how much time you two were spending together," he continued, each word like the tightening of a vise around Jamie's throat.

"It's not that much time," he choked out.

"So, what's the verdict?" Baz asked, bringing them back to the topic at hand. "Am I sending this contract over to Norm or what?"

All eyes turned to Gavin. "Do it. I don't think we'll have a problem selling the tickets."

"Great." Baz signed the contract and set it aside. "Now about using the high school cafeteria for the cooking demonstrations."

Jamie hardly heard as Baz and the guys debated the particulars of the next contract. Ethan had thanked him for spending so much time with Tessa. If he had any idea how Jamie had been spending that time with her over the last few days, the things they'd done...

His phone dinged as a message from Tessa popped up on his screen.

Tessa: Did I leave my phone charger at your place this morning?

He reached for his phone, flipping it face-side down, but not before Gavin's gaze swung from Baz to Jamie's screen, his brows drawing low as his eyes scanned the message. It wasn't the *most* incriminating message. If he thought about it hard enough, he was sure he could come up with plenty of reasons for Tessa to have been at his cottage that morning and to have left her phone charger behind. But he was a shitty liar, and Gavin knew it.

He met Gavin's eyes, soaking in the scrutiny he found there, the silent question slowly turning to disappointment.

"Guys!" Baz said. It clearly wasn't the first time he'd tried to get their attention. "Are you confident we'll have the volunteers for clean up or not?"

Jamie broke the staring contest with Gavin, turning to Baz. "We'll have the volunteers. Sign the contract."

He surveyed his friends, Ethan and Baz already off and talking about the logistics of volunteer management, Gavin staring at his hands. *So he doesn't have to look at me.*

"Excuse me," Jamie said, pocketing his phone and damn near sprinting from the room, leaving his friends to sort out the details.

He needed some air. Five seconds of quiet. Just a few minutes where he didn't have to pretend he hadn't betrayed his best friend twenty times over in the last few days alone. He paced to the end of the hallway and back, shaking his hands to dissipate the nervous energy coursing through him.

He doesn't know you've betrayed him. He never has to know.

Jamie wanted to go up to the roof, to throw himself into planning the restaurant's specials for the weekend, to get in his car and drive to Sugar Grapes just to see Tessa and prove to himself that she was his. But he couldn't do any of those things. He'd made a commitment to the town when he took on the food and wine festival, and those men in his office—the greatest friends he'd ever had—had all jumped in with both feet to help him. He couldn't bail on them now.

"Everything alright?" Gavin asked when Jamie pushed open the door and re-entered his office a few minutes later.

"Yeah. Sorry about that," Jamie said.

"I think we're done here for today anyway," Baz said, swiping his tennis ball from the corner of Jamie's desk and throwing it against the wall with a pointed look at Gavin as it *ka-clunk*-ed. "I've got to get to the office."

"Your office is your guest room," Gavin pointed out.

"It's still an office," Baz scowled. "Ethan, good to see you. I'll have the vineyard's month-end P and L to you by the end of the day."

"Thanks, Baz. You're the best damn finance manager around," Ethan said.

"Don't you forget it." *Ka-clunk.* "You coming?" he asked Gavin on his way out the door.

"You go ahead without me. Brodie's done with the lunch shift in a few minutes and he's going to give me a ride to the university."

Baz nodded and let himself out.

"Jamie," Ethan piped up from the computer. "I want to thank you again. For everything. I know you and Tessa didn't hit it off right away, but it means a lot to me that you've taken her under your wing. Made her feel welcome.

Mrs. White tells me that you guys even invited her to fill my seat on the trivia team while I'm out of town."

"You're getting reports from Mrs. White about us?" Jamie asked, a chill creeping up his spine. What else had Mrs. White told Ethan?

"Not me. She and Mom still talk almost every day," Ethan chuckled.

Of course.

"Anyway, thanks, man. You're a good friend," Ethan said. "The best, actually."

Jamie just nodded, unable to speak past the lump in his throat as Ethan signed off and the computer screen went blank.

Jamie sank into his office chair, his elbows braced against his desk, and cradled his head in his hands. The leather of the chair across from his desk creaked as Gavin sank into it. Jamie knew Gavin wouldn't be the first to speak.

"Say something," Jamie begged, his head still in his hands.

"What would you like me to say?" Gavin asked, his voice calm.

It was the voice Jamie imagined Gavin might use when he caught a student cheating on a test or plagiarizing a paper. The voice he likely used when Brodie had tried to sneak in past curfew every Friday night in high school. It was a voice that said he already knew what you'd done wrong and was just waiting for you to admit it. Gavin's brother had become a priest, but maybe it should have been Gavin who heard confessions for the way he wielded so much guilt with only seven words.

Jamie looked up at his friend, scraping his hand over his mouth. "Nothing," he said. "Don't say anything."

They sat in silence, staring at each other, until Jamie could feel Gavin's gaze crawling over him, assessing him.

But somehow still not judging him.

It would have been easier if Gavin was judging him.

"It was her," he said. "It was always her." Gavin's eyes narrowed in confusion and Jamie huffed out a breath, trying again. "I met Tessa the night before she turned up in Aster Bay. I went on a shitty blind date, and I wound up meeting Tessa."

"The girl from the hotel," Gavin said, the pieces slotting together.

"Except I didn't meet her for the first time a month ago. I met her six months ago, in an internet fan forum where she went by the name WhiskyBusiness. Only I didn't know it was her until Monday night."

"When you gave her a ride home from trivia."

He nodded, a strange sort of relief at finally saying it to someone mingling with his shame. Not just at what he'd done, but at the knowledge he was going to do it again.

"I didn't know—" He broke off, the empathy in his friend's face more damning than anything else. He didn't deserve empathy.

"And now you do," Gavin said. "Are you going to stop?"

Jamie shook his head, looking away. "I've been falling for this woman for months, and now she's here... I don't know how to stop."

Gavin blew out a breath, tapping his knuckles on the arm of the chair.

"What happens when she leaves?"

Jamie's gaze snapped to Gavin's even as he fought back the growl that gathered at the base of his throat. If he was honest with himself, there was a small—or maybe not so small—part of him that thought, with time, he could convince her to stay. He could figure out how to keep her and Ethan, too.

Gavin's eyes softened. "Jamie, she *is* going to leave again."

"I know," he said. He did know, he just wasn't ready to believe it.

"You've never been the casual-dating kind of guy."

"Maybe I've changed."

"Have you?"

He leaned his forehead against his hand, rubbing his forefinger back and forth as though he could wipe away the electrical storm behind his eyes. "This conversation would be a hell of a lot easier if you fucked up every once in a while, you know?" he muttered with a half-hearted chuckle.

Gavin huffed out a breath that could almost have been a laugh if it hadn't sounded so bitter. Jamie glanced at him curiously, but Gavin was no longer looking at him. "We've all fucked up, Jamie." He turned to Jamie with a strained half smile, then got to his feet. "I'm always here, man. If you want to talk."

"Yeah," Jamie said, struggling to decode the far-off look in Gavin's eye. "Same."

Chapter Twenty-three

Tessa climbed the steps of the white, Greek revival in the center of town, two large plastic platters of assorted cupcakes and pastries stacked in her arms. She drove her elbow into the doorbell, unable to free even a finger from her balancing act. When no one answered, she set the trays down on the wicker side table beside the porch swing and called, "Mrs. Blumenthal?"

"Around back!" came the answering shout.

Sighing, Tessa took up her trays and picked her way back down the porch steps, through the little gate at the edge of the driveway, and around the house. Dot Blumenthal's backyard was immaculately landscaped, lined with mature trees, their leaves painted in bright orange, yellow, and red for fall. An elaborate grape arbor sat at one end of the yard heavy with purple-black grapes, and a garden full of flowers in every color and variety was situated at the other. There, amidst the fiery orange daylilies and the purple asters that had given the town its name, stood Dot Blumenthal, her low-heeled pumps sunk into the dirt as she carefully pruned her flowers.

"Oh, Tessa, sweetheart, it's you!" Dot said, her face lighting up.

"Got your pastry delivery," Tessa said, as though the heavy trays in her arms weren't a dead giveaway. "Where would you like them?"

With a final snip, Dot tucked the pruning shears in the back pocket of her chinos and tugged off her gardening gloves. "Let's get those inside so the frosting doesn't melt," she said. "It's unseasonably warm today."

Tessa followed Dot through the back door of the house into a tidy, if dated, kitchen, the red Formica countertops and flower-patterned wallpaper spotless though worn around the edges.

"You can set those right over there on the table while I wash up," Dot said, moving to the sink to scrub any errant dirt from her hands. "I appreciate you taking such a large order at the last minute, dear. Cheryl DaSilva's baby was born yesterday."

"Oh! I hadn't heard. How's she doing?" Tessa asked.

Dot beamed. "Mother and child are both doing well. But poor Ricky seemed a tad overwhelmed when I spoke to him last night. With so many folks dropping by with their well wishes, and knowing how much of a sweet tooth Cheryl herself has, I thought it might be nice to bring them some of your delicious treats."

"That was very thoughtful of you," Tessa said.

"We all have to look out for each other," Dot said, drying her hands on a dish towel bearing a picture of a rooster.

Tessa glanced around the kitchen, taking in the bowl of silk fruit in the middle of the counter, old Mother's Day and birthday cards tucked in amidst the fruit. A black and white photograph of a young man in an army uniform with a stunning brunette on his arm hung on the wall, and finger paintings were stuck on the fridge with a magnet in each corner to flatten out the marks where they'd been folded into envelopes and mailed. Dot lived alone, long ago widowed, and Jamie had told Tessa that her children and grandchildren were overseas on an army base. Still, her kitchen was teeming with family.

"I must say, I wasn't expecting you to deliver them personally," Dot said.

"It's no trouble."

Tessa's gaze settled on a photograph in a clear plastic magnet photo frame on the fridge. In it, Dot, Ruth, Helen, and Judy sat with Tessa's grandmother, each raising a beer towards whoever was taking the photograph, laughter making their cheeks pink. The photo had to be at least thirty years old, judging by the hair styles and clothing.

"That was after your grandmother's pie won first prize at the church fair," Dot said, coming to stand behind Tessa and looking at the photograph fondly. "Sweet potato, I think it was. Louise always did know how to bake one hell of a pie."

Without thinking, Tessa reached out and ran a finger over the edge of the photo. She could practically hear her grandmother's laugh pouring from the picture.

"Would you like to stay for a bit and have a glass of cider with me?" Dot asked, looking at her fondly.

Tessa's shoulders relaxed in gratitude for the opening. "I think I would. Thank you."

Dot poured them each a glass of apple cider and produced a tin of rock-hard chocolate chip cookies from the refrigerator, arranging it all on a decorative wood tray and ushering Tessa back out into the yard, where a wrought iron table and chairs sat in the shade of a giant maple tree. Once they each had their glass and an inedible cookie on a crisp white napkin, Dot folded her hands in front of her and looked at Tessa with kind eyes.

"What's on your mind, Tessa Jayne?"

Tessa took a sip of her cider to buy herself a minute. How did a person go about asking questions they'd had their entire life?

One at a time.

"You and my grandmother were friends," she began, a hint of a question in the inflection of her voice.

"Still are," Dot said, beaming. "My late husband always said, 'That Louise Hart is too much mustard for one hot dog!'"

Tessa chuckled, not entirely sure she understood the phrase, but appreciating the spirit with which it was delivered and feeling more confident in coming to Dot with her questions.

"And you were friends with her when my parents...when I was born," she continued.

Dot leaned back in her chair, as though settling in for the conversation they were about to have. "Ah. Yes, I was."

"My mom always said there was nothing left for us in Aster Bay," Tessa said, picking her words carefully. "That we had to leave."

"I like to think there's a place for everyone in Aster Bay."

Tessa gripped the heavy glass of cider with both hands to ground herself as she met Dot's eyes. "The more time I spend here, the more I'm starting to think I'm missing part of the story. And you're the one who remembers how things actually were, right?"

"Generally," Dot said with a deferential tilt of her head.

"I want to know how things actually were. Before."

She needed to know the truth of why her mother had bundled her up and fled the town, why she'd never returned. Tessa had grown up in the shadow of that pain, hearing half stories told with thinly veiled bitterness towards her mom's hometown, *her* hometown. She couldn't reconcile the Aster Bay she'd grown up hearing about with the town she'd lived in for the past five weeks. The more time Tessa spent in Aster Bay, the more time she spent with Jamie, the harder it was to imagine leaving. But would staying be a betrayal of her mother's memory?

Dot smoothed her hands over her thighs, shaking her head. "You should be having this conversation with your grandmother. Or your father."

"I've heard what my father has to say. And I know what mom always said. But I also know she lied to keep me away from here. She told Ethan I wasn't interested in visiting him when she'd never even told me it was an option. I think maybe I need to hear this from someone who isn't so close to it, who hasn't spent the last twenty-five years living in the shadow of their choices. Please, Mrs. Blumenthal. I just want to understand. I've spent my whole life thinking no one wanted us here, except maybe my father."

"Well, that's just not true." Dot leaned forward, resting her hand on Tessa's. "We all wanted you here. Both of you."

"Then why did mom say we weren't welcome?"

Dot sighed. "Your mother had a hard time of it. Her parents weren't as understanding as Henry and Louise when your parents got pregnant. Francisco and Beatriz, they came to this country from the Azores with big dreams for their daughter, and they were the strictest Catholics this town has ever seen. Deacons at St. Anthony's, pillars of respectability. And then their precious baby girl went off and got pregnant out of wedlock and the baby's father wasn't even Catholic?" She clucked her tongue. "Not even Fr. Barry could talk any sense into them. And their friends were no help. Self-righteous fools. Your mother's parents laid down an ultimatum—your mother and father would marry as soon as they turned eighteen, or the Cordeiros would have nothing to do with her ever again."

Tessa felt like all the air had been knocked from her lungs. She remembered the fighting, the angry shouts of scripture that had followed them whenever they were with her mother's parents. Her heart ached for her mother, just sixteen and abandoned by her parents in every way that counted.

"Ethan wanted to marry her," Tessa said. "They've both told me that much."

"Ethan was always a good boy," Dot said with a fond smile. "Very responsible. Respectful. He wanted to do right by your mother, and by you. And your mother was such a sweet girl. Sharp as a tack, that one, and a spitfire to boot. But Stephanie was also a terrible people pleaser. She couldn't stand it if someone was disappointed in her, even when she was a child. And her parents' disapproval weighed heavily on her."

"I can only imagine," Tessa murmured, thinking of all the times they'd fled other towns over the years, all the times mom had told her to always leave before someone could leave you, that they had to be better, smarter, funnier.

"At first, when the fighting got particularly bad, you all moved in with the Harts. Louise and Henry were so happy to have you," Dot said, her face breaking into a wide smile. "I remember Louise standing right over there picking black-eyed Susans to decorate your bedroom with on the day you moved in."

Somehow the image Dot conjured was more painful than the one of her other grandparents with their fire and brimstone.

"What happened? Between black-eyed Susans and mom feeling like we had to go?"

"Ethan was ready to marry Stephanie, it's true. And they loved each other, the way you love the people you've grown up with. But everyone could see, plain as day, that they weren't *in* love. Your mother knew it, and she wanted more for herself. For you. And I think she was afraid that one day Ethan would regret marrying her. Your father, good man that he is, didn't understand the difference between loving someone the way he loved your mother, and loving someone the way a husband and wife should."

"So she said no," Tessa filled in.

"Actually, she said yes."

"Then why—"

"Louise knew if they married, it would end in disaster. By then, the Cordeiros had left town, ranting and raving the whole way about the shame and dishonor of their sinful child," she said, her lips pursed in disgust. "The friends they left behind were less than kind to your parents. Stephanie needed a support system, a family, and Louise and Henry wanted your mother to know that she had that family with the Harts. She didn't need to marry into it." Dot paused, sucking her teeth and staring at the black-eyed Susans that still dominated her garden. "Your grandmother told Stephanie as much, took her aside, woman to woman. Asked her what she *really* wanted. If she'd said she wanted to marry Ethan, Louise would have started planning the ceremony that very day. But what your mother really wanted was a fresh start, a place where she could leave the house without fear of running into people who were disapproving of her choices, without your father trying so hard to be a good man that he forgot how to be her friend."

"So we left," Tessa said, slumping in her seat, her mind racing as she rewrote the story in her mind.

How much of that story had come from her parents,

and how much had she filled in herself over the years? She wasn't sure anymore.

"Louise and Henry gave your mother enough money to go anywhere she wanted in the country and get established, with a promise that you'd always have a home here, in Aster Bay, with them. If Stephanie ever wanted that. Your grandparents didn't want you two to struggle. And, I think, your grandmother hoped your mother would see that someone was on her side. They helped support you both for several years, until one day your mother announced she was getting married and she didn't need their 'charity' anymore."

"That sounds like mom. She never liked accepting help."

"Just like her father," Dot said with a shake of her head. "It was never charity, Tessa Jayne. Your grandparents could afford it and they wanted to help. That's what family does. They take care of each other; they stand by each other. When your mother stopped cashing their checks, Louise started depositing them into a bank account for you, instead."

"The trust," Tessa said, pieces slotting into place.

"All they ever wanted was for you both to know how supported and loved you are. Louise and Henry, they don't always have the easiest time saying how they're feeling. But they show it. With black-eyed Susans and Sunday dinners, and sometimes with money."

"Thank you for telling me," Tessa said, turning her hand over under Dot's and squeezing the old woman's hand.

"You've had a home here your whole life, Tessa Jayne, just waiting for you to come claim it."

Chapter Twenty-four

Tessa was in the kitchen arranging the bouquet of black-eyed Susans Dot had sent her home with when Jamie arrived. He tapped on the door so lightly she might not have heard him if she hadn't been expecting him.

"Come in!" she called. "I'm in the kitchen!"

A moment later Jamie appeared in the doorway to the kitchen, his jeans clinging to his powerful thighs, the sleeves of his Henley pushed up to display his forearms, and that damn French tuck drawing attention to the taper of his narrow hips. Looking that sexy while just *standing there* shouldn't be a thing, yet somehow Jameson Chase managed.

He came up behind her and wrapped his arms around her waist as she continued snipping off the ends of the stems and dropping them into a vase. He pressed hot kisses to the curve of her neck, slowly pulling the collar of her slouchy cropped sweater aside to give him more access to the place where her neck met her shoulder.

"What's with the flowers?" he asked.

"They're from Mrs. Blumenthal," Tessa said, wedging the last flower into the vase.

"I think those are your grandmother's favorites," Jamie said.

She turned in the circle of his arms and draped her arms around his neck. "They are."

She stopped herself just short of telling him about her conversation with Mrs. Blumenthal that afternoon, about the way it left her feeling sad and at peace all at the same time. That wasn't what she and Jamie were doing—sharing those parts of themselves. Just like when he'd been DDB, those were the types of personal details they didn't share. The only difference was that now she got to touch him, taste him, *feel* him. She'd share other parts of herself, instead.

"What's that?" he asked, tilting his chin towards the counter.

She turned her head, catching sight of the notebook she'd been scribbling in off and on all day. It was open to one of her many lists of restaurants and off-the-beaten-path cafes she'd read about online, names of specific dishes she wanted to be sure to try, a handful of landmarks she'd always wanted to see.

"That's how I plan all my trips," she said. "Have you been to Italy?"

He shook his head, a line forming between his eyebrows. "No. I've never been abroad."

"Really? Why not?"

He shrugged. "I just never had a reason."

"Going is the reason," she said with a smile. "Seeing what's out there. Experiencing new things."

He grunted, his hands tightening and flexing on her waist. "I would have thought Italy was already on your list," he said.

She smiled. Of course he remembered her list of places she was dying to visit. They'd talked about it at length back when he was DDB and she was Whisky. "It is. Top of the list actually."

"Right. I guess Italy is a lot more exciting than Aster Bay."

He began to pull away from her, but she caught his shirt in one fist, pulling him back and kissing him until the tension melted from his shoulders and his hands closed around her hips again.

"Aster Bay's not so bad," she said with a smile. She flipped a page in her notebook to show him a different list, one of all the things Kyla and her customers at the bakery had been telling her she had to do and see before she left town.

His eyes snapped to hers, searching. Questioning. She wasn't ready to answer those questions, so she looked away, her eyes falling on the small toolbox he'd set down in the doorway when he'd come in.

"What with the toolbox?" she asked, arching her eyebrow.

He bent his head and captured her lips, licking into her mouth with lazy strokes of his tongue, like he could taste the answers she wasn't prepared to give if he kissed her long enough. He pulled back just enough to speak, but she could still feel the movement of his mouth against hers as he formed the words. "It's time to take care of your ghost problem, princess."

She laughed. "Oh, no. Not Bob."

"I'm afraid so," he said, drawing a line of hot kisses across her jaw, nuzzling into her hair. "I need my girl to be well rested. Can't have a ghost keeping you up all night." He drew back to look at her, a wicked gleam in his eyes. "That's my job."

She bit her lip, forcing down the wild flurry of butterflies in her stomach. *My girl.*

Careful.

With a playful roll of her eyes and a sigh she said, "I suppose if you must."

Jamie laughed, gave her ass a squeeze, and then stepped back to retrieve his toolbox. "Alright, show me where our friend Bob has been making the most noise."

There was something thoroughly domestic in a way Tessa had never before experienced in watching Jamie do the whole handyman thing. He oiled creaky door hinges and applied plastic weatherproofing to the drafty windows. He even tightened the screws on the wobbly towel bar in the bathroom, muttering to himself about Ethan letting things go too long without fixing them. With each minor home repair, each new tool pulled from his shiny toolbox, she felt that flurry of butterflies grow until she had a whole swarm in her belly, tangling and twisting, pressing against her rib cage from the inside like they'd burst from her chest if she let them.

Jamie stood from where he'd been bent over adjusting the tension on the knob of the radiator in the bathroom and caught her staring at him. "What are you looking at?" he asked, his boyish grin making him look younger than his forty-one years. When he smiled, a dimple appeared in his left cheek and his eyes crinkled at the edges. She couldn't help but smile back.

"Just admiring the view," she said.

He chuckled, dropping his screwdriver into the open toolbox on the floor and coming towards her. She backed away, gesturing to his hands, filthy with dirt and grease.

"Uh-uh. Not until you wash your hands," she laughed.

His eyes sparkled and he continued advancing on her, holding those dirty hands out like a threat. She knew what those hands could do—and it was far more than just tightening screws and oiling hinges.

In the kitchen, the oven timer beeped and she danced out of his reach, tossing a grin over her shoulder. "Dinner's ready," she said as she headed towards the beeping.

His growl followed after her. "What I plan on eating isn't in the oven."

She laughed, but the heat washing over her had nothing to do with the open oven door and everything to do with the promise in Jamie's voice. He reappeared behind her, hands now clean, just as she set the pie plate on the stovetop and closed the oven door.

"Smells great." He pressed his face into the hair at her neck again.

"Chicken pot pie," she said. "I'm working my way through those recipes you gave me."

"Mmm, then you read the part about letting it cool."

She reached for the recipe card on the counter. "I don't think—"

Jamie spun her around, pressing her back against the kitchen counter and capturing her lips. His hands stroked along the skin exposed between the top of her jeans and the bottom of her sweater, each pass leaving fire in its wake. He hoisted her onto the counter, wedging his hips between her knees so she could feel the solid length of him against her core. She canted her hips against his, swallowing the low rumble that fell from his lips with a smile of her own.

Those hands on her waist slid higher, pulling her sweater up with him until they had to part just enough for him to pull it up and over her head. He set it aside and kissed along her collarbone as he unhooked her bra, her breasts bouncing free when the underwire and lace fell away.

"This is hardly the way to cool things off," she teased, sliding her hands down his back to grip his ass and pull him in closer.

"Stay right there," he said, stepping back, his eyes dark and liquid. "Don't fucking move."

She wiggled on the counter, as though she might hop down, the slight movement shaking her breasts in a way that made his eyes snap to their straining tips. He only took his eyes off her long enough to throw open the freezer door, closing it with a look of triumph, a single ice cube held between his fingers. She dropped her hands back on the counter, arching her back to offer her breasts to him, eager for this new game.

He stepped between her thighs again, the width of his hips forcing her legs apart. With one hand braced on her thigh, his thumb stroking the seam of her jeans, he brought the ice cube down to one nipple. The cold was a shock, even as she watched the ice make contact with her skin, the sting of it drawing a gasp from her. She watched as he circled her nipple, as the tip pebbled and grew tighter, shiny with the melting ice. He moved to the other nipple, repeating the slow painting of her skin, then dropped his head and captured the first furled peak with his mouth. The sudden heat after so much cold was exquisite torture, an unexpected pleasure so great her clit throbbed in response.

As he moved his mouth to her other nipple, he used one hand to unbutton her jeans. "Off," he grunted, tugging on the zipper. She lifted her hips and wriggled out of her jeans and panties, letting them slide down her legs and onto the kitchen floor as he continued working her breast with gentle tugs of his teeth.

A fresh wave of wetness flooded her core as he stepped back to take her in, naked on the kitchen counter in her father's home, her father's best friend fully clothed and looking at every intimate part of her as though he intended to lay waste to her. The knowledge of who he was, of where they were, shouldn't have made it hotter, but it did. It made her want to claim him there more than anywhere else, to have him claim her.

That's how it always was with Jamie—her body and mind overwhelmed with need, with the addictive feeling of being wanted. Of wanting to belong to him in every way possible.

She arched her back further and brought one foot up to the counter, opening herself up for his inspection, a challenge glinting in her eye.

"I can see how wet you are from here," he said, his voice dark.

"Not wet enough," she said, dropping two fingers between her parted thighs to spread herself open for him. "Not yet."

He moved back between her legs, one hand driving into her hair with a firm enough grip to send sparks over her scalp. He kissed her like he'd consume her, like he'd drink all the air from her lungs. And then the ice was on her clit and she cried out against his mouth even as he swallowed her cries. Her legs began to close of their own accord, but he stopped them, his hips holding her open for him. He moved the melting cube back and forth over her swollen bundle of nerves, the heat of her core melting it faster, drips of freezing water sliding down over her pussy. He teased at her entrance, the rapidly melting cube and his rough fingers exploring every part of her.

She trembled with need as he kissed her, tugging on her hair and stroking her clit with the ice. So much sensation and yet not nearly enough.

Then the ice was gone. He brought the small piece that was left to her lips. She opened for him and he pressed the cube inside, the taste of herself melting on her tongue. And when he kissed her, his tongue swiped the cube from her mouth, taking it back for himself where it disappeared in the heat of his kiss.

He pressed two fingers into her entrance, pumping them slowly, exploring her. "How about now, princess?" he asked. "Are you wet enough now?"

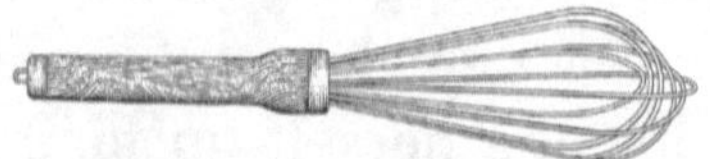

Tessa writhed on Jamie's fingers, bucking into his touch. He kissed her again, drinking the little gasps and moans from her lips as she drew nearer to her orgasm. He wanted to live inside those sounds, to spend all his days with his fingers buried in her heat, and the thought terrified him.

Tessa was only in his life temporarily—she'd been very clear on that account. For fuck's sake, she was already planning her next move. And even the moments they did have together were stolen, never meant for him. *She* was not meant for him. But when her pussy gripped his fingers, when she clasped his wrist, nails digging into his skin, and rode his hand with his name on her lips—fuck, it felt like she was his.

He dropped to his knees and sucked her clit into his mouth as his fingers continued to pump between her legs, curling and pressing into the spot that drove her wild. He looked up at her as she came undone in jerky shudders, their eyes locked as he licked her to a stunning climax. She was always beautiful, but never more so than with that heat in her eyes, that flush on her cheeks, ragged breathing making her chest rise and fall in a hypnotic rhythm as she came down from her orgasm. He kept his tongue on her as her climax receded, not yet willing to forfeit the taste of her. He could spend the whole day with his tongue between her thighs. With a final, slow circle of her clit, he leaned back, withdrawing his fingers from within her and sucking them clean as she watched.

She dug her hand into his hair and pulled him to his feet, crushing her mouth to his, licking her arousal from his lips. He shouldn't be standing in *this* kitchen with *this* woman naked on the counter, the taste of her coating his tongue, but there was nowhere in the world he'd rather be. Some wild possessive part of himself ran through the justifications in his mind as he flicked open his belt and undid his jeans, the heavy weight of his cock falling free into Tessa's waiting hand.

You didn't know she was his best friend's daughter the first time you slept together.

You've been falling in love with her for months.

You couldn't stop falling for her now even if you wanted to.

Even though it would make your life infinitely easier if you could.

"Jamie," she said, her breath hot on his ear as she roughly stroked his cock.

"Hmm?"

"Stop thinking so hard."

He released a strangled laugh and dug into his back pocket for his wallet. He retrieved the condom he'd tucked there earlier that day and tossed his wallet onto the counter.

"There's my boy scout," she said, her voice a liquid purr. "Always prepared."

"Hardly a boy scout," he said. He ripped open the package, guilt tangling with his need to be inside her. *A scout is trustworthy, loyal...* The words of the scout pledge he'd memorized as a child hammered in his mind.

She took the condom from him and rolled it down his length, guiding the swollen head of his cock to glide over the stiff bud of her clit.

"You're doing it again," she said, reaching up with one hand to stroke the furrow between his brows even as she kept a wicked grip on his erection.

"Doing what?" he asked, watching the way she teased herself with his tip.

"Overthinking. If you can think this much, I must be doing something wrong." She laughed but he heard the thread of self-consciousness in the sound and vowed to eradicate it.

He cupped her face, tilted it up to him, and bit her bottom lip. "You're perfect." Another nip, this time at the underside of her jaw. "Now put me inside you, princess. Let me feel how perfect you are."

She did as she was told, lining him up at her entrance, and he slid into her through the tight ring of her fingers. They both watched as he disappeared inside her, his cock framed by the open placket of his jeans and plunged into her soft, pink pussy. A sharp gasp fell from her lips as he seated himself fully all thought receded except *now* and *please* and *more.*

"Perfect," he murmured before capturing her lips.

She wrapped her legs around his hips, urging him on with her heels crossed at his lower back, and he fucked her like she was his. Like he had every right to this moment with her in this kitchen, to every moment he'd selfishly taken with her over the last few days, every moment he planned to steal with her in what little time they had left.

He fucked her like he could brand her, like he could carve his name into her most secret places with each thrust. And with each pump of his hips, each time he bottomed out and she gasped, he became more and more convinced that she was trying to do the same.

He pressed a hand low on her belly, gentle pressure across her pelvis, and he felt himself moving within her. Her nails dug into his back through the fabric of his shirt as she clung to him, her thighs beginning to shake around his hips.

"Let me hear you, baby," he grunted as he pistoned into her faster, harder.

"Jamie," she panted, her legs tightening around him.

"Louder."

He hooked one of her legs with his elbow, pressing her thigh back until it rested flush on his chest. The new angle drove him deeper, harder into that spot on her front wall, the one he pressed down on from the outside. She swore and her head fell back between her shoulders.

He captured one nipple between his teeth and growled against her skin, "Louder, Tess. Be a good girl and scream for me."

She cried his name as she came, her pussy clamping down around him so tightly that it pulled his own orgasm from him as well. He roared as his cock kicked within her, wave after wave of ecstasy buried in the heart of her, white hot heat singeing his spine and driving his hips into the cradle of her thighs over and over until his knees nearly gave out. He braced his hands on the edge of the counter to keep from collapsing.

When he met her eyes, she wore a lazy sort of satisfied smile. She pulsed around him a final time and he grunted at the overwhelming sensation. He turned his face to the leg propped against his chest, pressing an open-mouthed kiss just below her knee, then gently lowered her leg. She hooked it around his waist again, holding him inside her even as he began to soften.

He groaned into the curve of her neck. "I've gotta take care of the condom," he said.

She sighed and released her hold on him, planting her hands on the counter. He withdrew and turned his back to her to clean up. As he dropped the condom in the trash, she said, "Maybe next time we should skip the condom."

He spun around to find her still seated on the counter, her legs still parted so he had a clear view of every part of her. "Fuck, Tessa," he said, stepping back between her thighs and resting his forehead against her. "You can't say shit like that."

"Why not? I have an IUD. I was tested just before I left Vegas, and there's been no one but you—"

He kissed her and reached between her legs, cupping her pussy just to feel the heat of her against his palm. His cock was already growing hard and heavy again at the idea of being inside her bare.

She broke the kiss, laughing. "I take it you like the idea."

"Fuck yes, I like the idea," he said, taking her face in his hands so she had to look at him. "But, princess, if you let me inside you with nothing between us, then you're mine. Not just for a few weeks. Not just until you take off for whatever the fuck place is next on your list. *Mine.*" Her mouth dropped open as if she were going to argue with him, but he kissed her before she could say anything. "So you better be damn sure about what you want before you invite me inside your pussy bare."

He pulled back to meet her eyes, anxiety making his chest tight as he took in her shocked expression. He shouldn't have said that, shouldn't have issued ultimatums to the one woman he wasn't allowed to keep, and not just because she intended to leave.

But really, did it matter? Even if by some miracle he could convince her to stay, he still wouldn't be able to keep her. Ethan was going to come home eventually and he wasn't fool enough to think they could keep this up once her father was back in town. As it was, he needed to figure out how the hell he was ever going to look his best friend in the eye again. How he was going to welcome him back and fall back into trivia nights and late night burgers at the diner and all the thousands of other little moments where he'd need to pretend he wasn't a hollowed-out shell without Tessa, that he didn't lay awake at night as she slept beside him and try to triangulate some way—*any* way—that he could keep them both.

One way or another, in a few weeks, he would have to let her go.

Chapter Twenty-five

"Kyla, this is incredible!" Tessa scrolled through the website on the laptop in her father's office at Nuthatch while Kyla sat beside her, biting her lip and looking like she was going to be sick.

"You don't have to say that."

"I'm not blowing smoke, K. This is amazing."

Each page was beautifully designed, simple and easy to navigate with bright, bold images of the bakery and its desserts on every page. An events page highlighted the demonstrations and workshops Tessa would lead at the food and wine festival, some of the more playful shots Kyla had taken of Tessa and Jamie featured alongside links to buy tickets.

Kyla reached over and clicked on another tab. A clickable menu, each item displaying a photo of the dessert when you moused over its name, filled the screen. "There's an option to take orders online. So the next time Mrs. Blumenthal wants four dozen cupcakes, she could place the order in advance."

"Mrs. Blumenthal is never going to place an order online," Tessa said, mousing over each item to see the gorgeous photos pop up on the screen. "But this is a great idea. With the holidays coming up, we could encourage people to order their pies and things in advance without having to constantly man the phones."

She tried to click on the champagne and cream Swiss roll, but nothing happened. She tried again, frowning.

"The site isn't live yet," Kyla explained. "I wanted to be sure you liked it—"

"I love it." Tessa swiveled in the chair to meet Kyla's eyes. "Seriously. This is better than I ever could have imagined. You're really good at this." Kyla brushed off the praise, moving to log out of the test site. "I mean it," Tessa continued. "Have you ever thought about doing more of this?"

"What, website design?" Kyla scoffed, shutting down the laptop.

"Yeah, sure. Marketing and branding and stuff. Between the photography—"

"I'm not a photographer. Not anymore."

"Could have fooled me. And half of New England. Your photos are the reason Jamie and I are going to be on *Sunrise in the City* next week."

Kyla shook her head, waving Tessa off as they locked up Ethan's office and headed down the hall to Sugar Grapes. "I like working in the bakery. I only took those photos because Gavin asked me to."

"All I'm saying is, you have options."

"Don't you need a degree to do that stuff anyway?" Kyla asked skeptically.

Tessa shrugged. "I'm not sure. Gavin would know, though. You could always ask him."

"Ask me what?"

Tessa and Kyla turned to see Gavin walking into the vineyard's main building, a wide smile on his face and a small box held under his arm.

"Kyla was just showing me the website she designed for Sugar Grapes," Tessa explained.

"Yeah? I can't wait to see it. Kyla's always had a good eye," Gavin said. Kyla's cheeks flamed bright red.

"I was saying she should look into careers in marketing and branding, but she wondered if she'd need a different degree for that kind of work," Tessa said.

Gavin nodded in understanding, shifting the box from one side to the other. "It's certainly not a requirement. I'm sure there are plenty of people out there doing just fine without formal higher education, and there is probably a decent amount of overlap with your photography degree. But, since you asked me and I *am* a college professor, my vote is always going to be to get the degree."

Kyla nodded. "Thanks. That's what I thought." She moved past Gavin and Tessa and disappeared into the kitchen.

"Is she alright?" Gavin asked, concern marring his usually sunny features.

"I think she's just self-conscious," Tessa said.

"Maybe."

"What can I do for you? I'm all out of the strawberries and champagne cake pops, but I do have a fresh batch of the cabernet chocolate cupcakes with blackberry filling that I think you'll like."

"That sounds amazing. I'll take two to go," he said. Tessa nodded and moved behind the counter to box up his desserts. "The reason I came by today." Gavin set the box on the counter and removed the lid revealing a stack of glossy postcards, each featuring a close-up image of Jamie and Tessa. In the picture, she sipped her wine, arching an eyebrow at Jamie while he stared at her like he'd rather drink the wine from her lips than from his own glass.

Holy shit. How could anyone look at this photo and not

know that we're fucking?

"I thought you could put these on the counter to advertise the festival," Gavin said, oblivious to the swirl of arousal and guilt overtaking Tessa as she sealed the bakery box with a sticker. "There's a link on the back so people can buy tickets. We need to really amp up our efforts over the next few weeks to get the locals to come."

"Right. Of course," Tessa said, handing him the box of cupcakes. "We'll put them out today."

"Great. Oh! And before I forget." He reached into the inner pocket of his blazer and produced a folded flyer printed on orange paper. He handed it to her with a sheepish grin. "I didn't want to forget to give you that, too." She unfolded the paper, scanning the ad for a costume party-themed trivia night at The Rookery. "We haven't decided on what theme we should go with yet, but a cohesive group costume is worth the same number of points as a whole round of trivia. We can't afford to cede the points to Mrs. White and the rest of her gang."

"Who are they going as?" Tessa asked.

"Likely the same as every year. The Pink Ladies from *Grease.*"

Tessa laughed. It was too appropriate. "Well, if I have any ideas for you, I'll let you know. You could be the three Musketeers or something."

He gave her a look like she'd missed the point. "Tessa, we want you to play on our team again. The group theme has to have a part for you too."

"Oh!" Her chest warmed at the idea that these men wanted to include her, that maybe they were starting to be her friends.

Probably just because you're Ethan's daughter. Or because Jamie asked them to.

"I'll think on it," she said, folding the paper back up and tucking it into her back pocket.

Kyla re-emerged from the kitchen, a large tray of double-chocolate red wine cookies balanced on one hand. Gavin watched her for a minute, the smile sliding from his face into an unreadable expression, before he turned back to Tessa. "Right. I'll let you two get back to work."

Once they were alone again, Tessa moved to help Kyla load the cookies into the bakery case. "Do you and Gavin not get along or something?" she asked.

"What? No. It's just... I'm dating his son. I'm never sure how I'm supposed to act around him," Kyla said.

Tessa couldn't help wondering if Jamie would have the same difficulty with Ethan when he returned. Not that she and Jamie were *dating* exactly. They just hadn't gone more than twelve hours without mauling each other in nearly two weeks. Nothing awkward about that at all.

They placed the last cookie in the case and returned to the kitchen to retrieve trays of cupcakes next. As they returned to the front counter, Tessa asked, "Do you have any ideas for a group costume with three guys and one girl?"

Kyla paused briefly in her careful filling of the bakery case. "Goldilocks and the three bears?" she offered.

Tessa laughed, picturing Jamie, Gavin, and Baz in bear costumes. There was no way in hell Baz would put on fuzzy ears or a tail.

"Or you could pick four of the Muppets. Kermit, Fozzie, Gonzo, and Miss. Piggy?" Kyla suggested.

"I think I'm going to need something that doesn't require Baz to be an anthropomorphic animal."

Kyla rested a hand on her hip and pressed her lips together the way she did when she was thinking really hard. "Is this for you and your dad's trivia team?" Tessa nodded. "Oh, well that's easy then. *Star Wars.*"

"What makes you say that?" Tessa asked.

"Every year St. Anthony's hosts a spring bazaar to raise money for the food pantry and every year your dad and his friends volunteer to take turns in the dunk tank. After the second or third year, they realized they raised way more money if they dressed up in costumes to go in the dunk tank. No one wanted to dunk them, but they're more than happy to dunk Darth Vader," Kyla explained.

"Why wouldn't they want to dunk them?"

Kyla stared at her like she had asked what color the sky was. "Because those guys do so much for this town. Did you know Jamie personally cooks all the turkeys for the ecumenical Thanksgiving feast?"

"I don't even know what an ecumenical Thanksgiving feast is."

Kyla waved it away. "You will. You can come with me and Brodie this year. And you'll see that Jamie works his ass off. And your dad runs the toy drive at the women's shelter every Christmas. Gavin and Baz are always right there with them. Everyone knows if they need anything, those four will come through. My mom says Baz even shoveled the snow from the sidewalk outside the senior center once. Without being asked."

"Baz voluntarily did manual labor?" She couldn't picture it, what with the way he always wore a perfectly tailored suit and had not a hair out of place.

"I know," Kyla said. "Gavin got them all together to help build the animal shelter. Like, literally pitching in to put up drywall and nail...nails, or whatever you do to build a building. Brodie didn't even show up for his shift, but those guys, they were the first one there and the last to leave. So, of course, they volunteered to sit in the dunk tank for the spring bazaar. No one wants to sit in the dunk tank. Some years, it's barely sixty degrees at the spring bazaar and that water is freezing. But they volunteered. Because they always do."

"And then no one would dunk them," Tessa said.

"Right. So the next year, they all came dressed as Darth Vader. No one could see who was in the mask, but I'm pretty sure everyone knew. It just made it easier to dunk them." Kyla placed the last cupcake and turned to face Tessa. "So go with *Star Wars*. They already have a Darth Vader costume, obviously, and it shouldn't be too hard to put together Hans Solo and Luke and Leia."

"That's a great idea actually. Thanks," Tessa said, already running through what pieces they would need to find to put together the other costumes. It was easier to focus on the odds of finding a gold bikini in the local thrift store than the strange gooey feeling that had taken up residence in the center of her chest, like an underbaked cupcake.

"This spring, you can come with me and Brodie to the bazaar and take a turn dunking your dad," Kyla said, oblivious to Tessa's gooey raw batter feelings. "Brodie always likes to dunk his dad."

Except she wouldn't be in Aster Bay in the spring. She didn't know where she'd be—Italy or Sri Lanka or Croatia—but she wouldn't be there. For the first time, that thought didn't feel like freedom. It just felt lonely.

Chapter Twenty-six

"Do you even know what's in that?" Baz asked, eyeing the neon green liquid in Tessa's glass.

"Nope," Tessa said with a grin before taking another sip.

"It's a Midori sour," Jamie said.

He'd stuck to a gin and tonic himself, but he'd thoroughly enjoyed the glee on Tessa's face when Sam, the bartender, had presented her with the unnaturally colored drink. He'd also enjoyed the way her ass jiggled when she bounced on her toes, her thin, white, Leia costume barely concealing the fact that she was wearing a thong. That knowledge had been almost enough for him to drag her into the bathroom for a quicky.

"It tastes like a Jolly Rancher and it's delightful," Tessa said with a quirk of an eyebrow that dared Baz to question her taste. "I think our buddy Darth would appreciate it," she said, gesturing to the helmet Baz had left on the edge of the table.

"Darth will stick to his Scotch, thank you very much," Baz said.

Gavin sank into the seat next to Baz, setting his own neon green cocktail down on the table.

"Not you too," Baz grumbled.

"What? It's festive," Gavin said.

Under the table, Jamie slid his hand over Tessa's knee, his fingertips just disappearing into the slit at the front of her costume that had been torturing him all night. Her eyes widened a fraction of an inch and she took another sip of her drink as she pretended to pay attention to Baz and Gavin's bickering. He shouldn't touch her like that, not there, not with his friends at the same table and half of Aster Bay in the same room. But he couldn't help himself. It had been thirteen hours and twenty-four minutes since he last touched her and, in his estimation, that was far too long.

"Are you two ready for *Sunrise in the City*?" Gavin asked.

"As ready as we'll ever be," Tessa said. "Kyla will have no problem keeping Sugar Grapes going for twenty-four hours while I'm gone. Especially now that we've hired some more staff."

"And Anabel prefers when I leave her to run Lemon and Thyme without my interference anyway," Jamie said, his hand sliding higher on Tessa's thigh.

"You have the talking points I sent over?" Gavin asked.

Tessa nodded. "We do. Really, it will be fine," she said with a laugh. "Oh, and Baz, I looked over those projections you sent over."

She and Baz talked about budget projections and cost savings and return on investment, and she was breathtaking. Confident and competent, she fit so perfectly—in the town, with his friends, with him. He felt like he was standing in the eye of a storm, and she was the storm, all around him and ready to rip his world apart. So why did he have the overwhelming urge to throw himself into her chaos, to let her tear down the life he'd built and shape it into something new, something inextricably hers?

"Really, boys? *Star Wars*?" Ruth Greene asked as she and Dot Blumenthal approached their table.

"What's wrong with *Star Wars*?" Gavin asked.

"Nothing's wrong with it, dear," Dot said. "It is, perhaps, a tad uninspired."

"Everyone will know it's you in the dunk tank this year," Ruth chided with a pointed look at the Darth Vader helmet.

"I'm pretty sure everyone already knew, Mrs. Greene," Baz said.

Ruth tsked as if that were hardly an excuse.

"But you do make a handsome Hans Solo," Dot said, squeezing Jamie's shoulder. "I always did like that Harrison Ford. And his holster."

Tessa nearly spit out her Midori sour, laughter dancing in her eyes.

"And who are you supposed to be?" Ruth asked, eyeing Gavin.

Gavin smiled and pulled on the brown faux fur coat that he'd discarded as soon as he'd arrived. He zipped the coat up to the top, flipping up the hood. "I'm Chewbacca." He tilted his head back and did his best impression—which wasn't very good.

This time Tessa did laugh, her fingers twining with Jamie's under the table. A wave of peace that he had no right to washed over him and he fought the urge to pull her into his lap.

For a moment he could picture it, what it would be like if Tessa were really his, if they didn't have to hold hands under tables and pretend they hadn't spent the night tangled in each other's arms. They'd go to trivia at The Rookery on Monday nights and brunch at The Dockside on Sunday mornings before the church-going crowd arrived. They'd tease Gavin about his horrible impressions and they'd run the food and wine festival every year. They'd have hectic days in the bakery and the restaurant, and at night they'd fall into bed and make love until they were both too tired to think. And then he'd wrap her in his arms until morning came and they did it all over again.

They'd build a life in Aster Bay, one filled with laughter and good food and even better friends and maybe even a raven-eyed baby or two… He could see it all and he wanted it so badly his chest ached. Tessa turned her brilliant smile on him, laughing at some joke at Gavin's expense that he'd missed in his daydreaming, and he wondered what he would do to be able to see that smile for the rest of his life. To be able to kiss it off her lips right there in the middle of trivia night.

Anything.

The answer was immediate and so clear it knocked him off balance. He'd do anything to have forever with her.

But, of course, that was the problem, wasn't it? Because she wasn't his to have, and he wasn't even certain she wanted to be.

Tomorrow, when they were away from Aster Bay and its prying eyes and all the reminders that he was not supposed to fall for his best friend's daughter—tomorrow they'd talk about all the things they'd been avoiding talking about. Things like what happened when Ethan came home, when the festival was over, when Sugar Grapes closed for the season?

She squeezed his hand, a silent question in her eyes to match the thousands of questions swirling in his mind. He took a sip of his gin and tonic and squeezed back.

Chapter Twenty-seven

"Tessa?" Jamie's voice rang out through the darkened house.

"In here!" Tessa called from her bedroom.

"Why are all the lights off?" he asked, his voice getting closer.

"Because I was going to wait for you on the front porch, but then I realized I hadn't packed my blue blouse and I thought maybe blue was a better color for promoting the festival because blue is kind of like purple and purple is the color of red wine. I don't know why they call it red wine when it's really purple."

She whipped another set of hangers to the end of the closet. When had she accumulated so much clothing? She was pretty sure she'd arrived at Ethan's with only two bags, and now she had a closet full of clothes. She'd never had a closet full of clothes before—too cumbersome when it came time to move again.

"And now I can't find the blue blouse. Oh! Maybe I should wear a Nuthatch t-shirt? I don't have shirts with the Sugar Grapes logo but I could promote the vineyard at least. Or maybe—"

Jamie's arms closed around her waist from behind, his chin resting on her head, and she broke off mid-sentence, melting back into his solid form behind her.

"Breathe, baby," he said, his voice level and calm and somehow still deep and sexy enough to do all sorts of inconvenient things to her when she needed to find something to wear on TV. "I'm sure whatever you packed will be fine."

Tessa sighed, pushing another hanger out of the way half-heartedly. "Kyla came by after work and helped me pick out three options."

"What's wrong with those options?"

"Nothing. But what if they're not the *right* options? What if my perfect television-debut outfit is still in this closet?"

"It's not." His lips brushed her hair and she softened against him even further. "And it's just a local morning show."

"According to Gavin they're the biggest morning news show in New England. That's not *just* anything," she argued, but she let herself lean back against him and wrapped her arms around his to pull them tighter around her waist.

He nuzzled into her hair. "They are going to love you no matter what you wear." She sighed and turned in his arms to meet his lips in a quiet kiss. "Now can we stop tearing apart your closet and get on the road? You'll be beautiful in anything. I do like this skirt, though. Did you dress up just for me?" he asked. His hands dropped to squeeze her ass through the stretchy fabric of her pencil skirt, as if to punctuate his point.

"You wouldn't tell me where we were going for dinner. I wanted to be prepared for any dress code."

He hummed in approval, the calluses on his palms snagging on the fabric as he ran his hands appreciatively over her backside. She loved how much he loved her curves. He pulled her against him, and she could feel the beginnings of his erection pressed against her belly.

She laughed. "I thought we had to get on the road?"

"You're right," he sighed, stepping away. But that hungry look lingered in his eyes as he snagged her bag from the edge of her bed, holding out his other hand for her to take.

As they stepped out onto the porch, he dropped her hand, walking ahead to put her bag in the car while she locked up. In less than two hours they'd be in an entirely different city, where she could hold his hand outside of the four walls of her father's house or Jamie's cottage, where she could kiss him on the street if she wanted without worrying that someone's nephew's cousin twice removed would see and report back to her father.

He held the car door open for her and she hesitated for a fraction of a second, wondering just how bad it would be to rise up on her toes and kiss him anyway. What were the odds that someone would see them?

And would it be so bad if they did?

Jamie grinned, the edges of his eyes crinkling and that dimple in his left cheek popping out. "Whatever you're thinking about, yes, please," he said.

"You don't know what I'm thinking about," she teased, taking a step closer to him. Too close to just be friendly. Closer than she should stand next to him in her father's driveway.

His eyes sparkled. "I know I'm going to like it." His pinky stroked the side of her hand, a single point of contact that made her heart pound and heat rush between her legs. "Anytime you're thinking dirty thoughts, you get this look on your face..." He huffed out a breath, shaking his head. "It's fucking adorable." She shuffled a half step closer, her breasts brushing his chest. A low rumble sounded in the back of his throat. "Get in the car, Tess."

She slid down into the passenger seat of his car, never taking her eyes off him. He leaned towards her as though he might kiss her, then seemed to remember where they were and closed the door behind her instead. She swallowed down the disappointment.

Stupid. You know he can't kiss you here, she thought. Still, she couldn't help the pang of longing to have him claim her, to kiss her and touch her and not care if her father found out, even if she knew that was asking too much.

They pulled out of her father's driveway in silence, winding through the streets of Aster Bay. As they passed the town common, they waved at Natalia, out walking her dogs, the black labs chasing leaves as they fluttered to the ground. At the light at the top of the hill, Ricky DaSilva drove by in his pickup, the back loaded down with crates of produce, honking and waving in greeting as he passed.

"Oh, that reminds me," Tessa said, pulling her notebook out of her purse. She flipped past pages of notes, past the sketches she'd drawn of the view from the roof of Lemon and Thyme, of the list of her favorite farmer's market finds. On a clean sheet, she began jotting down notes.

"What's that?" Jamie asked, glancing over.

"I told Ricky I'd make the cake for the baby's christening. This morning, while I was in the shower, I had an idea," she said, her pen moving faster over the page. "What if, instead of a regular layer cake, it's a vertical layer cake made from a cardamom banana cake—because Cheryl loves Grama's banana bread so much—and a caramel cream cheese frosting, because—"

"Ricky will eat anything with caramel," Jamie said, nodding.

"Exactly," she grinned. "I just wanted to write it down

before I forgot." She glanced at him, the crinkles around his eyes and his dimples on full display as he suppressed a smile of his own. "What?" she asked, suddenly self-conscious.

"Nothing," he said. "It's perfect for them. They're going to love it."

At every stop sign, someone else passed by outside—Carla getting into her car at the diner after a long shift, Mrs. Blumenthal trimming the bushes in front of her house, Norm in his banana-yellow convertible shivering against the chill in the air. At the edge of town, they passed the goat farm and Tessa jotted a note in her notebook to stop by when they got back to town to bring Michelle her latest goat cheese ice cream creation.

She realized suddenly that she knew the names of every person that had waved at Jamie's car, that they all knew her. She had stories about these people now—the day she'd met with Norm about the festival's contract with The Barclay and he'd tried to play hardball while also reminiscing about playing capture the flag with her parents as kids; the time Ricky had shown up at Sugar Grapes with an unexpected delivery of quince because she'd mentioned in passing wanting to experiment with them; or the time Natalia had covered the register at the bakery when Tessa was short staffed so she could run to the bathroom. She knew their favorite cupcakes and their allergies, who was off gluten and who needed a cup of tea with their donut. But she also knew that Ricky had been practicing his swaddling on squashes, that Mrs. Blumenthal video chatted with her grandchildren every Saturday morning, that Pastor Davis secretly checked the football scores on his phone during the hymns.

Somehow she'd collected all these people the same way she'd accumulated all that clothing, and she couldn't help but feel like they'd collected her as well.

Jamie pulled the car onto the highway, his hand settling on her knee now that they were out of town. "You're awfully quiet over there."

"Just looking at the trees," she lied, uncertain even as she said it why she was lying. "We didn't get colors like this in Vegas."

"Were you in Vegas long?" he asked.

"About four years."

"And before Vegas?"

"Before that was about six months in Tampa, and before that was six years in South Carolina. That's the longest we stayed anywhere. Before South Carolina, we bounced around a lot, moving every year or so—Detroit, Portland, Kennebunk, Atlanta. Oh, and there was the year we spent in Virginia. And before that, four or five years in Phoenix. I was still pretty young then. I don't really remember the details."

It was the first time she'd listed it out like that in years, and she felt somewhat lighter for it. She'd learned early on that when you moved as much as she and her mother had without a job or something to justify it, people started to look at you strangely, started to whisper about why you moved so much. No one ever considered it was just the way Stephanie Cordeiro was—they'd stay in one place until something went wrong, until her mother had reason to worry that someone might be angry with her or might try to discard her first, and then they'd leave. It had taken Tessa years to realize that not everyone operated that way.

Jamie's fingers stroked the inside of her knee. "That must have been hard. Moving around so much." His words were careful, but they didn't sound judgmental. Just cautious. Like he recognized that she was peeling back another layer of herself and letting him see this messy corner of her life that she usually kept hidden from view.

"Yeah, it was," she said, sinking into her seat. "It's nice to stay in one place for a while. In Vegas, there were different people around every night. Even my co-workers changed all the time. It was like moving while standing still." He hummed like he understood what she meant. "I know I've only been in Aster Bay a few months, but it already feels more like—"

She stopped herself, glancing at Jamie, unsure how he'd react. Maybe he liked the idea that she was temporary. Maybe he didn't want to hear that she'd been thinking about sticking around for a while.

His hand slid higher up her thigh. "Like what, princess?"

"Like home."

The corner of his mouth kicked up and that tiny movement was like the clouds parting. Relief washed over her and she placed her hand on top of his, sliding it even higher up her leg, under the hem of her skirt. His fingers stroked over the smooth skin there and he made that low rumbly sound again.

He kept his eyes focused on the road as his fingers slid higher and higher up her thigh. His entire body went tight when his fingertips brushed the exposed curls at the apex of her thighs. She let her knees drop to the side and he stroked a finger over her slit in gentle passes, like he was hardly aware he was driving her wild.

"Jamie," she whined, canting her hips into his touch.

"What's your rush, baby? We've got a long drive." He slid one finger through her folds, just up to the first knuckle, sliding it up and down the length of her pussy. "Is this what you were hoping for when you decided not to put on panties?"

"Actually, I was hoping you'd finger me at dinner."

The pad of his finger found her clit, gently sliding over the stiff little button. "Seems to me you don't want to wait all the way until dinner." He pressed slow, firm circles over her clit and her breathing grew heavier. Jamie glanced at her, the smirk on his lips making it clear he knew exactly what he was doing to her. "Seems to me you want my fingers now."

"I always want them."

"Good girl."

He played with her clit with deliberately unhurried slides of his fingertip. Every time her orgasm began to take shape, he'd gentle his touch, drag his finger through her growing wetness and paint it over the place where she ached for him.

"We have another hour before we get to Boston," he mused. "How many times do you think I can make you come before we get there?"

"Only one way to find out."

He glanced at her, his eyes dark and hungry as they roved her face and the place where his hand disappeared beneath her skirt. "Pull up your skirt, princess. I want to see you."

She did as she was told, sliding the stretchy material up around her hips. Any truck that pulled up alongside them would be able to see her—see them. After weeks of hiding, the idea that someone might see Jamie's hands on her only made her wetter.

"Now you," she said, tilting her chin towards the obvious erection tenting the front of his pants.

He shook his head. "It's hard enough to focus on the road with my fingers in your pussy. We're not getting into an accident today." She pouted, but she knew he was right.

He laughed at her disappointed expression. "Don't worry, princess. You can have my cock all you want when this car stops."

She quirked an eyebrow at him, sliding her hand down his wrist and using two of her own fingers to press two of his into her pussy. "Anywhere I want?" she asked.

"Anywhere but moving vehicles," he confirmed, fucking her slowly with his fingers.

She withdrew her own fingers, now coated in her wetness, and held them up to his lips. He turned his head just enough to suck them into his mouth, scraping his teeth along the pads of her fingers as he licked her juices from her fingers, never taking his eyes from the road.

"What if I want you in the parking garage at the hotel?" she asked. He growled around her fingers. "Right here in your front seat where anyone could see us. What if I can't wait until we get to our room to have you inside me?"

She pulled her fingers from his mouth and gasped as he curled his fingers inside her pussy.

"You want people to see how badly you need my cock?" he asked.

She was on fire, her hips moving restlessly as he drove her towards orgasm with his clever fingers and his dirty words, but it was this—the idea of someone seeing them together, of not trying to hide how much she wanted him— that had her hovering on the edge.

"Yes," she gasped.

"Me too," he said, his thumb doing dangerous and wonderful things to her clit.

"I want everyone to know that I—" She broke off on a moan.

"That you what, Tess?" His voice was rough, like sandpaper on her skin.

"That I'm yours," she said.

"Then come for me."

Her hips shot up from the seat, driving his fingers deeper as the orgasm rolled through her. She rode his hand until her thighs stopped shaking, then she slumped down in her seat, his fingers still inside her.

"Fuck, you're beautiful," he groaned.

"That's one," she said with a wicked grin.

He laughed. "That sounded like a challenge, princess."

She shrugged, her breathing slowing. "Maybe it is."

With a determined growl, he got back to work.

Five.

The answer to how many times he could make her come with his fingers alone before they got to Boston was five.

Chapter Twenty-eight

In the end, they skipped the tour of the city Jamie had planned to take her on. He hadn't been able to wait even five minutes after checking into the hotel to get her naked, spread out on the bed for him. After burying his face between her thighs and licking her to an orgasm that left his chin wet with her arousal, they decided to order in room service rather than get dressed and leave the cocoon of their hotel room.

They ate bowls of clam chowder loaded with tiny oyster crackers and shared an overpriced lobster roll in bed, Tessa dressed only in Jamie's shirt, him wearing nothing but his jeans. She snagged the last piece of lobster claw meat that had fallen onto the plate and popped it between her lips.

"What is that flavor? Tarragon and…?" she asked, licking the dressing from her fingers.

"Celery salt," Jamie said, dragging the last bit of toasted bun through the bits of dressing that had remained on the plate.

"Hmm. I'm going to have to steal that." She leaned against him in the giant bed, her bare feet teasing at the cuffs of his jeans.

Jamie set the empty dishes aside and pulled Tessa into his lap, his hands running up and down her thighs, just below the hem of his shirt. A thousand things thrummed through his mind—*Every day could be like this. Stay with me. I think I'm falling in love with you.* But what he said was, "You look good in my clothes."

She grinned. "I'm glad you think so because I don't plan on giving this shirt back."

He laughed and leaned in to capture her lips.

"What was it like growing up here?" she asked.

"Somerville isn't exactly Boston. It's smaller. Quieter."

"Not as small or quiet as Aster Bay, though."

He chuckled. "Definitely not."

"And you lived there your whole life?" she asked, drawing patterns in his dusting of chest hair with her fingertip.

"Until college." He caught her hand and pressed it to his lips, then held that hand to his chest and leaned back against the quilted headboard. "By then, my brother Daemon had already moved to New York to become an actor. My parents were great, but they weren't around much anymore. Mom traveled for work—insurance—and dad wanted to go with her more often since we were older."

He shrugged, as though he hadn't been so lonely he could hardly breathe most of the time, as though he hadn't missed the days of family dinners and board game nights from when he and Daemon were children.

"I got into culinary school in Providence and it seemed like the right move," he continued. "Far enough from home that mom and dad wouldn't pop in unannounced, but not so far that I couldn't go home whenever I wanted to."

"When did you move to Aster Bay?" she asked.

"Pretty much right away. I met Ethan and Baz at orientation. Baz was giving Ethan a hard time because he'd decided not to move into the house Baz and Gavin had rented and they needed a third roommate."

"Why didn't he—" She stopped herself, the realization making her face fall. "Oh. For me. He didn't move in with them for me."

Jamie tightened his grip on her hand. "That was part of it. Your mom didn't like the idea of you visiting him at a house he shared with a bunch of other college guys. Can't say I blame her. You two were living with the Harts by then, anyway, and there was talk of a wedding. It made sense for him to stay there."

"So you moved in with Gavin and Baz."

"And the rest is history," he said, running his thumb over the back of her hand.

"Did you always know you'd end up staying?"

"No. But after my parents died... I didn't have a home anymore. Daemon was touring the country with some show, and I didn't want to go back to that house alone. We sold the house and I used my half to put a down payment on my cottage. You know the rest." He ran his free hand up her thigh, focusing on the slide of his skin over hers as he framed the question he'd been afraid to ask her for weeks. "Have you ever thought about doing something like that?"

"Buying a cottage?" she asked, an amused look of confusion wrinkling her brow.

"No. Choosing a place and making it yours."

His heart pounded against their hands where they lay on his chest as he waited for her answer. She twined her fingers with his, keeping her palm pressed to his heart.

"Yeah," she said, her voice soft. "Lately, I think about it all the time. Choosing a place...and a person."

Reckless hope swelled in his chest as he surged forward and kissed her, imbuing that kiss with all the things he was afraid to hope for.

She broke away, framing his face with one hand. "But what would that even look like, Jamie?"

"It would look like this," he said, gesturing between them. "More of this. You could keep the bakery, or you could open another one that's not connected to the vineyard." His pulse raced and his words tumbled over themselves in his rush to paint the picture for her, to help her see just how perfect their lives could be. "We could grow the festival into the biggest and best food and wine festival in New England. You could move into my cottage, or we could get a place of our own."

He pressed his forehead to hers, closing his eyes against the images that came next—Tessa dressed in white and agreeing to be his wife, Tessa round with his child, endless Saturday mornings at the farmer's market, waking up with his arms around her each morning and falling asleep beside her each night.

"I know it's fast, but—"

"I like your cottage," she said softly, her hand tangling in his hair. "What about Ethan?"

He pulled back so he could meet her eyes, so she could see that he meant every word. "I'll tell him about us."

"I've only just started to get to know Ethan, but even I know he's not going to be okay with you and I being together."

"Let me worry about that. If I can keep you—" He broke off, clearing his throat, and met her eyes again. "I'll talk to Ethan."

Her voice was small when she asked, "What if he doesn't understand?"

"Then I'll make him understand."

Her eyes darted between his, the corners of her lips

pulling down. "I was supposed to come here for a fresh start. To rebuild a relationship with my dad, not to come between him and his best friend," she said, her voice catching.

"Hey," he soothed, pulling her closer and dropping a kiss on her temple. "Ethan is my family, but you…" *You're the love of my life.* "We'll figure it out."

She nodded. "We'll tell him together."

He loved her. He loved her resolve and her courage and her bright, beautiful heart. There had never been any chance that he would be able to let her go, even if keeping her meant he risked losing Ethan. Somehow, he'd make Ethan understand. He wasn't naïve enough to think Ethan would accept Jamie and Tessa's relationship right away, but he had hope that with time, when Ethan saw how happy they made each other, he'd come around. He had to.

"Tell me more about what we'll do," she said.

Tessa slid her hand down his chest to flip open the button on Jamie's jeans, his cock kicking in anticipation of her touch. She slid her hand into the opening of his pants, wrapping her fist around his rapidly hardening cock and giving it a slow pump.

He released a shaky breath, his own hands sliding under the edge of his shirt where it rested on her thighs. "We'll go strawberry picking in the summer," he said, dragging the shirt up and over her hips. "And we'll go swimming in the bay when the days get hot and humid."

He was fully erect now, his cock jutting from the opening in his pants as she slid her hand up and down his shaft, but he wanted to go slowly. To savor this moment.

"Rumor has it there's a private cove at the edge of the beach at The Barclay," she said.

"There is," he confirmed, struggling to follow the thread

of the conversation when her hands were on his cock.

"I'd like to go there at night and swim naked under the stars."

He cursed under his breath and pulled the shirt over her head, drawing one of her nipples into his mouth. She let out a little moan as he played with the stiff peak.

"What else?" she asked.

He paused just long enough to push his jeans down over his hips, allowing her better access to his cock. She grinned and slid down his body, taking his jeans with her, before crawling back up the bed towards him. She was like a lioness, all hidden strength and grace, and her tits brushed his leg when she took him in hand once again.

"What else, Jamie?" she repeated, dragging her thumb over the slit at the top of his crown.

"We'll go to the open-air concerts in the park in Bristol in June," he said, sliding one hand down the line of her spine to cup her ass, his fingertips digging into the porcelain curve. "And to Waterfire in Providence. I'll take you hiking in the woods in Tiverton."

She dipped her head and took the tip of his cock between her lips, licking away the pearl of precum that had formed there. He gripped her ass tighter as pleasure began to coil at the base of his spine.

"What else?" she asked again, before dropping back down onto his length, taking him so deep he hit the back of her throat.

He slid his fingers between her cheeks to stroke her most secret places as she bobbed on his cock, and he fought down the urge to buck up into her mouth. But as his fingertip grazed the tight circle of her back entrance and she moaned around him, it took all his restraint not to come on the spot.

"We'll go sledding at St. Anthony's," he said, his voice gritty and dark as his pleasure built. "And when you're red-faced and cold, I'll take you home and warm you up." He slid his finger into her pussy to slick it with her arousal before pressing it to her pleated rim. He slipped in up to the first knuckle, loving the way she shuddered beneath his touch, increasing her speed as she swallowed him down. "I'll make love to you in every room of the cottage. On every surface. Until you know it's your home as much as mine."

She lifted her eyes to look at him through her eyelashes as she continued to suck his cock, the desire—not just to fuck, but to build that life together—that he felt in his chest reflected in her raven-dark eyes.

"Fuck, princess, look at you." He circled his finger, sliding in deeper when she lifted her hips to press against him.

"I want that," she moaned.

"Which part?"

"All of it. All of you."

He caught her chin and tilted her lips up to his, holding her still for his kiss. He pulled his finger from inside her, loving the way she whined in protest.

"Ride me, baby."

He reached for the box of condoms he'd dropped on the nightstand, but she stilled his hand.

Tessa straddled him. "Can I?" she asked, using one hand to line his cock up with her entrance.

He stared at the place where she held him, her skin against his skin, and realization rocked through him as he recalled his own words.

If you let me inside you with nothing between us, then you're mine. Not just for a few weeks. Not just until you take off for whatever place is next on your list. Mine.

He met her gaze and knew she was thinking of it, too.

"Are you mine, princess?" he asked.

Holding his gaze, she nodded, then slid down onto him in one smooth stroke, her intense heat washing over him. He'd never tire of the sight of himself disappearing inside her, of the way she stretched to make room for him, the way her eyes fell closed when he bottomed out. He'd never tire of anything about her.

She cupped her breasts, pinching her nipples and rolling them between her fingers, as she rode him in slow waves of her hips, his hands clamped onto her thighs to hold her steady.

"What else?" she gasped as she impaled herself on his length over and over again.

"Stay with me and find out," he said, moving one hand to play with her clit. "Don't go to Italy or France or wherever the fuck you were going to run away to. Don't run away at all. Stay here and be mine."

"I will," she said, slamming down on him harder and faster.

"Say the words, princess." He clenched his teeth to stave off his orgasm. Not yet. He wouldn't come yet, not before she did.

"I'll stay with you."

She gripped his wrist, holding his hand to her clit as she trembled, her pussy clamping down around him in wave after wave of pleasure. He roared her name as he came, driving his hips up into her again and again as his vision went white and fuzzy at the edges and fire tore through his body. She swayed above him, falling against his chest. He moved to help her off of him, but she wrapped her arms around him, pressing her hips against his with a little noise of protest.

"Not yet."

He banded his arms across her back, tucking her against him and pressed a kiss to her forehead as he softened inside her. "Not yet," he agreed.

Mine.

Chapter Twenty-nine

Baz: How long until you guys are on? I don't think I can take much more of this.

Gavin: This is the top-rated local morning show in New England.

Baz: They just did ten minutes on the best places to go leaf peeping. Who the fuck goes leaf peeping?

Ethan: My mom.

Gavin: My mom's entire book club did a day trip up the coast to go leaf peeping.

Jamie: The people who watch these morning shows.

Baz: Jesus Christ. I thought we were trying to advertise to a younger demographic, not your moms.
Baz: Ask Tessa. She'd agree with me. No one her age is watching this shit.

Gavin: All press is good press.

Jamie: She says you're right. But she also says to stop complaining because you're not the one who had to be up at 4 a.m. to do this show.

Gavin: You're welcome, by the way.
Gavin: For getting you on TELEVISION.

Ethan: I think you hurt his feelings.

Baz: Can we back up to the part where she said I was right?

Jamie: No.

Gavin: Ethan, how are you even watching this? You can't get local Boston stations in Florida.

Ethan: The wonders of modern technology, my friend.

Jamie: Tessa sent him a link to stream it online.

Ethan: The wonders of modern technology AND daughters.

Baz: Is anyone else watching this shit? No way are New Hampshire's leaves any more peepable than Rhode Island's.

Jamie: Did the big bad local news anchor offend you, Baz?

Ethan: He's not wrong. Aster Bay has some top-notch leaf peeping.
Ethan: According to my mom.

Gavin: See if you can work that in, Jamie. Like a segue.

Jamie: I'm turning off my phone now.

Gavin: Break a leg!

Ethan: You've got this.

Baz: Don't fuck it up.

Tessa speared another cranberry on the end of a long wooden skewer and plunged it into the bubbling pot of sugar on the stovetop. She and Jamie had been at the small television studio where *Sunrise in the City* was filmed for hours. The producers had decided at the last minute that it would be great to periodically cut back to the two chefs as they worked in the studio's makeshift kitchen, until they finally ended the segment with an interview and the overly coiffed hosts taste testing their dishes. It was an odd way to cook, but not terribly different than when guests in Vegas would press their faces up against the window of Marisa Sinclair's bakery to catch a glimpse of someone icing a cake.

She swirled the fruit through the syrup, then set it aside on a rack to cool before shifting on her feet and skewering another red berry for dipping. Why did she agree to wear heels and a pencil skirt for this taping? Though she kept catching Jamie staring at her ass, so it wasn't all bad.

Beside her, Jamie shook a dry pan toasting pine nuts with one hand and whisked his chardonnay browned butter with another. She caught his eye as he set the pine nuts off the heat. He dumped the nuts into a small ramekin on the workstation that would look good on camera when he plated up his dish—the producers had been very clear that they were to plate their dishes on camera while the hosts interviewed them—and poured a generous swirl of oil into the pan, preparing to fry his sage leaves. She smiled to herself, knowing both the sage and the pine nuts were her additions to his dish, the small mark she was leaving on his plate.

It felt good to work like this, side by side with Jamie. They couldn't speak or it would interfere with the filming at the anchor's desk mere steps away from the kitchen set, but every glance, every time their hands brushed on the workstation or he placed his hand to her waist as he stepped around her, felt like an entire conversation. She thought of all the times they'd have together in the future when they would prep a meal side by side like this—all the Friday nights alone in his cottage, all the holidays and birthdays. Maybe they'd bring back Sunday dinners, the two of them cooking her grandmother's recipes and some of their own and welcoming their friends and family for a weekly meal.

A twinge of nerves hit her as she considered how many of those moments depended on Ethan being okay with his daughter and his best friend being together, but Jamie seemed sure that it would work out, and he knew her father better than she did. For the hundredth time, she swallowed down the fizzy panic, the pre-emptive alarm bells urging her to get out, to leave before Jamie could decide she wasn't worth the trouble. When she looked at Jamie, when he looked at her, she felt like maybe, just maybe she was worth it after all.

Jamie dipped a spoon into his browned butter sauce,

capturing the smallest amount on the tip of the metal curve, and held it out to her with a questioning eyebrow raise. Her stomach flip-flopped as she realized he was asking her opinion on his sauce. She leaned forward, his hand beneath the spoon brushing her bottom lip as she sipped the sauce from the spoon. The nutty brown butter combined with the rich reduced champagne and the bright herbs as it coated her tongue. She licked the last drop of it from her top lip, fighting the smile when his eyes heated at the sight, and nodded. It was perfect. *They* were perfect.

Tessa lifted a cooled, candied cranberry from the wire rack and held it out to Jamie to taste. The firm berry in its sticky candy coating shone under the studio lights like a jewel held between her thumb and forefinger. Rather than taking the berry from her fingers with his own, however, Jamie held her wrist and leaned forward to capture the tips of her fingers, and the berry with them, between his lips. His tongue swiped the cranberry and he sucked her fingertips clean, before he righted himself with a smirk, her pulse pounding between her legs.

Holy shit, this man.

He gave her the smallest of nods and returned his attention to dropping sage leaves into his now-hot oil, and she had the strangest desire to poke her finger in the dimple on his cheek.

"We'll be back, with chefs Jameson Chase and Tessa Cordeiro after these words from our sponsors," the female host, Wendy, announced and Tessa could practically feel the camera sweeping over her as she began scooping what was left of her white chocolate buttercream into a piping bag.

Those final moments, as Wendy reapplied her hot pink lipstick and Gene, the other host, called for a refill on his coffee, flew by in a whirlwind of retrieving her uncut Swiss roll from the chiller and dropping candied cranberries into the designated ramekin. Before she knew it, they were counting them back in.

"Good morning, Chefs. We can't wait to taste what you've been working on all morning," Wendy said as she and Gene sauntered onto the kitchen set.

"Good morning, Wendy. Thanks for having us," Jamie said with an easy smile as he effortlessly formed another agnolotti.

"You two are the co-chairs for Aster Bay's Food and Wine Festival this year, isn't that right?" Gene asked, his smile reaching all the way to his eyes as he surveyed their work.

"That's right," Tessa said as she began slicing her Swiss roll into thin slices that would show off the perfect swirl of cake and buttercream. "We think people are really going to love all the new programs we've got in store for them this year."

"Like axe throwing and spa treatments?" Wendy asked with a quirk of her eyebrow that wasn't entirely friendly.

Jamie chuckled, setting aside one perfectly formed agnolotti and starting the process over with another one. "It's a little unconventional, we know, but Tessa and I feel strongly that we want this festival to show off all that Aster Bay has to offer, not just our incredible food and wine."

"Chef, your restaurant, Lemon and Thyme, has been a fixture in Aster Bay for the last several years, and before that you were the Executive Chef at another popular local spot. But, Tessa," Wendy began, turning that sharp eye her way, and it wasn't lost on Tessa that Wendy had referred to Jamie as 'Chef' but was using Tessa's first name instead. "You're a newcomer. Your bakery only just opened a month ago."

"Sugar Grapes is a pop-up bakery at Nuthatch Vineyards, bringing back a beloved Aster Bay fixture for the holidays,"

Tessa said, her smile tight as she recited the line Gavin had written for her about the bakery.

"Bringing back?" Gene asked.

"Tessa's from Aster Bay originally," Jamie said, all charm and ease. "Sugar Grapes was her grandmother's bakery until Mrs. Hart retired some years back while Tessa was working in Las Vegas under a James Beard Award-winning pastry chef. There was no one better to take over Sugar Grapes or to co-chair this festival. As the chair of our Merchant's Association likes to say, Aster Bay is in Tessa's blood."

Tessa's heart pounded as she listened to Jamie list off her qualifications and claim her for the town, pride in his voice. She hadn't realized how badly she'd wanted to be claimed, not just by Jamie but by Aster Bay. To really be one of them.

"Well, now I'm even more excited to taste your food," Gene said, stepping closer.

Jamie demonstrated dropping the agnolotti into the boiling water. As he placed a baked lobster tail in the center of the white plate and surrounded it with a ring of al dente pumpkin agnolotti, he talked about the theory behind offering package vacations to Aster Bay as part of the festival, the goal of attracting a younger crowd and showcasing that Aster Bay was more than just a beach town. He added fried sage leaves and pine nuts with meticulous precision and spooned a swirl of his chardonnay brown butter over the top as he described the popularity of their girls' weekend package. With a quick wipe of the rim of the plate—not that it needed it; the plate was pristine—Jamie spun the plate to face Gene and Wendy and held out a fork to each of them.

After a pause to let the camera capture the full effect of the plated dish, they each took a bite, Gene raving about the delicacy of the pasta dough and sweet pumpkin filling and Wendy marveling at the tender cook on the lobster.

He made it look so easy, to plate and chat and smile and charm them all without missing a beat. Nerves bubbled up within Tessa as the hosts stepped towards her and she felt the cameras shift to focus on her food. Being charming wasn't as easy for her, and she certainly didn't present pristine plates the way Jamie did. What if her food looked childish compared to his? What if the candied ginger crystals didn't look like gemstones as she'd intended and they just looked like a child's craft project? What if this was just like Vegas all over again, and the food that she'd poured her heart and soul into was just a new embarrassment for the people who had trusted her? What if—

Jamie's hand settled low on her back and all her racing thoughts calmed. She could do this.

"Tessa, tell us about this beach bonfire. I understand that was your idea," Gene said kindly as his eyes roved the confections on her station.

"I like to think it was a team effort," she said with a smile, reaching for the Swiss roll to slice off another piece, careful not to press too hard so she maintained the swirl in the middle. "Jamie and I went for a walk, and we realized that one of Aster Bay's most beloved natural assets—the beach—is underutilized in the off-season. But what if it didn't need to be?"

The more she talked, the easier it became. Jamie's hand fell away from her back as she moved about her station, but she still felt him there beside her, a silent presence firmly in her corner, ready to support her if she needed and happy to step back and let her shine. The realization sent warmth tingling through her and, combined with the adrenaline of being on camera, converged in a throbbing ache between her legs.

I love him.

The thought should have been more surprising. She'd certainly never had that thought about anyone else before. But it didn't feel surprising—it felt inevitable.

She couldn't wait until they were alone so she could tell him.

"I understand you've gotten the local university involved," Wendy said.

Right. Still interviewing.

"That's right, Wendy. Our good friend is a professor there and he helped us connect with the art department. There will be ten visual arts majors constructing a giant gingerbread house out of sand as the centerpiece of our beach bonfire." She piped a swirl of buttercream on top of the Swiss roll slice and drizzled it with cranberry coulis. "We'll have mulled wine and red wine hot chocolate and make s'mores by the bonfire. It might be chilly, but how often do you get to have a wintertime beach bonfire?"

She dropped a trio of candied cranberries on top of the plate and dusted it with the finely diced candied ginger before sliding the plate across the workstation to the hosts.

Gene didn't need to be invited. He grabbed a fork and dug into the decadent cake, groaning as he ate it. "That is the best cake I've ever eaten," he said.

"It is quite nice," Wendy agreed, sliding her fork through the cranberry coulis that had pooled on the edge of the plate.

"These are just two of the dishes we'll be serving at the opening dinner for the festival next week. And there will be tastings, demonstrations, and workshops all weekend," Jamie said as a producer off-camera swirled their finger in the air in a signal to wrap it up.

"Tickets are still available, but we do expect to sell out," Tessa chimed in, taking half a step closer to Jamie.

"Trust me, folks," Gene said into the camera, "you don't want to miss your chance to taste this food. You better believe I'll be buying a ticket."

Wendy rattled off the website where people could purchase tickets and thanked them for coming, then handed off the segment to the local weatherman who stood across the set in front of a giant green screen.

And then it was done. The cameras turned away and PAs rushed in to clear their workstations and usher Jamie and Tessa off set.

Once off camera, she slumped against the wall, leaning her head back and closing her eyes. Her feet ached and, now that the adrenaline had worn off, she was tired, but she couldn't keep the smile from her face. They'd just killed it, and she knew it.

And she loved him. God, she loved him so much.

Jamie rested his hands on her hips and stepped close enough that she could breathe him in, the clean scent of cedar and soap enveloping her. He leaned close, pressing his lips to her ear, and growled, "You were incredible. Tell me, princess, you wearing any panties under your skirt today?"

She laughed, turning her head to capture his bottom lip between her teeth. "Take me home and find out."

Chapter Thirty

As his car crossed the town line into Aster Bay, Jamie reluctantly extricated his hand from Tessa's, placing it firmly on the steering wheel so he wouldn't be tempted to touch her again. She'd come on his fingers twice since they'd begun driving home and it still wasn't enough. It would never be enough.

She sighed beside him, and he glanced her way, feeling the melancholy of that sigh in every part of himself. She wriggled in her seat, setting her skirt to rights as she asked, "When do you want to tell him?"

No need to ask who the 'him' in question was. Ethan. The specter of her father—his best friend—took shape between them like a physical presence.

"I'll call him this afternoon. I just need to check in with Anabel first and see if she needs anything. I don't want to rush this conversation."

"Let me know when you're ready. I'll come over and we can call him together."

"No, Tess. This is one phone call I need to make myself."

"He's my father. You don't think I should—"

"No," Jamie said firmly. "He's going to be angry, and you

don't deserve any of that anger. Let him vent it on me."

Tessa rolled her eyes, an adorable smirk lifting one corner of her lips. "It's not like you did this on your own. I'm the one who started banging my dad's best friend."

"It's not the same," he said. He stared out the windshield, avoiding her eyes, as he admitted the part that weighed the heaviest on him. "I lied to him. I should have told him about us that first day when you showed up in my restaurant."

She scoffed. "Yeah, because that would have gone over well."

"I've had so many opportunities to tell him, and I never did. Every time he asked about you, I could have told him what was going on, and I didn't. There's nothing Ethan values more than honesty and I betrayed his trust." He glanced at her. "I need to be the one to tell him. After everything he's done for me, I owe him that much."

Her hand landed on his thigh, squeezing lightly. "Okay. And you'll come find me when you're done."

He nodded, swallowing down the lump in his throat and hating when she pulled her hand away, even though he knew it was the right thing to do. They were too close to the town center now, too close to where they could be seen. And the last thing he needed was for anyone to see them together before he had a chance to tell Ethan himself.

Jamie steered the car into the driveway at Ethan's house—somewhere along the line he'd started thinking of it as Tessa's house—and the gravel crunched under his tires. He turned off the engine and sent Tessa a soft smile. "Back to reality," he said.

She sighed that melancholy sigh again and he vowed to never give her a reason to make that sound again.

He retrieved her bag from his trunk, Tessa leaning one hip against his car and watching him with an attentiveness that made him want to push her up against the car and kiss her right there in the driveway.

"If you don't stop looking at me like that—" he warned.

"Is that a threat? Or a promise?" she laughed, turning towards the house. She paused, her posture stiffening. "Is that Ethan's truck?" she asked, gesturing to the back of the pickup visible along the side of the house.

Just then, the front door of the house flew open. Ethan stood in the open doorway, arms crossed over his chest and jaw tight.

Fuck. What happened?

"You're home early," Tessa said moving towards her father.

Jamie approached his friend where he stood like a statue on the porch. "What happened? Is Henry alright? Louise?" He set Tessa's bag down and scanned Ethan's eyes for some clue as to what had happened, but Ethan's gaze was firmly fixed on Tessa. "Talk to me, man."

Ethan's eyes snapped to Jamie's, fire flashing in his gaze for a fraction of a second before his fist collided with Jamie's jaw with a sickening thwack. Jamie stumbled back, clutching his face. Blood rushed in his ears, dulling the sound of Tessa's startled shriek. He'd never been punched before, at least not like that. He'd had schoolyard scuffles like any kid growing up, but he'd never been clocked by a grown man who threw the punch like he intended for Jamie to go down and stay down.

"What are you doing?" Tessa screamed at her father, her hands pulling at Jamie until he turned towards her.

She took his face in her hands tenderly, examining the throbbing place where Ethan's fist had made contact, but Jamie never took his eyes off of Ethan's, barely feeling Tessa's touch.

"You know," he said, getting to his feet.

"Yeah, I fucking know," Ethan barked. "The whole goddamn world *knows*." He took a step like he intended to punch Jamie again, but then thought better of it as his eyes focused on Tessa, her fingers still pressing lightly against Jamie's rapidly swelling jawline. "You were supposed to be mentoring her, not giving people another reason to gossip about her. Now when you Google her name, the first thing that comes up is you asking if she's wearing any—"

"What the fuck are you talking about?" Jamie asked, stepping out of Tessa's reach and towards his best friend.

Ethan put up a hand and took a step back, a warning that Jamie shouldn't get too close.

"Your mic was still broadcasting when you asked my daughter about her goddamn underwear," Ethan said.

Jamie's thoughts turned to static as his last hopes of getting Ethan to understand slipped through his fingers. How would Ethan ever understand this? Not only had Jamie lied to him, repeatedly and purposefully, not only had he been sleeping with Ethan's daughter behind his back, but he'd also been caught saying filthy things to her on live television. He had promised to help Tessa see that the people in Aster Bay could view her as more than a walking scandal, and then he'd gone and done the one thing that would ensure that never happened.

"Gavin's been trying to get a handle on the story all morning," Ethan continued, rage simmering beneath his words.

"What story?" Tessa asked, still not connecting the dots.

Jamie held Ethan's eyes as he answered her, his hands beginning to shake. "That the chefs in the photos of the festival are sleeping together," he guessed.

Ethan grunted an affirmation. "I've had four calls from Norm already wanting assurances that you two aren't mismanaging festival funds to finance your—affair," he spat.

But Jamie couldn't worry about Norm or the festival right now. He couldn't care if the entire town thought he was scum for what he'd done or who he'd done it with. Not when he was so close to losing Ethan, the man who more like a brother than his actual flesh and blood sibling.

"Can we talk about this?" Jamie asked, his throat so tight he was almost surprised he got the words out at all.

"The time to talk was before you went and—" Ethan shook his head like he couldn't even bring himself to say it. "You lied to me."

"I did," Jamie said, his heart slamming against his rib cage. This was not how this was supposed to happen, and with each icy glance Ethan sent his way Jamie could feel his best friend slipping away, walling himself off. And Jamie couldn't even blame him.

He had made this mess. He had lied to his best friend for weeks. If he had any hope of fixing this, he would have to face Ethan's wrath.

"Get the fuck off my property," Ethan snarled through gritted teeth.

Jamie stumbled back a step, the disgust in Ethan's voice slamming into his chest. His heart splintered under Ethan's vitriolic glare with fault lines he hadn't known existed. After all their years together, all the things they'd been through and all the times they'd stood by each other, this couldn't be the way it ended.

Tessa reached out to grip Jamie's hand as she turned to face her father, but he pulled his hand away. Her sharp intake of breath at his side, the way her shoulders immediately sagged, were like daggers in his spine. But he couldn't worry about that now. Just like he'd fix things with Aster Bay, he'd fix things with Tessa, too, *after* he fixed things with Ethan. She knew him better than any woman ever had—she'd understand.

"I said, get the fuck out of here," Ethan repeated.

"We didn't want you to find out like this," Jamie said, grasping at any chance to get Ethan to hear him.

"Then you should have fucking told me," Ethan spat, the low menace in his tone brooking no argument.

"You're right. I screwed up. Jesus Christ, Ethan, don't you think I know how badly I've fucked up here? But you're still my best friend," Jamie said, the panic that had been ricocheting around his mind spilling out into his voice.

He always knew Ethan had a temper, that there were some things he held sacred—family and honesty chief amongst them—but Jamie had also thought their friendship was sacred. At least, it was to Jamie.

There had to be something he could say, but he was unable to think with his heart flailing in his chest and his blood racing. And it was clear Ethan was in no place to listen. He needed to calm down and then Jamie would try again. He'd try again every damn day for the rest of his life if he had to, whatever it took to make Ethan listen, to make him understand how sorry he was, how he'd never intended to hurt him, how he'd never planned on falling in love with his best friend's daughter.

But he *was* in love with her, and he couldn't give her up. Not now that he'd finally found her.

"I don't know who you are," Ethan said, his voice cold enough to make the hair on the back of Jamie's neck stand on end. "I don't fucking know you at all."

"You have to know we didn't want to hurt you," he said.

"I don't know that at all," Ethan said, his eyes going wide and hard.

"Ethan, you are one of the most important people in my

life," Jamie said, struggling to keep his voice calm. "Tell me what to do. Tell me how to fix this."

All he said was, "Go."

Jamie stumbled down the porch steps, away from the two people who meant the most to him in the entire world. His feet were heavy and clumsy as the panic in his chest rose in his throat, his stomach lurching.

"Wait, Jamie! I'll come with you," Tessa called, following after him.

"Like hell you will," Ethan snapped.

Her step faltered, but she kept her eyes on Jamie. "Let me come with you," she said. Then, softly, just for him, "He doesn't get a say in who I—"

She broke off and Jamie hung on that pause. *Say it, princess.*

But she didn't.

Jamie swallowed around the lump in his throat and turned back to Ethan. "I know you don't believe me, but I'm so fucking sorry. When you're ready to talk, I'm here." He turned to Tessa, her big raven-dark eyes shimmering with frustration and something feral, like a caged animal. The words were inadequate, but that didn't make them any less true. "I'm sorry."

As he pulled out of the driveway, Tessa still standing in the driveway in shock and Ethan staring down Jamie's car like he could make it spontaneously combust with his eyes, Jamie had the distinct feeling that he was leaving something vital behind, but whether it was Ethan or Tessa—or both— he couldn't be sure.

Tessa stood next to her father and watched as Jamie drove away, wishing she was in the car with him. *He didn't want you to go with him. He left you here in this mess.*

Once Jamie's car was out of sight, Ethan bent to pick up Tessa's bag, but she snatched it before he even reached the handle. "I don't need your help," she snapped, cradling the bag against her chest.

"*You're* mad at *me*?" Ethan asked incredulously.

"You *punched* him!" she said, her voice going high and shrill.

Ethan scraped his hand over his mouth, the anger draining from his face. In that moment, he seemed so old, so tired. "Why'd you really come here, Tessa?" he asked her softly, a wounded look settling in his eyes. "The money's been yours, no strings attached, from the beginning. I'll sign the trust over to you today."

"It's not about the money," she said, but the accusation felt like oil on her skin, a shame she couldn't wash away.

"If you wanted to hurt me, there were easier ways than spending the last month and a half coming between me and my best friend."

Her mouth fell open as she struggled to make sense of his words. "You think I did any of this to hurt you?"

"What am I supposed to think? Who knows how long you've been lying to me?" He shook his head. "I raised you better than this."

"You didn't raise me at all," she spat.

Hurt flashed in his eyes and she instantly regretted the words, but it was too late. Besides, he'd hurt her, too. Between the hurt and regret and the constant refrain of '*run, run, run*' echoing in her brain like a drumbeat, she couldn't think of how to fix it.

"Right," he said after a minute, turning away from her

and stalking towards his truck.

"Where are you going?" she asked.

"I don't know," he said, pulling open the door to his truck.

And then she was alone again, feeling like her chest was going to cave in as yet another person she loved drove away from her that day. She glanced around the front yard of her father's house, a place she had started to think of as home.

Until I ruined it all.

She sank down until she sat on the top step of the porch stairs and pulled out her phone. Her hands shook as she dialed. Jamie answered on the first ring.

"Are you alright?" he asked, concern in every word.

"Come away with me," she said when he answered.

"We can't run away from this," he said, his voice raw on the other end of the phone. "Ethan will come around."

"Do you really believe that?"

"I don't know." There was a long pause before he continued, "I have to believe it."

"Or we could go."

"Go where?"

"Italy. Argentina. Moscow. Anywhere. Let's just go," she said, her voice thready with adrenaline.

"And what about our lives here?" he asked.

"I don't have a life here!" she shouted, the panic rising and choking her from within. "I don't—Just come with me. Jamie, we could disappear. Just the two of us."

"He's my family, Tessa. He's *your* family." She winced at the recrimination in his voice.

"He won't let us be together. He won't—"

"You don't know that."

"We could just go," she said, her voice small, pleading for something she knew would never be.

"I have to fix this. This is my home. Ethan is my family.

I'm not going anywhere."

She swallowed down the sob she wouldn't let herself cry. She'd almost believed they could figure it out. When she was lying in his arms in that Boston hotel room, it had all seemed so simple—Jamie wanted her to stay with him, and so she would. She should have known better.

He was choosing Ethan. He was choosing Aster Bay. Because how could she ever hope to measure up? How could she compete with twenty years of memories, of friendship that amounted to family? She couldn't. And she wouldn't stay and wait for him to leave her.

"Okay," she whispered. "I have to go."

She hung up, sliding the phone back into her purse. Something inside her snapped then as she pushed inside the house, past the place where Jamie had fucked her on the kitchen counter, place the drafty windows he'd fixed and the couch where they'd curled up together to watch *Brilliant British Bakes.* In the guest room once again— *because that's all you ever were: a guest, a temporary visitor in a place that wasn't yours to keep*—she threw open the too-full closet and stuffed clothing haphazardly into the empty suitcase that she'd kept beneath the bed. It only took a few minutes to tear apart the room, shoving the most important of her accumulated belongings into the bag until it was so full it was difficult to zipper shut.

Then, without looking back, she left her father's house.

Her hands shook as she gripped the steering wheel of her rental car, turning out onto the main road that would lead her out of Aster Bay, retracing the route she and Jamie had driven earlier that day. Only this time she didn't know where to go.

Chapter Thirty-one

Earlier that day

8:50 am
Missed call: Gavin West

8:51 am
Missed call: Gavin West
Missed call: Sebastian Graham

8:52 am
Gavin: Why is your phone off? Call me.
Gavin: Jamie, it's important.

Baz: What the fuck is going on? Did you just say what I think you said? On fucking television?

8:55 am
Missed call: Gavin West
Missed call: Ethan Hart

8:58 am
Missed call: Gavin West

9:02 am
Gavin: Where the hell are you?
Gavin: God dammit, answer your phone!

Baz: Who the fuck turns off their phone?

Gavin: Ethan knows.

Baz: Everyone fucking knows. Maybe next time check that your mic is off before you go asking someone about their panties.
Baz: Or lack thereof.

Gavin: Really? How was that helpful?

9:07 am
Missed call: Ethan Hart

9:11 am
Missed call: Gavin West

9:13 am
Gavin: JAMIE!

Baz: Texting in all caps doesn't actually make your text go through any louder.

Gavin: Shit, Jamie, you need to call me.
Gavin: Ethan is home.

10:00 am
Gavin: WHERE ARE YOU?

11:27 am
Jamie: I'm here.

Jamie: I'm at the restaurant.

Gavin: Thank God. I was about to send out a search party.
Gavin: Ethan knows about you and Tessa.

Jamie: I know.
Jamie: *picture of a bruise blooming on Jamie's cheek*

Baz: Fuck

Gavin: On my way.

Baz: Meet you there.

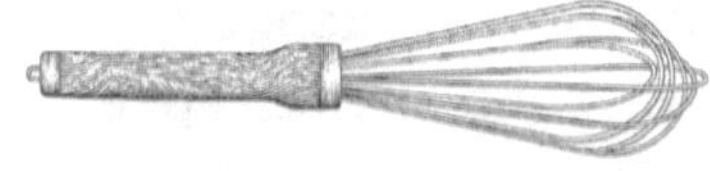

It was too cold to be on the roof of Lemon and Thyme, but maybe the cold was what Jamie needed to convince himself that it was all real. He'd really fallen in love with his best friend's daughter. He'd really lied to Ethan for weeks. He'd really thought that somehow this would all end with him getting to keep them both.

He propped his elbows on his knees and stared out at the bay. He wondered how long it would be before others in the town sided with Ethan. After all, Jamie hadn't grown up here like Ethan had. He wasn't really one of them.

If Ethan didn't forgive him...

He squeezed his eyes shut, the harsh November wind whipping against his skin, and prayed to whatever deity was listening that he hadn't just destroyed one of the most important relationships in his life.

Gavin and Baz pushed through the door onto the roof, a

look of relief washing over Gavin's face when he saw Jamie. Gavin pulled his coat around himself tighter and sank down beside Jamie, staring out at the bay alongside him as though Jamie hadn't just blown apart their friend group. A beer bottle appeared in his line of sight, dangling from Baz's fingertips.

"Little early for that, don't you think?" Jamie asked.

Baz shrugged, still holding out the bottle. "Thought you could use it."

Jamie accepted the bottle, taking a sip before setting it aside. It just made him even more nauseous. The last time he'd sat on this roof and drank a beer, Tessa had been sitting in his lap as she tried—and failed—to convince him that leftover cake scraps were an acceptable substitute for lunch.

"Where's Ethan?" Gavin asked.

"At home, last I saw him," Jamie replied, gesturing lamely to his swollen cheek.

"Your mic was hot," Gavin said.

Jamie snorted, eyeing his phone where it lay silent beside him. "I know."

After turning on his phone to the flurry of frantic texts and missed calls, Jamie had found a clip of the interview online. His voice, clear as day, carried over the weatherman's discussion of wind speed. *Tell me, princess, you wearing any panties under your skirt today?*

A heavy metal rendition of the overture to *The Marriage of Figaro* blared from Baz's coat pocket. He pulled his phone out and flashed a glance Jamie's way. "It's Ethan," he said, before answering the phone and stepping away to take the call.

Jamie dropped his head in his hands, scrubbing them through his hair. "You guys should go. I don't want anyone to take sides here."

"Who's taking sides?" Gavin asked.

"Jamie, is Tessa here?" Baz asked, holding the phone against his ear.

"No. I left her at Ethan's," Jamie said, his stomach dropping.

"She's not here, man," Baz said into the phone. His lips pressed together in a tight line as he held Jamie's gaze.

Jamie got to his feet, taking a step towards him, but Baz held his hand up and shook his head, taking a step back as he continued to listen to Ethan on the other end of the phone. Falling back, Jamie reached for his own phone.

It had been nearly two hours since she'd called, begging him to leave town with her. His breath caught in his chest. *No. She wouldn't...* He tapped out a message, cursing as his fingers fumbled the spelling in his haste to reach her.

Jamie: Where are you? What happened with Ethan?

He stared at the phone, waiting for the status to change, to indicate that she had read his message, but it didn't budge. He blew out a frustrated breath and called her instead. It went directly to voicemail.

"Her phone is off," he said, staring at the useless device in his hand in disbelief. "Maybe she went back to the cottage," Jamie said, as if saying so could make it true.

He knew she wouldn't be at the cottage. With a certainty that sank into his gut like lead, he knew she was gone.

Baz hung up with Ethan and slid the phone back in his pocket. "All her stuff is gone. Well, not *all*, but enough," he said.

Jamie fell back a step, feeling like he'd been punched all over again.

She left. She promised to stay and she left anyway.

"Ethan doesn't know where she went?" Gavin asked.

Baz gave a tight shake of his head. "He went out to cool off. Drove around town a few times. When he got home, she was gone."

"Maybe she just did the same thing he was doing," Gavin said. "Maybe she just needed some air and she'll be back soon too."

"She had to take all her stuff for that?" Baz asked, making it clear just what he thought of that idea.

"She's not coming back," Jamie said, the words burning his throat like acid.

"You don't know that," Gavin said.

"She asked me to run away with her and I said no," Jamie said, dazed as he replayed that conversation in his mind. How had he missed it? How had he not understood that she was going to leave whether or not he went with her?

Baz swore under his breath.

"She's running away." Jamie slumped against the side of the building, the ground shifting beneath his feet as his stomach lurched. "Just like she did that first night."

"Just like her mother," Baz mumbled.

"Jamie, think," Gavin said. "Where would she go?"

He thought of all the places she'd talked about visiting—Italy and Sri Lanka and the French countryside. He thought of all the places she'd lived before coming to Aster Bay—Vegas and Phoenix and South Carolina. He thought of her most recent stepfather in Colorado and her grandparents in Florida.

Fuck, she could be anywhere.

"I don't know," he said helplessly.

Chapter Thirty-two

Jamie: Where are you? What happened with Ethan?

Tessa stared at the message. *What happened with Ethan?* Not "are you okay?" or "why did you leave?" or "are you coming back?" No, the most important question Jamie could think of asking her was about her father.

She darkened the screen and slid the phone into her purse as the cab pulled up outside the modest one-story, stucco home with a red-tile roof. She paid the driver and gathered her bags from the trunk. As the cab disappeared down the palm tree-lined street, it occurred to her that she'd left one place where she was no longer welcome and come to another that might also not want her. After all, she hadn't seen her grandparents in years. Would they even recognize her? What if Ethan already told them what happened? What if they were just as disgusted with her as he was?

The door to the house opened slowly, a petite woman with a reddish-brown bob and wire-frame glasses appearing in the doorway. She dried her hands on the edge of the ruffled, red gingham apron that she wore loosely tied around her neck and waist.

"Is it really you?" she asked.

Tessa swallowed, the sound of her grandmother's voice washing over her like a wave, pulling her under, tempting her to drown in the rush of memories of being a little girl and hearing that voice call her in for dinner.

"Hi, Grama," she said with a watery smile.

Her grandmother nearly ran down the front walk to meet her, sweeping her up in a hug far tighter than Tessa would have suspected a woman of her age was capable of. She pressed Tessa against her, clutching her head to her chest.

"It's good to see you, baby girl," she said, her voice thready with emotion.

Tessa sank into the hug, dropping her bag on the sidewalk and gripping the older woman back. "I'm sorry it's been so long," she choked out, tears gathering in her throat in a hot tangle.

Grama tutted. "You're here now." She pulled away, holding Tessa's shoulders as her eyes swept over her face. Something softened in her gaze, like with that simple look she'd found the rough, broken edges behind Tessa's tight smile, but if she had, she didn't say anything. "Come in, come in. Gramps will be so glad to see you."

"How's he doing?" Tessa asked as she picked up her bag again and followed her grandmother up the walk.

"He's still asking me for bacon every morning, so he can't be doing too poorly," she laughed.

"Lou, who was it?" her grandfather called from the living room as Grama closed the front door behind them.

They rounded the corner into the living room, Tessa's shoes clacking against the tile floors. There, in an old orange and brown paisley easy chair, was her grandfather. His glasses were pulled down to the edge of his nose as he assessed the folded newspaper in his hand, a pencil poised to fill in the next clue in the crossword puzzle.

"Come and see for yourself," Grama said, ushering Tessa further into the room.

Gramps lowered his paper, looking up at the doorway for the first time. "TJ?" he asked, narrowing his eyes.

"Remember, it's Tessa now," Grama prompted. Then, confidentially to Tessa, "Your father told us."

"Right, right, I remember," he said, getting to his feet.

Tessa couldn't help the smile that overtook her at the sight of her grandfather, the way his presence took up the entire room even after all these years. She hadn't realized how much she'd missed her grandparents.

"Come here, Tessa Jayne, and give an old man a hug," he said with an impish grin as he held his arms out to his sides. She wrapped her arms around him, nestling her cheek against the warmth of his chest, and he enveloped her with a chuckle. "I suppose I'll have to have a heart attack more often if it means I get to see both you and your father in the same week," he said.

"Henry!" Grama scolded. "What a thing to joke about."

Gramps laughed that big belly laugh that shook his whole body, and Tessa's with it. Her grandmother ignored Gramps' laughter, turning her attention back to Tessa.

"Let's get you settled in the guest room," Grama said. "I just put fresh sheets on the bed this morning after your father left. Then maybe you'll help me finish making dinner. You must be famished."

Tessa followed her grandmother down the hall to a small, clean guest room. "Thanks, Grama. I won't stay long."

"You stay as long as you'd like," she said, glancing at Tessa's bags. "I hope you've got something fit for the Florida heat in those bags."

"I'll be fine," Tessa said.

"I'll leave you to it then. Come find me in the kitchen when you're ready," Grama said. Then, with a fond pat of Tessa's cheek, she turned and left Tessa alone in the guest room.

Tessa sank onto the bed, tossing her purse onto the bedside table. For the first time since Ethan had punched Jamie, she let herself take a deep breath, let the sadness sink into her bones. It was hard to reconcile her sudden flight from Aster Bay with the warm welcome she'd received at her grandparents, the easy way they'd taken her in, assuming she'd stay with them without even asking the question. Assuming she belonged there.

Her whole life she'd had to fight to carve out even a tiny corner of a place for herself, a corner she'd surrender over and over again when the walls caved in. Easier to admit defeat, to move on to somewhere new where the people didn't look at her askance, didn't hold the memories of her wrongs. And yet, here in this place with the grandparents she'd wronged over and over, the people she and her mother had abandoned, here she didn't need to fight for her place at all. It was there, waiting for her with clean sheets on the bed and everything.

You didn't need to fight for your place in Aster Bay. They were waiting to welcome you, too.

Maybe they had been, but that was before. By now, the whole town must have heard what she'd done, that she'd come between Ethan and Jamie and jeopardized the success of the festival in the process. If they couldn't repair what she'd broken, the town would blame her. She'd never be able to go back. The thought was a punch to the gut, a bright burst of pain that leveled her with its intensity. She'd never mourned the places she left behind before.

She shook off the thought and went to meet her

grandmother in the kitchen. Grama stood at the sink scrubbing potatoes with a natural bristle brush and humming to herself. Without looking up from her work, she tilted her head towards the cutting board on the counter, a freshly washed pile of carrots and celery stalks waiting beside a large yellow onion and a shiny chef's knife.

"Would you mind dicing up those veggies? My arthritis is acting up today." She turned a quick smile in Tessa's direction. "Lucky me that you turned up."

The two women worked side by side to the sound of Tessa's knife moving through the vegetables, Grama's humming, and the splash of water in the sink as she washed a whole bag of potatoes. When she was done chopping the vegetables, Tessa moved on to trimming and tenderizing the tough cut of beef her grandmother would turn into Swiss steak.

"Aren't you going to ask me why I'm here?" Tessa asked as she set the meat aside.

"Do you want me to?" Grama asked. When Tessa didn't immediately respond, Grama glanced up from peeling the potatoes with a soft smile. "I figure you'll tell me when you're ready."

Tessa was leveled by the unquestioning acceptance. In any other place, with any other people, she would be suspicious, but she knew her grandparents could have no ulterior motive. They simply welcomed her into their home as though she visited all the time, as though they weren't relative strangers.

Grama seared off the meat as Tessa began chopping the potatoes and dropping them into the prepared pot of water on the stove.

"Does your father know you're here?" Grama asked after a minute.

"No."

"Does anyone?"

"No."

Grama clucked her tongue. "You'll tell him—your father and anyone else who might be worrying about you, wondering where you've gone. After that is up to you, but you won't hide out here while your father's making himself sick with worry."

"I'm sure he's not—"

"He is," Grama said firmly. She removed the meat from the pan and scraped the mirepoix off the cutting board into the hot oil. Without looking at Tessa, she added, "I'm sure Jamie is, too."

Tessa paused in her chopping, her mouth dropping open and shame flooding her. "How did you—did Ethan—"

Grama gestured to the refrigerator with her spatula. "Anyone with eyes can see how that boy feels. His emotions have always been written all over his face."

Tessa followed the end of the spatula to the photograph held on the fridge with a magnet in the shape of a flamingo. It was a poor-quality copy of one of the promotional photos she and Jamie had taken for the festival, likely printed on a home computer. In it, Tessa was throwing sprinkles at a cupcake, smiling at the camera, while Jamie looked down at her with such adoration in his eyes it made her heart twist in her chest. What she wouldn't give for him to look at her like that again.

"Do you love him?" Grama asked. For the first time since they'd started cooking, the older woman turned her full attention to Tessa, studying her face.

Tessa swallowed. "Yeah. I do."

"Hmm. That *is* complicated," Grama said, turning back to her skillet. "I don't suppose your father is too happy about that."

Tessa huffed out a laugh. "That's putting it mildly." She returned to chopping the potatoes. "What should I do?" she asked in a small voice.

Grama put her hands on her hips and surveyed the kitchen. "Well, right now I think you should finish up chopping those potatoes. After that I'm planning on opening a bottle of wine and having a glass while this dinner finishes cooking. You're welcome to join me."

"I meant—"

"I know what you meant, baby girl. One step at a time."

12:23 pm
Jamie: Where are you? What happened with Ethan?

3:57 pm
Jamie: Baby, please just let me know you're alright.

8:03 pm
Tessa: I'm okay.

Jamie: Where are you? I'll come to you.

Tessa: I'm in Florida.
Tessa: With my grandparents.
Tessa: I think I need to stay here for a while.

Jamie: How long?

Tessa: I don't know.

Jamie: The festival is next week.

Tessa: I need to figure a few things out.

Jamie: Can't we figure them out together?

Tessa: I'm sorry.

Jamie: I don't need your apology. I need you here with me.
Jamie: What happened to staying? What happened to not running away?

Tessa: I'm not running away.

Jamie: That's not what it feels like.

Tessa: I just need some time.

Jamie: And then you'll come home?

Tessa: I don't know where home is.

Jamie: It's here. With me.
Jamie: But if you don't know that by now, maybe we both have some things to figure out.

Chapter Thirty-three

"Go," Anabel said with a laugh as she shoved at Jamie's back, pushing him towards the door. "Get out of my kitchen."

"*My* kitchen, you mean," Jamie said.

"You're gumming up the works, Chef," Anabel said, crossing her arms. "You've got my whole crew on edge with all your muttering and growling and menu changes."

"That menu—"

"Is *fine.* You approved it last week. And the crew is solid. Well, except for Brodie, but that's nothing new," she said with an eye roll. "We can't have two chefs running lead or my line is going to be a mess. So, unless you want to help out with the prep station, either you go, or I go."

Jamie released a frustrated sigh and scrubbed his hand through his hair. It had been like this for the last week. Seven days since Tessa left without so much as a goodbye... again. Seven days since he'd thrown himself headfirst into the restaurant so he wouldn't have time to think about the gaping hole in his chest. After sixteen-hour days at the restaurant, he'd stumble home and collapse in a bed that still smelled like her, too tired to even dream before getting up at the crack of dawn and doing it all over again.

Compartmentalize, focus on work, and for fuck's sake stop rereading her damn texts. That had been his mantra for seven days. None of it had helped.

He knew he was driving his kitchen staff—and the skeleton crew working under Kyla to keep Sugar Grapes afloat in Tessa's absence— crazy, but he didn't know what else to do. Ethan wouldn't talk to him, Tessa was off "figuring things out," and the only things he knew how to fix were in the kitchen. The fish delivery was delayed? He could rewrite the menu, put lamb on special and get the servers to push the pork. Kyla couldn't decipher Tessa's half-written recipes? He could take them home and write them out in clear, step-by-step instructions for the untrained bakers at Sugar Grapes. The food and wine festival was this weekend and he needed to come up with a vegan, gluten-free option for the opening dinner for Pastor Davis' niece? Done.

If only he could fix his relationships so easily.

How many days did she need to spend holed up in Florida before she realized her home was in Aster Bay? With each day that passed, he became less convinced that she'd ever come back, and in his darkest moments he wondered if she'd ever intended to stay with him at all.

"Don't you have stuff to do for the festival or something? The opening dinner is only a few days away," Anabel said, waving her hands as if she'd shoo him out the door.

He had far too much to do for the festival, including finding back-up plans for all the programs and demonstrations Tessa was supposed to lead. He was already pulling overtime to prepare her parts of the menu—with Kyla's help, thankfully—but he couldn't be in two places at once during the festival itself, so he wouldn't be able to cover her demonstrations and workshops. Finding someone else to take them, though, meant admitting that she might not come back, and he hadn't been ready to do that. With less than forty-eight hours to go, though, it was time to take Gavin and Baz up on their offer to help find coverage for Tessa's programs. Anything they couldn't cover, they'd have to refund.

"Okay, I'm going," Jamie said, holding his hands up in surrender as he backed out the kitchen door. He couldn't help but poke his head back in and call, "But don't overcook the pork. And make sure those fingerlings get crisp before you plate them. And—"

A barrage of side towels pelted him as his entire crew turned en masse, Anabel right there out front, and chucked the linens at him.

"Okay!" He dodged the last of the towels. "Kitchen's yours," he said to Anabel.

"Thank God. Now will you get out of here already?" she said with a smile as she shook a pan on the stovetop.

The dining room of Lemon and Thyme was quiet in the midday lull between lunch and dinner on a weekday, but he spotted Helen, Dot, Ruth, and Judy lingering over a bottle of wine in the corner. He'd been avoiding Helen and her friends all week, not wanting to have to explain how he'd let things get so fucked up so fast. But they continued to show up at the restaurant every other day for lunch, their quiet show of support something he wasn't sure he deserved.

He stopped a server on her way past. "Send four bread puddings over to table twelve with my compliments," he said, tilting his head towards the table in the corner.

"Yes, Chef," the server said, ducking into the kitchen to place the order.

Jamie made his way down the hall to his office, where he knew he would sit and stare at the schedule for the festival for the hundredth time without even starting to make alternate plans. He pulled his phone out and thumbed back to the group text he had with the guys, the last message of which had come in just that morning. Ethan still hadn't responded even once to the group chat since learning about Jamie and Tessa.

Yet another thing to worry about, he thought. *Bad enough I've ruined my relationship with him, but now I'm dragging the other guys down, too. And Tessa's not even here...*

He pushed open the door to his office and froze in the open doorway. The overhead light was off, but the lamp on his desk had been turned on, and Ethan sat in the chair opposite the desk nursing a beer. A second bottle sat on a coaster in front of Jamie's chair.

Without turning to look at him, Ethan inclined his bottle towards Jamie's chair. "Have a beer with me," he said.

Jamie let the door swing shut behind him and took the seat across from Ethan. He lifted the beer that had been waiting for him and took a long pull from the bottle.

"Ethan—"

He held up his hand to stop Jamie from speaking, his eyes trained on the top of the desk. When he spoke, his voice was calm and low. "You lied to me."

Jamie swallowed hard. "I did."

"I fucking hate that."

"I know."

"She's my kid. You don't get to lie to me about my kid." Ethan lifted his eyes to meet Jamie's for the first time. Jamie nodded, every muscle in his body pulling tight. Ethan shook his head and took another sip of his beer. He wrinkled his nose and stared at the label on the bottle. "This beer is shit."

Jamie laughed, a halting sound born of anxiety and disbelief. Ethan was still mad, but he was *there.* He was *talking*. It was progress at least.

Jamie set his beer down and leaned back in his chair, scrubbing his hands over his face. "Fuck, man, I'm sorry."

"So you said." Ethan took another sip of the beer, made the same disgusted face, and then pushed the beer away from him. "This thing with you and Tessa... What is it exactly?"

Jamie eyed his friend warily. "You want to know..."

"I'm trying really hard not to picture any of the details," Ethan said, wincing, "so you can spare me those. But I need to know what the hell we're talking about. Is it serious? Or—"

"Or do you need to punch me again?" Jamie asked.

Ethan smirked. "Sorry about that."

"It's okay. I deserved it."

Jamie met his friend's eyes across the table and made a decision. He couldn't have this conversation with Tessa's father, not without making a mess of it anyway, but he could talk to his best friend. So that's what he would do.

"I love her," he said, the words making his throat tight. "I'm in love with her. And I think I have been for months." Ethan's brow wrinkled. "Do you remember Whisky? The girl from—"

"The internet. Yeah, I remember. What's she got to do—"

"It was Tessa," Jamie said. "All this time, it was Tessa. I didn't know it until a few weeks ago but once I knew...I couldn't un-know. You know?"

Ethan let out a breath and slumped back in his chair. "Your internet girlfriend was my daughter."

"She wasn't my girlfriend then."

"But she is now?"

He didn't know how to answer. Was Tessa still his? Had she ever been? Yes, she'd said she was his, but then less than twenty-four hours later, she'd jumped on a plane without telling him and they'd barely spoken since. He had no idea if she was even coming back. She'd run, not just from the mess with her father, but from him. True, she'd asked him to go with her, but she hadn't trusted him enough to stay. To fight by his side for the life they'd imagined having together. Maybe he was the only one who had wanted that life all along.

He didn't know what they were anymore. But he knew he still loved her, still wanted her.

"I hope so," he said at last.

"You never were the casual fling kind of guy," Ethan said, shaking his head. "I just never thought you'd end up with my daughter."

"Me neither," Jamie said, huffing out a laugh.

"Does she love you back?" Ethan asked.

And fuck if that wasn't the million-dollar question.

"I don't know. I thought she might, but then..." Ethan nodded, understanding all the things left unsaid in that pause. "I asked her to stay. Here, in Aster Bay. With me. I asked her to move in with me. We were going to tell you when we got home from Boston. We had always planned on telling you."

"You should have told me sooner. You should have told me as soon as something happened," Ethan said.

"I know."

"Why didn't you?"

"I didn't want to lose you," Jamie said, the excuse sounding so feeble when he spoke it out loud. "I knew you'd be angry—"

"Fuck yeah, I was angry. You were— with my *daughter*," Ethan said. "There was never a scenario where I didn't hit the roof over this shit." Ethan braced his arms on the edge of the desk and leaned towards Jamie. "But, Jamie, you're family, man. Did you really think we'd fight and that would stop being true? Did you really have so little faith in me?"

"She's your daughter," Jamie said helplessly.

"And as much as I hate to admit it, she's an adult who can make her own choices. I missed out on seeing her grow up. She turned into this incredible woman, and I had nothing to do with it. Do I wish she hadn't chosen to—" He waved his hand around as if to indicate the words he wouldn't say. "—with my best friend? Of course, I do. But that's not up to me. Doesn't mean I fucking like it, and it sure as hell means there better never–and I mean *never*—be a time when you say any locker room shit about her to the guys. But I'm not severing ties with anyone because you couldn't find someone who's not my kid to fall in love with."

Jamie didn't know what to say, how to express the immense relief washing over him, the awe at this unbelievable grace his best friend was granting him.

"You can be angry at the people you love, and it doesn't mean you love them any less. You might not understand why they make the decisions they make, you can wish they'd choose something else, and you can still want them in your life. That's family, man. Maybe not always the family you're born into, but definitely the family you choose. You and I are family just as much as Tessa and I are. I don't think I've ever been angrier at another person than I was the day I found out about you two, but I never for a second stopped loving either of you."

"Are you still angry?" Jamie asked.

"That depends," Ethan said, raising one eyebrow. "You done lying to me?"

Jamie laughed. "Yes. I will never lie to you again, I swear."

"Good," Ethan said. After a moment, he asked, "You heard from her?"

"Not since the day she left. You?"

Ethan shook his head. "Not since she called to tell me where she was, which I am well aware she only did because my mom made her."

The now-familiar weight of missing Tessa sank into Jamie's bones, like a chill he couldn't warm up from. "I don't know how to make her understand…"

"That's your first problem. You can't *make* her do anything. I might not know Tessa as much as I'd like, but I knew her mother, and I'd recognize Steph's penchant for self-preservation anywhere. All you can do is give her all the information and pray she makes the right choice." A haunted look flashed across Ethan's face, the flicker of a memory. "But if you try and corner her, she'll just run again, further and faster."

"Then what do I do?" Jamie asked, helplessly.

"You wait."

Chapter Thirty-four

Tessa pulled another tray of failed chocolate chip cookies out of her grandmother's oven, tossing it on the stovetop with a clang. That was five batches in a row, each one worse than the last. She'd forgotten to add the salt to the first batch. On the second, she'd mixed up the measurements of sugar and flour. On the third, she'd over softened the butter. Mistake after mistake. She couldn't remember the last time she'd made so many mistakes in the kitchen.

On the counter, her notebook sat unopened, taunting her.

"Why don't you take a break?" her grandmother's gentle voice came from the kitchen doorway.

"I'll buy you a new sheet pan," Tessa said, scraping the blackened cookies off the tray and into the garbage.

"There's no need for all that," Grama said. She slid open the window over the kitchen sink and began fanning smoke out the window, one wary eye on the smoke alarm on the ceiling. "But maybe we could talk about what's bothering you before you use up all the butter in West Palm Beach?"

Tessa thought of the text sitting on her phone, the one that had arrived mid-day and she still hadn't answered, even though it was long past sunset.

Jamie: I miss you.

She missed him so much she felt like her chest was caving in with the weight of his absence, but she didn't know how to fix it. By now, with the festival only two days away, she'd not only betrayed her father and destroyed Jamie's oldest friendship, she'd also let down the entire town. How could she make any of that better?

She put the scorched pan back on the stovetop and sank onto a stool at the kitchen island, watching as her grandmother bustled about the kitchen making tea. She'd memorized this dance over the last ten days, the way Grama made tea, flitting from cupboard to cupboard because she could never remember which one she'd stashed the box of tea in the day before. (It was never the same cupboard twice.) When the tea was ready, Grama slid a mug across the island to Tessa and stood on the opposite side, her hip resting against the counter.

"Have you called them? Either of them?" Grama asked.

"I don't know what to say. And every day that I don't say something, it gets harder to figure out how to start."

Grama nodded, holding her mug between both hands, the steam curling into the air in front of her face. But she didn't say anything. It was what she did—stared at a person with that sympathetic grandmother stare until they broke down and spilled their secrets. It's how she got Gramps to admit he'd been stopping at the McDonald's a few blocks away for a Big Mac when he went out for his afternoon walks.

"I made everything worse," Tessa said at last. "I went to Aster Bay to get to know my dad and instead I pushed him away and destroyed his most important friendship at the same time."

Grama clucked her tongue. "That would be quite the thing. But I don't think you did any of that at all."

"Ethan punched Jamie. He told him to get off his property. He—"

Grama shook her head. "Those boys are brothers, and they fight like brothers, too. But that also means they'll forgive like brothers. Ethan always did have a black and white sense of morality, especially when it comes to honesty, so I have no doubt that he felt perfectly justified in punching Jamie. And I'm sure Jamie felt justified in not telling your father sooner about the two of you. They'll talk it out and they'll be just fine, if they aren't already."

"That's not how things work. When someone gets angry like that..." Tessa trailed off, taking in her grandmother's concerned frown. "My mom always said it was better to be the one to leave than to be the one who was left."

"And so you came here," Grama said. She sank onto the stool beside Tessa, turning to face her. "And who did you think was going to leave you, baby girl? Your father, or Jamie?"

Tessa shrugged, focusing her attention on her tea.

"Your mother... Well, I won't say she was wrong exactly, more that her viewpoint was skewed. Your mother's parents were not the most forgiving of folks," Grama said. Tessa snorted at the understatement. "I see you've heard about them."

"Mrs. Blumenthal told me about why we left Aster Bay when I was a kid. She told me about my other grandparents," Tessa admitted.

"I shouldn't be surprised, I suppose. Dot is practically the town historian," Grama said with a soft smile. "So you know that your mother was taught from a young age that love could go away if you disappointed someone, or made them angry, or defied them. But, baby girl, what your mother didn't stick around long enough to learn was that's not love at all. That's manipulation. And there's no room for that in love."

Grama gripped Tessa's hand and stared into her eyes. How had Tessa gone so many years without this woman in her life, without her warmth and her wisdom?

"Your mother was like a wounded bird. She didn't know how to accept love from our family, so we gave her freedom instead. And there were days when we were dreadfully angry that she'd taken you away and never came back, that the two of you were out there without a family. But our anger was never greater than our love. Your father and Jamie are both good men. Their anger will never be greater than their love."

"What if he doesn't want me anymore?" she asked, the question slipping out before she could stop it.

Grama squeezed her hand. "Oh, child, of course he wants you."

"I don't mean Ethan. I mean—"

"I know perfectly well who you mean," Grama said. "You're asking the wrong question, Tessa Jayne."

"What's the right question?"

Grama smiled. "What if he does?"

Tessa blinked away the tears that had gathered in the corners of her eyes. "Grama, I don't know what to do."

"What does your heart tell you to do, baby girl?"

Run.

The familiar refrain sounded in her head, but for the first time it wasn't telling her to run *from* something— instead, all she wanted to do was run *to* the people and place she had come to love. She rested her hand on the notebook, her thumb fanning the edge lightly as though she could soak up the dreams she'd written within its pages through touch alone.

"I think I need to go home," Tessa said, "to Aster Bay."

Grama squeezed her hand again. "Henry, get your shoes on!" Grama called to Gramps in the other room. "We're taking Tessa Jayne to the airport."

Tessa watched from her father's front porch as the line of cars drove away from Nuthatch. She recognized Baz's BMW and Natalia's SUV, Gavin's hatchback and Kyla's beat-up Honda Civic. At the back of the line was Jamie, his focus on the dirt road that led off the vineyard property. He didn't see her sitting in the shadows on the top step of Ethan's porch, huddled in her jacket against the cold November wind, but still Tessa's breath caught at the sight of him. Her fingers clenched around the thick down of her jacket, itching to touch him instead.

Soon. She had some things to make right first.

Finally, Ethan's pickup truck rumbled down the dirt road and turned into the driveway, his headlights sliding over her where she sat. She raised a hand to shield her eyes from the blinding light, so she didn't see him get out of the car, but she heard the door slam, heard his boots crunch on the gravel.

"Tessa?" he asked, something that sounded like relief and hesitance all jumbled up in his voice.

"I hope it's okay that I came here," she said, getting to her feet.

"Of course, it's okay. You're always welcome here," he said. "This is your home. If you want it to be."

She nodded. "I do."

He bounded up the steps towards her and swept her into a hug. She froze, unused to hugging her father, but only for a moment. She wrapped her arms around him and turned her face into his embrace.

"I'm sorry," she said, tears already burning her throat. "I'm sorry I lied to you. I'm sorry I came between you and Jamie."

"I'm sorry too. I shouldn't have lost my temper like that."

Tessa pulled away, wiping her eyes. "I never meant to hurt you."

"I know that too. I never should have implied otherwise," he said, giving her a tender sort of half smile. His eyes fell to her bags by the door and his smile widened. "Let's go inside. It's freezing out here."

She laughed in relief and nodded, following him inside and letting him help her with her bags. After they'd left her things back in the guest room, he made them hot chocolate, dumping powdered cocoa mix with freeze-dried marshmallows into mugs of microwaved milk. It was the best damn hot chocolate Tessa had ever tasted.

"What made you come back?" Ethan asked warily when they were settled on the couch in the living room.

Tessa watched the rehydrated marshmallows swirl in her cup. "I couldn't let everyone down by not holding up my end of the deal for the festival."

"Is that the only reason you came back?"

She met her father's eyes, noted the uneasy way he shifted in his seat, the tight set of his lips. "No," she said. "But I'm not sure you'll like the other reasons."

"I like any reason that gives us a chance to start over. To get to know each other."

She smiled tentatively. "I'd like that." She took a sip of her hot chocolate as she gathered her courage to ask about

Jamie. "Are you… Have you and Jamie…"

"We're all right," Ethan said, putting her out of her misery. She released a breath as a fragile peace bloomed in her chest. Her father studied her from the other side of the couch. "This thing with you and Jamie—is it serious?"

She nodded, tears pricking at the edges of her vision. "I love him." She swallowed down the stinging in her nose and set her mug down on the coffee table. "Please don't hate me."

"Hate you?" he repeated, his eyes going wide. "T, I could never hate you. I'm sorry that I haven't been there for you or told you enough how lucky I am to be your father. You are the best thing to ever happen to me, kid. Hate you? No, T. I love you too much for that."

She launched herself across the couch and, for the second time that afternoon, found herself comforted by her father's embrace.

"Doesn't mean it's not goddamn awkward," he said, the smile in his voice evident.

She laughed, holding him tighter.

"We're gonna be okay, kid. All of us. Just glad you're home."

"About that," she said, straightening up. "I need to make things right. I want to show you—and Jamie, and everyone else—that I'm not going anywhere. But I need your help."

"Anything, T. What do you need?"

"Can we start with your spare key to Lemon and Thyme?"

Chapter Thirty-five

A kitchen was a chef's castle. His temple. A sacred place.

True, over the last month and a half he hadn't spent as much time in the Lemon and Thyme kitchen as he used to, but it was still *his*. And he did not like showing up at his restaurant after hours to find someone in his kitchen without his knowledge. Especially after the week he'd had. A week with no sleep and no Tessa and a rapidly dwindling supply of hope that he would ever get through a day without wanting her. Without missing her so much he could hardly breathe.

When he received the call from Ethan that he'd spotted a light on in Lemon and Thyme, Jamie had chalked it up to Brodie being left to close down the kitchen the night before after the rest of Jamie's staff had gone over to Sugar Grapes to plan for festival coverage. The restaurant would be closed today, so no one should have been there, but then Jamie had arrived and it wasn't just one light left on—the entire kitchen was lit up.

Jamie unlocked the front door of the restaurant and entered the darkened dining room, the faint sound of the *Brilliant British Bakes* theme music carrying through from the kitchen. His breath caught in his chest as hope flared to life behind his sternum. With stilted steps, he made his way towards the kitchen, the blood moving through his veins with a buzzy feeling, like his very cells were vibrating.

He pushed through the doors from the dining room and forgot how to breathe. Tessa's back was to him as she swayed to the music and worked at one of his workstations, a kitchen torch in her hand. His hungry eyes roamed over her, taking in every curve, every strand of hair that flowed over her shoulders. She stilled, her spine straightening as though she knew she was being watched, and very slowly she turned to look at him over her shoulder.

"What are you doing here?" he asked, half expecting her to disappear like smoke on the wind.

"I would think it's obvious," she said, tilting her head towards the torch in her hand.

"I've never known someone to break and enter just to fix themselves a snack," he said.

"What about to apologize?" she asked.

He searched her face, letting himself wade in her raven-dark eyes, wanting to keep his guard up. But he knew he had no defenses against her. This was Tessa, Whisky, the woman he'd been waiting for his whole life. He wound through the workstations, his hands clenched to keep from shaking as he made his way to her.

"What are you making?" he asked.

Tessa held up a notecard, Louise's neat handwriting scrawled across the front. "Sweet potato pie."

She stepped away from the workstation to show him the pie resting on the counter, the sugar crust topping she'd been torching bruléed to crackling perfection. "I thought it was time I made you that pie." She flipped the card over and held it out to Jamie. "And I thought maybe there were some traditions we might want to revive."

Jamie took the card. On the back, she'd written the date, but the rest of the card was blank. "I don't understand," he said.

"I was hoping you could help me decide what to write. What we're commemorating," she said, her voice shaky with nerves. He met her eyes, his fingers gripping the recipe card. "We could commemorate that I'm moving to Aster Bay. Permanently."

He sucked in a breath, his chest bursting, but he held himself back as she continued.

"Or my very first lease in my own name." She reached into her back pocket and pulled out her notebook, retrieving a folded piece of paper from within its pages and placing it on the counter. "I cashed out my trust this morning and put down a deposit on the empty storefront across from Natalia's shop."

"That's great," he said, his voice sounding foreign to his own ears. *Ethan must be so happy.*

She tapped the front of her notebook and handed it to him, gesturing for him to open it. He flipped through page after page of notes about Aster Bay—where to get the best berries, her favorite flavor of goat cheese, which chutney from the farm stand was the best for eating with crackers straight from the jar. Sketches of the view from the roof of his restaurant, from the back porch of his cottage, the second floor tasting room at Nuthatch. Lists of special events throughout the year—the spring bazaar at St. Anthony's and the ecumenical Thanksgiving feast, the Easter egg hunt on the town common and the polar plunge at the beach. Bursts of inspiration with ideas for the recipes they'd inspired scrawled in the margins.

On the last page, she'd written a menu: sweet potato

pie, beet cake with bourbon custard, bananas foster with cardamom caramel and goat cheese ice cream, cheesecake bars with honeycomb crumble, fig and peach pie, Bakewell tart Swiss roll. On and on, the recipes she'd dreamed up or perfected over the last few weeks.

"We could celebrate the opening of my new bakery," she said, her voice unsure. "I've even hired my first staff. Kyla and Cheryl."

His chest ached with pride, his blood thick and slow as he processed her words.

She took a step towards him, setting the notebook aside and twining her fingers with his. "Or that I'm sorry for running away."

He rested his forehead against hers, his free hand landing on her waist. He needed to touch her, to ground himself with the feel of her skin on his skin.

"I'm so sorry, Jamie. You were right. I was scared and I ran. This is my home." She pressed her free hand to his chest, just above where his heart hammered against his rib cage. "You are my home."

"What happens the next time you get scared?" he asked.

"I won't run."

"How do you know?"

"Because I love you." He pulled back to meet her eyes, warmth filling his chest. "And my love is greater than my fear."

He captured her mouth, drinking the words from her lips. She released a little sob against his kiss, throwing her arms around his neck and pressing herself against him. She tasted like spun sugar and home and *his*. They broke apart, panting, and he leaned his forehead against hers again.

"I love you, too," he said, holding her closer. "And I know what we should commemorate."

Still holding her against him with one hand, he reached over and picked up the pen that lay on the counter next to the recipe card, scribbling: The first time we said I love you.

"You were worth the risk," she whispered.

He kissed her again, softer this time. "Let me take you home, princess."

She smiled, the curve of her lips lighting up her entire face. "I already am home."

Epilogue

One Year Later

"You boys ready to lose?" Helen asked as she sauntered up to Ethan, Baz, Gavin, and Jamie's usual table.

"I have a good feeling about tonight," Gavin said.

"You're down a man," Helen said. "And she's your best player."

"I'm here!" Tessa said, rushing to the table from the front door, the gust of cold wind and snow flurries chasing her inside. She unwound the thick scarf from around her neck, her cheeks bright with cold, and her engagement ring glinting under the lights of The Rookery.

The sight of his ring on her finger still made Jamie wild with need. It had been a year since Tessa had moved into his cottage and made it a home, nearly six months since she'd agreed to become his wife, and he was just as desperate for her as he had been that first night. He shifted in his seat, subtly adjusting himself. Her father was at their table, after all.

"Hi," she said with a knowing quirk of her eyebrow before she planted a soft kiss on his lips and slipped into the empty seat between Jamie and Ethan. "Hey, dad. Sorry

I'm late," she said to Ethan. "We had a last-minute rush on the drunken pear gingerbreads."

Helen sucked her teeth. "Fools. That's why I bought mine yesterday morning. Can't leave these things to chance."

"Not when we sell out so often," Tessa said with a grin. "I'm going to need to hire more help soon to keep up with the holiday rush, especially now that Kyla's only working part time."

Jamie wound his fingers through hers, pulling their intertwined hands into his lap. "Enough shop talk. You are officially off duty for the next week."

"Yes, Chef," she said, her eyes dancing wickedly.

His cock gave an answering twitch. *You'll pay for that later, princess.*

"Where are you two off to this time?" Dot asked as she came up beside Helen at the table's edge.

"Dublin," Tessa replied, practically bouncing her seat. She may have settled down in Aster Bay, but her love of travel hadn't diminished. This would be their third trip that year, and Tessa already had their next two trips planned.

"My brother is producing a new musical there, and my sister-in-law is playing the lead," Jamie said.

"It's the perfect excuse to visit Ireland." Tessa beamed at his side.

"As if you needed an excuse," Baz grumbled into his beer.

"You've earned a break," Dot said, shooting Baz the kind of warning look that had sent second graders scrambling to clean up their desks. "Who would have thought our little food and wine festival would be named one of the top ten food and wine festivals in the Northeast two years in a row?"

Jamie and Tessa had agreed to co-chair the festival for a second year, building on the success of their first outing. The gingerbread sandcastle and bonfires were big hits and had become an annual part of the festival, as had Jamie's pasta making demonstrations. This year, they'd even expanded the festival to include tours of Ricky's greenhouse and goat cheese tastings at Michelle's goat farm. Each night, sore and tired from the long hours of demonstrations, workshops, and tastings, Jamie and Tessa had stumbled into bed, where they'd lain awake in each other's arms as Tessa rattled off the hundreds of new ideas she had for next year.

"I never had any doubt," Jamie said, squeezing Tessa's hand. Together they were unstoppable, breathing new life into the little town that had loved them both before they knew how to accept it.

The school bell rang at the front of the room as Mike Greenhall took his place at the podium. "That's our cue," Helen said with a wink. "Good luck, boys. You'll need it."

She and Dot danced away to their table where Ruth and Helen waited with a fresh round of margaritas. Mike began running through the rules of the game, as if they weren't all regulars who played each week. Tessa slid their interlocked hands higher on his thigh and he did his best not to lean into her touch. They'd made a promise to Ethan—no PDA, at least not when Ethan was around—but damn if Tessa didn't make that promise nearly impossible to keep sometimes.

"You all packed? Have your passport?" Ethan asked Tessa as he took another sip of his beer.

"Yes, dad," she said with a roll of her eyes, but her smile gave her away. "And Cheryl's going to take over your weekly breakfast delivery while Jamie and I are out of town."

"She doesn't need to go to any trouble," Ethan protested, his eyes lighting up in excitement despite his words.

Tessa laughed. "Enjoy it while you can. When I'm back, there'll be no more chocolate muffins for breakfast."

When Tessa had taken over Ethan's weekly delivery, she'd swapped out most of the sweets for quiches, quinoa and egg cups, and banana oat muffins. Ethan grumbled about it whenever Tessa was within ear shot, but they'd all seen the way he scarfed down the food and refused to share. He loved every bite, not just because it was delicious, but because it had been made with love by his daughter.

"But I may have left a cheesecake in your fridge," Tessa added with a wink.

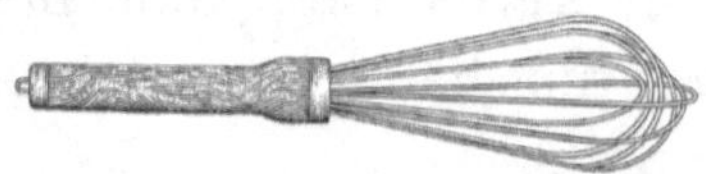

"I'm telling you, something is going on with Gavin," Tessa said later that night as she put her toiletry bag into her suitcase and zipped it closed.

Jamie carried the suitcase into the living room and placed it beside his own at the front door so they would be easy to grab in the morning when Ethan arrived to drive them to the airport. Tessa followed him.

"Gavin is the most stable one of us all," Jamie said. "I think you're imagining things."

"He hardly said anything at all tonight," she continued, pulling her hair free from the bun she wore when she worked. Her hair tumbled over her shoulders, swinging across her back as she turned and headed back into their bedroom.

"It's the end of the semester. He's always more focused on work this time of year," Jamie said as he shed his sweater and tossed it into the hamper.

"I don't think it's work he's focused on," Tessa replied.

She shimmied out of her jeans. She hadn't worn panties—again—and his cock swelled behind the zipper of his jeans as the knowledge that she'd been bare all day.

Just like he'd asked.

She continued, "I think he's seeing someone."

"What, like a woman?" Jamie said skeptically as he undid his belt and kicked the bedroom door closed.

"Yeah." Tessa removed her sweater and threw it in the pile on the floor with her jeans. Jamie snorted as he picked up the pile and moved it to the hamper. "Why is that so hard to believe?"

"Gavin doesn't date," Jamie said, adding his jeans to the dirty laundry.

"Ever?"

"Not since his divorce. Not really." He turned to face Tessa just as she unhooked her bra, her breasts tumbling free. He wrapped his arms around her and planted a sucking kiss to the place where her neck met her shoulder as he walked her back towards their bed. "I'm done talking about Gavin for tonight."

"Oh yeah?" she asked with a laugh. "And what did you want to talk about?"

He dropped a hand between her legs, cupping her possessively. "No more talking."

Her calves hit the edge of the bed and she sat, her hand in his hair pulling him down with her. "We have an early morning," she said, her voice thick with desire.

"We'll manage," he said as he sank to his knees between her thighs.

Despite her words of protest, she dug her hand into his hair and guided him where she wanted him, his stubble scraping against her inner thighs.

"We can sleep on the plane," he growled as she spread her knees, revealing herself to him. He ran his thumbs over her swollen folds, his fingers growing slick with her desire. "And you didn't forget your panties this morning because you wanted me to leave this pussy alone," he grunted before pressing his mouth to her.

She threw her head back as he licked her, steadying herself on the bed with one hand.

"Still want to go to sleep?" he asked.

The hand in his hair tightened, guiding him back to the stiff bud of her clit. He chuckled and sucked it into his mouth, nursing on it until it was swollen and pulsing against his tongue.

"No, but I don't want to sleep on the plane either," she said, panting as she ground herself against his face.

He slid two fingers into her wet heat, loving the way her body clutched at him as he entered her. "What did you want to do instead?" he asked. "Were you hoping I'd fuck you at thirty-five thousand feet?" He pumped into her steadily, slowly stroking her front wall.

"I just wondered how many times I can come before we get to Ireland," she said, her hips bucking up to drive his fingers deeper within her.

"Greedy girl," he tsked.

She laughed, the sound breaking off on a moan when he returned his tongue to her clit. "You love it," she teased.

"Fuck, I can't wait to marry you," he said.

Just three more months. In three more months, she would be his wife. The thought alone was enough to have beads of precum pooling on the tip of his cock.

He hooked his fingers, coaxing her orgasm forward, sucking and stroking until she cried out, her thighs shaking against his ears as her taste flooded his tongue. When her orgasm subsided, she reached for his cock and they both groaned as her fist closed around him. She stroked him from root to tip.

"I don't know, princess," he said, his voice gravelly. "I don't think you can be quiet enough. Can't have the entire plane knowing how much you like it when I play with your pussy."

"I can be quiet," she said, licking her lips and guiding him up onto the bed as she slid back to make room for him.

"I guess you won't be wearing panties again tomorrow then," he said, cursing when she ran her thumb along the sensitive ridge on the underside of his cock.

"I wouldn't dream of it," she said, her eyes dancing.

He pushed her back on the bed and crawled over her. "Good girl," he said as she guided the head of his cock to her entrance.

He filled her in one smooth stroke, seating himself fully. Her legs wrapped around his back, urging him deeper. He captured her lips, licking into her mouth and tangling his tongue with hers, breathing her air. Jamie clasped her hands, sliding them above her head as he slowly worked himself in and out of the cradle of her thighs.

He watched as she came undone beneath him, in awe that he was the one who got to see her like that, to make her feel that way. It never got old—the feeling of her climax pulling him under, the look in her eyes, the way she cried out his name as she came. He fell over the edge after her, pumping his own release deep inside her.

Jamie pulled her against him, her back flush with his front, and wrapped his arms around her. She was all loose limbs and heavy eyelids as she wriggled back against him, pressing the ripe curve of her ass to his groin with a happy sigh. He nuzzled his face into her hair.

"I love you," he said.

She turned her head and planted a sleepy kiss to his bicep. "I love you, Chef."

The End

Love Song Series
Irreplaceable

Indiscreet

Undeniable

Aster Bay

Whisking It All

Just For Show

First Comes Marriage

Visit my website to learn more and download free bonus content:

Acknowledgments

As always, there are so many people who have made this book possible.

To my husband—Thank you for supporting this crazy dream of mine. And more than that, thank you for reminding me to take breaks. Every recovering people pleaser needs someone to remind them that it's okay to rest once in a while, and—even though I don't always listen you—I appreciate your reminders more than you can know.

To my mom and John—There are not enough words to thank you for the ways you support me. From all the little (and big) ways you make my life easier and more comfortable, like watching my son to inviting me to raid your refrigerator when I run out milk, to the ways you endlessly celebrate my successes and let me vent when things feel too hard, I am so lucky to have you in my corner. Thank you for not only being my parents, but also my best friends.

This book is dedicated to my aunt, Ann. For all the ways you have cheered me on, for every copy of my books you have handed to a friend, for being more big sister than aunt—thank you.

I am forever grateful for the friends and family members who have supported this crazy dream of mine. Thank you to Megan, Phil, John, Mindy, Alysa, Devon, and Denise.

Being an indie author can be lonely at times, which makes it even more special when you make a connection with another indie author. From brainstorming, reading early drafts of Jamie and Tessa's story, pushing me to make this the best book possible, sharing advice, and just generally understanding this insane, wonderful ride we're on, I am grateful for the friendship, camaraderie, and unhinged text messages. Thank you Ginny B. Moore, Liz Alden, Sophie Snow, and Maria Secoy.

Last but certainly not least, thank you to each and every person who has read one of my books, talked about them on social media, left a review, or recommended them to their friends. I always dreamed of writing a book, holding it in my hands and knowing someone else would read it—you have made my dream a reality. I am forever grateful to be a part of the romance community.

About the Author

Cara Dion writes steamy, contemporary romance, often with a forbidden or age gap relationship.

Cara has always had an overactive imagination and spent much of her teenage years watching 80s and 90s romcoms with her aunt. She read her first romance when a friend snuck one of their mother's Harlequins into their Catholic school and passed it around like contraband, but she didn't return to romancelandia until the pandemic.

She has been an English teacher, professional musician, and nonprofit administrator. When she's not reading or writing romance, Cara loves cooking, Broadway musicals, and all things Disney.

Cara lives in a small town in New England with her husband, son, and two very demanding cats.

Follow Cara on Instagram at caradion.author and contact her at cara@caradion.com. Visit the website and join Cara's newsletter to get insider information on upcoming books and exclusive content.

www.ingramcontent.com/pod-product-compliance
Lightning Source LLC
Chambersburg PA
CBHW021338310726
48971CB00001B/188